To Mike.

I

Ian Collinson

Ian Collinson
Landham 2009.

Weathervane Press

Weathervane Press

Published in 2009 by Weathervane Press
22a Hilton Crescent, West Bridgford, Nottingham NG2 6HT
www.weathervanepress.co.uk

ISBN 978 0 9562193 0 5

Designed and printed in Nottingham
by Parker and Collinson Limited.

One

'Excuse me,' a voice called from the field's edge.

Glancing up from his notebook, he saw a young woman on a horse.

'Are you going to say 'can I help you'?' he asked.

'Why would I say that?'

'Isn't it what people like you do in these situations?'

'Which people; what situations?'

'Is this conversation going to consist entirely of questions?' he sighed.

Before she could stop herself, she laughed, then sauntered the horse a little closer to where he was lying, on the bank of a small pond surrounded by trees in the middle of the field.

'I didn't begin with a question,' she replied softly.

He pretended to be deep in thought, swivelling his head as if following a Wimbledon rally. 'Hmmm,' he considered, 'I think perhaps it was an enquiry of sorts.'

'I suppose it was,' she conceded.

'You were intending to establish,' he continued, 'how I came to be sitting in the middle of your field!'

'What makes you think it's *my* field?'

He held up his hands in surrender. 'Ok. Ok. You win. Just go easy with the questions, already!'

She looked down, assessing him with a tolerant smile. He was about her age, early-twenties, and sensibly dressed for casual walking in a navy fleece, jeans and trainer-style boots. He had straight, longish black hair and dark blue eyes.

'It is actually my Dad's field,' she admitted, 'and there is actually no footpath to this part of it.'

'Guilty as charged!' he exclaimed, springing to his knees and unsettling the horse a little, 'I am indeed trespassing on your land but I couldn't help noticing this little oasis and thinking, 'I bet there's a lovely pond tucked away up there,' and, since there was no livestock to disturb I decided to investigate.'

She nodded towards the notebook, which his rapid movement had tipped on to the grass. 'And did you find inspiration here?'

For the first time he seemed less assured. 'A thought did strike me, yes,' was all he replied.

'Which was?' she persisted.

'Is. Gone, alas!' he lamented. 'Like the person from Porlock, you distracted me at the vital moment and the masterpiece is lost forever!'

'You flatter yourself, I think,' she laughed, 'and in any case you got some of it down, I saw you scribbling away as I rode towards you.'

'Just sketchy fragments; nothing of substance I assure you.'

'Is it a poem?'

'Not this,' he gestured dismissively, 'this is merely a poor, stillborn thing, never to grow to maturity.'

'Well read it anyway; read it and I will forgive you your trespasses.'

He inclined his head a little, 'thine is the kingdom,' he murmured, smiling to himself. 'Very well, you give me no choice. I will share these scraps with you if I must.' He looked up at her. She had brown eyes and long dark hair, which flowed from beneath her plain black helmet. He lifted the notebook with a flourish and moved to a sitting position.

'Swallows dive with spitfire wings, laugh at the lumbering airbus grinding warily overhead, curving at stalling speed the longest way down to Castle Donington.'

The horse tensed, shivered a little then farted softly and deposited a neat pile of steaming glossy turds onto the grass. They looked at each other and laughed. She patted its neck.

'I'm afraid Darcy isn't into poetry, but I liked it,' she hesitated for a second, 'well, I must be off,' then added theatrically, 'you are forgiven!' and turned the horse to trot away.

'I thought horses had names like 'Game for a laugh',' he called after her.

'That's race horses!'

'What's your name?' he called again, rising to his feet now.
'Jess, what's yours?'
'Sam,' he answered, 'Samuel Taylor.'
Jess waved as she cantered to the track at the bottom of the field and disappeared from view.

Sam arrived back home by mid afternoon. It was Sunday and his housemate Matt was flat out on the sofa watching the football. He picked his way carefully through the detritus on the living room floor and flung open the curtains. Matt did not even blink. He turned and surveyed the squalor. 'What a dump!' they both said simultaneously. Sam glanced towards the TV.
'How's it going?'
'Ok.'
Sam let out a strangled cry and turned to the screen, deliberately obstructing Matt's view but provoking no reaction at all.
'Nil-nil in the eighty-ninth minute and you've nothing better to do than watch this crap?'
'Nope.'
The final whistle blew, the referee choosing to show some compassion and play no added time.
'Satisfied?' asked Sam aggressively.
'It's a result.'
'Of course it's a bloody result! What else is the end of a football match?'
Matt began to mimic the reader of the final scores on the BBC, leaving Sam to predict the away team's score from his intonation.
'Brighton and Hove Albion Nil, Leyton Orient…' 'Nil' Sam guessed.
'Notts County 2, Accrington Stanley…' 'Three,' he suggested.
Matt sipped the remainder of his lager as their game continued, then gently lobbed the empty can onto a small pile in the middle of the floor. He punched the air as it came to rest neatly on the top.
'I'm sorry Matthew, I've misjudged you. Here I am complaining about you turning our lounge into what appears to be an abandoned squat, when all the time you have been

carefully constructing a conceptual art installation. This should be in Tate Modern, you could win the Turner Prize for it mate!' He ripped open an imaginary envelope. 'And the winner is.... Matthew Mullins with 'Living Room', a shocking and uncompromising study of life on the margins of *sub*urban society.' He hung an air microphone in Matt's direction, inviting him to spout in Post Modernese, but he refused to play. Sam had finally managed to provoke his nonchalant flat mate.
'Ok Mr self-righteous prick! What have you been doing all morning that's so fucking brilliant?'
Sam told him all about his walk and the meeting with Jess.
'Nice one mate!' exclaimed Matt. 'She's definitely up for it and probably loaded to boot. Get in there!'
'I don't know,' hesitated Sam, 'farmers are having a tough time at the moment'
'Yeah right! Probably had to turn the heat down on the jacuzzi!'
The door abruptly swung open and a dishevelled girl entered, dressed only in a T shirt of Matt's, which bore the slogan 'Give germs a chance' beneath a line drawing of a grinning hairy bug. She had clearly only just woken up.
'Who are you?' she asked Sam accusingly.
'Sorry for intruding,' Sam replied, 'I just happen to live here.'
'Sorry, sorry' Matt intervened, 'this is err…this is um….'
'Jenny,' she prompted him, 'and I was just coming down to say I can't get the shower to work.'
'That would be because it doesn't,' explained Sam helpfully, 'our landlord's not being very co-operative at the moment on account of us being a bit behind with the rent, you see.'
'Well why don't you move then?' Jenny asked angrily, 'this place is an absolute -'
'Dump!' they all cried in unison. The lads both giggled and slapped palms.
'I'm off,' Jenny snapped and stomped back upstairs.
Sam looked enquiringly at Matt, who responded with an expansive, continental sort of shrug, and a hand swivelling 'so, so' gesture.
After a few moments Jenny came thumping back down, breezed through the room without a word and was just opening the front

door when Matt called, 'I didn't get your number!'
'Good!' she snarled as the door slammed.
'Was that my fault?' asked Sam, not troubling to disguise his indifference.
'No, no I think she generally wasn't too impressed. It's been a while since I changed the sheets and what with the shower being kaput, well….'
'That's more than enough info thanks mate. She's probably gone straight down the clap clinic!'
'Are they open Sundays then?' Matt enquired with genuine curiosity.
'How the hell would I know?'
'Oh course, sorry,' acknowledged Matt, whose frequent and apparently effortless success with women was a constant source of annoyance and bewilderment to Sam. 'Maybe your luck's turned,' he suggested, 'sounds like horse girl's there for the taking.'
'How could you possibly know that?'
'Well she didn't laugh at your poem did she?'
'Firstly, it wasn't a poem and secondly, most intelligent people don't as it happens. How come I've ended up sharing a house with a brainless, rugby playing, alcoholic philistine?'
'Same reason I've ended up with a pseudo intellectual loser who has only fleeting acquaintances with the world of work I suppose. Nobody else would have us mate.'
Sam's resentful silence indicated that his friend was probably about right.

Jess trotted back to the farm at a brisk pace. Sunday lunch was still a family ritual at home and she liked to help her mother with the cooking. Dismounting, she led Darcy into a small paddock beside his stable. She deftly unbuckled the saddle and bridle, draping them over the fence as she turned him out. He would be fine there until after lunch. She patted his neck and pressed her cheek against him then ran to put the tack away, kicked off her boots and stepped into a pair of old trainers.
As she jogged through the yard she saw Mark, her father, belting the coupling of the muck spreader with a lump hammer.

He was forever bashing or welding recalcitrant bits of metal.
'That'll fix it Dad!' she called cheekily as she sped by.
'Bloody things seized up again!' he grimaced. 'I was going to try and get Dumbles done before lunch but there's no chance now. I'll douse it in easing oil and leave it till this afternoon.'
'OK. I'll give you a shout when we're dishing up.'
Jess smiled to herself as she slid off her trainers and jacket and dumped them in the porch. But for that rusty coupling, Sam would have had shit sprayed all over him as he lay there pontificating. She quickly washed her hands and dashed into the kitchen.
'Hi Mum! What needs doing?'
Christine, her mother, was just lifting the foil off a roasting tin containing a large joint of pork. She cautiously lowered it back into the oven and slid a tray of potatoes and a dish of stuffing onto the shelf above.
'You can do the veg if you like, love. How was your ride?'
'Lovely thanks,' she replied as she took a thick slice off a large swede and began peeling it, 'but I really shouldn't have left all this to you.'
'Nonsense!' said Christine, 'it's months since you've been out riding on a Sunday.'

As she briskly prepared the vegetables, Jess thought about Sam. There was something about him that appealed to her; he seemed intelligent and a bit quirky, rebellious even. She wished now she had found out more about him instead of hurrying away, perhaps exchanged numbers.

Jess was lonely. She had been half way through the first year of a degree course in English at Leeds University when her mother was diagnosed with breast cancer. Christine responded well to the initial treatment and, apart from spending more weekends at home than originally planned, Jess completed her first year without interruption. Although Christine appeared to have beaten the breast cancer, secondaries were discovered on her liver during that summer. Since this was inoperable, chemotherapy was the only recourse so Jess decided to defer her second year and stay at home to support the family. Months of chemo debilitated Christine but succeeded only in arresting the growth. Eventually, early in the new near, she had taken the decision to discontinue her treatment. Nothing more could be done now; she perhaps had only months to live but was resolved to carry on normally for as long as possible. Jess knew all this of course, but her younger brother Tom had not been made fully aware of the seriousness of the problem. He was about to do his 'A' Levels and the others agreed that it would be best to protect him until the exams were out of the way. Jess found this difficult at times because Tom was inclined to be lazy and thoughtless and she often had to bite her tongue when remonstrating with him.

Christine suddenly looked utterly exhausted.

'Mum, why don't you let me finish off here and have a rest before we dish up?' Jess suggested. Her Mother did not object, silently making her way into the sitting room. Jess had just got all the vegetables boiling when Tom, still in pyjamas, drifted into the kitchen.

'I'm starving, what time's dinner?'

Jess turned to look at him. He was short for his age with a pale complexion and curly brown hair.

'You look like you need feeding up, squirt,' she teased.

'Well that's better than being fat!'

Jess had put on some weight since coming back home but it didn't concern her. She decided to sidestep a slanging match, which, after all, she had initiated.

'It'll be about ten minutes. Just time for you to get a shower and put some clothes on.'

'Yes Mother. Where is Mum by the way?'

'She's just gone to get Dad in, so you'd better get a move on.'

When everything was ready and keeping warm in the oven, Jess slipped into the lounge. Her mother was lying on the sofa, a hand resting protectively across her stomach. Jess knelt beside her.

'Are you going to be able to eat any of this, Mum?'

'Just a bit.'

'Ok, I'll go and fetch Dad.'

She was just starting to get up when Christine suddenly clasped her hand.

'Thanks love,' she whispered, 'I couldn't do this without you, you know that don't you?'
A wave of emotion flooded through Jess, but she knew she must not cry. Squeezing her Mother's hand, she hurried from the room, not trusting herself to speak. Stamping her trainers back on, she ran out to find Mark. He was already on his way up to the house, having finally brokered a union between tractor and spreader.
'You managed it?' She enquired, careful to modulate her voice.
'Eventually. How's Mum doing?'
Jess could not hold out. 'Oh Dad,' she sobbed, 'she's totally worn out. I don't know how much longer we can keep this up.'
Mark clasped her to him tightly.
'I know it's hard, love but it's what she wants. Tommy will be through most of his exams in a week or two and we have to try to keep things on an even keel till then.'
'But I don't know if we can!' Jess wailed.

The food was all a bit dried up and overdone by the time Jess had got everybody served but Tom was so hungry he didn't notice this, or the fact that Christine hardly ate a thing. On the pretext of urgent revision he excused himself as soon as he had finished and nobody objected; it was just a relief to be over another hurdle on this final lap. Jess cleared away and washed up as her parents dozed on the sofa.

As soon as she could, she ran back down to the paddock. Since she was fifteen, Darcy had been her best mate. Several of her school friends with enough land or money had bought a horse at around the same time and he was the only survivor.
Jogging through the farmyard she noticed a few swallows skimming low over surface of its muddy puddles. She stopped abruptly and watched them carefully for a moment.
'They do have Spitfire wings!' she laughed.

Darcy was nibbling the longer grass at the bottom of the paddock when Jess arrived. She clambered onto the fence and sat for a moment enjoying the view over the Vale. It was a lovely late spring afternoon with real warmth in the sun and a gentle breeze. Eventually he noticed her and ambled over.

‘Ok buddy,’ she whispered, ‘it’s time to give you a good brush down.’
Jumping off the fence she led him over to the stable where she reached in and grabbed a pair of heavy brushes. With both hands she dragged one across his broad flanks, gently smoothing out the matted hair.
Jess saw the tractor heading over towards Dumbles, muck spreader trailing along behind, and decided it was time to go back to the house to see how her mum was doing. She quickly finished brushing Darcy down, forked some hay into the manger and turned towards the paddock gate where she noticed Tom sitting on the fence in her favourite spot.
‘How long have you been perched up there?’
‘A while,’ he replied glumly.
‘What’s up? It’s not like you to risk exposing yourself to fresh air and sunlight for long.’
Tom looked down at the ground for a moment as if weighing up how best to express what he wanted to say. ‘Something’s up with Mum isn’t it?’ he mumbled eventually.
Jess felt as though she had been thumped in the chest and struggled to find a reassuring reply, knowing that her hesitation had already given the game away.
‘Isn’t it?’ Tom reiterated.
‘Yes,’ Jess whispered, ‘she’s quite poorly.’ And despite her best efforts, she began to cry.
‘I know what you’re all thinking,’ Tom continued calmly, ‘that I need protecting from all this so it doesn’t affect my revision, but it’s not working. Something is obviously wrong and not knowing is just making things worse.’
Jess nodded. She had been half expecting this to happen eventually.
‘Is she going to -?’ He couldn’t finish the question before tears came. Jess walked over to him and held his arms. He pressed his face into her shoulder.
‘Don’t think about that,’ she said as firmly as she could. ‘It’s a step at a time at the moment and the next one is navigating your exams. Can you do that for her Tom?’
He nodded into her shoulder and she put her arms round him

now, holding him tightly. They were not especially close but had never hated each other like some siblings they knew.
‘Thanks sis,’ he croaked, ‘thanks for telling me.’
‘Our secret, yeah?’ she murmured.
‘Ok,’ he agreed.

Two

On Monday morning Sam was dashing out for an interview. He tended to work for about six months at a time building up a fund to keep him going for as long as possible while he concentrated on his writing. He had just come to the end of his reserves, but was now struggling to find a job. Normally he would work in a call centre but the few who were recruiting found his employment history wanting. The interview was with And Software, a company that designed computer software and sold it by mail order.

Things had got off to a bad start because Matt, who had promised to wake Sam and give him a lift to the business park, had gone off to work without doing either and he was late. Fortunately the manager doing the interviews agreed to see him at the end and Sam was eventually shown into his small and rather untidy office. He was about Sam's age and seemed very easy going.

'Hi Sam,' he began, 'my name is Martin Smith, Sales Manager here at And Software. Make yourself at home.' He pointed to a chair facing his desk. 'Being late's not the best way to impress a potential employer, Sam. What went wrong?'

Sam decided dishonesty was the best policy.

'The bus driver had a heart attack and we had to wait for a replacement,' he explained matter of factly. Martin looked shocked and concerned. 'He'll be fine apparently,' Sam added hastily, 'I got him into the recovery position, called an ambulance and gave him mouth to mouth until the paramedics arrived. They were certain he'll pull through.'

'Wow, pretty impressive.' Martin whistled. 'Have you trained to do stuff like that?'

'Can't say too much about it I'm afraid,' said Sam

confidentially, 'all a bit hush-hush.' Martin thumbed through the application form but drew a blank. 'This is strictly off the record,' Sam continued conspiratorially, 'but I'm sure I can trust you, I'm part of the Special Operations Reserve Division.'

'Never heard of that one,' said Martin, sounding unconvinced.

'Of course you haven't. That's the whole point. I'm a sleeper you see; undercover, I can be called on at a moment's notice. That's why my employment record looks a little patchy.'

'Right,' Martin nodded hesitantly, 'I see. How does a degree in English qualify you for that kind thing exactly?'

'You have to write a lot of reports,' explained Sam.

'Don't you think you're a bit over qualified for this post though?'

'It's what I need right now.' Sam allowed a waver into his voice. 'My last assignment was, well let's just say it was demanding.'

'Quite, of course,' said Martin, briskly moving on. 'As you know it's a very low basic wage here but you make it up with commission. That tends to mean we often get all sorts of dreamers and no-hopers applying. It'll be quite a coup to have someone with your background on board Sam.'

'Thank you Martin, and I'm sure I can rely on your absolute discretion.'

'Indeed, absolute,' agreed the manager, shaking Sam warmly by the hand. 'I shouldn't really tell you this but the job offer will be in the post to you tonight.'

'Thanks. I'll look forward to that. Let's hope there are no major incidents for a month or two at least.'

Sam arrived back home determined to make the most of his last few days of freedom. His latest project was a thriller set in Canada but he had never been there and was having difficulty setting the scene. Most of his previous efforts were campus stories and he had to admit the characters and plots were all unremarkable, hence the change of genre and location. He could carry on writing after going back to work of course but it tended to have a detrimental effect on his output.

It was starting to dawn on Sam that he might not make it as a writer, at least not as quickly as he had first expected. Even getting agents to take an interest was difficult; never mind publishers. The agent who turned down his last book liked his style but had no demand for the type of thing he was writing; it was all too arty and inconsequential. He really wanted thrillers so Sam sent him synopses for three, set in Canada, Alaska and Siberia called 'Thine is the Kingdom', 'For Ever and Ever' and 'Amen.' The agent replied by return saying that he had a publisher who was very interested in the project and if he could get a few chapters out quickly there was the possibility of a book deal and a sizeable advance.

The Canada book opened with a skidoo chase but he had no idea how fast you could go in a skidoo and was trying to find out on the internet. He had just found a useful site when he heard the front door open.

'Hi honey, I'm home!' Matt called.

This was the reason, in addition to a chronic shortage of funds, why Sam needed to get a job. Matt worked as a driving instructor and most people wanted lessons before and after work or at weekends, so he was often at home during the day. He bounded up the stairs and burst into Sam's room.

'Your twelve o'clock cancelled,' said Sam.

'A no show actually, which is good because I still get paid and I have nothing booked in till three so we have time for a leisurely lunch. Fancy going up the Maid Marian for a two for one?'

Sam disregarded what he took to be an attempt at smutty innuendo and declined the offer. There was no point, Matt couldn't drink before a lesson and the food was terrible.

'Although I am hopeful that a modest celebration will soon be in order,' he added, looking significantly at his friend.

There was a pause while Matt slowly pieced it together.

'Oh shit! The interview! I'm really sorry, mate, I completely forgot. How late were you?'

'Pretty late,' Sam confirmed, 'but let's just say I managed to turn it to my advantage; I was more or less promised the job.'

'Great, we can start catching up with the rent.'

Matt was usually good at keeping on top of the bills but he had just paid the balance on his holiday and things had started to

slip.
'Yeah, I'll pay you back every cent once I start shifting that software!'
Matt looked at his friend and nodded, smiling, though he was thinking Sam was surely the last person on earth you would offer a telesales job to.
'I'm going to make a quick omelette,' he said, turning towards the door, 'fancy one?'
'I would if we had any eggs.'
'I'll nip round the inconvenience store and get some,' said Matt amiably, 'chucky eggs are on me!'
In so far as he had a conscience, Matt was clearly still feeling guilty about the interview. As he descended the stairs, Sam called after him, 'how fast do skidoos go?'
Matt stopped for a moment and considered.
'Not sure mate. We don't do lessons on them at Pass Masters I'm afraid.'

Peter Spencer, a close friend of the family, had given Jess a part-time job at his solicitors practice in Nottingham. It was mostly clerical work, answering the phone and audio typing, but it was ok. It got her out of the house and earned her some money and Peter was a very understanding boss. The problem was his son Jack. He and Jess had been at school together and he had always been keen on her but the feeling was not mutual. In the second year of a law degree, he spent a lot of time at the office during holidays and a fair amount in term time too. The problem was, he seemed convinced that Jess would eventually come round to his way of thinking. Though he never said anything directly, she got the impression that Peter would like nothing better than to have her as a daughter in law, and she also suspected that her father nurtured similar hopes. They both seemed to be blind to the fact that it was the last thing on earth she wanted.

It was an unusually quiet Monday morning and Jess found herself with a little time on her hands. The more she thought about Sam, the more he interested her. She barely knew him of course, but she liked what she had seen. He seemed sensitive,

artistic and funny, all the things that Jack would never be. She smiled to herself as she thought about him.
'A penny for your thoughts, Miss Beresford.'
It was Jack. She wondered how long he had been standing there and coloured a little, hurriedly getting back to checking some purchase invoices. One of her jobs at Spencer's was ordering the office stationery. The practice had been using a small local firm for years and she liked the old chap who called in to take the orders. He had been a help to her when she first started, explaining all the different products and indicating how many were normally ordered at a time. Jack wandered over to her desk and studied one of their invoices, shaking his head.
'Parkinson's are so expensive. Look at the price of those legal wallets.'
'I know they're a lot,' Jess defended herself, 'but we've tried cheaper ones and they just fall to bits.'
'We can get the best for much less than this though. I know because I play squash with the rep from Cuteprice Office Supplies. I've asked him to give you a call actually. Make sure you see him, name's Gary Swift.'
'I get people calling all the time, Jack. You get what you pay for.'
'We'll see what Mr Swift has to offer shall we? It's always the right price at Cuteprice.' Jack said this without a trace of irony and Jess struggled to keep a straight face. Fortunately someone else had caught his eye and he was already moving off to bother them.

Jess usually managed to get away at about three o'clock. This gave her a chance to pick up some shopping and still arrive home in time to help with the evening meal.
Everything was under control in the kitchen when she got in so she went off to find Tom, on study leave now, as she had not had a chance to speak to him since their conversation in the paddock. She found him lying on his bed, staring up at the ceiling.
'Don't bother to knock,' he said apathetically.
'How's it going?' asked Jess, trying not to sound too earnest.

‘What?’
‘Oh, life, university and everything,’ she tried, which earned her a half smile.
‘I am working actually,’ he explained, ‘enclosures, corn laws, Luddites and rotten boroughs all meshing round in my head like a Rubik’s cube.’
‘Sounds vaguely promising; I can come back later if this isn’t a good time.’
‘If you want to do something really useful,’ he grinned, ‘I could murder a peanut butter sandwich.’

The family usually ate together but there was often a shortage of conversation at the table. This evening was different; Tom had clearly decided to make an effort. He asked Mark about rising food prices and how much extra was likely to find its way back to the farm. Jess was worried that her parents would suspect something but they seemed to be enjoying this new articulate version of their son. Mark, true to his profession, explained that input costs were rising just as fast and any benefit would be negligible.

The farm had been in the family for generations. It was really too small to punch its weight economically but Mark had resisted offers from bigger neighbours whilst eschewing opportunities to expand. Much of the land was too hilly for efficient arable farming and was down to pasture; sheep and dairy, with the larger, flatter fields for winter wheat or oil seed rape. In his head, he knew it was no longer viable but his heart did not want it to go under on his watch. Jess suddenly realized how hard it must have been for her parents trying to keep this failing business afloat for so many years. She thought of the cost of keeping Darcy, the vet’s bills they had never once complained about, and felt guilty. Christine was from a farming family too and had always been actively involved, particularly in the office. She was explaining to Tom about subsidies, set-aside and wildlife zones, things she had never talked about in detail before.

During a brief lull in the conversation Tom suddenly looked pointedly at Jess. ‘Anyway, who was that bloke you were

talking to down Dumbles on Sunday morning?'
Jess was shocked. He must have been gazing out of his bedroom window and watched the whole encounter. For some reason, she blushed.
'Oh he'd just strayed off the footpath a bit and I was pointing out that he was actually trespassing,' she explained, trying to sound offhand.
'You seemed to be getting on pretty well.'
She threw him an angry look. 'We had a chat. Yeah, he was quite nice actually.'
Christine smiled at her conspiratorially. She was less of a Jack Spencer fan than her husband.
'I must put a sign on that gate,' muttered Mark, 'people often walk straight up the field.'
'Get his number sis?'
'No! Course not!' she cried, wishing she had.

Three

On Wednesday morning a letter arrived from And Software offering Sam the job and inviting him to call to arrange a start date. He rang straight away to accept and was offered a place on an induction course the following morning. He was asked to read and sign the contract sent with the letter and take it in with him.
'They don't hang around,' he muttered, skimming through the densely printed pages, grimly noting just how low the basic wage was. The hours were not what he expected either; there was some evening work. That was ok though, he liked to write in the mornings. He knew several people who had worked for Andsoft, most of whom said they were a pretty reasonable employer. Maybe it would work out all right.

Matt gave him a lift the following morning. He was early so they badged him up in reception and showed him through to the canteen, which was deserted. There was no early shift because accounts and after sales were dealt with by a different call centre. He wandered over to the hot drinks machine and inserted a pound, selecting a white coffee. The machine whirred and gurgled but no cup appeared and his coffee spurted into the vacant space and straight down the drain. He looked around in confusion but there was no one to ask. Wondering whether to try again, he noticed an adhesive note lying on the floor. 'This is a green machine!' he read, 'no cups supplied. Please use your own mug!'
He pressed it back onto the fascia where he assumed it belonged and took a seat at one of the tables. After a few moments the note fluttered gently back down onto the floor like an autumn leaf.

People were starting to walk past the canteen entrance on their way to the workstations. Sam glanced up to see Martin Smith in the doorway beckoning him over.

'Hi Sam, glad you decided to come on board,' he said enthusiastically. 'We'll just shoot over to my office to go over some paperwork then I'll hand you over to HR for your induction.' He set off at speed and Sam had to hurry to keep up. 'Tomorrow and Monday you'll get some product training. In fact if you could familiarise yourself with the 'bible,' as we call it, over the weekend it will help you get off to a flyer. On Tuesday CRM will do some sales training and for the rest of the week you'll ride pillion with one of the seniors in telesales to get some live experience. Ok?'

Sam nodded. He had worked for big companies often enough and knew that HR stood for Human Resources, a term he hated, and CRM meant Customer Relationship Management. He had been expecting Martin to make a reference to the tale he told at his interview, but it was never mentioned.

The induction was uneventful. He was photographed, given a proper ID badge, a door entry swipe card, two white polo shirts with the company logo, a black ampersand, embroidered on, briefed on the dress code (no jeans or trainers) and given various health and safety, rules and regulations type booklets. He was then ushered into a room to watch a series of corporate videos. The person doing the induction was reassuringly cynical about the whole process. He was supposed to sit with Sam during these but said he would go completely insane if he saw them one more time and bunked off to the canteen. He told Sam he could go home when the films had finished provided he promised to read all the company rules stuff, sign the slip to say he understood it and bring it back with him the following day.

As Sam sat half watching the videos, Jess was meeting Gary Swift of Cuteprice Office Supplies and he was exactly what she expected, pushy, cocky and over familiar. She handed him a list of products they ordered regularly and asked him to email a quote with his best prices.

'Cool,' he drawled, 'but aren't you going to give me an idea of

what you are paying; something to aim at?'
'I don't think that would be very fair.'
'Ok, no problem, I can easily blow Porky's prices out of the water.' Jess almost smiled. Geoff Parkinson was rather overweight. 'But I don't think you quite get how we work. There are all sorts of incentives I can offer you like gift vouchers and air miles. For instance, if you were to give me your current buying prices, I could guarantee to beat them and put you on double air miles for the first three months of the contract. It's a win-win situation.'
'Contract?' queried Jess.
'Yes, that's right. It's in your interest. If we can lock you in for twelve months we can guarantee to hold your preferential pricing for the whole period.'
'I don't think we'll want a contract and I'd prefer you to quote blind if you don't mind. I'll stick with Squeezyjet for my trips abroad, thanks.'
Gary was clearly irritated but he remained ingratiatingly enthusiastic.
'Fine, fine,' he said, 'you're the boss.'
He left her with a pile of catalogues and priority access to their on-line ordering system. As soon as she had shown him out, Jess sat down heavily and sighed. The thought of young Mr Swift descending on her every week was more that she could bear. She was just getting ready to leave when Jack breezed into the office.
'How did it go?' he asked, casually.
'I gave him a list of stuff to price up and he left all the regular sales literature,' she replied matter of factly. 'He's going to email me their best prices in the next day or so and I'll do you a spreadsheet comparison.'
'Fine,' said Jack a little uneasily. 'I asked Gary to open an account for us anyway so that everything would be in place if we do decide to give him the business.' Jess did not reply and carried on tidying her desk. 'Oh, and before you go, could you just give me that list of our current buying prices?'
She looked at him blankly with barely disguised contempt. It was obvious that the decision had been made and the air miles

account already opened. She briskly attached the file and emailed it to Jack.

'On its way.' she said curtly.

'Thank you darling,' he grinned, 'what would I do without you?' Jess did not respond. 'Oh and while I think about it are we still on for the Young Farmers' disco next week?'

Jess was taken aback, having completely forgotten that he had asked her weeks earlier about this. At the time, she had just been evasive, hoping he would let the idea drop.

'It's difficult with my mum and everything,' she said hurriedly as she logged off.

'But she really wants you to go. Your dad was telling mine the other day. They worry that you never go out any more.' He moved towards her and she scooted round the opposite side of her desk, grabbed her bag and bolted for the door.

'Not sure if I'm free,' she called over her shoulder. 'I'll check and let you know.'

'You'll enjoy it, you know you will.'

'I'm sure I shan't,' she snarled through clenched teeth as she hurtled down the stairs.

Four

On Sunday morning Sam rose early, determined to get a couple of hours in on the novel. Matt had woken him at five a.m. as he fell up the stairs, mercifully unaccompanied, and he decided to get straight on. The product training on Friday had been very intensive. He was given some publishing software and a photo-editing suite to take home to play with and was impressed with all of it. For the first time in a long while he felt genuinely optimistic about starting a new job.

He typed steadily on the laptop but his mind kept wandering. Jess had been in his thoughts all week. They had made a connection and he desperately wanted to see her again but could not work out how to contact her. Matt had a mate who worked at the Land Registry and said he could easily find the name and address of the owner of that field, but Sam only wanted to use this as a last resort. It seemed a bit sneaky and not the way he wanted to find her. His plan was simple; go back there at the same time and see if she showed up. That was the only option open to Jess if she felt the same way about him, the only possibility of encountering him again. He set out early to make sure he got there in good time.

Jess was thinking along exactly the same lines, though she did not often ride on Sundays. The bridleways were usually at their busiest with small children and dogs to contend with and she always had plenty to do in the kitchen. Today she had decided to go on foot because several paths converged at the bottom of the field and they were not all bridleways. If Sam were true to his word, he would stay out of Dumbles because the sheep were back in.

In the event Sam arrived almost an hour earlier than planned.

After a fine start, it had turned cloudy, spotting with rain, and a gusty wind was strengthening. He had not expected to see livestock in the field and was uncertain what to do next. Stupidly he had brought neither a waterproof nor a map. He knew roughly the direction in which Jess had ridden off so he decided to explore that way. The path was clear enough as it followed the stream but at the next gate it veered off up the hill towards the village. If she lived in a farmhouse nearby it was very unlikely she had taken that route and he could not tell which way she might have gone. It started to rain heavily and Sam felt angry and foolish. How naive to assume he could breeze out there a week later and just bump into her again. How arrogant to think she would take the trouble to seek him out. He turned back and sat for a while on the fence at the bottom of Dumbles as if willing her to come trotting down the hill on Darcy. Although his fleece was shower proof, he was starting to get seriously wet. People probably rode in all weathers but he began to think it was increasingly unlikely that she would be out in this. He jumped off the fence, re-crossed the stream and dejectedly set off back the way he had come.

Jess was just entering the top of Dumbles as Sam disappeared from view into the trees at the bottom. She had seen the rain clouds blowing in and was suitably dressed in cagoule and over-trousers. She was hoping Sam had decided to take shelter among the trees surrounding the little pond where they met. Her heart sank as she drew level with it to find no sign of him. She carried on to the bottom of the field and waited for a while by the gate knowing it was unlikely he would be hanging around in this weather. She was about to give up and head back to the house when her mobile rang. It was in her jeans pocket and by the time she had burrowed into her waterproofs the call had diverted to voicemail. She clicked on missed calls; it was Tom. What on earth did he want? He was normally far too mean with his credit to call her and if he did he would usually hang up quickly so she had to call him back. Before she could do this, it rang again. It was Tom again! She was worried now. She jabbed the answer key. 'What's up?' she barked anxiously.

'He was there!' Tom exclaimed.

'Who?'
'Him, the guy you met last week! He was sitting on the fence right there but he's headed off along the path towards Thorpe's plantation.'
'Is this a wind up?' she asked with panic in her voice, already setting off in that direction.
'Go now and you might just catch him. Go!' was all Tom shouted as he hung up.
Jess stuffed the phone into her jacket pocket and squelched off at a trot towards Thorpe's. Luckily Sam had stopped for a while under the shelter of the taller trees in the hope that the rain might ease. It did seem to slacken a little, so he ducked back onto the path and set off briskly as Jess rounded the corner. She was just in time to see him as he dropped down the slope to the new concrete bridge that re-crossed the stream. She shouted his name at the top of her voice but the wind roaring in the trees drowned her call. Sam plodded on and Jess stopped, knowing there was no chance of catching him now. She stood breathless, rooted to the spot, watching him disappear out of her life.

Sam could never explain what made him look round at that moment. It was as though some primeval sixth sense kicked in just when it was most needed, a throwback that has survived from a time when we needed to know were being watched. Whatever the reason, he did look round. He turned back from the stile and walked uncertainly towards her. She pushed back the floppy hood that was obscuring her face, hoping the moisture on her cheeks looked like raindrops, and smiled.
'Jess!' exclaimed Sam with an incredulous laugh. 'It really is you!'
'Look at you,' she grinned, 'like a drowned rat!' and they both laughed.
'How on earth did you find me here?' he asked in amazement.
'I have spies everywhere,' was all she replied.

There was nothing for it but to take Sam up to the farmhouse and dry him out. As they squelched back the way they had come there was a momentary awkwardness between them. Suddenly and unexpectedly arriving at where they both wanted to be had

caught them off guard and they were not sure what to do next.
'Where's Darcy then?' asked Sam, immediately reprimanding himself for being so predictable.
'He's a bit old to be out in this weather,' Jess replied. She decided to be more direct. 'Did you finish the poem?'
'No, no. It was just jottings really, you know, bits and bobs.'
'Is that why you came back?'
'How do you mean?'
'To finish the poem.'
'Oh that, no, not really,' he said but was thinking, 'she came out in this weather, she somehow spotted me in the distance and ran after me. Say it man, say it.'
'I came out this way because I wanted to see you again,' he said at last.
'Is the right answer!' exclaimed Jess and they both laughed with a mixture of happiness and relief.
'For a poet you're bloody inarticulate!' she chuckled and Sam just grinned and nodded. She looped her arm through his and leaned into him as they marched up to the farm.

Sam was literally soaked to the skin. The house was built to cope with all this, having a shower just off the back porch. Jess opened the kitchen door to explain to her mother, only to find Tom standing there with a towel, a pair of jeans, boxers and his favourite T-shirt neatly folded in his outstretched arms.
'Hi. I'm Tom, Jess' brother. Saw you coming up the field and thought you might need these,' he said, handing the stuff to his sister.
'Cheers mate, I'm Sam by the way.'
'Nice to meet you! I'll leave you two to get your kit off then,' he grinned.
Jess glared at him but Sam just laughed.
'What have we got here then?' asked Christine as she peered into the porch.
'Oh hi Mum! This is a friend of mine, Sam. He got soaked this morning so I thought he could get dried off and have some lunch with us.'
Christine looked puzzled but not particularly concerned.
'Yes, of course, there's plenty.' She turned to him. 'Hello Sam,

nice to meet you. I haven't heard Jess mention you before. Have you known each other long?'
There was a pause, then Tom looked theatrically at his watch.
'One week…precisely,' he announced.
'Haven't you got work to do,' Jess hissed. Then turning away, 'I'll just explain the eccentricities of the shower to Sam then come and help you with lunch Mum.'

As Jess entered the kitchen, a very muddy Mark was making his way through the yard having spent much of the morning trying to clear a blocked drain in the top field. She did not pay much attention as the back door banged but when her father did not appear after a few moments she gasped, dropped her knife and bolted for the porch. It was too late. Mark had already stripped off and marched into the shower room where Sam, who had just finished, was standing, towel in hand. They stood facing each other for a few seconds as Sam hurriedly wrapped the towel around himself.
'You must be Mr…' he began, then realised he had no idea what their surname was.
'Beresford, Mark Beresford.' Mark informed him tersely. 'And you are?'
'Oh hi Dad!' Jess exclaimed as she rushed into the porch. 'You've met Sam then.'
'Yes we're thoroughly acquainted thank you Jess. I'd better wait out here for a moment I think.'
'No, don't worry Dad. Sam can finish getting changed in my room. Grab the clean clothes, Sam, while I chuck your wet stuff into the tumble dryer.'
Fortunately the kitchen was deserted because Christine had gone for a lie down. They hurried up the stairs and Jess showed him into her room.
'Make yourself at home,' she grinned, 'I'll go and finish doing lunch. Come down when you're ready.'
Sam sat down on the bed. It felt odd to be trusted so unreservedly. They hardly knew each other yet here he was alone in her room with all her precious things arranged on her desk and her laptop and purse left openly on display. He looked

around. Stuck to the wall were photos of Jess with groups of friends, partying and on holiday, all the regular stuff. As he dried himself, he flicked through her CD collection, nodding approvingly. Not quite up to date but who bought CDs these days? Recollecting himself, he quickly squeezed into Tom's clothes, and, grimacing in the mirror at the Lord of the Rings T-shirt, tidied his hair and slipped out of the room.

Lunch was a bit awkward. Tom monopolised Sam, quizzing him on football, music, computer games and mobile phones, about all of which he appeared to give the right answers. Mark and Christine had little knowledge of or interest in any of those subjects and Jess was busy dishing up. Once she was sitting down it was no better; there was so much she wanted to say to Sam but it was impossible with an audience. The conversation was spasmodic, with Sam telling them about his new job at Andsoft, which Tom thought was really cool, especially if you got free software. They both veered off into a byzantine discussion about photo editing and in the end it felt more comfortable for everyone to just let them get on with it. None of this mattered to Jess; it was just a prelude, like sound checks at a gig that had to be patiently sat through before things got going in earnest. All that mattered was Sam was there, Sam was there and making a good fist of keeping the show on the road too, even if some members of the cast were not performing.

At the mention of washing up, Tom did his usual disappearing act. Mark and Christine wandered off for a snooze and at last the opportunity arose for some private time together, albeit at the kitchen sink. Jess took cups of tea through to her parents and came back to find Sam up to his elbows in foamy water. She walked up to him and hugged his arm.

'You were brilliant!' she exclaimed, 'and I'm so sorry about all that.'

'About all what?'

'You know, my dad blundering in on you and having to sit down to a meal with a bunch of people you've never met before and my geeky little brother…'

'It's really nice having one's arm embraced like that but it

makes doing dishes a bit tricky,' said Sam, sidestepping the tribute. Jess just smiled and stood close to him as she dried, leaning into his shoulder.
'Well, you've been thrown it at the deep end with my family, so now you have to tell me all about yours,' she said as they sat down at the kitchen table with a coffee.
'Ok. Well I was born in York -'
'What happened to t'accent lad?'
'My dad was in the army so we moved around a lot. I've lived all over; Germany, Hong Kong, Pembrokeshire, loads of places.'
'Sounds brilliant!'
'It wasn't really. I don't remember much about most of it and anyway I was often at boarding schools back here.'
'Ok. Siblings?'
'Just a big brother, Dave. He's five years older so we never had much in common and were never at the same school. He's living in Oz now with a wife and kid so I don't think he'll be coming back any time soon.'
'Parents?'
'Would it help if you shone a lamp in my eyes?' Sam suggested, but Jess just waved this away. 'Dad took his army pension years ago and tried a few jobs but never settled so last year they went over to live with Dave and Suzy. He's in real estate and has done really well. They built Mum and Dad a little bungalow in the garden. It's worked out brilliantly.'
'Yeah, baby sitters on tap! Any plans to visit?'
'I couldn't afford the flight even if I wanted to.'
'And you don't?'
'Not really; not at the moment. I'd feel out of place and painfully unsuccessful.'
'Last question, for the moment anyway, what brought you to Nottingham?'
'Uni,' was the simple answer. 'I came here to read English five years ago and it's been home ever since.'
'So let me guess, you're a struggling writer who's working in call centres to make ends meet?'
'Yep, that's pretty much it. My parents aren't impressed. It cost

them a lot to get me my degree and now they think it was a waste of my time and their money, especially as Dave has prospered without an A Level to his name.'
'Well you'll just have to prove them wrong, won't you?' said Jess encouragingly.
He told her about the possible book deal and how important it could be, even if it wasn't the kind of thing he really wanted to write.

By the time Jess had brought him up to date with her life, it was getting late. She went to fish his clothes out of the tumble drier and took him back upstairs to change. She logged onto her laptop and they and linked up on Facebook.
'We're friends now,' Jess laughed, 'it's official!'
Sam reluctantly said he should be off home as it was his first proper day at work the following morning. Luckily Mark was about to visit his sister in Nottingham and offered him a lift, but as he was late it meant leaving in a rush. Jess was disappointed they hadn't said goodbye properly. She went back upstairs and lay on her bed trying to take in what had happened. It had been a strange but brilliant day and she felt happier than she had for ages. She sent Sam a text saying, 'So glad we met!' finished off with a smiley and an x. He replied, 'Can't wait to see you again.' Jess was soon chatting online with her friends in Leeds telling them all about him. Having someone special in your life, someone to think of and talk about was like an emotional Satnav; she would never feel lost now.

Five

Jess was woken by sunlight beaming through the gap in her curtains. She jumped out of bed and looked out. The storm had blown itself out during the night and left a glorious cloudless morning. Everything had been rinsed clean by the rain. The fields and sky shone in the brilliance of the new day. Perhaps it did not occur to Jess that there could be another reason why the world looked so wonderful. She decided to get up right away even though it was earlier than usual.

It was far too lovely out to wear one of the dull suits she had bought for work. Jess flicked through her wardrobe and her hand alighted on a yellow summer dress she had not worn for ages. She took it out and held it up to herself in front of the mirror. 'This might be a tight squeeze,' she thought as she tried it on. It was a bit tight round the tummy but she could get away with it. She rummaged around for her favourite tan sandals. Having plenty of time, she spent longer on her hair and makeup than usual, finally walking over to the wardrobe to appraise the results in the full-length mirror. Her legs looked a bit anaemic but there was no time to apply fake tan and in any case she didn't care; she felt great!

Walking into the kitchen she was surprised to see Tom at the table munching his way through a plate of scrambled eggs. Of course, brain food; it was his first exam. The rest of the family assumed she had risen early to wish him luck so her flicker of guilt about forgetting was only momentary. Tom did a double take as she waltzed into the room.

'Wow! What's the fashion show in aid of?' he exclaimed.

Christine turned round from the sink and smiled approvingly.

'It's got legs!' she squealed.

Jess twirled in a little jiving movement. 'Well, it looked such a

super day, I just felt like dressing up a bit.'
'And why would that be?' asked Tom.
'Just did, that's all,' she laughed. 'Anyway, Sigmund, have you got your head together for Psychology?'
'Piece of piss,' he replied smugly and Christine pulled a face.
Jess took her lunch box out of the fridge, grabbed an apple and took a bite.
'No breakfast?' her mother asked.
Jess patted her stomach and shook her head.
'Does my tum look big in this?' teased Tom, but there was no malice in his voice.
'I think she looks fab,' said Christine, as Mark walked in from the yard.
'Day off?' he asked, noticing the dress.
The others all grinned conspiratorially.
'What a difference a boy makes,' Tom sang tunelessly.
Jess coloured a little but it felt nice to have her relationship with Sam acknowledged. For the first time in ages there was an air of optimism in the house that morning. It was the perfect way to send Tom off for his first exam.

As she was early Jess offered to give Tom a lift to school. It was their first chance to talk alone since the momentous events of the previous day.
'It was great what you did Tom, calling me yesterday.'
'Certainly seems to have perked you up, sis.'
'Yeah, he's nice. I know it's early days and all that but I can't help wondering it's kind of like fate he should just show up out of the blue last week. Anyway, you certainly seemed to hit it off with him.'
'Makes a change to have someone normal to talk to in that house.'
'I know. I'm so sorry. It must have been hard for you.'
'It's harder now though in a way. I'm beginning to wonder if they know that I know.'
Jess smiled. Her little brother was starting to develop a half decent sense of humour. She pulled up outside the school and he jumped out.

'Good luck!' she called.
'No sweat,' he replied, calmly waving her away.
Jess sped off back towards Melton road. She loved this old car, a battered Fiesta that had been in the family for years. Originally her mother's, it had become a sort of family pool car now. Jess had learned to drive in it and Tom was supposed to be but this had been rather neglected due to Christine's illness. Jess resolved to make time to take him out regularly as soon as his exams were over. She certainly owed him one.

A few heads turned as Jess walked to her desk. She got on well enough with the other clerical staff at Spencer's. The fact that she was a family friend and allowed flexible working might have caused resentment but it had not been a problem. She worked closest with Kerry, who though a little younger was more experienced, having worked there since leaving school.
'You're looking very glam for a Monday!' she cried cheerily.
'It's the sun,' smiled Jess, 'it really bucks me up.'
'Shame it didn't make an appearance over the weekend.'
Jess nodded her agreement as she logged on to her terminal. She was relieved to see no email from Gary Swift. Geoff Parkinson was due to call and she was hoping to be able to give him one last order before the inevitable happened. Her heart sank as her phone rang; she could see from the display it was Jack.
'Morning darling,' he murmured, 'do you think you could just pop and see me for a sec?'
She did not reply but immediately crossed the office, knocked once on Jack's door and walked straight in.
'Ooh you look nice! Haven't seen you in that little number since my eighteenth.'
Jess remembered with horror that it had been bought especially for his party, at which she had nominally been his partner. Wearing it now was sending out all the wrong messages. She sat in the chair facing his desk. He was shuffling through some spreadsheets and she could see various columns highlighted in yellow.
'Gary got back to me last thing Friday and I've been doing some work on it over the weekend.' He handed copies across

the desk. 'I think you'll have to agree it's pretty conclusive.'
Jess scanned through the list. It was showing an overall saving of over twenty percent.
'If these are definitely like for like then I can't really argue. Not that it's my decision anyway.'
'I don't want you to feel I'm going over your head though.'
'So long as they match the quality and service we get from Parkinson's I've got to accept it's a very competitive tender. But Gary mentioned something about a contract. What does that involve exactly?'
'Oh that's to our advantage. We get these low prices guaranteed for twelve months.'
Jess had nothing more to say.
'I knew you'd agree. Gary's calling in later today to finalise things.'
'I'm expecting Geoff actually. I was going to give him an order. What do you want me to do?'
'Perfect opportunity to tell him.'
Jess just nodded. Although it would be hard, she wanted to tell Geoff herself and make it clear the decision was not hers.
'Is that all, Jack?' she asked coolly.
'Just one more thing. Do I get the impression from your choice of attire that you've made your decision about that disco?'
'I'm afraid that would be the wrong conclusion, Jack. The fact that I had completely forgotten when I last wore this dress should tell you all you need to know. I'm seeing someone else, so I'm afraid I won't be available.'
'Couldn't you have told me this sooner? It's a bit late to ask someone else now.'
'I'm afraid not,' said Jess, walking towards the door. 'Why don't you ask Kerry? She seems to think you're wonderful.'

Sam's day began early too. One of his jobs on Saturday had been cleaning up an old bike that lay abandoned in the outhouse, originally an outside toilet, in the back yard. It was filthy but basically serviceable and since he vaguely remembered somebody saying you got a small bonus for cycling to work, he decided to give it a try. He was not on the shift system so was due to start at eight all week. By the time he had managed to park his bike and stash his helmet and jacket in a locker, it was time to meet up with his mentor for the week, Gill Smith, a senior sales exec. On Friday he had been left on his own at a PC to go through some product tutorials and generally familiarise himself with the whole suite of programmes, trial versions of which he was given to take home. He was fairly computer literate and made good progress on Saturday. The plan now was to concentrate with Gill on the 'features and benefits' of each product and learn them bullet point fashion. He tapped on the door of her office and was invited in to find himself standing face to face with Gill Benson, his old college girlfriend.

'Hello, Samuel,' she said, clearly enjoying the advantage of surprise, 'nice to see you again after all this time.'

Their relationship had not ended amicably. Gill dumped him very publicly during the Summer Ball at the end of their second year and they had spent their final year avoiding each other.

'Gill! Oh my god, hello,' stammered Sam, 'You're obviously -'

'Married,' she finished for him, 'yes, to Martin, which is how I know all about you and your little performance at the interview.'

'Oh god.' said Sam.

'Don't worry soldier boy, your secret's safe with me, so long as you play your cards right that is. Luckily dear little Martin is very trusting, bless him, a useful quality in a husband don't you think?'

Sam gulped. Gill walked right up to him and rubbed her hands across his chest.

'You've filled out a bit since I last had you. Are you any better in bed these days Samuel?' She broke his name up into three distinct syllables, lingering on the last one.

'Look Gill,' Sam tried to assert himself, 'I can live without this shitty little job. You've got no power over me you know.'

'I think I have. Lying at an interview, getting a job under false pretences, it's not just a sackable offence; it's fraud.'

'Bollocks!' Sam exclaimed. 'I'm not wasting any more time here. I'm off.'

He turned to leave but Gill skipped round him and stood between him and the door.

'I like a man who stands up for himself,' she purred. 'I don't remember you being so cocky,' and reached down and squeezed his crotch. Sam winced and backed away, 'you have no right to treat me like this!' he cried.

'I can think of a lot of men would be only too pleased,' she boasted, though she was indeed a stunning figure; tall with green eyes and a mane of dark wavy auburn hair, like a pre-Raphaelite heroine.

There was an awkward pause, and then her manner changed abruptly.

'The fact is, Sam, it's Martin whose job is in the balance. You are the latest in a string of duff appointments. Fortunately he didn't refer to your little special agent fantasy on your record because you 'swore him to secrecy' but if it ever came out that he swallowed such a blatant lie it could be the final straw and we simply can't afford that at the moment.'

'Well I wasn't planning on telling anybody.'

'Good,' said Gill, 'because you are going to be my star pupil, a real high flier and Martin is going to get all the credit for it.'

After that it was as though nothing had happened. Gill became brisk and professional and they spent a couple of hours intensively running through all the packages. Eventually she broke off.

'That's great. You've really got a handle on all this stuff but how do you feel about actually selling it to real live punters?'

'I don't see why not. It's a good product, they're all existing customers and the deals are really attractively packaged. What's not to like?'

'We'll make a salesman of you yet Samuel Taylor! Go and get some lunch and come back here in an hour.'

Sam stumbled out of Gill's office feeling shell-shocked. Deciding he needed some fresh air, he headed for the small garden area round the back of the building. He turned on his mobile hoping there would be a text from Jess but there was not. He wanted to send her a message but he couldn't really say that he'd just been touched up by his ex from university. In the end he just thumbed in 'Heavy morning! Hope your day going well. Call you tonight.'

By the time Jess got back to the general office, Geoff Parkinson had arrived and was sitting by her desk. He stood as she walked towards him and they shook hands. She was horrified to see the Cuteprice catalogue clearly visible in her filing tray. 'Oh well,' she thought, 'might as well get straight to the point.'
'I see you've had a visit from Mr Swift, then.' Geoff clearly had the same idea.
'Yes, I'm afraid he's a mate of Jack's and he got his foot in the door.'
'He's a mate of anyone who can get him an order. I expect he's claiming to undercut us by a sizeable margin?'
'He is,' Jess nodded, 'and I'm very sorry to say the decision has already been made. I've been told to start ordering from him today.'
Geoff softened a little. 'I know this isn't your fault Jess and I'm probably wasting my breath but if you take my advice you won't sign a contract with them.'
Jess raised an eyebrow. 'That did strike me as being a bit dubious I must say.'
'That's an understatement. The small print says they have the right to substitute out of stock products for a suitable alternative. I'm sure I don't need to tell you what that amounts to.'
Jess nodded again; their contract prices were a fiction. They would wriggle out of them before the signature had dried by sending inferior substitutes.
'It was good of you to warn me, Geoff.'
'Well it's in my interest too. They'll still want to supply without a contract. You may lose out on some perks but at least you'll be able to boot them out when you find out how awful they are.'
'And come back to you begging for forgiveness,' smiled Jess.
'Something like that maybe,' said Geoff, getting up to go.
Jess decided it would be best to run this by Jack immediately. She walked quickly over to his office, tapped on the door and entered. Peter was standing by Jack's desk.

'Oh, sorry.'
Peter looked up and smiled.
'Hello Jess. You're looking very glamorous today. How's Mum?'
'About the same thanks. Shall I come back later?'
'No, don't worry if it's quick,' said Jack, 'I'm sure Dad won't mind.'
'I've just told Geoff Parkinson and he pointed out something that's quite important.' Jess explained, trying not to be too specific.
Peter looked puzzled. 'Just told him what, Jess?'
She just looked across at Jack and waited. Already the colour was draining from his face.
'We've had a much lower quote from a competitor and we decided to give them a try, didn't we Jess?'
'Without consulting me?' There was an edge to Peter's voice. 'You seem to have forgotten that Parkinson's are a very good client of ours. It's not just a matter of saving a few coppers on sticky tape, it's reciprocal business.'
'Well that's the thing,' Jess said, hoping to retrieve the situation. They both looked up at her expectantly. 'Geoff said whatever you do, don't sign their contract. Then we can boot them out as soon as we like.'
Peter laughed patronisingly. 'You seem to be forgetting that we are a firm of solicitors, Jess. We wouldn't sign anything without putting it under the microscope first would we Jack?'
Jack had his head in his hands now.
'I already did,' he said very quietly, 'and gave it to Gary at the gym last night.'
Jack assured his father he would see Gary when he called and get him to tear the contract up. He would understand; it wouldn't be a problem. But Gary never came. When he was half an hour overdue a girl called Lisa rang from Cuteprice to say he was running late and had asked her to take the order. The very first item Jess gave her was out of stock, but they 'had an alternative of similar quality.'
It was going to be a very long twelve months for Jack Spencer.

Sam was given some respite from Gill after lunch. The purchasing manager of an important buying group arrived unannounced and she was deployed to look after her. Sam was allowed to spend a few hours working through some more tutorials and was glad of the opportunity to consider his predicament. He could not decide whether Gill was seriously interested in him. He had already heard plenty of gossip about her. It was an open secret that she had slept with most of the senior management. He needed to keep out of her way for the next few days at all costs, even if it meant pulling a sickie. He was just starting to feel better about things when a pair of hands suddenly clamped over his eyes.

'Sorry to leave you all on your own. Did you miss me?'

Sam did not move or say anything so Gill released him and looked at the screen.

'What have we been up to then?'

Again Sam did not respond. They were in a secluded room used for meetings and training and were unlikely to be disturbed. He was trapped.

'Martin's away on a course for couple of days. How about coming round for some supper tonight, catch up on old times?'

'Why are you doing this?' groaned Sam. 'I didn't know who Gill Smith was of course but in the short time I've been here I've heard all sorts of things about you. You seem to be able to swim with much bigger fish than me whenever you fancy so what exactly is the attraction?'

'Don't you see? I just fancy a minnow. I want to be top of the food chain for a change. Now stop wasting my time and make sure you come to my office at five sharp.'

'Ok,' muttered Sam grimly, 'I'll be there.'

'That's better,' she said as she turned to leave, 'make sure you come.'

'I said I'll be there.'

She nodded and walked briskly away.

Sam sat in silence for a few moments, then stood up and walked down to the main reception. He took off his badge and handed it with his swipe card to the girl at the desk.

'You have to take these with you otherwise you won't be able to

get in tomorrow,' she explained patiently.
'I'm not coming back tomorrow.'
'Well you'll still need them for your next shift.'
'I'm not coming back ever. Can you tell HR for me please?'
The girl looked concerned.
'There are people to talk to if you have a problem,' she began, but Sam was already on his way. As he hurried out he realized he had left his cycling gear in the locker. There was no way he was going back for it now. He just turned and ran as fast as he could for the main gate.

Jess did not read Sam's text until she had pulled up at home. She felt a bit guilty for not checking her phone earlier but it had been the weirdest of days. She knew he was working until five so there was nothing to do but reply saying she was looking forward to speaking later. As soon as she sent this, her phone rang.
'Hey! Did they let you out early?' she asked cheerily.
'No, just broke out and made a run for it.'
'Seriously, how come you finished early?'
'Seriously, I just walked out.'
'Why?'
There was a silence. She could hear Sam breathing heavily and was really worried.
'Sam, what's happened? Where are you?'
'I've just been running that's all.'
'I'm going to come and get you now. Where can I meet you?'
'Is it easy to get to the Nottingham Knight?'
'Yes.'
'Ok I'll walk up there and wait for you.'
Jess was about to start the car and head straight back to town when she remembered Tom's exam. She could not just drive off without seeing how he had done. She sat undecided for a moment, then suddenly jumped out of the car and ran in to the house, making Tom and Christine jump as she burst into the kitchen.
'How did it go?' she asked breathlessly.
'Hey sis, chill. It's only a bloody exam. It was harder than I

expected but nothing to panic about. Why are you in such a state?'

'I just had a call from Sam,' she explained, 'he sounds in trouble and I have to go and meet him.'

'What sort of trouble?' asked Christine.

'It's to do with work. I don't know any more than that. Sorry but I really have to go now. I'll call you.' And with that she hurried away, adding as an afterthought over her shoulder that she was glad the exam had been ok.

'That's a shame,' said Christine looking over to where Jess had been standing. 'She seemed on such good form this morning and now she's all flustered. I'm not sure if that boy is going to be good for her. We don't know anything about him. Can you send Jess a text asking her to let us know where she's meeting him?'

'Might not be such a great idea, Mum. She's a big girl and Sam didn't look all that dangerous to me.'

Jess sped into the pub car park and found a space near the entrance. She quickly checked her face and hair in the mirror. It was all somewhat best before but there was no time to fix it. Her dress looked a bit crumpled too but it would have to do. She walked briskly into the bar and spotted Sam in the corner hunched over a pint of lager. He stood up and waved as she approached and they embraced rather awkwardly.

'You look nice,' he said, stepping back to admire her. 'Do you normally dress up for work?'

Jess just shrugged. It wasn't what she had come to talk about.

'I'd have got one in for you but I've no idea what you drink. What would you like?'

'Oh nothing for me thanks. I'll just have a sip of your lager if you don't mind. So what's been going off today?'

Sam began to tell her about it. They were sitting next to each other in an upholstered corner seat and Jess squeezed up tight, holding his hand. She became increasingly angry as Sam recounted the events of the morning.

'Don't forget I work at a solicitor. You need to speak to Nigel. He's red hot on employment law. They'd get slaughtered in a tribunal!'

'But would they? The company have done nothing wrong. It's just the behaviour of one individual.'

'And what a cow! What a thing to do, especially to someone you were once close to.'

Sam began to relax having talked it over. It was great to have someone who really cared about your feelings.

'Thanks for coming over. You've been brilliant. I can't tell you how much it means to have you on my side.'

Despite her confidence that litigation would be successful, he was inclined to forget about the whole thing. He just wanted to put it behind him and move on. By way of changing the subject, he asked Jess how her day had gone.

'Funny you should mention that,' she sighed.

It was after ten by the time they had finished picking over her day. Sam suddenly realised he was starving but Jess said it was too late for her to eat and offered to run him home via the chippy. She was curious to see his house, a Victorian terrace near the Melton Road shops. Sam invited her in and she was tempted but decided she really needed to get home. It was going to be a difficult day at the office. They chatted for a while longer and Jess tried again without success to persuade him not to throw up his job. Sam thanked her again for coming over, and they kissed. Jess wished she didn't have to go but knew her parents would worry if she were any later. She kissed him again, pinched a few of his chips, promised to ring him from work in the morning, and headed home.

Matt was in his customary place on the sofa when Sam walked in.

'That was a long shift,' he called as Sam tried to find a clean plate in the kitchen. Giving up, he brought the polystyrene tray through.

'It was the shift from hell,' he said, slumping into the armchair. He fast-forwarded through his day. The more he recounted it, the worse it seemed. Matt was less sympathetic but probably more realistic.

'You shouldn't have done a runner mate, that won't improve

your case at all.' He helped himself to a chip. 'Can I finish these?' Sam nodded. He didn't really want to say too much to Matt, particularly about his previous relationship with Gill.
'Think I'll get off to bed,' he sighed, 'I'm bushed.'
'Where have you been all this time anyway?'
'Jess came over and took me for a quiet drink to talk me down.'
'That's nice. Still going well with her?'
'It's good but we need to spend more time together and do some fun things. It's all been a bit crap so far.'
'What sort of fun things?' asked Matt.
'All sorts.'
'Well don't forget I'm off to Xante with the gang next week so you could invite her over and fool around a bit here.'
'Well I could if the council would agree to fumigate the place first.'
'Yeah, we do need to start making a bit of an effort.'
Sam did a double take. 'I must be dreaming. Did you really say that?'
'It is a bit of a pigsty. Let's blitz it one evening this week.'
'I can carpet bomb it all day tomorrow if you like, so long as you agree to do your bit and help keep it that way.'
'I think you should go in, if only to make a complaint.'
Sam shook his head. 'I can't go back now. I just couldn't face it. Anyway, don't change the subject. What's this super nanny thing all about? I noticed you haven't been bringing any trophies back lately. Has word got round that you live in squalor?'
Matt seemed to want to talk properly for a change. Usually he was very flippant and shallow, avoiding revealing too much about his feelings but tonight he was different.
'It's made me think, you meeting Jess. I've realised I'm sick of one-night stands and casual sex. I want a proper grown up relationship too; one that's got the potential to develop into something really significant and lasting.'
'I hope you're right about that, Matt but you can't possibly know about me and Jess. I'm in the relationship and even I don't know it yet.'
'No,' said Matt, 'I can tell. It's what you want, you've been

ready for this for a long time now and you want to make it work. I'm jealous mate, I really am.'
'You going to have a quiet fortnight in Xante then?' asked Sam with a grin.
'Seriously mate, it's going to be the last big bender then I'm going to change. You just see if I don't.'
'Well it'll be good to share with someone who occasionally washes up and cleans the bathroom,' said Sam standing up and clapping his mate on the shoulder. 'Don't wake me tomorrow. I'm having a lie in.'
'What about the cleaning?' Matt shouted after him.

As Jess sped back home she remembered she had promised to ring. There was no point now; her mother would have gone to bed ages ago. As she walked in she was surprised to see Tom sitting at the table tapping away at his laptop.
'Sorry I didn't ring.'
'Mum was a bit worried but I said you'd be fine. They asked me to wait up and text you if you weren't back by ten.' Jess looked up at the clock, it was almost eleven. 'I knew you'd be ok,' he shrugged. 'What was the problem with Sam anyway?'
Jess gave a brief summary of Sam's experience, concluding that she had tried to convince him it would be best to go back.
'Bet he doesn't.'
'Well I think that would be a shame. There were lots of things he liked about that job and it's not right that one person should be able to wreck it.'
Tom nodded without looking convinced.
'Did Jack Spencer get hold of you?'
'No. Did he call?'
'He came round, seemed a bit agitated, said he needed to see you urgently.'
'Well he never rang me.'
'Perhaps he guessed you were with your lover,' said Tom, lingering on the last word.
'Probably,' said Jess, refusing to be provoked. To change the subject, she asked Tom about his next exam. They talked a bit about how their mother was doing, so much easier now Tom

knew, then she excused herself and headed upstairs.

Jess sat up in her room for a long time going over the day. She wondered what Jack could have wanted. She thought about Sam, sent him a text to say she was thinking about him, then waited for a while but no reply came.

Six

Sam had not set his alarm but still woke early. For a moment he wavered. Jess and Matt were both insistent that he should go in but there was just no way. He would call HR at nine o'clock and confirm that he had resigned; another kick in the nuts for his flimsy CV.

He picked up his phone and noticed a message envelope. With a tingle of excitement, he saw it was from Jess. He was just wondering whether it was too early to reply when his phone started ringing. It was not a number he recognized but he answered it without thinking.

'What happened to you last night?' It was Gill and she sounded worried.

'How did you get my number?'

'Your application of course. I assumed some of it must be factual.'

'I've left. You've got no power over me. You can get lost!'

'You can't leave.'

'I already did.'

'No you haven't. I picked your ID up from Mandy on reception and told her you were the victim of a beginners prank. As far as the company is concerned you have not resigned. I think I explained Martin's job is on the line and it's important you don't fail. I need you Sam.'

He so nearly hung up on her but something was nagging him.

'So why were you so obnoxious yesterday? How was that going to help exactly?'

There was a pause. He could hear her breathing unevenly.

'I think I'm having some kind of a breakdown,' she said eventually. 'It won't happen again I promise. You have shown real aptitude so far and people with your potential don't come

up that often.'
'It's probably something to do with the pathetic basic salary.'
'The targets are very achievable and there are lots of perks.'
'Like a blow job in the training office?'
'Look, I've said I'm sorry.'
'Actually, you haven't.'
'Well I am; I am sorry. I'll arrange for you to buddy up with someone else on the sales team for the rest of the week and I'll keep out of your way.'
'I could report this you know. I've already spoken to a solicitor.'
'Don't push your luck. I know you need this job and you lied at the interview don't forget.'
'Not in writing.'
'It was recorded.'
He didn't believe her but he'd had enough now anyway.
'OK. I'll come back, but only because I do like the look of the job. Leave my things in reception, I'll pick them up on the way in.' He terminated the call before she could reply.
He could hear Matt moving around downstairs. It was half seven already. Maybe he could scrounge a lift from his new caring sharing flatmate.

'This is a pain,' said Matt as the traffic moved slowly along Wilford Lane.
'I know, I'm sorry.'
'No I don't mind giving you a lift, it's just that everyone's assuming I'm the learner and making suicidal efforts to overtake me.'
Sam smiled and decided to quickly try calling Jess. She answered on the second ring.
'Hi. How's it going?'
'I'm going in.'
'Good. I know it's hard but I think it's the right decision. Well done.'
'Thanks, and thanks for your support last night, it really helped. Matt agreed with you too, for what that's worth.'
'Hey!' shouted Matt, 'Do you mind?'
Jess could hear him and there was a smile in her voice as she

asked. 'Was that him?'
'Yeah, he's giving me a lift in, bless him.'
'Hello Jess!' called Matt.
'Say hi,' she said. 'I want to meet him.'
'Why? She says she wants to meet you! Why do you want to meet him?'
'I want to meet all your friends. I want to know everything about you.'
'You're so nice. When are we meeting again?'
'Tonight if you like; I'll want to know how you got on.'
'OK. I'll call you later.'
'OK. Good luck.' She so wanted to say 'love you' but the conversation just petered out with them both saying 'bye' softly several times.
'I so envy you,' Matt said as he dropped Sam off at the gates.

As Jess drove in to work she decided it would be best to see Jack straight away to find out why he had called round. She was surprised to see that his dark green mini was not parked in its usual spot. Maybe he had gone back to Bristol to revise for the exams.

Talking to Sam had made her a bit late and she hurried up the stairs to the office. The conversation between the other girls died as she walked in. As she started up her terminal, Kerry got to her feet and walked up to her desk.
'Mr Spencer said to tell you as soon as you arrived that he wants to see you in his office,' she said morosely.
Jess was beginning to get the impression that whatever had gone wrong was clearly being perceived as all her fault.

Peter Spencer seemed troubled as he motioned her to the chair facing his desk. He dispensed with asking after her parents and the usual pleasantries.
'Jack won't be working for the practice any more,' he began bluntly.
'I suppose he has a lot of work to do for his exams now.'
'You know it's not that. Yes he's got exams but it's not the reason he's gone. He won't be coming back, ever.'
Jess gasped. 'You've fired your own son?'

‘He resigned. I think he felt his position was untenable after making such a blunder. I have to be fair to the other partners. Anyone making an error of judgement like that would have to be severely reprimanded and I can’t bend the rules for my benefit. He was irresponsible and inept. If this ever gets out it will make us a laughing stock. He felt it would be best for both of us if he quit.’ He paused for a moment as if trying to regain his composure and there was a quaver in his voice as he concluded, ‘I can’t pretend I’m not devastated though.’

Jess was too shocked to say anything and sat quietly as Peter seemed lost in thought for a while.

‘Anyway, he has at least confirmed that you are completely blameless in this sorry affair and has asked me to apologise for the awkward situation he has put you in.’

Jess suddenly burst into tears. She felt guilty about the way she had treated Jack the day before and was genuinely upset for him. Peter waved a box of tissues in her direction. She helped herself to a couple, blowing her nose noisily, and let out a shuddering sob.

‘I’m so sorry,’ she gasped.

‘You have nothing to be sorry about but you do have to be clear about one thing; the office staff are not to be told about what has happened and why Jack has gone. How much do they know about what went off with this boy from Cuteprice?’

‘Unless they overheard me talking to Geoff, Mr Parkinson, which is unlikely, they won’t be aware of Jack’s involvement.’

Peter Spencer rubbed his chin. ‘Good,’ he muttered. ‘You see we think we can get out of this contract quite easily. Jack is not an authorised signatory and we doubt if Cuteprice will fancy mixing it with us if we cancel immediately. We would prefer it if the office staff never find out what happened though.’ He looked at her significantly.

‘I certainly won’t say anything but I get the impression from the atmosphere out there this morning that they know something’s up.’

‘You are referring to young Kerry I suppose?’

Jess just shrugged.

‘Did you know,’ he continued ‘that Jack invited her to the

Young Farmers' disco? They won't be going now of course and I suspect that's what's bothering Miss Foster.'
'Oh dear,' said Jess, starting to cry again, 'that's my fault too. Perhaps I should resign as well. I won't feel right working here after all this.'
'That's not what we want,' said Peter firmly, 'and not what you deserve either. Why don't you take the rest of the day off while things calm down here? Come back tomorrow and make a fresh start.'
Jess agreed this was probably the best plan. She gathered her things up and slipped out while the others were on break.
'God, what a pair,' she thought as she drove away.

Mandy was already at her post in reception at Andsoft when Sam walked in. She smiled grimly at him and reached under the counter for his things. Looking over her shoulder she murmured, 'I'm not supposed to be talking to you about this but just tell me one thing, has that cow Smith been bullying you?'
'I just over-reacted to something, that's all. It's sorted now but thanks for your concern.' He took his badge and swipe card and moved towards the staff entrance. Mandy gave him a knowing look as he turned away. 'You're not the first and you certainly won't be the last,' she hissed. 'If it happens again see Keith Edwards in HR. He's been trying to nail her for months.'
Sam spun back for a second and their eyes met, 'I'm new, the job's important to me and I don't want to make trouble.'
'I understand,' she nodded, 'but remember what I said.'
He bowed his head in silent acquiescence and walked away.

The morning passed quickly. Sam shared a terminal with Ross McKenzie, one of the more experienced 'Outgoing' telesales workers.
'We call this section Outgoing because we're calling people up; people who have bought from us in the past but have gone a bit quiet. Here is my call list for today. Double click on the first name and it brings up his history,' he pointed at the screen, 'these are the products he's bought and today I've got an offer he can't refuse: software upgrades for all these applications for just £9.99!'

Ross used the same approach for each call, asking first whether they were still using the packages and what they thought about them. He then moved on to explain the advantages of the latest versions, all the time getting agreement that this or that feature would be really useful. He would then tell them the list price for all the upgrades and finish up by saying: 'If I were to tell you that for today only you can have all of this for just £9.99, what would you say?'
They almost all said 'Yes', and each time Ross would wink and smile at Sam, who wondered if he would be able to make it seem quite so easy.

Jess decided to go straight home and take Darcy out.
Walking upstairs to get changed she heard her mother call from the bedroom.
'Mark, is that you?'
Jess walked in to find her in bed.
'What are you doing at home at this time of day, love?'
'It's a long story Mum, I'll tell you later. More importantly, what are you doing up here, are you feeling worse today?'
Christine looked sheepish. 'I didn't want you to know, but when Tom goes to school I take myself off to bed. I just feel so exhausted all the time.'
'Oh Mum!' Jess cried, tears springing into her eyes, 'why didn't you tell me? I would have taken time off work.'
'That's why I didn't tell you. You've sacrificed enough already.'
Jess sat on the bed and clasped Christine's hand. 'It's nothing special working at Spencer's you know. You're more important to me than anything and if you're not coping, I need to know. Now I'm going down to sort some lunch out for Dad. Can I bring you a bit of soup or something?'
'I'm not hungry now thanks love and your father is quite capable of making himself a sandwich when he's ready. You get on with what you were planning to do. Are you going to meet Sam?'
'I'm going to make you some soup whether you like it or not and I'm sure Dad could do with more than bread and cheese,'

she said, getting up to go. As she walked out, she could see her mother was already drifting back to sleep.

Jess quickly changed out of her work clothes and ran out to find Mark. He was just pulling into the yard in the tractor. Ignoring his question about why she was home early she asked angrily, 'Why didn't you tell me Mum has been spending all day in bed? She looks terrible. It's not fair keeping quiet about that!'

Mark suddenly looked drawn as the mask of cheerfulness slipped from his face. 'She really ought to be in hospital, you know but she's so stubborn. She is absolutely determined to get Tom through these exams if it's the last thing she does.'

'It will be at this rate!' exclaimed Jess. 'Look, Tom may seem a bit dozy at times but he's not stupid. He's guessed that something's up and I haven't denied it. He knows that Mum's had a relapse.'

Mark seemed stunned. 'I can't believe you told him. We -'

'He worked it out for himself!' Jess interrupted, 'and I wasn't prepared to lie to him. He was so grateful to be treated like an adult for a change. I would never have volunteered it but honestly it was the best thing that could have happened!'

'Well make sure you don't tell your mother,' said Mark angrily.

Suddenly something snapped inside Jess.

'Stop being such a bloody martyr!' she yelled, 'and stop treating me and Tom like kids. If Mum needs to be in hospital then let's get her admitted. It's crazy behaving like this. Who's benefiting exactly?'

Mark hardly reacted to this outburst. He just stood there looking a bit hurt and crestfallen. 'It's not hospital your mum needs,' he said finally, 'it's a hospice; that's the next stage and there'll be no coming back from there.'

Without saying another word he turned and walked slowly towards the house.

Jess was shocked for a moment. She knew things were bad but not as serious as that. She called after her father but he did not turn round as he entered the back porch.

Jess felt so overwrought she decided it would be best to go out on Darcy for a while. She walked pensively down to the

paddock and sat in her usual place on the fence. He soon spotted her and wandered over.
'At least someone's pleased to see me,' she said pressing her forehead against his and patting him on the neck. An airliner droned slowly overhead and she watched it for a while and wished Sam was there.
'I'll just have to make do with you, won't I?' she whispered to Darcy.

Sam called Jess as soon as he got in from work.
'I'm so glad you had the bottle to go back, well done!' she said.
'I can hear birds singing. Are you outside?'
'Oh yeah!' she exclaimed, 'I'm out on Darcy. I needed to clear my head.'
She went on to tell Sam about Jack's resignation.
'Have you got anything planned tonight?' asked Sam.
'No, not really. Want to meet up?'
'Of course! Look, it's the Poetry Café in town tonight. I normally go and read there. I think you might enjoy it. It will take your mind off work and you can meet all my eccentric poet friends.'
Jess agreed to pick him up at eight. She did not mention what happened with her parents. It still felt a bit too raw to talk about.

As Darcy plodded back up the hill to the paddock Jess noticed Tom wandering up the farm track, plugged into his ipod. She trotted over to meet him and dismounted, walking alongside.
'How were Economic History and Business Studies then?'
Tom pulled a face. 'Tougher than I expected; didn't really get the subjects I wanted but you know how it is with essay papers, you just have to massage the question so you can write what you want.'
'Ok,' Jess said without sounding too convinced, 'so you've got a bit of a break now haven't you?'
'Yep, three more next week and all over on Thursday!'
'Great, so are you still planning to head off to Cornwall?'
'It's all a bit up in the air. None of the girls are being allowed to go at the moment so that's going to like totally wreck things.'

'How are things going with Amy?'
'Nowhere. She's still obsessing about Danny Prince even though he dumped her at Christmas. It's like she doesn't even see me.'
Jess could sympathise with Amy to some extent; Dan was a nasty piece of work but he was a bit of a hunk. She wisely chose to keep this observation to herself though. When they reached the paddock, Jess led Darcy in and Tom helped her with the saddle and bridle. He didn't seem to be in a rush to go in so they sat together on the fence while Darcy drank from the trough and ambled off down the slope.

Their relationship had changed since their talk the previous week. Tom had emerged from being a self-centred virtual reality geek to become someone who she felt she could share her feelings and concerns with. It was weird really; in the space of a few days she had found two people to confide in where previously there had been no one. Continuing their previous conversation, she pointed out that he could still go to Cornwall with the lads and that it might actually be better camping without a bunch of girls to contend with.
'That's a bit sexist sis. They all did really well on the Duke of Edinburgh expedition, but I see what you're saying; I expect they can only last so long without hair straighteners.'
Jess was about to mention the episode with her parents when Tom asked her how things were going with Sam. He was really pleased when she told him they were meeting again that evening.
'By the way, do you know what Jack Spencer wanted last night?'
'Not really. He said he needed to speak to you urgently and would give you a call. I assumed he was upset about you and Sam.'
'No, I think it was probably something to do with work but he's gone back to Bristol for his exams now so I suppose it can't have been that important.'
Jess went on to tell Tom about their mother and how she had lost her temper with Mark. Tom seemed a bit shocked by this and Jess wondered if she had made a mistake mentioning it.

'Maybe it's time to tell her that I know,' he said after a pause, 'after all you've told Dad now and it would be so much better if she didn't have to make the effort while I'm at home for the next few days.'
Jess put her arm round his shoulder and gave him a hug.
'You're such a star!' she said. 'You've grown up such a lot in the last week.'
'Maybe I was grown up all the time but nobody noticed.'
'Maybe.'
'You two look very conspiratorial!' It was Mark, who had walked up without them noticing.
'Tom's just joined the escape committee. We wondered if we could have a vaulting horse in the paddock.'
'Darcy might get jealous,' chuckled Mark.
'Or too friendly,' suggested Tom.
'Yes, could get very messy,' agreed Mark. 'Anyway, how did the exams go today?'
Tom put a fairly positive spin on his performance and then, announcing he was in urgent need of a peanut butter sandwich, took himself off without another word.
'He's gone so that we can talk,' Jess explained. 'We have so underestimated that boy, Dad.'
'And I've underestimated both of you. I came down here to apologise, Jess. It's been like having tunnel vision for the last few weeks. These exams have been the only thing your mum and I could focus on. Tonight we'll all sit down and talk properly, four adults together.'

Jess was running late by the time she set off to pick up Sam. As Mark promised, they sat round the kitchen table and talked and it had been a very productive meeting. The very fact that Tom knew yet could still handle his revision and exams was a huge relief for Christine. She seemed to visibly strengthen during the discussion. It was agreed that Jess would take the rest of the week off work so that Christine could have a few days complete rest. The fact that she was planning to hand her notice in was not mentioned. She decided to talk to Sam before finally making up her mind.

It was half eight by the time Jess collected Sam. They parked up by the Playhouse and hurried down Maid Marian Way to The Yard, the bar where the Poetry Café was held. This was through a narrow entrance off Angel Row, which opened up into a courtyard. The bar was on the first floor above an empty shop. It was a long, narrow room with an atrium ceiling. There were no seats left so they found a space by the bar and Sam ordered two bottles of Czech lager. He shook hands with several acquaintances and introduced them to Jess but she didn't catch their names. He waved to Declan, the MC who mouthed 'second half,' to which Sam nodded and gave thumbs up. He hissed to Jess that the first half was full so he would have to read after the break. She nodded and smiled. It was all so strange and exciting. She loved the way Sam had whispered in her ear.

Declan moved into an area of the bar that was vaguely spot lit and stood patiently waiting for the din to subside.

'Hello!' he shouted.

'Hello!' chorused the regulars, rather raggedly.

'I'll just try that again,' Declan said. 'Hello!'

The response this time was suitably raucous.

'Welcome to Stance, open mike night at the Poetry Café! Tonight as always we have a fine selection of talented writers to educate and entertain you for the open floor. If you want to read and haven't got you name down, we have some space after the break, during which there will be a raffle…' He paused here and a few people cheered with exaggerated enthusiasm.

'During the interval we will be having a raffle,' he repeated and this time everyone whooped and hollered hysterically.

'Thank you,' he said solemnly then displayed the dubious prizes one by one, all of which were all applauded with similar fervour.

Declan began the evening by performing one of his own poems. His writing was witty and intelligent with a delivery similar to stand up comedy.

'Good isn't he?' Sam whispered to Jess and she smiled and nodded.

The open floor part of the evening was of more variable quality.

The poets were not introduced by Declan, just told who to follow. Most read rather then recited from memory, some were very nervous and hesitant whereas others were extremely voluble and waved their arms around wildly. Some chatted to the audience and introduced their work whilst others just read their poem and sat down quickly, but everyone was given enthusiastic applause. To close the first half, Declan introduced the guest poet, who had come up from London. He was an Anglo Caribbean called Smartman who was very stylishly dressed in a cream suit and fedora hat. His work was delivered in Jamaican dialect and performed with expert timing in a deadpan style. He talked about the Brixton riots, the 'sus' laws and the persecution that black people experienced during those times. He spoke with anger, passion and humour too and no bitterness. He was given a massive cheer at the end.

At the start of the interval, Sam went to get more drinks and buy the mandatory raffle tickets. He got chatting at the bar to one of the performers, a tall man in his forties with long unruly black hair, dressed in a battered green corduroy jacket and jeans. He was one of the regulars, an extrovert whose poems were always slightly deranged, as if written whilst under the influence; which they probably were. By the time Sam got back to Jess she was deep in conversation with a woman called Lauren, who had read in the first half. She was another regular who wrote cleverly observed poems about family and gender issues, which were always wry and witty. In her mid thirties, she was a divorcee with two 'pro teen' children as she put it. She had long fair hair and wore a full-length dark cotton print dress with a short, colourful embroidered waistcoat. As Sam approached she smiled and asked him if he was reading in the second half.

'Have you heard him before?' she asked Jess, who shook her head. 'Oh he's great,' she continued 'we've all been dying to meet the subject of all those love poems.' She waved a hand which held an unlit cigarette and began to make her way down the stairs. 'Nice to meet you Jess,' she called over her shoulder.

Jess looked quizzically at Sam.

'Maybe she's right,' he said, 'perhaps you are the subject of these poems; it's just that I hadn't met you.' They both laughed as she squeezed herself against him.

'Love poems,' thought Jess, 'that should be interesting.'

The interminable raffle finally drew to a close. It was the sort where you fervently hoped you would not win a prize and in this sense Sam and Jess were lucky. Declan came round telling performers the running order for the second half. Sam was on straight after him. Jess worried that she would put him off but he was faultless, performing two poems from memory along with a bit of banter with the audience during the introductions.

'You were great,' Jess said as he worked his way back to her. 'I liked that one called 'Arithmetic of Love', it reminded me a bit of some of the metaphysical poets like John Donne.'

'Thanks,' he said, 'yes it was supposed to be a sort of affectionate pastiche of their work; not that I'm comparing myself to them of course.'

'You're way better!' she said, standing on tiptoe to kiss the 'as if' expression from his lips.

'Do you mind if we go soon?' she asked, 'it's getting a bit late.'

'No, course not. I would have liked to see Smartman's second set but there are loads of floor performers to get through yet. We'll go straight after this one.'

A slight, rather pale young man with a shock of red hair had taken the stand.

'Hello, I'm Ned,' he said. 'I want to start by improvising a poem on a theme suggested by the audience, so don't stop to think, just shout out the first thing that comes into your head.'

'Red-hot sex!'

It was Jess who had called out first. She put her hand over her mouth and looked at Sam uncertainly but the whole house erupted in cheers and shouts of laughter. People were nudging Sam or slapping Jess on the back and making arm-flexing gestures. It was a while before the hubbub died down.

'Any more suggestions?' Ned asked nervously and everyone said 'No way!'

'Well that's fine, I can do red-hot sex!' he said brightly.

There was a general muttering of 'not what I heard' from the crowd and more laughter.

Ned's poem was full of innuendo with a lot of panting, gasping and extravagant gesticulating. It was not terribly good but everyone enjoyed it. When Ned had finished, Sam started quietly waving goodbye as they moved towards the exit. This caused further amusement, with calls of 'early night then?' as wolf whistles, yelps and howls accompanied their exit.

They walked hand in hand through the courtyard but before they burst out into the main thoroughfare, Sam bundled Jess into the doorway of the empty shop. He held her really tight and kissed her hard on the lips.

'You were fab tonight,' he whispered in her ear, 'I really loved being with you. I think you're gorgeous.'

'Thanks,' said Jess, 'I think you're more than gorgeous. You can kiss me again if you like.'

'You up for a bit of red-hot sex then?'

'Oh yeah,' she breathed, 'but not right here.'

Seven

Next morning, Jess lay in bed thinking about the previous day, the turmoil at work, the row with her dad and the Poetry Café with her crazy outburst.

'They'll all think I'm a right slapper,' she thought with a smile. It was good though because it had moved her relationship with Sam up a gear, even if in the end nothing happened. It was late by the time they got back to his house and when he invited her in, she declined. No doubt the place was still a tip and although keen to meet Matt, she wanted Sam to herself. It had been impossible to talk properly at the Yard Bar because it was so crowded and there was not enough time on the journey home. In the end their parting had been a bit of an anticlimax, just a quick snog in the car before she had driven away. Sam was such a strange mixture; so sensitive and articulate in some ways and yet tongue tied and clumsy in others. 'Typical bloke,' she sighed. But it was good not to rush things; she knew Matt was off on holiday and they would get their time together soon enough.

Jess decided to send Peter Spencer an email at work booking holiday for the rest of the week. She was just spending a few moments deleting stuff from her spam filter when she noticed an email from Jack that had been there for a few days. He must have changed his web mail provider because the message had not been allowed through to her inbox. Jess opened it apprehensively. She felt obliged to read it but had a feeling that it was going to spoil her holiday mood.

'Hi Jess

Tom has probably told you that I called to see you tonight. I was going to ring you but couldn't pluck up the courage.

Mainly I just want to say that I am SO SORRY. I have behaved

like a complete prat. I have let you down, and my father and my whole family too.
I am self-centred, arrogant and immature and you are so perfect and intelligent and lovely. You were right all along about that business with Gary Swift but I was so certain I knew best. I can't believe I was so ignorant and I am afraid you will never forgive me and that I have lost my chance with you now.
Jess I want you to know that I LOVE YOU. I have always loved you and I kind of took it for granted that we would be together one day. Please tell me there is still a chance.
I have so much work to do for my exams but I just can't concentrate. I can't get you out of my head. All I need is some sign from you that I can still hope and that if I can change and become a better person you will find room in you heart to forgive me.
I have told my Dad that you were totally blameless for the fiasco at work and it was all my fault.
Please take pity on me and give me a straw to cling to. Just say it is not completely hopeless. That is all I ask.
Your penitent friend
Jack.'
Jess could not bear to see people suffer and her first inclination was to reply but she soon realised that was impossible. Someone in Jack's state of mind would interpret any form of reply, however negative, as a lifeline. She decided the best thing was to do nothing. It was already too late in any case, and she could just deny ever having received the email if it was ever mentioned. Yes, the recycle bin was the best place for that message and before she could stop herself she clicked on the delete icon.
'Gone,' she said to herself, 'and good riddance!' She knew it was the right thing to do but she knew too that an aftertaste of guilt would stay with her for the rest of the day.

After saying goodbye to Jess, Sam had felt similarly mixed emotions. He didn't have long to dwell on them though because he walked in through the back door to find the kitchen piled high with bulging bin bags. From within he could hear the rev and rattle of the vacuum cleaner. As he moved towards the sitting room, the washing machine clicked round to spin and leapt into epileptic convulsions. In a state of shock Sam peeped round the kitchen door to discover Matt belabouring the sitting room carpet with the asthmatic hoover.

'Oh my god!' shouted Sam, 'your really mean business don't you?'

Matt switched off and the motor droned down through the octave of its limited range.

'This is crap!' he said, 'it's not picking up at all.'

'Well maybe the bag needs changing.'

'What bag?'

Sam kicked the plastic carcase of the thing. 'I think you'll find there's a paper bag full of toxic waste in there.'

Matt reached down, flicked the slide on the front and it popped off to reveal the bag in question, which was so full it had burst. A wad of grey matter flopped out and a cloud of vile smelling dust puffed into the air.

'Shitshitshit!' screeched Matt jamming the cover back on, 'this is just making things worse!'

Sam laughed, unplugged the machine and carried it through the kitchen into the back yard. 'There's no time to loose, we have to go directly to theatre!' he cried in an American accent. 'We're going to need everything you've got! Oh and bring the Marigolds could you old boy?'

Using the light from the kitchen window Sam reopened the patient. Matt arrived with an unhygienic looking pair of rubber gloves and a pack of bags for the cleaner. 'Found these under the sink. They look as though they might fit in there.'

'OK, clear everyone, I'm going in.' Sam flipped open the wheelie bin then deftly unfastened the punctured bag and gently lifted it in. He took a replacement from Matt and fitted it with similar dexterity.

'I think it's going to be -'

'OK' they both said together.

Back in the living room, Sam looked up at the ceiling and noticed cobwebs.

'Aren't you supposed to dust before you hoover?'

'Why?'
'Well there's no point sucking all the crap up off the floor and then flapping a load more down.'
A lengthy debate followed concerning the pros and cons of dusting first, with Matt growing increasingly impatient. 'Surely any cleaning is a step forward in our current situation,' he grumbled.
'Well that's certainly true mate and I'm very grateful but in future I think you'll find it better to dust first.'
'You'll make someone a lovely housewife.'
'I'll go and do battle with the evil empire in the bathroom then.'
'The Force is strong in that one. By the way, they're supposed to be coming to fix the shower tomorrow so don't bother making it all spotless just for some sparky to mess up.'
'There's not much danger of that,' muttered Sam.

It was late by the time Sam got to bed and although he was pleased they had at least made a start on the house, he was concerned about the novel. He had planned to do some work on it before turning in but was too tired by the time he had got to grips with the bathroom. He needed to get a few chapters in to the agent while the publisher showed interest and he reluctantly decided it would be best if he didn't see Jess again until the weekend.

The sun was just coming up as Mark Beresford trudged across the farmyard towards the house. He stopped for a moment to take in the glamour of the morning sky; another day rinsed clear by a night of rain. A few long wisps of cloud were layered above the rind of rising sun, their underbelly glowing bright cerise beneath the dove grey of their surfaces. It was a stunning spectacle and despite his weariness from the troubles of the past year, Mark could not help being moved. He stood open mouthed for a moment, entranced.

As he stumbled into the kitchen, Mark was surprised to discover Jess, up and dressed, standing at the stove frying bacon and eggs.
'I thought you were having a few days off.'
'I am indeed,' she said brightly, 'and the first job of the day is to

give you a decent breakfast. Do you want fried bread?'

'I'd love fried bread,' Mark patted his paunch, 'but I'm not sure if I need it!'

'Nonsense! It'll do you good. Ready in two minutes!'

Mark walked over and gave Jess a hug.

'Thanks love,' was all he said before hurrying off to wash his hands. It was true; he hadn't had a decent breakfast for ages. In fact for weeks he had done nothing but snack during the day.

When Mark sat down to the table, Jess joined him with a bowl of slimming cereal. 'Aren't you having some of this after going to all the trouble of cooking it?'

'Now I do need to lose a few pounds.'

'I don't think so,' smiled Mark.

The door opened and Tom drifted in wearing his school football shirt and shorts.

'What on earth has got into you two?' Mark exclaimed. 'I didn't expect to see the lie-in king till lunchtime at least!'

'It looked such a nice morning I decided to go for a run. Anyone seen my trainers?'

'Probably in the back porch where you left them.'

'Thank you Mother.'

For a second, like a glitch in a digital broadcast, the room froze as they all registered the unintended significance of Tom's remark. Just as quickly it returned to normal and he went off to rummage in the porch.

'How is Mum this morning,' asked Jess softly.

'Zonked out again,' sighed Mark, 'I'm beginning to think her prescription for painkillers must be wrong. They said at the hospital the medication would make her drowsy but it seems to be knocking her out.'

'Why don't you have a word with Rupert?'

Robert Best had been the family GP for as long as the children could remember. Jess had mistakenly called him Rupert Bear as a child and it had stuck as a family nickname.

'Yeah, good idea,' said Mark rubbing his chin thoughtfully, 'I'll see if I can give him a call later.'

Tom stuck his head round the door to announce his departure.

'Do you want a fry up when you get back?' Jess called after

him.
'You bet!' he yelled back.
'I won't bother washing up yet then,' said Jess as she yawned and stretched.
Mark finished his tea, thanked Jess for the breakfast and went back out to finish off after milking. Although it was relentless, he liked the routine of farm life. Getting up early had never bothered him and there was plenty of variety on a mixed farm like his. The problem was it had not really been a viable economic proposition for years; the farm was a bit of a relic, the last of an extinct species still clinging on at Dumble Hill. In truth Mark felt completely trapped by circumstances. He knew he would have to make some tough decisions eventually but Christine's indeterminately limited lifespan overshadowed everything else. Even thinking about it was difficult. Mark knew he needed some help and support but he had no idea where to find it.

Jess peeped into her parents' bedroom to see if her mum was awake. She stood silently for a moment until Christine's eyes flickered open. She smiled in recognition.
'Hi Mum!' Jess said brightly, 'fancy a cup of tea?'
'It's ok thanks; I'm getting up in a minute,' Christine replied unconvincingly.
'Well I've taken time off so that you can have a rest so why don't you have a lie in today? You can have breakfast in bed if you like! Shall I bring you some toast?'
'I'm getting so lazy!' Christine groaned, 'but if you've taken time off specially I suppose I'd better cooperate.'
'Good! I'll be back in a sec,' smiled Jess.
As she was doing the toast, Tom burst into the kitchen.
'That was quick!'
'Yeah, I just remembered something.'
'What?'
'I hate fucking running!'
'Walk then.'
'I'm not mad on that either.'
'Well I'm not sure you've earned a cooked breakfast.'
'Two eggs and make sure the bacon's crispy,' called Tom as he

disappeared upstairs.

Sam was up early too. Now things seemed to have settled down a bit he decided it was time to start the regime of writing for an hour before work. He had tried this in the past and always found it more successful in the summer when it was light and warm first thing.

He sat at the narrow table in his room and scrolled through the first chapter. He had certainly packed a lot in: the discovery of a body, a skidoo chase followed by a gunfight in which the cornered hero was saved by the miraculous intervention of a polar bear and an escape stowed away in an empty lorry returning south on an ice road over a frozen lake.

'What was the bloody lake called?' he said to himself as he tried to dredge it out of his sleepy brain. Matt might remember; they had watched a series on the TV about it. Anyway, he had to introduce some more characters in the next chapter. The hero needed to meet a sidekick to buddy up with, possibly a native American or a French Canadian. He began sketching out a character on a post card, a bit like a sort of literary Top Trump. He liked the French idea, a John-Claude Van Damme type maybe. Next he needed an impossibly beautiful heroine to fall in love with the hero. Maybe she should be the French Canadian. That might work; a sultry accent like in Bond movies. Sex scenes at thirty degrees below zero were going to be a challenge but maybe wearing thermal underwear would add a kinky slant to it; probably not. He would have to invent some kind of refinery or smelting plant where it was always hot. In fact the bad guys could have their headquarters there. Yes, an environmental slant, the callous rape of pristine tundra.

Sam's head was beginning to ache. Writing a thriller was turning out to be more difficult than he expected; it was the detail that drove him mad. The hero for instance, whose name was Max Million, could not possibly just pull out a gun, it had to be a Smith and Wesson 9mm semi automatic with twin carburettors, rinse hold and a dual grill. He made a note on another card, 'FIND OUT ABOUT GUNS', saved his work and shut down the laptop.

Although Matt had now finished work for his holiday, he was up and about too. Sam found him downstairs admiring his handiwork.

'Looking good isn't it?' he said brightly as Sam came down.

'It's starting to look normal, Matt. Let's keep things in proportion.'

'Well I've got all day, so as soon as the shower's sorted I'll get those bags down to the tip and have a go at the kitchen.'

'God, you're serious about this aren't you. What time are you off by the way?'

'Can't wait to get rid of me can you? Not till one a.m. tomorrow morning so we're setting off for Brum at about ten. I was hoping I might get a chance to meet the lovely Jess before leaving. Will she be coming round tonight now the place is almost respectable?'

'I'm not sure, mate; I'll send you a text later.'

'I thought maybe we could get some pizza in or something.'

'Maybe not,' Sam thought as he quickly made a coffee and some toast.

'Is that really why you tidied the place up; just to meet Jess?'

'Well, the experience last week with, what was her name?'

'Jenny, I think.'

'Yes, Jenny made me realize things had got to change.'

'Well thank you Jenny.'

Sam grabbed his jacket, promising to contact Matt later as he hurried out the back to get his bike. The previous day at work had been ok and he felt optimistic as he pedalled off down the road.

At lunchtime Sam decided to give Jess a call. He walked outside to the garden area and sat in the sun. The morning had gone well, with a different team called 'Inbound Sales.' Their job was to deal with people who were not live customers but were responding to mailings and adverts. The tasks were to find out a bit more about them, capture accurate data, sell them the offer they were responding to and, most importantly, try to add value to that order. Generally the offer was virtually a give away, sometimes only requiring postage to be paid, so it was important to hook them with a 'for today only' additional offer. Although the customer was being manipulated to some extent it did not concern Sam because the supplementary offer was good value. They were perfectly free to say no, and plenty of them did.

'Hi hon!' Jess picked up after a couple of rings, 'I was hoping you were going to call. How's the world of software shovelling?'

'Quite good actually, they said I could take some live calls this afternoon. How's everything?'

'Better thanks. We got the doctor in to see Mum because she's so dopey and he was furious because the hospital is basically ODing her on painkillers. He's cut the dosage right back to get them out of her system and she's brighter already.'

'Won't she be in pain though?'

'Yeah but we can ease the dose back up a bit if necessary instead of her being totally battered all the time.'

'Excellent, that's brilliant news, well done!'

'Well it was Dad really.'

'Look I was wondering about tonight. Matt is dead keen to meet you before he jets off to Chavland; he's even tried to tidy the place up a bit, so we wondered if you would like to swing by and perhaps have a bite to eat or something?'

'Oh I'd love to but we're taking Mum out for a meal tonight. We feel there'll be a window where she's still benefiting from the painkillers without being totally comatose so we're going over to the Crown. I'm so sorry but we're having such a nice day and everyone's really up for it.'

'Don't apologise; it's great news. I'm really pleased you're having a lovely time. Matt will be back from Xante soon enough. What have you got planned for this afternoon?'

'I might take Darcy out again and then I promised to help in the office. The paperwork is a bit behind with Mum being ill.'

People were starting to drift back inside.

'Look babe, I've got to go. I'm really pleased your mum's perked up. You have a great time tonight.'

'Wish Matt a good holiday. I so want to see you tonight.'

'I'll call you tomorrow and we'll definitely do something.'

'Most definitely! Thanks for ringing. Love you!'
'Love you!'
There, he had said it.
Jess closed up her phone and held it close to her as though doing so would somehow prolong her contact with Sam. Then, feeling rather self-conscious, she quickly stuffed it back in her pocket and got on with clearing up the lunch things. Christine had decided to do half an hour in the office and sort things out so that Jess could finish them off and get stuff posted or filed and generally tidied up.
'You leave me to it and go off for your ride,' Christine insisted. 'It's good to see you with a bit of colour in your cheeks.'
Jess did not need coercing; it was a perfect afternoon.
Christine began sorting through various piles of paper on the desk. Mark had kept on top of all the immediate tasks but there were some important applications to fill in for environmental funding, introduced in place of the recently suspended grants for set-aside, which were getting close to their deadline. Some of these could be filled in online and she hoped Jess would be able to complete them if she gave her the figures. Judging by the pile of account reminder letters from suppliers, Mark was behind with the purchase ledger. When she saw the bank statement she could see why, they were frequently going significantly above the overdraft limit. Christine held her head in her hands. She was slipping away and at this rate the farm would quickly follow her into oblivion. The same thing had happened to her parents but it came sooner since they did not own any land. Dumble Hill farm had survived longer because they had subsidised it by gradually mortgaging the estate away. There was nothing left now, no collateral; the family silver was all in hock. Instead of making her despair, their predicament filled her with new energy and a determination to steady the ship before she had to abandon it; to leave it in the best possible shape. She would explore every avenue for subsidies, grants and funding to drag in as much as she could before she succumbed.
The last letter in the pile was the one she had been dreading. It was from the bank. It stated that their unauthorised borrowing was in breach of the overdraft agreement. Under these

circumstances they had the right to terminate facility and demand immediate repayment of the debt. It gave them one month to get back inside their limit. The letter was three weeks old.

When Jess came back into the office after her ride, Christine tried to look unconcerned but Jess could tell something was wrong.

'You haven't done too much have you Mum?'

'I am a bit tired. Can I quickly run through the things I need you to do?'

Jess soon got the hang of the online applications and she had helped with routine office tasks before. She flicked through the pile of supplier account reminders.

'Do you want me to pay some of these?'

'I think they might have to wait a while longer. We're a bit short of readies at the moment.'

'No change there then!'

'No, not even loose change I'm afraid.'

'Oh very good Mum, very witty!'

Jess clearly had no idea how serious the situation was, and that suited Christine fine for the time being.

'Don't spend too long on this now; we've got a date tonight don't forget.'

'I won't,' smiled Jess as she deftly navigated through the screens of the first application.

'The last supper,' Christine thought grimly as she carefully made her way back to the house.

In the kitchen she found Tom munching his way through a peanut butter sandwich the size of a phone book.

'I hope you still have an appetite at the Crown!' she exclaimed, 'we're going early don't forget.'

'No worries on that score, Mum,' he replied, 'trust me.'

'Don't forget your sister will probably give you half hers and I doubt if I'll be able to eat very much.'

'I can handle that,' he drawled, and Christine had no doubt that he probably would.

'Run and find your dad when you've finished that and remind him not to be long.'

Tom waved his mobile in the air. 'I'll just send him a text, Mother. We don't all inhabit the communications dark ages you know.'

'Bit of fresh air wouldn't hurt you.'

'It could do irreparable damage,' he smirked as he thumbed out a message to Mark.

The Crown was a gastro pub that served better than average food at reasonable prices. It was always busy, particularly on Wednesdays when they had a two for one offer. The family arrived early and went straight through to a table.

'Couldn't you have found something a bit smarter, Tom?' asked Christine as they studied the menus.

Tom pointed to the label on his sleeve. 'Hello! Look, River Island!'

'What does that mean?'

'It's just so that people know it was ridiculously expensive,' explained Jess.

'Oh I see, designer scruffy. You could at least have brushed your hair.'

'He probably spent ages getting it to look like that, it's the style Mum.'

Christine sighed. She had always taken an active interest in the kids' taste in fashion and music but suddenly she seemed to have become old and out of touch.

'Are we having starters?' asked Tom hopefully.

'You can if you want love but I doubt if we will,' said Christine looking at Jess, who shook her head. 'Will you have one with him Mark?'

Just then someone slapped Tom on the shoulder. He turned round in surprise to see Amy standing behind him dressed in a white blouse and black skirt.

'Hi,' he smiled. 'I didn't know you were working here.'

'I was going to wait till I'd finished my exams but they were desperate so Mum let me start today.'

'Cool. How are the exams going?'

'Don't ask. How about you?'

'Same really, but don't tell them.'

'You could get on here when you get back from Cornwall, they're always short staffed.'
'You definitely can't come then.'
'Definitely. Your sister's looking good; she seeing someone?'
Jess was wearing a grey long sleeved T-shirt dress in a velvety fabric that looked expensive. She was had a hint of make up and her newly washed hair was glossy and lustrous. They watched her for a moment as she chatted with Mark and Christine.
'Yeah, she just met this bloke in one of our fields, weird isn't it? He's ok though.'
'Quick, pretend to ask me something about the food,' hissed Amy.
Tom noticed the restaurant manager heading towards them at speed. He held the menu up and pointed to the prawn cocktail.
'No sir, we always use the finest quality fresh prawns.' Amy said loudly as the manager arrived, eyeing her suspiciously.
'Everything all right here?' she enquired. They all nodded and she turned to Amy, 'I think you've got confused dear, your tables are in the bay window over there.'
'Sorry Mrs Anderson,' said Amy pinching Tom on the arm in thanks as she hurried away. He exchanged glances with Jess who gave him an optimistic 'maybe there's still a chance' look. Tom was glad that Amy would not be serving them; that would have been just too gross.
'Was that Amy Kienewicz?' asked Christine. Tom nodded.
'What a pretty girl she's turned out to be, she used to be such a dumpy little thing at junior school.'
'Haven't you asked her out Tom?' asked Mark.
'Oh Dad!' groaned the children and Jess poked her finger into her open mouth in a 'puke' gesture.
Mark and Tom both ordered rump steak, which came with a pile of chips and a side salad whereas Jess and Christine had sea bass on a bed of green beans and mash.
'Looks like it's Beefeater versus nouvelle cuisine!' grinned Jess.
'God, I'd send that back if I got it as a starter never mind a main!' laughed Tom.
'It's quality that matters, not quantity,' said Christine primly.
'Yes,' said Jess 'this fish is perfectly cooked and tastes

wonderful.'
As Tom was demolishing his plateful with rhythmic efficiency, he paused for a moment, deep in thought.
'You know when Sam came for lunch he only ate the vegetables. It that because he doesn't eat pork or is he a veggie?'
'He doesn't describe himself as a veggie because he eats fish. He doesn't eat red meat. I'm not sure about chicken.'
'I just don't get that. Surely you either eat animals or you don't,' Mark grumbled.
'Well I haven't really talked to him about that. We're probably going to cook together at his place this weekend so I'll find out then.'
'I hate vegetarians,' Tom snorted.
'I'm sure Sam would be interested to hear such an intelligent and well constructed argument.'
While this conversation was taking place, Jess noticed that her mother had hardly eaten a thing. She was just moving the food around on her plate.
'I don't know if I can manage all this,' she sighed.
'Want to swap plates Mum?' asked Tom, who had already cleared his.
He was about to reach across the table when he was frozen by a ferocious glare from Jess.
'What is it Mum' asked Jess, 'don't you like it?'
'It's lovely but I'm just not very hungry.'
'There's no rush,' said Mark, 'have a little rest and eat a bit more in a minute.'
'It's ok thanks. I think Tom can finish it if he wants to.'
'Actually Mum I'm stuffed. Let's get some water and see if you feel better after a drink.' He discretely waved Amy over and whispered to her.
'Sure babe!' she said and quickly returned with a large jug of tap water with ice and lemon.
Christine drank a full glass and smiled. 'Thank you Tom,' she said, 'that was a really good idea,' and began to eat some fish.
Jess winked at her brother and gave him a discrete thumbs up sign.

When Sam arrived home from work he was pleased to see Matt had taken the rubbish away and made a start on the kitchen. The cooker still looked like it needed shot blasting and the sink retained its coating of indescribably greasy scum but the floor was clean and the worktops appeared to have been wiped over. Matt, however, was nowhere to be seen. Sam peeped into Matt's room to see if his suitcase had gone and was amazed to find the room not only tidy, but also completely empty. He stepped inside and wandered around in disbelief, opening drawers and cupboards and finding them all cleared. He raced down the stairs to check Matt's things; the TV, stereo, coffee maker, even the lethal toaster had all gone. How could this be? Why would he do that? Sam wandered back into the living room and suddenly noticed an envelope standing prominently on the mantelshelf. He roughly tore it open.

'I'm sorry mate but I owe three months rent and there is no way I can pay it. I've cancelled my holiday and moved to a driving school 'somewhere in the north of England'. I'm not going to tell you where so you can't be accused of lying when they come after me. I'm afraid rent arrears are the least of my financial troubles. Just ignore any mail that comes for me - I won't want it. In case you're wondering, the guy fixed the shower. You'll have a few nights with Jess before they get possession and change the locks. I hope you enjoy it. Don't give anyone any money. It's all in my name and you won't be liable for a penny. I know you owe me for half the bills and rent but forget it. It's been a laugh sharing with you and I'm sorry it had to end like this but it was the only way.

Look after yourself and good luck with Jess.

Matt.'

Sam slumped into the armchair and gasped in disbelief. He read through the note again but still could not understand. He felt guilty because he was a month late with his share of the rent but Matt had been so laid back about it. Now he knew why. He badly wanted to ring Jess but they would just be going out and it didn't seem fair. In any case he needed time to get his head round it.

After a few moments, he walked to the corner shop and bought

a large aerosol oven cleaner and some surface spray. If the place was immaculate, Matt should at least get the deposit knocked off his arrears.
Sam emptied the kitchen as he cleaned it then made a snack and sat down to look at adverts for house shares in the local paper. Nothing affordable caught his eye. It was the wrong time of year really because all the students would be moving out soon. He remembered there was a notice board at work where staff could place small ads. Maybe he could find something there. However long he might have before the notice to quit, he just wanted to be out of there as soon as possible.

Christine decided to go straight to bed as soon as soon as they got back from the Crown and Tom disappeared to do some revision, so the party dispersed almost immediately. The meal had not been a massive success but just doing it was important and there was tacit agreement as they went their separate ways that it had been worthwhile. Jess decided to try giving Sam a call.
'Hi' he said bluntly.
'What's up? You sound a bit subdued.'
'I'm in shock'
'He cleaned the kitchen?'
'He's gone.'
'Well, yes,' said Jess looking at her watch, 'he'll be checking in now I should imagine.'
'His room is empty. He hasn't gone to Xante. He's done a runner.'
'Like a moonlight flit you mean?'
'Well, a daylight one, but yes.'
'Where does that leave you?'
'Homeless.'
'Can't you take over the lease?'
'We're three months in arrears; I'm not going to be top of the landlord's Christmas present list. Anyway I couldn't afford the deposit and besides it's totally freaked me out. I can't get out of here fast enough.'
'Sam, you're scaring me. Do you want me to come over?'

There was a silence.
'Sorry Jess, I'm being a total arse. How did the meal go?'
'It was fine thanks, but you haven't answered my question.'
There was another silence. Jess snuffled as she tried to stifle tears.
'Please don't cry. This isn't about us. Everything's fine with us. I'd like to be with you more than anything but not here, not now.'
'Where are you going to go?'
'I might be sleeping on friends' floors for a bit, I don't know.'
Jess could not hold back any longer. She had been so looking forward to spending the night with Sam once Matt had gone, cooking a meal with him, sleeping with him, and now it had been snatched away from her. She began to cry.
'Jess, Jess, Jess. Listen to me. Can't you understand how weird this feels for me?'
'Not really, I mean it's not like it's the house where you were born and your family just disappeared. I think if I were you I'd squat there for as long as I could and make the most of it.'
'Yeah. Maybe you have a point. I mean, I don't think I can possibly be liable for any of the debt.'
'I can help you look for a new place!' said Jess brightening a little.
'I'd like that.'
So it was decided that Sam would be up front with the landlord and promise to go quietly to save the cost of repossession if he could have a few days grace to find a new place. It was agreed that he would call Jess the following day to let her know the outcome.

Jess sat thinking in her room for ages before going to bed. For the first time she wondered whether she had been too impetuous over Sam; after all she hardly knew anything about him and his mood earlier had scared her a little. But that was stupid. She was just going to sleep with him, not marry him! And in some ways it was good that he let things get to him; it showed he was emotional and sensitive, unlike some of her previous boyfriends. She told herself to chill and just live for the

moment; if it all worked out it would be brilliant, if not there was no harm done.
Her friends in Leeds kept asking if they had 'done it yet' when they were chatting on Facebook. It was ok for them; they had the privacy to shag themselves senseless whenever they wanted. In a way, Jess was glad that she and Sam had not had the same opportunity for casual sex.
'Let's hope that landlord plays ball,' she thought to herself as she finally drifted off to sleep.

Mark sat down with a glass of brandy after the others had gone upstairs. It was such a relief to have Christine back after she had been so out of it for the past few days. The time they had left together was finite but they could still enjoy themselves before she became too ill.
Just as Christine had tried to keep herself going for Tom's exams, so he wanted to keep the farm afloat for their last few months together. He locked up and put the lights out before heading upstairs. On the landing he could see light under Tom's door so he knocked and looked in to say goodnight. Tom was just too slow minimizing the screen of Death Crash Three. Mark was not clued up about computer games but he knew it did not look like revision. He decided to be tolerant.
'I was going to say don't work too late,' he said with a wry smile.
'Just having a break, Dad.'
'Whatever,' he said, mimicking his son's slanguage. 'I just wanted to say you and Jess were great at the Crown. I know it's not your idea of a night out but I think Mum really appreciated it.'
'Do you think I can work there when I'm back from Cornwall?'
'Why not? I'm sure Amy could teach you everything you need to know.'
'Funny!'
'Anyway don't stay up too late. I don't believe you're doing 'A' Level Crash Test.'
'Did you hear about the P.E. student Dad?'
'No, what was that?'

‘He wanted to do ‘A’ Level Playing Field.’
‘Glad you’re not dong ‘A’ Level Comedy.’
‘Well, my results might be a bit of a joke.’
‘Ok. You win. Night night sleep tight.’

It looked as though Jess was already lying down, so Mark washed and stepped quietly into their room.

‘Is it late?’ Christine asked.
‘I thought you’d be well away by now.’
‘I think I’ve already had enough sleep for the rest of this week.’
‘No it isn’t very late. How do you feel?’
‘A bit sore but I’d rather have this level of discomfort and be compos mentis.’
‘Did you get much done in the office today?’

Christine decided to keep quiet about having seen the letter from the bank.

‘Yes it was good. I got to grips with most of the cross compliance stuff. The rules are slightly different to set-aside. I showed Jess where to fill in the forms on-line, gave her the figures and left her to it.’

‘Oh that’s good. I don’t know what we’d do without that girl.’

‘It’s not fair, Mark. She was so happy at Leeds. She shouldn’t have to sacrifice it for the family.’

‘She can go back.’

‘But it won’t be the same. Her friends will be in their final year.’

‘She’ll make new friends.’

‘I’m worried that she won’t go back at all now.’ Christine was on the verge of tears. Mark put him arm round her.

‘You know she wouldn’t have had it any other way.’

‘I know, but it doesn’t make it any easier. And here am I half killing myself to get Tom through these exams while she’s doing part-time clerical work. What must she think?’

‘She’ll think you’re amazing, like we all do.’

‘She’s such a good girl. Did you see that look she gave Tom when he was about to eat my fish?’

‘Yes, he looked like he’d been shot.’

‘I felt obliged to eat it after that!’

‘She’s been brilliant with him though. She recognized a level of

maturity in him that we didn't spot.'
'Whatever happens,' said Christine 'we can be very proud of those two.'

After talking to Jess, Sam paced uncomfortably around the house. It felt strange, like when you've only just moved in somewhere. He decided that if he was going to stay a few more days, he might as well do some work on the book. He opened the document, scrolled through it, stopping occasionally to glance through odd paragraphs, and read the chapter he was working on. He probably only needed another couple of thousand words before there would be enough to send off to his agent.
He had just finished a scene where Million had been captured by a hit man called Hogshead and his cronies. They had been told by the evil megalomaniac Sternbum to take him alive; he wanted to see the look on his face as Hogshead made him squeal. They were taunting him in a basement room of the refinery. Million noticed pipes slung beneath the ceiling that ran just above head height.
'Hey Hogshead!' he called, 'I assumed you were called that because you had a face like a pig, but I was wrong; you look like a pig's ass!'
The big man grunted and charged towards him, intending to head butt him in the guts. Million jerked himself free from his captor's grasp, vaulted off the back of the onrushing assailant and swung onto the overhead pipes. 'Shoot the bastard!' growled Hogshead but Million was too quick for them. He rotated the wheel of a huge valve and a jet of scalding steam geysered down, engulfing the men below. He shinned along the pipe until he was out of range and slid down beside the door. Locking it behind him, he straightened his tie and walked briskly along the dimly lit corridor towards the exit.
'Turkish bath anyone?' he drawled.

Eight

Jack Spencer drove back home before dawn to miss the traffic on the motorway. His exams had been virtually back to back over three days and he was shattered. None of his friends had finished and he did not feel like celebrating anyway so he decided to make himself scarce. As he pulled into the drive, he noticed his Mother's red BMW parked in front of the double garage. She was a partner of an executive recruitment agency called Just the Job, and was free to work from home when she wanted.

Walking in, Jack was relieved to see she was on the phone in the office. He quickly made a coffee and disappeared up to his room. He checked his emails but there was still no reply from Jess. It was not like her; even if she was mad, she was not the type to just blank him like that. He sent Kerry a text asking if Jess had arrived at work. Only after it had gone did it occur to him that he was being a bit tactless. The reply, 'She's off till Monday nobhead,' rather tended to confirm this. So she was at home. Perhaps her mother was worse. He wondered whether to visit but needed to know how Jess was feeling first, so he decided to risk texting her.

'Just found out ur off work. Hope everything ok. Did u get my email?'

Jack lay on his bed waiting and tried to empty his mind. The exams had gone very badly and he had more or less decided to quit. He was just trying to work out how to tell his mother when she tapped on his door and walked in.

'Hello darling,' she gushed, 'why didn't you tell me you were coming home this morning? How did the exams go? You must be exhausted!'

'I am rather tired Mum.'

'I just wanted you to know I've given your father hell about his ridiculous decision to let you go. I've told him to reinstate you immediately or suffer the consequences!'
'It's nothing to do with you Mum.'
'What?'
'It's none of your business.'
'It most certainly is.'
'No, actually, it's about me and Dad and something stupid that I did and Dad was right to let me go. So just for once will you stop trying to run my life and leave me alone?'
'You're obviously tired.'
'I am tired, tired of you. And while we're at it you might as well know that I've decided not to go back to Bristol in September; I'm jacking it in.'
Theresa looked horrified. 'Does your father know this?'
'Not yet but I think he'll understand.'
'Oh he'll understand all right. I've had to fight him every step of the way to get you where you are today Jack. I know you don't appreciate it but one day you'll see'
'I see that you are a self-centred, domineering cow who tries to manipulate everything and everybody to conform to your view of the world!'
'You are clearly overwrought and irrational at the moment and there is no point trying to reason with you but let me make one thing clear, you are not leaving university. I'll never live it down.'
Jack looked at her coldly. 'You'll have to live it down. I'm leaving and there's nothing you can do to stop me.'
'We'll see about that,' said his Mother as she stormed off along the landing.
Jack's coffee was cold but he drank it anyway. He had not smoked for years but he badly wanted a cigarette. He lay for a long time waiting for a text that was never going to come. In the end he picked up his phone and thumbed in another message.
'I just want you to know I'm sorry. I won't bother you any more. I will always love you. Jack.'
He pressed send, then tore the back off the handset, pulled out the sim card and threw it out of his window. As he was doing

this, his father's car rolled onto the drive. Jack quickly ducked out of sight.
The front door slammed and he heard raised voices in the living room. From his mother he heard 'if you are a man you will go and talk to him right now and make him see sense,' and from Peter 'it's got to be his decision as far as I'm concerned.' It was good to hear his father standing up to his mother but what would the consequences be? Jack was worried. He was the cause of the fight that might finally destroy their marriage. The argument raged on and on. Jack buried his head under the pillow. He wanted to stop it but didn't know how so he stood up, opened his window wide, and stepped out.

Sam was nearing the end of the induction programme at work and was back in Outgoing sales being mentored by a team leader as he worked through a live call session. The evening shift was by far the busiest in this section as they tried to catch people after work. It ran until eight pm but Sam was just doing a couple of hours to get a feel for it, knocking off at five. The punters varied enormously in their response; some were dismissively offhand, while others were very talkative and clearly rather lonely. In a way they were the most difficult. Staff were encouraged to engage with customers, but there was a long list to work through and if a call did not appear to be leading to a sale it had to be terminated. Sam was finding it hard to pull the plug on these calls. After finally extricating himself from a particularly lengthy one that did not lead to a sale, his mentor, Dave Beale, prodded him in the back.
'You're not a fucking social worker you know. I mean I don't mind; you can play Samaritans all day if you like but how are you going to eat? You have to hit your target to make commission at this place and you're way off track at the moment.'
Sam knew he was right. With the next call he was more focused and managed to add on a photo-editing package to the free upgrade that was on offer.
'Result!' cheered Dave. 'There's no marks for just shipping the free stuff. You really need to get at least one item added to the

basket to make it worthwhile. The freebie is a hook; when they bite you got to reel 'em in and make that sale!'
Sam tried to look enthusiastic. Selling just didn't give him the same kind of buzz that it clearly gave Dave.

During his lunch break he called Matt's landlord to explain about his disappearance and offer to hand over the keys as soon as he found somewhere else to live.
'Do you have the lease?' he asked, which Sam confirmed. 'Well, it's a bit unusual,' he continued, 'but I suppose if you're willing to surrender the lease and go quietly it might be in my interest to give you a little time. How long do you need?'
'I should be able to get fixed up within the week I imagine'
'And do you honestly not know where Matt has gone?'
'I genuinely have no idea.'
'I'll make a deal with you then. If you let me in tonight to check the place and see what repairs need doing, you can have until next Friday.'
Sam agreed to this and arranged to see the landlord at eight. He sent Jess a text to say that they were still on for the weekend but he would be tied up that evening.

Sam hurried to the staff area and scanned the notice board. There were a couple of 'fourth person wanted to share' ads but he was not sure if he really wanted to do communal living any more. What he really wanted was a place of his own. It would have to be a bed sit of course, and a pretty crappy one at that, but it would be worth it just to have a door that you could close when you got home and not have people in your face and their stuff everywhere. He and Jess could go out looking over the weekend; it would be good involving her in the search.

Jess was working in the farm office when the text arrived from Jack. Christine was sleeping in after the late night so she had decided to finish filing the environmental assessments. The problem was that once started, each one had to be finished and submitted because there was no way to save them. She decided to reply later.

She had just managed to complete the last form when the second text came in. There was something about the way it was

worded that concerned her. 'I will always love you.' It sounded final, as though they would never see each other again. Assuming Jack was still in Bristol, Jess decided she had better phone him but the call diverted to voicemail without even ringing. This worried her, so she called Peter on his direct line but ended up on his voicemail too.
'Sorry to trouble you Peter, I just wanted you to know that I've had a text from Jack that sounded a bit desperate. I've tried to call him but it's as though his phone is out of order. I know there's not much you can do and it's probably nothing but I just have this strange feeling that something is wrong.'
As she recorded this, an inert Jack was being stretchered into an ambulance.

Sam arrived home and let himself in to the empty house. It still felt strange. He sat on the sofa like it was a dentist's waiting room. The thought suddenly struck him that he had not tried ringing Matt on his mobile, 'how stupid,' he muttered, reaching for his phone. There was no answer, which was no great surprise, but he decided to leave a message anyway.
'I don't suppose you'll get this but I just want you to know that I'm handing the lease over to the landlord and moving out.' He paused for a second, not sure what else to say. 'I don't get why you did this mate, and I'm still a bit in shock, but if you need any help or anything doing or whatever, just call me, ok. Take care then, see you then, well maybe.'
Sam hung up. He was crap at leaving messages but that had to be one of his worst. Why didn't he think of calling Matt last night? He might have been able to persuade him to come back and sort things out. 'As if,' he thought grimly, 'I'd have stood a better chance of selling him some software.'

Sam walked through to the kitchen and rummaged around in a cardboard box full of stuff he had taken out of the cupboards and made himself a snack. He decided to go and start up his laptop. On the way, he noticed how filthy the stair carpet was. It seemed a shame to leave it like that after the effort they had made with the rest of the house so he gave it a good vacuuming. 'Suppose I should have dusted first,' he thought with a smile.

Before starting work on his story Sam decided to see if he could check his bank balance. Andsoft had agreed to pay him weekly for the first month and it should have hit his account by now. Fortunately, the plug had not been pulled on the broadband and he was able to access his Internet banking. He knew he was only going to get basic pay for the first week, commission would take a while to come through, but he still could not believe the figure on the screen; well under two hundred pounds. Surely that was less than minimum wage? Maybe they had put him on an emergency tax code or something. Sam put his head in his hands. It had barely taken him below his overdraft limit. He was going to have to be a bit more ruthless on those phones.

The landlord arrived promptly. He looked round the sitting room suspiciously as Sam let him in.

'Looks quite tidy,' he muttered.

'Shall I just leave you to look round then?'

'Yeah. Is there anything that needs attention? I think you have a problem with the shower?'

'We got that fixed actually.'

'Oh really. Who by?'

'I don't know. Matt arranged it the other day.'

'I'll have to get it checked, but never mind.'

Sam sat down and left him to it. He heard doors and drawers opening in the kitchen and then upstairs.

'That all seems to be in order,' he said on reappearing, evidently surprised.

'So you'll promise to be out in one week?' Sam nodded and was handed a business card. 'I'll take your copy of the lease with me now. Just put all the keys through the letterbox when you leave. Make sure you get the meters read and cancel any other services.'

'I'm sorry about the arrears,' said Sam. 'I can give you some money I owed Matt if it helps.'

He softened a little, 'thanks, but that will just complicate things really.' Hesitating in the doorway, he asked, 'What sort of accommodation are you looking for?'

'Just a bed sit, round here if possible. It's quite handy for work.'

'Where's work?'

‘Andsoft.’
He nodded, looking carefully at Sam as if weighing him up. Eventually he said, ‘I do have one available at the moment, in one of those larger houses on George Road. Do you know where I mean?’
‘Yes, sounds perfect but I’m rather surprised that you’d consider letting it to me.’
‘It would be on a monthly lease at first, paid in advance. As soon as you fell behind you’d be out.’
‘Can I see it?’
He scribbled the address on the back of the card. ‘I’ll be there Saturday morning decorating; call round if you like.’
Sam watched him walk off down the street and felt bad. Doing his own decorating, he was clearly not wealthy and they had just deprived him of a quarter’s rent.

Having nothing planned for the rest of the evening, Sam decided to do some more work on the story. His agent wanted the opening chapter and one each from the middle and end. It was this latter one he was working on. He quickly called Jess to report back about the landlord’s visit and they finalised their plans for the following day.
Sam had already started the later chapter. Max Million had cornered Sternbum in the control room. He had discovered that the refinery was just a front for a nerve agent processing plant. Sternbum was planning to hold the whole of North America to ransom with his deadly new discovery. Million levelled his Mauser 9mm semi-automatic at him.
‘It’s game over Sternbum, give yourself up!’
‘On the contrary Mr Million, the fun is only just beginning.’ With a leer, he opened his raised right hand to reveal a small phial. ‘There is enough Passado in this little bottle here to wipe out a city the size of Pittsburgh.’
‘Worse things could happen.’
‘Such a comedian Mr Million. Well you won’t be laughing in a moment. If I smash this onto the floor, not only will you be dead in a millisecond but the air conditioning will pump it into the atmosphere and destroy every living thing within a hundred square miles.’

'Including you of course.'
'Except me, I have the antidote in a capsule cemented to my wisdom tooth and I have plenty more Passado.'
'I thought that was a kind of tomato puree.'
'Stop wasting time! What's it to be Million? Drop the gun now and you can leave here a free man, hesitate and you will die writhing in agony.'
'How do I know that really is a lethal substance in there and not just your aftershave?'
'You are about to find out!' screamed Sternbum as he flung the phial onto the tiled floor. Max Million watched in horror as it hurtled down, hit the ground with a loud crack, then bounced past him at head height. He stuck out his left hand and caught it cleanly without taking his eyes off the evil madman.
'Howzat' he said calmly, 'advantage Million, I believe.'

Peter and Theresa Spencer sat in stunned silence as they waited in A&E. Neither of them dared to risk uttering a single word in case the argument flared up again. Peter clutched a plastic cup of cold coffee and stared absent-mindedly at the comings and goings of the walking wounded. It was a quiet day in Casualty.

Eventually a young man dressed in chinos and a white open neck shirt walked over to them.
'Mr and Mrs Spencer?' They nodded expectantly.
'Hi, I'm Rob, the Doctor looking after Jack.' This was a surprise. Apart from a photo I.D. badge clipped to his waist, there was nothing about his appearance to indicate it. 'He's going to be fine,' he added quickly to put them out of their misery.
'Thank God!' exclaimed Theresa and, as if this news had released some kind of emotional valve inside her, she burst ferociously into tears. The Doctor waited a moment as if expecting Peter to comfort her in some way.
'We've been sitting here for over two hours thinking he was dead,' was all he said.
'He was very lucky; his right shoulder took most of the force of the impact. He might not play tennis for a while but it will

recover. The bang on the head was a secondary impact. He was just stunned and winded really when the paramedics brought him in; all the seriously vulnerable areas like neck and spine appear to be fine.'
'You mean he can come home?'
'We have to keep him in overnight for observation but we can probably medically discharge him after the ward round tomorrow,' Rob paused here, hoping to get Theresa's attention as well. Peter nudged her.
'Did you hear that? They might be able to discharge him tomorrow.'
Theresa gave them a dazed look from behind a soggy tissue.
'I said medically discharge,' Rob continued, 'but he'll need a psychiatric assessment. Somebody Jack's age does not normally fall out of a first floor window by accident and there's no sign of alcohol or drugs in his blood. We need to know why he ended up on your drive.'
'It's our fault,' said Peter dully, 'we were having a huge row downstairs and he must have just jumped on impulse.'
'I see,' said the doctor thoughtfully. 'It's a rather drastic way to stop an argument isn't it?'
'It only postponed it,' said Theresa with a menacing look in her eyes.
'Jack's over twenty-one and any problems you two have are really none of our business but he does need to at least see a counsellor before we would consider him fit for discharge. We're going to move him to Ward B3 and let him sleep for a bit longer. The best thing you can do is go home for a few hours and come back after six pm at visiting time.'
'Can we just see him before we go,' asked Theresa.
'Of course, follow me.'
The Doctor walked briskly through some double doors into a corridor with curtained compartments along it. He opened the third one along to reveal Jack lying on a bed in a neck brace with his right arm in a sling and what appeared to be an ice pack strapped to his forehead. He looked deathly white and there was a bank of monitors blipping away on a trolley beside him.
'Oh my god,' whimpered Theresa, staggering as if swooning.

'Don't worry about all the technology. He's breathing unaided and is not in any danger. We don't want him to sleep for too long though. They'll keep a close eye on him on B3. It's in West Block by the way. Do you know your way around this gulag?'
'We've done our share of visiting here, I'm sure we'll find it,' said Peter humbly. 'I'm sorry to put you to all this trouble.'
'We just patch 'em up Mr Spencer, you don't have to apologise to me.'
Peter nodded and the couple walked slowly towards the exit.

On the journey back, Theresa was the first to break the silence.
'None of this would have happened if he'd gone to the High School.'
'Oh don't start that one again,' groaned Peter.
'But it's true. He would have had a much more suitable circle of friends and he wouldn't have become infatuated with that insipid little Jessica Beresford.'
Peter sighed. Rationally he knew there was no point in continuing this conversation. They had been through it all a thousand times before and they were never going to agree.
'For a start, Jess is not insipid as you say, she is an intelligent, very capable and attractive young lady and in any case she is the daughter of my best and oldest friend so they would have met anyway.'
'If they hadn't been classmates it would have been different. Jack was a fish out of water at that school.'
'If you remember, it was the school he wanted to attend and as far as I recall, he was perfectly happy there.'
'How did he know what was best for him at the age of eleven? I had all but persuaded him to sit for the High until you interfered.'
'I could see what you were doing to him Theresa, the pressure you were putting on him. It wasn't fair.'
'Fair, Fair?' she screeched. 'Don't talk to me about fairness! Look what it's done to him; broken by his unrequited love for the daughter of a white trash hillbilly!'

Peter braked hard and Theresa shot forward, then jerked back as the seat belt locked. He swerved the car violently into a lay-by and skidded to a halt, slamming Theresa back into the belt.
'What the hell are you doing?' she yelled.
'Never say that again!' he screamed in her face. 'Mark is my closest friend; his wife is dying of cancer. Yes, they are struggling financially but that's not so unusual. Now get out of my car!'
'How dare you!' spluttered Theresa. 'You have no right to shout at me like that and I will not get out of the car. How do you expect me to get home from here?'
'Right,' said Peter through clenched teeth. He unclipped both seat belts, got out of the car, stamped round to the passenger side, opened the door, grabbed her by the shoulders, dragged her out of the seat and dumped her heavily onto the tarmac. She sat there panting in disbelief, then began thumping his legs and struggling to get back in. Peter slammed the door and locked it with the remote.
'You cannot leave me here!'
'I can and I shall.'
'But how will I get home?'
'Phone a friend, ask the audience, I don't give a shit!' shouted Peter as he jumped back into the car, revved the engine and sped away, tyres spinning on the chippings at the road's edge.

It was after five by the time Peter arrived back at the house. He tried ringing the office but the answering machine was already on, so he dialled in and remotely listened to his voicemail. His heart froze when he heard the message from Jess. He replayed it several times then immediately called the Beresford's.
'Hi Tom, it's Peter Spencer. How are the exams going?'
'Exceptionally average thanks Peter. How are you?'
'Oh, you know, been better. Um, I don't suppose your sister's around?'
'I think she's down the paddock. Can't you manage a few days without her?'
'Ha! Well probably not, but I was just ringing about a message

she left me actually.'
'Try her mobile.'
'No it's ok; I've got to rush off somewhere. Can you ask her to call me on mine when she's got a minute?'

Peter stuffed a few things into a holdall and headed back to the car. He was not planning to return that night. As he sped back onto the main road he passed a dark green Land Cruiser. It was their neighbour Tasha Barrington's car and he could guess who the passenger was.

When Peter arrived on the ward, Jack was conscious and sitting up in bed.
He smiled sheepishly as he saw his father walk in.
'How are you feeling?' asked Peter gently.
'Thick headed - in more ways that one. Where's Mum?'
'Oh she'll be along later. I'm just so relieved to see you looking better,' he paused, 'am I allowed to ask what happened?'
'I jumped out of my bedroom window.'
'We probably shouldn't be discussing this now.'
'I think I have to see a shrink.'
'It's just counselling, a routine thing, formality.'
'I think I need to see a shrink.'
'I'm sorry, Jack. Your Mother and I, it was very wrong of us, rowing like that.'
'It wasn't the rowing. That's normal.' He stopped abruptly and pressed his hand to his forehead. 'Oh my head. It feels like it's splitting in two.'
'Perhaps you should lie down for a bit. I didn't mean to push you.'
'I think I need to see a shrink! I think I need to see a shrink! I think I need to see a shrink!' chanted Jack, getting louder with each repetition.
Visitors and patients in nearby beds looked up in consternation. A nurse hurried across the ward and drew curtains round them. He held Jack's hand.
'Would you mind stepping outside please?' he asked.
There were some chairs by the reception desk so Peter waited there, shocked by his son's abnormal behaviour. Someone

ducked in through the screen then reappeared almost immediately and walked briskly towards him.
'Hi, I'm Steph, one of the doctors here. I take it you are Jack's dad?' Peter nodded. 'Ok. He's calm now but we think it would be best not to disturb him again tonight. Is Mum here?'
'No, she was coming later.'
'I see. If he's feeling up to it, we'd ideally like to start counselling in the morning. We're keen to involve parents. How would you feel about that?'
'I'm not sure. I think we might mess things up. I'm not really a fan of that sort of thing.'
'Well have a think about it. We have to see what he has to say first anyway.'
Peter wandered away from the ward feeling perplexed and profoundly disturbed. Jack's deranged behaviour had been frightening.
As he passed through the automatic doors of the main entrance he switched on his mobile and sent Theresa a text warning her not to come and saying that he would spend the night in a hotel in town to give them both a chance to calm down. He did not expect a reply and none came as he drove down to the Holiday Inn.

Nine

Jess was awoken in the morning by a tap on her door and Tom's head appeared.
'Good grief' she exclaimed, 'Banquo's ghost!'.
'Thought you'd be awake,' he croaked, 'I just remembered Peter Spencer called yesterday afternoon, something about a message?'
'Oh that,' Jess groaned, 'he probably thinks I'm crazy. Well it can't have been that urgent or he'd have called my mobile.'
'He said could you call him on his.'
'I'll email him at work later. Fancy expecting you to remember to give me a message.'
'Well I have, haven't I?'
'Up to a point, Lord Copper.'
'What?'
'Literary reference, Waugh, don't worry your pretty little head about it.'
'Which war?'
'Evelyn.'
Tom decided it was time to retreat.
'Well I've done my duty. I'm off back to bed.'
'You don't fancy making a cup of tea?'
'Exactly right'
'Lazy arse,' giggled Jess.
Tom shuffled back to his room. It was nice to see his sister happy but all that euphoria was too much to take at this time of the morning.
Jess lay back in bed. She really ought to make the most of it and have a lie in but she was too wide-awake now. She was just deciding what to do when there was another knock on her door and Christine walked in with a cup of tea.

'Mum what on earth are you doing? You shouldn't be running up and downstairs with beverages!'
'I haven't run anywhere. I've got a kettle in the bedroom remember.'
'Whatever, you've got enough on your plate without looking after me!'
'Maybe I want to look after you,' she said gently lowering herself onto the edge of the bed and kissing Jess on the forehead. 'It is your day off after all.'
'Oh Mum!' cried Jess, flinging her arms round Christine. She tried hard not to squeeze too tightly but her mother still winced.
'Sorry,' she said, releasing her.
'Don't apologise. It's nice to have a hug, even if it hurts a bit. Do you think Tommy wants a cup?'
'I should leave him. He's been up actually but he seemed a bit dopey.'
'No change there then.'
They both laughed affectionately.
'Look, I'm going to get up now and do a couple of hours in the office. This seems to be my best time of day at the moment and there's still quite a bit of catching up to do down there.'
'I'll come and help you then,' said Jess glugging her tea.
'No, you have your lie in. It would suit me best to leave you some stuff to do later, like yesterday. Did that work ok?'
'Yeah, it was fine but that on-line filing was a pain.'
'Why do you think I left it to you?'
'Nice one Mum.'

Peter Spencer toyed with a bit of scrambled egg in the hotel dining room, then returned to his room and tried calling the ward. After holding for a few minutes he was told Jack had slept well, eaten his breakfast and was sitting in the day room. They had strapped his shoulder but, apart from painkillers, were not planning any further treatment. He was due to see the counsellor at eleven so they suggested that Peter should visit after two. He tried phoning home but there was no answer. Theresa had probably spent the night at Tasha's. He tried her mobile but it went to voicemail. He left a message telling her when he was visiting Jack. It was too early to call the office switchboard but one of the partners was an early bird so he tried his direct line. 'Nick, it's Peter. Yes I'm fine but Jack's had a bit of an accident. No, not too serious but he's in the Queen's so I won't be in this morning. Can you get Kerry to go through my diary and cancel everything today? I don't think there was anything that can't wait. Yes I know, the older they get the more trouble they become! Look, I'll let you get on. Tell them to call my mobile if they need to but it might be switched off. I'll probably be able to call in last thing this afternoon.' He switched off his phone and lay on the bed dozing for a while, having hardly slept. It had been strange at breakfast, all those professional types with their busy schedules ahead of them, that focused expectancy, and him with nothing planned but a hospital visit. Now his morning was completely free and it seemed peculiarly precious, a little bubble blown out of his life where he had some time to reflect. After a while he checked out, dumped his bag in the car and walked over to the nearby marina. There was a hump-backed footbridge where it joined the canal. He walked onto it and leant on the rail at its apex. Despite the rush hour traffic on the boulevard it was calming to stand there looking across the rows of narrow boats with their perfect reflections in the flat calm of the moorings. How wonderful it would be to live in one of those. He descended slowly to the far side, deciding to follow the towpath for a while. It occurred to him that although he knew it must rejoin the Trent further upstream, he had only a vague idea where the canal ran. He walked under the ring road, past a small boat yard and through an industrial estate until eventually entering the flat, open countryside of the Trent flood plain. Occasionally a barge would putter by, each helmsman greeting him like an old friend. He felt as though he had stepped out of his life and though he must eventually turn round and rejoin it, he would not arrive back at the same place.

Christine was busy emailing in the office. She had decided to respond to the letter from the bank by asking their manager to write to Mark and arrange a meeting so that they could consider their options and formulate a rescue plan. It was a flagrant bid to buy a little time but it seemed to be the only way to postpone the inevitable. She emailed or faxed a few of the suppliers who had sent final demands explaining that due to her illness they had been late with their grant applications this year. They were mostly large, impersonal organisations and unlikely to be moved by such a plea to the extent of restarting deliveries but it might help stave off legal action for a while. She finished off by collecting an electronic bank statement for the day, and then wished she hadn't; they were still seriously the wrong side of their overdraft limit. She decided not to print it. Instead she made a list of things for Jess to do before dragging herself back into the living room. She had done too much and was now exhausted. Instead of trying to struggle back upstairs, she lay on the sofa with her head pounding.

Jess showered and sat wrapped in a towel straightening her hair. She stood up and opened her wardrobe.

'I so need some new clothes,' she said to herself.

Selecting a few things to take to Sam's, she chose the grey dress she had worn at the restaurant for the coming evening. Until then, jeans and a jogging top would do fine.

She banged on Tom's door.

'What?' he groaned.

'Want a cooked breakfast?'

'Yeah, obviously.'

'Well you have to be up and dressed to qualify. You've got ten minutes.'

'Get a life.'

'Got one thanks. Ten minutes, yeah?'

'Alright. Now go and be cheerful somewhere else please.'

Jess smiled to herself as she bounded down the stairs, then remembered how long this had taken her mother and felt guilty. It seemed wrong to be happy after so many months of anguish. In some ways it was impossible to be truly, blissfully happy with the spectre of terminal cancer haunting the family. No, spectre was the wrong word entirely, it was no apparition, but an awfully tangible, concrete reality and it was a reality that had ruined all their lives. Her mother was giving it one last run for its money, punching the tiger on the nose before it suffocated and devoured her. It was not just Sam; it was the incredible guts and determination of Christine that was causing this temporary euphoria. They were standing on the deck of a stricken vessel and they were playing rock and roll!

Jess put the kettle on and jogged down to the paddock to let Darcy out. He seemed a bit disgruntled because she was rather late.

'So sorry, your Lordship!' she whispered as she stroked his nose. He whinnied and trotted off down the slope. 'Suit yourself then,' she called after him and hurried back up to the house. She tried the yard entrance to the office on her way through but it was locked. Looking through the grimy window she could see it was empty. 'Hope she's ok,' she thought as she sped inside. Guessing that her mother would be resting in the living room she rushed in and found her lying face down on the sofa, her cheek blanched.

'Mum,' she whimpered and knelt beside her, but there was no response. She grabbed the hand of the arm the trailed on to the floor and it was icy cold.

'Mum, Mum,' she said with panic in her voice and Christine's eyes fluttered open.

'Oh,' she moaned weakly, 'I must have dozed off for a moment.'

'Mum you're freezing, I thought,' Jess stopped herself but it was too late.

'You thought I'd snuffed it?' said her mother faintly with a thin smile.

'Don't be silly,' Jess snapped, 'I'll fetch my quilt and try to get you warmed up a bit.'

She bounded up the stairs and leaned for a moment on the inside of her bedroom door. She let out a stifled sob and stuffed her fist into her mouth. It was unbearable, this awful realization that one day soon she might find her mother like that and would not be able to wake her.

When she got back downstairs, Christine was sitting up. She took the quilt and patted the cushion next to her. 'Sit down a minute,' she said gently. 'Sorry if I scared you,' and she put her

arm around her daughter and kissed her softly on the cheek.
'Oh Mum,' sobbed Jess, 'never do that to me again!'

It was the last day of Sam's induction and he was due for an assessment. Most of the observations by supervisors he had worked with were positive. His product knowledge, telephone manner and general attitude all scored well, but the area where he fell short was rather important, selling. He was not shifting enough boxes. It was not unusual but it needed to be addressed. His review should have been with Gill Smith but, much to Sam's relief, she was off sick and it fell to Dave Matthews, one of the section leaders, to comment on his performance. He was a very laid back character and Sam felt comfortable with him. They sat in Gill's office and he looked through all the reports.
'Blah, blah, blah, bollocks, bollocks. What a waste of time!' He threw the reports up into the air.
'Look mate, it's a very simple job this; we sell soft ware.' He half sang the last four words like the quarter past chime of the town hall clock.
Sam laughed; this was going to be a breeze.
'I don't know why you're looking so happy because you're not doing it. Why is that?'
The smile froze on Sam's face.
'I think it's just inexperience, Dave. I need to be a bit more ruthless, that's all.'
'Fair enough, if you can do that, fine. But the thing is we make it very easy; we virtually give the fucking stuff away. We must have those add on sales. Now tell me honestly, can you sell?'
'Honestly?' asked Sam and Dave nodded encouragingly, 'I guess it's not my strength.'
'Good. That's good. I wanted you to be honest and I agree with your self-assessment. Now we can help you if you like but there is 'another way,' as they say.'
Sam looked anxious. He had not expected Dave to be this critical.
'Don't worry mate, I'm trying to help you here. Thing is it's no good for either of us if you don't 'ex sell'; see what I did there?'
Sam smiled uneasily, 'I'm not sure where this is going, Dave.'

‘Ok, I’ll stop fannying around. You tick all the right boxes but one: selling, so how about going onto the technical support line? It’s a better basic but there’s no commission, but if you don’t make your sales, you won’t last long here anyway. So what do you think?’
‘I thought a different call centre handled it.’
‘That’s after sales but we have a small section here to support premier customers and our sales teams, who can either ask a quick question themselves or put the caller through if they’re really struggling.’
Sam thought for a moment.
‘Yes,’ he said decisively, ‘I would be interested in that, so long as the basic isn’t too basic.’
‘Ok. In that case I think it would be a good idea for you to spend an afternoon with them observing just to get a feel for it. If you think it’s right for you we’ll put you through the mother of all product-training modules. You need a good grounding in all the suites but we’ll want you to develop a specialism, so that you would know, say, photo editing inside out.’
‘I get the picture.’
‘I make the jokes.’
Sam felt relieved. Dave was clearly shrewder than he made himself out to be. ‘Thanks Dave,’ said Sam as they shook hands, ‘that was really helpful.’
‘Round pegs in round holes, it’s not rocket science mate. I’ll have a word with the head geek and see if I can pencil you in for Monday. Knock off for lunch now and come back here at about two.’

Peter Spencer had walked further than he intended, all the way to Beeston lock. He stood for a long time watching the river cascade over the weir. He loved the raw, elemental power of the white water as it tumbled down the steps of the dam. He found it soothing and at the same time thrilling to watch it surge over the lip and roar away down stream. The noise seemed to shut out the world and purge his mind.
Suddenly he realized he should be getting back. It was past noon and he had a fair way to walk back to the hotel. In the end

he went straight to the hospital but it was two thirty by the time he reached the ward.
The nurse at the desk looked puzzled. 'I'm sorry, I've only just started my shift, but I can't see his name down here.'
'I rang this morning and they said to come after two.'
'Oh here we are, Jack Spencer, yes he's been discharged. Your wife picked him up at two o'clock. Sorry if you've had a wasted journey.'
Peter was dumbfounded. He felt Theresa must have done this deliberately to score points in some devious, misguided way.
It was three thirty by the time he got back to the hotel. He went into the bar and ordered a snack and a beer. He really did not feel like dragging himself into the office now. He turned on his mobile. There were no texts, missed calls or voicemails waiting for him so he rang Nick. Nothing untoward had taken place and all his appointments had been rescheduled so he decided to give it a miss. He assured Nick that Jack was fine and everything would be back to normal on Monday morning. He tried ringing Jack but his phone was still out of order.

Peter felt more human after some food and drink but he was not comfortable. He felt outmanoeuvred and he was not sure what to do next. He did not want to go home; in fact he was not sure if he would ever feel like going back there. He and Theresa had fallen out many times before but this was on a different scale. For the first time, he could imagine himself not living there anymore. A conceptual shift had taken place and he no longer thought of that house as his home. He no longer had a home, and he was glad. He decided to head for the Beresford's. He wanted to find out what Jess knew about Jack and it would be good to chew things over with Mark, to whom he had often turned in times of discord.

When Sam returned to the office after lunch, Dave was nowhere to be seen. He stood in the corridor like a naughty schoolboy. Eventually a very pretty Asian girl approached him.
'Sam?' she enquired. He nodded. 'Hi, I'm Raj,' she continued, 'Dave Matthews asked me to meet you here. He's arranged for you to spend the afternoon with us in Tech Support?' Her

intonation implied a question.
'Fine,' said a surprised Sam, 'the sooner the better!'
'Ok then, follow me!' She grinned and spun round, heading towards the accounts offices. 'We're in a corridor behind Purchases,' she explained as Sam hurried along behind her.
Tech support consisted of a single four terminal workstation and a narrow oblong desk for clerical support. He had expected racks and shelves stuffed with manuals but it was completely paperless. All the data was stored electronically on the hard drive.
Raj rolled a spare operator chair up to one of the terminals. They were all in use, the support workers talking rapidly either to sales staff or punters. You could tell which by their manner.
'This is Ricky,' she whispered, 'probably the most knowledgeable techie in the world. Just eavesdrop for a while to get a flavour of the sorts of questions we deal with. You probably won't understand a word he's saying but that's ok because none of us do.'
Sam quickly decided it would be better than Sales. Having that level of knowledge and being able to use it to help people really appealed to him. He listened to Ricky taking the caller through a complex series of commands. 'Right click on this, open the drop down and select properties, double click on that, enter on the other,' and so it went on until the problem was resolved. When the call was over, Ricky rotated on his chair and clasped hands with Sam. 'Hi buddy,' he said, 'welcome to the hive.'
'Why do you call it that?'
'Because it's cramped and noisy and we always get stung,' cut in Raj who had been standing behind Sam.
'How do you mean stung?'
'Some of the calls we take are premium rate,' explained Ricky, 'we earn serious money for the company but we never see any of it. Our working conditions are crap and apart from the Christmas bonus, we get no incentives.'
'So why do it?'
'We're the elite man, like fighter pilots and besides you get to work with the incomparably beautiful Raj.' He winked at her and she looked at Sam and grimaced.

‘Talking of which,’ she diverted, ‘it’s time you baled out isn’t it?’
Ricky glanced at his watch and nodded. He quickly closed his session and vacated the place for Raj, who had been waiting to relieve him.
‘Seriously mate, the really good thing about this job is there are no bosses, no one breathing down your neck. So long as we keep taking the calls and sorting people out they leave us alone. And we’re a great team, all equals, all good guys.’
‘Sounds perfect.’
‘Well, I wouldn’t go that far, but it has its good points. So what do you think? Want to give it a whirl?’
‘Yep, think so.’
Sam found his own way back to the office. Dave had arrived now and they went through the tech support contract. The salary was almost double the basic in Sales, still not great but it suited Sam; at least he had a guaranteed wage. When they had finished, Dave said he could knock off. On Monday he would start two weeks of intensive support training.

Jess had just got back from a ride when her mobile rang. Surprised to see Sam calling her mid afternoon, she was a bit concerned. When she learned it was because he was already home, she was delighted.
‘Come as soon as you can!’ he exclaimed.
Jess quickly unsaddled Darcy. It had been a short, very gentle ride and he did not need brushing down. She hurried into the kitchen where Christine was just getting a pie out to defrost.
‘Sam got home early,’ she said breathlessly, ‘so if it’s ok with you, I’ll have a quick shower and head straight over.’
‘Of course love, you certainly deserve a weekend off.’
‘What about me?’ complained Tom, who was sitting with his feet on the table flicking through some notes in a jotter.
‘Pass these exams and you’ll get three years off,’ grinned Jess.
‘Don’t tell him that for goodness sake,’ said Christine turning from the freezer.
‘Hey, feet off please young man!’
Tom slouched off grumbling about not being allowed to do

anything.
'You sure you'll be ok this weekend?' asked Jess looking anxiously at her mother.
'Don't you worry about me; you go and have a lovely time.'
'Thanks Mum, but you see the thing is Cat and Ali have invited us up to Leeds next weekend and I really want to go but I'm not sure if I can.'
'I can't see a problem with that. Tommy will have gone to Cornwall by then so me and your dad can have a bit of peace.'
Jess threw her arms round her mother. 'Thank you, thank you, thank you,' she cried jumping up and down.
'Steady, you'll have me over in a minute!' Christine complained half-heartedly.

Abandoning the grey dress for jeans and a T-Shirt, Jess was changed and ready in minutes. She shouted goodbye to her brother, who had retreated to his room. Mark made a timely appearance for a cup of tea, and wished her well as she flew through the kitchen.
'It's lovely to see her sparkle back,' smiled Mark after she had left.
'Let's hope it doesn't all end in tears,' cautioned Christine.
Minutes after Jess had sped down the farm track, Peter Spencer's Jaguar slowly turned on to it. It was not unusual for him to just turn up at the farm on a Friday evening to see how they were getting on. He had been very supportive during Christine's illness. Often he would arrive with a bottle of red, but today he was empty handed. As usual, he let himself in through the back door and walked straight into the kitchen where he found them both sitting together at the kitchen table with a mug of tea. For a second before they looked up, Peter had a snapshot of a couple that, despite so much recent adversity, were absolutely united. Mark's hand rested gently on his wife's. They did not appear to have been talking, just enjoying a quiet moment together, minutes whose scarcity value increased with each passing day.
'Oh, I'm sorry, I shouldn't have just barged in like that.'
'Don't apologise, mate,' said Mark getting to his feet and shaking him warmly by the hand, 'drag up a chair. There should

be some tea in the pot if you fancy a cup.'
'I'd love one actually, no don't get up Chris, I can help myself.'
Peter sensed that she resented his interruption a little and he felt guilty.
'It's ok, I've got to put this pie in the microwave,' she said getting carefully to her feet, 'you sit yourself down.'
'You've just this second missed Jess,' said Mark. 'She's gone off to Nottingham to stay with her new bloke for the weekend.'
'I didn't know she'd got one.'
'Oh it's all very recent, a bit too sudden in some ways, but it's certainly put some colour in her cheeks.'
'Actually I was hoping to have a word with her about Jack.'
Peter went on to recount the events of the previous twenty-four hours. Mark and Christine were horrified.
'It's just that Jess left a message on my voicemail at work. I think Jack must have sent her a text or something just before he jumped and she was concerned enough to ring me about it. I just wondered if it would shed any light on his actions. This new boyfriend might have something to do with it I suppose. He's still holding a candle for her, you know.'
'You're not suggesting,'
'No Chris, please don't misunderstand me, I'm quite sure Jess is completely blameless. It would just be useful to know what he said.'
'So when did you last talk to Theresa?' asked Mark.
'We've had no direct communication since I dumped her in that lay-by.'
'Oh Peter,' said Christine, 'I'm sorry, but that's unforgivable.'
Mark gently placed his hand on her arm to indicate that was sufficient judgement.
'I think you need to go home now Pete, especially if Jack's there.'
'I just can't,' he said pitifully, burying his head in his hands. 'I was going to ask if I could spend the night here.'
Mark and Christine looked at each other and she imperceptibly shook her head.
'At least call,' said Mark.
Just then Tom burst into the kitchen.

'Any danger of being fed, oh, hi Peter, is anything wrong?'
Peter instantly brightened, 'Jack's had a bit of an accident but he's going to be fine. Did you give Jess that message by the way?'
'I only forgot temporarily,' said Tom cautiously.
'What's that supposed to mean?' asked Christine tersely.
'Well, I told her this morning and she said she'd get hold of you at work.'
Christine tried to communicate by eye movement that Tom should leave the room.
'What?' he asked before finally grasping her meaning and departing with a shrug.
'She'll probably be at Sam's by now if you want to call her,' suggested Mark, provoking more daggers from Christine.
'No, it's not that urgent. I wouldn't dream of disturbing her.' After a pause, he added, 'I should go home.'
'Yes,' said Mark.
'There was something I was wondering though. The way I feel at the moment, Theresa and I will at the very least have to spend some time apart. If that did happen, would you be willing to let that flat you built for your Mum?'
Christine's mother had spent her last years in a small specially built apartment just behind the farm office. It had been empty for a while.
'Surely it won't come to that.'
'I think it might. I'll pay you the market rent of course.'
'You will not.'
'Well give it some thought. I'll give you six months up front if you say yes.'
As Peter left, Mark was thinking about the impossibility of taking that kind of money from his friend. Christine was thinking about the overdraft.

The front door flew open as Jess pulled up outside Sam's and he rushed out to greet her. She jumped out of the car and they embraced in the middle of the road, laughing and jumping up and down. Sam took her bag and they walked inside. She was momentarily surprised that the front door led straight into the

sitting room.
'This is nice,' she said looking round the room.
'Nice and empty.'
'Minimalist.'
The TV and stereo belonged to Matt and had disappeared, leaving behind just a sofa, armchair and small dining table. Sam showed her round the rest of the house.
'I have to be honest, this is the first time I have ever seen it looking remotely presentable,' Sam smiled.
They decided to try to avoid the Friday rush and go straight to the supermarket.
'I got paid yesterday but I'm still a bit financially challenged,' said Sam apologetically.
'That's fine, I'm buying!'
As they drove to the store, Sam told her about the developments at work.
'That sounds perfect!'
'Well, that's not the word I'd use but the idea of working in small, friendly team is very attractive, plus I'm not under pressure all the time to make targets.'
'I have to say Sam, I never had you down as a salesman, which is a compliment actually.'
'Yeah, you have to be so pushy. I don't mind call centre type work, I've done it loads, and this will be good because the caller will actually want to speak to you instead of being suspicious or mad about something.'
They had to park a long way from the store but it didn't matter. They walked hand in hand along a pedestrian corridor between rows of cars. Jess noticed that some of the people plodding by with laden trolleys looked up at them and smiled.
'I wouldn't mind looking at the clothes,' said Jess as they walked in, 'they're pretty good here.'
'Well let's just get the minimum we need and I'll queue while you look upstairs,' suggested Sam.
'Good plan. Right what do we want? You don't eat fish I suppose?'
'I do actually.'
'Some veggie!'

‘I never said I was! I just don’t eat mammals.’
‘Let’s just concentrate on what you do eat for now. How about a nice bit of swordfish?’ Sam nodded. At the fish counter Jess held back to see how involved he would be and was pleased to see him looking carefully at the display.
‘Those two pieces look fine. Shall we get some Tuna as well for tomorrow? Or I could have that and you choose a bit of steak or something?’
‘Tuna’s good!’
Sam selected two thick pieces and sought her approval. ‘This is nice,’ thought Jess. In her experience, boys and shopping simply did not mix.
They got some fresh vegetables, bread, milk and eggs and two bottles of wine. As he was heading towards the checkout, Sam turned back,
‘Um, this might not go through on my card?’
‘Oh course! Sorry, I forgot.’ She took her purse from her bag and handed it to him. Sam looked bemused for a moment. Jess assumed it was because it was pink and sparkly.
‘Suits you sir!’ she laughed.
‘I’ll see you in ladies underwear,’ Sam said, louder than was necessary and as heads began to turn, Jess hurried off giggling.
They met up again about twenty minutes later. As Sam handed back her purse, Jess showed him some of the things she had selected.
‘What do you think to this summer dress?’ It was an open weave linen fabric in a rich kingfisher blue.
‘I love it. I think it will really suit you; why don’t you try it on?’
‘Would you mind?’
‘Course not; there’s no rush. Try on everything you’ve chosen if you like.’
This was too good to be true; a boyfriend who didn’t mind hanging round outside changing rooms!
‘A little fashion show!’ laughed Jess, hugging his arm tightly.
In the end, she bought the dress, an emerald green skirt and a couple of tops to go with it. Sam was genuinely interested and even suggested that another top she had chosen ‘did not quite go.’

On the way out of the store, Jess spotted a photo booth. 'Let's get a photo together as a memento!' she cried.
'That's silly!' exclaimed Sam. 'We could take a much better picture for nothing with our mobiles!'
'I know but it's not the same! Come on!' she insisted, taking him by the hand and dragging him over to the booth. 'I always used to do this with friends,' she laughed as she clambered onto his knee on the stool. 'Say cheese!'
The sticky sheet of four snaps slowly emerged from a slot in the side panel and shivered as it was blown with a jet of warm air. Jess carefully lifted it out and showed it to Sam and they laughed. They both the same rather bemused look on their faces. 'Perfect!' Jess giggled.

'Thanks for letting me try all these on,' said Jess as they loaded the stuff into the car.
'Oh I don't mind a bit of shopping,' said Sam. 'The problem is, women shop differently to men.'
'How do you mean?'
'Well you were shopping like a bloke just then.'
'Thanks.'
'No, I mean it. You wanted some new stuff, so you just went in and bought it, job done, end of story. If you'd been in town, I bet you'd have tried all that on, then gone to two or three more shops and done the same, then gone for a cup of tea, then gone back to a couple of the shops and maybe ended up buying one dress. That's just completely beyond the male comprehension.'
Jess laughed. He was exaggerating but there was some truth in it.
'Yes, I suppose we enjoy the process of shopping whereas for men it's a functional thing, a necessary evil.'
'Exactly. I'm not saying I didn't enjoy it but my patience might have been wearing thin by the third or fourth store.'
'Noted,' smiled Jess.

Matt had left a few cans of lager behind so they put the wine in the fridge and made a start on them. They sat together on the sofa and Jess rested her head on his shoulder.
They sat in silence for a while. There was no need to talk. The

little, sparsely furnished sitting room had finally provided them with the space and peace and time alone together they had needed from the day they first met.
'Happy?' murmured Jess eventually.
'Blissfully,' sighed Sam. He turned to face her and they kissed. 'This is a perfect moment,' he murmured.
Jess undid a button of his shirt and slid her hand in, gently stroking his chest.
'That feel nice?' she whispered in his ear.
'Mmmm,' sighed Sam, kissing her again.
Jess swung round so that she was kneeling on the sofa facing Sam, sitting on his legs. She held his face in her hands and looked at him closely for a moment.
'Your eyes are such a deep, dark blue,' she whispered and they began to kiss harder and deeper. 'I love how you kiss,' she sighed.
'You're so lovely,' he murmured. He slid his hands under her T-Shirt and unhooked her bra, gently stroking her nipples, which began to harden at his touch.
'That's nice.'
'You're so soft, so beautiful,' he moaned. He roughly tugged her shirt over her head and began hungrily kissing and sucking her breasts. She pulled frantically at the buttons of his shirt as he undid the cuffs then lifted it away and threw it across the room. He wrapped his arms around her and squeezed her to him tightly. She gasped for breath and wriggled with delight and they kissed again, harder and harder. He unbuttoned her jeans, tugged them down and gently stroked her.
'Oh, that's good,' she breathed and pressed herself down on his hand moving rhythmically to his touch. She frantically undid his jeans and as he hitched them down, his cock bobbed up and she caressed it gently.
'Hello my little boy, hello my darling,' she cried, 'let me kiss him, oh let me kiss him.'
'Oh god, oh no, I'm going to come,' he screamed.
'Oh no no no,' she laughed, 'not yet my baby. I want to feel you inside me first! Come inside me, come inside me!' Straddling him, she pressed herself down hard. 'Oh yes! Oh yes!' she cried

as she pumped rapidly on top of him.
'Oh my god, oh my god!' yelled Sam as he lost control. 'I'm so sorry, I'm so sorry,' he panted.
Jess kissed him hard on the lips. 'It's ok, baby, it's ok but stay inside me, stay inside me!'
Still clinging to each other, they rolled over so they lay side by side on the sofa. Jess pressed herself to him tightly.
'I always come too soon,' he groaned bitterly.
'It was fine, it was fine,' Jess gasped, 'Just to feel you inside me was wonderful, believe me.'
After a while, Sam fetched his quilt and they lay together for a long time, caressing each other, whispering and kissing as it grew dark outside.

When they were ready to make love again Sam kissed and stroked her until she was beside herself with excitement. He rolled over and squashed her until she squealed then thrust himself deep inside and she gasped at the strength of his penetration.
'Fuck me! Fuck me hard!' she cried as she drew him into her, squeezing him tight. She dug her fingernails deep into his arching back and wrapped her legs around him until they seemed to merge into one writhing, sliding creature. This time as his thudding ejaculation pumped deep within her, she came with him; a long, slow, shuddering orgasm which shook her whole being and left her body quaking with a pleasure of immense, indescribable intensity.

They lay clasped together, drifting in a hazy semi-consciousness for what seemed like hours and spent the whole night on that sofa, the food and the wine remaining untouched in the fridge.

The house lights were on as Peter Spencer pulled into his drive. With a sinking feeling he stepped out of the car and walked slowly towards the front door. He had felt this way so many times before, working late, taking the longest way home, anything to postpone the moment of arrival. He let himself in, braced for the inevitable onslaught but at the same time not really caring; he had made his decision, it was over between

them and Theresa could do nothing to him now.
'Peter, thank god you're back!' She was halfway up the stairs, turned towards him as he walked in.
'What's wrong?' he asked anxiously.
'When we got home he went straight to bed. He was sleeping so deeply I nipped to the farm shop to get a few things.'
'You left him?'
'I was gone minutes. When I got back he had locked himself in the bathroom. I knocked on the door, he said he was fine, wanted a shower, so I left him to it.'
This was no time for an argument so Peter began to ascend the stairs. Brushing past her he asked, 'how long has he been in there?'
'I don't know, half an hour maybe. The shower's still running but he won't answer me. I kept banging on the door but he was ignoring me and you know how long he spends in there sometimes.'
Peter knew this was true. It could all be perfectly innocent. Jack might emerge any moment in his dressing gown, blissfully ignorant of the anxiety he had caused. He listened at the bathroom door. He could hear water splashing into the tray but there was no sound of movement. He banged hard on the door,
'Jack, Jack, it's Dad! Can you hear me?' There was no response. He tried barging the door but it was very solid. He ran at it and kicked it hard but it held firm. He rushed back downstairs. Theresa had not moved. She was gripping the banister, shaking in terror.
'Call an ambulance!' he yelled as he raced back outside. Running towards the garage he pressed the remote to operate the automatic up and over door. It shuddered, and then began to open with agonising slowness.
'Come on, for fuck's sake!' he growled through gritted teeth. Ducking down, he dived beneath it. Hanging on the wall from a nail was a rusty old crowbar that had been there since they moved in. He snatched it and sprinted back inside. Theresa was shouting hysterically to the emergency services. He leapt back up the stairs and jammed the end of the crowbar into the doorjamb just above the handle. He yanked it towards him using

all his weight. The door and fame cracked and splintered until the lock was forced and he could push his way in. Jack was lying unconscious, fully clothed on the bathroom floor. By his head was an empty paracetamol bottle and a few of the tablets were scattered around on the carpet. Peter had no idea what to do. He could hear Theresa still talking to the ambulance service so he ran back down and snatched the handset from her.
'This is the boy's father. He's taken an overdose of paracetamol and is unconscious. What do I do?'
'Try to stay calm sir. May I have your name?' He impatiently gave it. 'We have a vehicle on the way to you now sir. Are you with the patient?' The phone was cordless so Peter took it back into the bathroom. He gave the dosage details from the bottle and estimated that Jack might have taken about fifty tablets. He confirmed that Jack was still breathing. 'Right sir, I want you to stay with the patient. Do not give him anything to drink; do not try to make him sick. Please stay on the line while I relay this information to the paramedics. They will have everything ready to help the moment they arrive.' Peter held Jack's hand and pressed his forehead to the cold rim of the washbasin while he waited, straining to hear the distant wail of the approaching siren.

Ten

Sam took a moment to focus when he woke, then as he recollected the night a wave of euphoria surged through him. Jess was sleeping with her back to him, facing the sofa. He saw the smooth curve of her shoulder lifting gently as she breathed. He wanted so much to wrap his arm around her and feel the soft warmth of her breast against his skin, but was reluctant to wake her. When she shifted a little in her sleep, he folded her in, wrapping her up in him. He kissed her imperceptibly on the cheek. She shifted once more and unconsciously snuggled herself deeper into the cradle of his embrace. Sam wished there was some way of capturing this moment. This feeling of her, this feeling inside, was so immense and he wanted somehow to burn it into his mind, but the brain was no good for this; it would remember the day but this feeling, this feeling, this feeling, he needed all of his body and all of his mind to drink it in, drink it all in and even then it would not be enough. Nothing could contain this storm surge that was flooding through him.

'I love you,' he breathed softly in her ear. Her eyelid fluttered and she gently drifted into wakefulness.

'Hi babe,' she murmured drowsily.

'You ok?' he whispered.

'Yeah, but I'm going to wet myself if don't go for a pee in a minute.'

The first thing to do that day was view the bed-sit. The house itself was a large Victorian semi that looked in need of a bit of care and attention. As usual with this type of property there was just a random array of anonymous bell pushes by the front door, so Sam called the landlord on his mobile. He came down and let them in. The hall was a bit shabby and depressing with the inevitable piles of mail and magazines for absentees that nobody thought to forward or throw away and a dusty floor that no one ever swept. Yet peeping through this cloak of neglect were little reminders of what had once been a lovely family home: the few surviving panes of stained glass in the front door, a scatter of patterned tiles on the hall floor and the faded elegance of the ragged treaded staircase. As they ascended the stairs, it occurred to Jess how sheltered her life had been. Even as a student she had lived in modern purpose built accommodation with an en-suite room.

The room itself was quite tiny. It must have been a box room or perhaps for a maid. It looked out over the garden through a narrow single sash window. In the corner beside this was a square pot sink with an instant electric water heater and a wooden drainer. On the other side of the window was a small electric cooker and next to this a drop leaf Formica table with a single bent wood chair. Along the adjoining wall was a light oak melamine wardrobe with a not quite matching chest of drawers. Opposite this was a single bed with an open fronted cabinet and lamp and there was a small fridge between the foot of the bed and the sink. The blue carpet and curtains looked quite new and the walls and ceiling were freshly painted.

Jess gripped his arm and whispered, 'I love it; it's like that Van Gough painting!'

Sam seemed less impressed. 'How much is it?' he asked cautiously.

'Two hundred a month including rates and there's a prepayment meter under the sink for the electricity.'

Sam nodded thoughtfully. This was less than he had been paying Matt.

'Can I see the bathroom?'

This was next-door. It contained the original bath and washbasin with a modern shower cubicle in the corner.

'It's an instant electric shower with a coin timer and there's a prepayment gas meter for the bath water.'

There was an ancient, ferocious looking Ascot heater fixed to the wall above the bath. The floor covering appeared to be authentic buff coloured linoleum. Despite looking a bit like an

exhibit in a museum of suburban life, the room was quite clean and serviceable.
'The toilet's next door and there's another with a shower downstairs. I'll leave you both for a few minutes to think about it while I put my stuff away.'
They walked back into the room. The sun was streaming in through the window. Sam sat down at the table and pretended to type.
'What do you think then?' asked Jess excitedly.
'It's like a bloody prison cell!'
'It is quite compact.'
'You like it don't you?'
'Yes!'
Sam stood up and opened the cupboard under the sink. It was mostly taken up by the electricity meter. 'There's no storage space!'
'You've got no stuff!'
'True.'
He sat on the bed and bounced a few times. 'This feels ok actually.'
'Very important!'
He looked under the bed and pulled out a battered old convector heater. 'There's nowhere to put this.'
'We can turn the oven on if it's cold!'
Sam looked up at her, shook his head and smiled.
'Ok, you win. I'll take it'
Jess grinned and jumped up and down, clapping her hands like a child.
They walked back outside to where the landlord was loading decorating gear into his car.
'Did you say you wanted a month's rent up front?' asked Sam.
'Yes. In cash please. After that you can pay by standing order if that's ok.'
'How soon do you need the money?'
'Today really; I've got other people who want to see it if you don't have it.'
Sam looked at Jess and shrugged. There was no way he could do that.

'Do you want to wait while we find a cash machine?' she asked. Sam looked at her in amazement.
'If you can have the cash later this morning I'll call round to the house with a copy of the lease and the keys. It would suit me if you could move out this weekend actually. I'll let you have till Saturday in the bed sit before the rental period starts.'
'It's a deal,' said Sam, and they shook hands.
They walked by a store with a cash machine on the way home. Jess withdrew two hundred pounds and handed it to Sam.
'It's going to take me a while to pay this back you know,' he said apologetically.
'You'll just have to do some jobs for me instead then!' She stopped, pulled Sam towards her and gave him a lingering kiss on the lips.
'I'm really busy at the moment,' he said and she boxed him playfully on the chest with both fists.

Sam decided to start packing as soon as they got back to the house. Because the bed-sit was so small, he would have to be ruthless with his stuff. He began by sorting through his book collection, packing the ones to take in a box and leaving the others in a pile for Oxfam.
'You should burn them like Jude Fawley,' said Jess, idly flicking through the reject pile.
'Oh yeah, Jude the Obscure, brilliant title for a novel! Do you like Hardy?'
'I love him but its all so tragic and sad. You need a bit of a laugh sometimes. What's this?' she asked opening a small pamphlet of poetry, 'how's that for a title, 'Brine' by Anna Parsons. Why did you buy that?'
'I think it's quite a good title actually, astringent and elemental. I went to a reading she did in town and I usually end up buying the book.'
'Sucker. No wonder you're skint. Not much book here for £6.99.' She began reading the quotes on the back cover. 'Oh god, listen to this: 'With Brine, Parsons has consummately lifted contemporary poetry clear of the jejune, elevating it to a level where it can safely be called 'art'. These poems are hard won and the product of an intelligent sensitivity that is all to rare in

the modern age.' Don't get David Ambrose to do the puff on your novel; you won't sell a single copy!'
Jess read a few of the poems while Sam continued to pack, then dropped the book back on the pile.
'When do I get to read 'Thine is the Kingdom' by the way?'
'While I do this if you like,' said Sam opening up his laptop and double clicking an icon on the desktop.
'I'm not sure if I want to, I mean what if I don't like it?'
'I shan't mind at all; it's just work. I badly need that advance.'
'You mean you haven't lifted it clear of the jejune?'
'Well obviously I've lifted clear of the jejune,' he said in a silly voice.
'I should hope so.'
There was a knock on the front door. Sam picked up the wad of cash and, waving it provocatively at Jess, hurried downstairs leaving her in the company of Max Million.

Peter Spencer was waiting in a small interview room in the psychiatric department of the Queens Medical Centre. A doctor entered carrying a medical record file.
'Mr Spencer?' Peter nodded. 'Hi, I'm Sanjay, one of the psychiatric team. I'm sorry we've kept you waiting.' They shook hands and the doctor sat opposite him. 'Jack's stable now. They caught him early enough in A&E to flush most of the paracetamol out before it got into his bloodstream. He's sleeping at the moment and is comfortable.' Peter nodded. They had already told him in casualty that Jack would be ok.
'What happens now?' he asked.
'Well, we have to write a care plan. Jack clearly has some major issues that have pushed him into crisis. We need to talk to him about this as soon as he feels ready and find out what the problem is, then see what can be done to resolve it.'
'Shouldn't you have done that before?'
'Well I think we should Mr Spencer, but Jack is an adult and he chose to discharge himself after one counselling session. That's his right and we didn't feel there were grounds to apply to detain him.'
'Section him you mean?'

'If you want to use that term, yes section him. Is your wife with you tonight?'
'No she was too distressed. She felt it was all her fault. She's with a friend at the moment but knows Jack's out of danger.
'And was it?'
'What?'
'Was it all her fault?'
'Not all, obviously, no, but she did make some errors of judgement.'
'Such as?'
'Well bringing Jack home for a start. He clearly needed help. And then leaving him on his own this afternoon.'
'So you weren't consulted about the discharge?'
'No.'
'Is that normal?'
'I might as well be frank with you Doctor, um, Sanjay, we are having some problems at the moment and when Jack fell, jumped from his bedroom window we were in the middle of a blazing row.'
'I see. We'll come back to that if you don't mind. Let's just talk a bit more about the discharge. When did you find out that Jack had gone home?'
'When I came to visit this afternoon.'
'And how did that make you feel?'
'Well pretty angry obviously, not for wasted journey but because I thought it was the wrong thing to do and Theresa should have known that. She did it to get one over on me.'
'So you were angry with your wife about it?'
'Yes.'
'You felt it was a deliberate attempt to undermine you?'
'Yes.'
'But your son discharged himself. He was free to walk away so maybe she did the right thing taking him home.'
'I'm sorry, but I don't really see where this is leading. I mean Jack's the patient isn't he?'
'Of course and we'll have a good chat with him when we can but we have to get the full picture and family is obviously very important.' He flicked through some pages of handwritten

notes. 'He mentioned something about a girl to the team member who counselled him. Can you help me at all with that?'
'Yes. He was upset because a girl he's close to has just got a new boyfriend and it's rather dashed his hopes.'
'How significant do you think that was?'
'I think it was one element in a mixture of things. He was also very stressed about his university exams. He had just told Theresa that he was going to throw it up and not do his final year. That was what we were arguing about.'
'And the girl?'
'We certainly had argued about Jess as well. Did he mention that?'
'I can't tell you what he said I'm afraid. You've been very helpful Mr Spencer, thank you. We need to see Mrs Spencer, and do you think Jess would be willing to talk to us?'
'I really can't say. I must stress she has never regarded Jack as a boyfriend. It's all one way I'm afraid. I will talk to her though.'
'You know her then?'
'She works for me; she's the daughter of my oldest friend.'
The doctor nodded thoughtfully for a moment then snapped the file shut, thanked Peter again and briskly left the room.
Peter did not feel like travelling all the way home to an empty house. He still had his overnight things in the car so he drove down to the hotel and checked himself back in.

Sam was a while sorting things out with the landlord and Jess had time to read all three chapters of the book. She heard the front door slam as Sam thundered upstairs and walked in jangling his keys.
'We're in!' he cried excitedly.
Jess jumped up and hugged him.
'I'm so glad!' she said breathlessly. 'Let me see, let me see!'
'It's not very exciting,' he said handing them over, 'a Yale for the front door, another for my door and the long one is for the shed.'
'The shed?'
'Yes, there's an old shed round the back where I can keep the bike and he said it would be ok to put a few boxes there as my

room's so small.'
'Does that mean 'Brine' will be preserved?'
'Ha! Probably. It's easier than lugging this lot down to Oxfam.'
'It's their loss. A shed, how exciting! Meet me there tonight, Mellors, I want to see what tools you've got!'
'I've got just the tool for you my lady!' he said, grabbing her roughly and crushing her to him. They kissed long, hard, passionate kisses, undressing each other frantically. She knelt on the bed and he thrust into her from behind. He squeezed her breasts as he pulled himself onto her and drove himself in with short jabbing strokes. When he came, the ejaculation was immense. He felt as though he was exploding inside her. They collapsed down onto the bed and held each other breathlessly.
'That was just incredible,' he gasped, 'was it good for you too?'
'It was fine,' she said, 'you're so powerful Mellors.'
'Was I too rough?'
'No, no. It was exciting, I liked it,' and she had, though it wasn't her favourite way.

They lay in bed for a while dozing and chatting by turns. The feeling of cosy contentment was blissful. In the end hunger forced them downstairs. They had skipped breakfast and it was nearly two o'clock.
'Can we sleep in the bed sit tonight?' asked Jess excitedly.
'If you like,' Sam nodded. He spent the next half hour phoning meter readings through to utility suppliers while Jess loaded some boxes into the Fiesta.
They did a couple of trips together in the car and then Sam was to follow her on his bike. When the final load was ready he posted the keys through the letterbox.
'How does it feel?' asked Jess.
'I'm not sorry, though I am worried about Matt.'
'He'll probably be ok.'
'I suppose so,' said Sam, climbing onto his bike. 'Race you!' he cried and pedalled furiously off down the road with a manic laugh. Jess stood and watched him go. Silly boy, she might as well let him win.

The shed turned out to be rather damp and ramshackle but it

would do for the things Sam wanted to store in it. They put a pan of water on the stove for a cup of tea and Jess helped him put his clothes away. She held up an Andsoft polo shirt and traced the embroidered ampersand logo with her finger.

'It's an odd name. Does A.N.D. stand for something?' she asked.

'I can tell you all about if you like. It was in one of the corporate videos I had to watch. How long have you got?'

'Summarise.'

'Ok, well a lot of people think it stands for something like Associated Nano Dynamics, but that's not the case at all. The real reason is quite fascinating actually. Honestly. Remember Sir Teddy?'

'Oh, The Hardware Store, yes. What ever happened to him?'

'Well, about ten years ago he decided to develop software to go with his computers so he invested millions and it was planned that when it launched, the company name would change to the Hardware…'

'And Software Store! So what happened?'

'Oh he got cold feet at the last minute, decided the sums didn't add up and pulled the plug. The management did a buyout and it was spun off before even being launched, and the rest is history!'

'Ha! That is quite a good story actually, especially since the abandoned child fared better than its rejecting parent.'

The water finally boiled and they sat on the bed together with their tea.

'This is nice,' sighed Jess. Then her mobile rang. It was Mark.

'Hi Dad, everything ok?'

'We're all fine here thanks love. Are you ok?'

'Oh we're just perfect thanks.'

'Look, I'm sorry to bother you but there's something you need to know. It's about Jack. Peter just called to say that he took an overdose last night. He's going to be ok but they're keeping him in the QMC for a few nights.'

Jess went white. 'Oh my god!' she cried and Sam looked anxious, assuming it was about Christine.

'I wondered if you should visit since you're in Nottingham

anyway.'
'Of course, of course, I'll go this afternoon.'
She took the ward details and visiting times and promised to call Mark back later.
'It's Jack Spencer, you know, Peter's son? He's taken an overdose and he's in hospital and I think it might be my fault.'
'Your fault?'
'Well he sent me this email kind of grovelling and begging forgiveness about what happened at work and stuff and I just deleted it without replying. Since then he's sent me a couple of texts that were a bit weird and I ignored them too. Maybe I should have spotted the danger.'
'How exactly? I mean, I assume he didn't say he was going to top himself.'
'Of course not, it's just that he was obviously distressed. I did tell his Dad about it.'
'Then you've nothing to reproach yourself for.'
'No but would you mind if I visit this afternoon?'
'I'll come with you.'
'You don't have to. You'll probably have to wait in the corridor.'
Sam insisted and they decided to set off right away. When they got there Jess was allowed straight on to the ward and, as she suspected, Sam was asked to wait outside. He hated hospitals but had never been in a psychiatric department before and his writer's brain was busy soaking up atmosphere. He saw a familiar face walking towards him and struggling to place it out of context, suddenly realised it was Martin Smith from work.
'Hi, Martin!' he called softly.
Martin stopped in his tracks and went through the same process of recognition.
'Samuel Taylor?' he enquired. 'Have you come here to visit Gill?'
'Gill's a patient here?' he asked incredulously. He had to be careful because Martin almost certainly knew nothing about their relationship at university.
'Yes. Most people don't realise it but she's very fragile mentally. I have a terrible time with her you know. Something

pushed her over the edge while I was away on a course for a few days and she cut her wrists. If a colleague hadn't called round she probably wouldn't have survived.'
Sam commiserated.
'Anyway,' continued Martin, 'here I am going on about my problems. If you haven't come to see Gill, who are you visiting?'
'Oh it's just routine,' said Sam trying to sound evasive.
'Surveillance?'
'I really can't say Martin, I'm sorry,' he muttered looking furtively up and down the corridor.
'Had I better not mention to Gill that I've seen you?'
'Don't mention it to anybody at all please Martin. You haven't seen me.'
'No, right, of course not,' he spluttered, hurrying away.

Jack was propped up in bed when Jess arrived on the ward. He looked terrible because the bruising had all come out where he had banged his head in the fall and his arm was still in a sling. He lay there gazing out of the window.
Jess put her hand to her mouth.
'God Jack, what on earth have you been doing to yourself?'
He looked at her as though his eyes were slightly out of focus and smiled wanly.
'Oh Jess, hi. I know, I look like I've done a fifteen rounds with Mike Tyson don't I? Don't worry it's all pretty superficial. Thanks for coming. There's some chairs stacked over there if you want.'
He seemed remarkably calm and Jess wondered if he was on medication. She perched on the edge of the bed,
'How are you feeling?'
'What, physically or mentally?'
'Well, both really.'
'Ok then, physically I have a bump on the head, which looks much worse than it is, a sprained shoulder is much worse than it looks, and my gut feels like it's been hit by a train. Mentally I'm fine.'
Jess laughed, which seemed to please Jack. 'So how did you

manage to get so beat up?'
'You probably don't know; the overdose was my second attempt. Before that I jumped out of my bedroom window.' He was so offhand it was quite alarming.
'Oh Jack! What on earth made you do that?'
'It was just an impulsive thing. Mum and Dad were having one of their epic rows downstairs and I just lay there thinking this has been going on for as long as I can remember and I just wanted to make them stop, to make them actually think about me for once.'
'Well I guess that worked.'
'I'm not sure. It stopped that particular argument all right but I don't think it actually changed anything. The main reason Mum let me discharge myself from that admissions ward was that she didn't want me moved in here. She didn't want her son to have been in a psychiatric ward. What would they say at the bridge club?'
'Surely not.'
'She said as much on the way home. She didn't give a shit whether or not I needed help, she just wanted me out of there.'
'So that's why you did the OD?'
'Yep.'
'It wasn't about me then? I mean that text you sent me was a bit scary.'
'I just wanted you to know that I've seen the light Jess. I was arrogant and stupid just like my mother. I want to break free from her control and find myself; become a different person. I know now that I'm not worthy of you, Jess and I never will be. That's what I was trying to say in the text. This isn't about you, it's about her.'
'Not worthy? That sounds a bit extreme! How's your dad coping with all this?'
'He needs to leave her. He can't contend with her; she's too strong for him.'
'Do you think he can do that?'
'I don't know but I can't be the buffer, can't referee that marriage any longer. All my life I've been walking on eggshells, trying to make sure nothing happens to spark off another punch

up. I can't do it any more Jess, I just can't.' He put his good hand up to roughly smear tears away from his eyes. Jess grabbed it and pulled it away, holding it in hers.
'It's ok to cry Jack. Come on, don't bottle these feelings up.' She squeezed his hand tight as he wept bitterly for a few moments. Suddenly she was aware of someone standing behind her.
'You must be Jess,' a voice said. She looked round and nodded.
'I'm Sanjay, one of the team looking after Jack. Thank you for coming in, this is just what he needed. Feeling better, Jack?'
Jack nodded. Jess released his hand and passed him a tissue. He wiped his face and blew his nose loudly. They all laughed.
'Yes, I feel everything is very clear now and I know exactly what I want to do. We've got a house in Bristol for next year. I'm going to leave home and move down there permanently, get a job for the summer, do some retakes probably, and be independent; break away from my parents.'
'And how will they feel about that?' asked Sanjay.
'That's their problem.'
'Ok, and what about Jess here?'
'I've been such a prat. I just hope you'll forgive me one day and we can be friends.'
'Of course we'll be friends you dick head!' cried Jess, tears springing into her eyes now. She leaned over and hugged him and he winced. 'Oh sorry,' she said.
Sanjay walked Jess back to the reception desk.
'Sometimes it takes a crisis like that to really find yourself. Thank you for coming in, Jess you've had a really positive effect on Jack's treatment.'
Peter and Theresa Spencer were walking down the corridor as Jess left the ward.
'What's she doing here?' hissed Theresa acidly.
'Mark must have got hold of her.'
'Well she's the last person Jack will want to see.' Theresa nodded coldly at Jess and walked by her onto the ward. Peter stopped to talk. She put her hand on his arm,
'I'm so sorry about all this. How are you coping?' she asked.
'It's been terrible. Theresa and I are hardly speaking. We both

blame each other.'
'And me?'
'No Jess, I don't blame you at all. You're a victim if anything.'
'It's poor Jack who's the victim I think; he just never allowed anyone to see it before.'
'Has he opened up to you?'
'Yes. He seems remarkably clear and lucid considering what's happened over the last couple of days.'
'Good, that's good.'
Theresa remerged from the ward and glared at them.
'You'd better go,' said Jess.
'Will you come in to work on Monday?'
Jess hesitated, 'I don't know.'
'Please!' said Peter urgently.
'Yes, alright then,' Jess nodded, 'I will.'
'Thank you,' he whispered as he hurried away.

It was after six by the time Sam and Jess got home. They had planned to go to the cinema in Nottingham but it would be too much of a rush to get there now. They decided to open a bottle of wine and have a leisurely meal together.
An elderly man was standing outside the front door smoking a cigarette. He was rather shabbily dressed in an old sports jacket and cord trousers.
'Hello,' he said cheerily, 'are you the new residents of the broom cupboard?'
'Well, I am anyway. There certainly wouldn't be room for both of us. My name's Sam and this is Jess.'
'Hello samandjess, welcome to heartbreak house. I'm Roland by the way.'
'Why do you call it that?' asked Jess.
'Oh we're just a collection of failures and misfits, the fractured detritus of broken homes and wrecked relationships.'
'You'll fit in ok then Sam,' said Jess.
'Oh don't worry, we're all perfectly,' he jerked his head a couple of times, 'normal here.'
'Pleased to meet you Roland,' said Sam, shaking hands.
'Like wise, and you too young lady. That's my domicile,' he

indicated the ground floor front room with his thumb, 'just ask if you need anything.'
They thanked him and went inside.
'He seems quite a character,' said Jess as they walked up the stairs.
'Yes, he sounded rather educated didn't he? I wonder what he does.'
'I shan't be surprised if we hear the clacking of a manual typewriter later on,' observed Jess wryly and they exchanged a smirk.

'Right, how are we going to do this?' asked Sam, opening the fridge.
'Open the wine for a start!'
'Good plan. Thank goodness for screw tops, I've no idea where the cork screw is!'
He found a couple of tumblers, wiped them on his shirttail and poured liberally.
'To a happy new home!'
'A happy home,' he echoed and was about to clink glasses when Jess lifted hers away.
'And,' she added, extending the vowel, 'to us!' She leaned forward and kissed him as they completed the toast.

Sam had an old Japanese wicker steamer that had been reprieved from the charity shop, so they put potatoes in a big pan with vegetables tiered above them.
'You could really do with a microwave; it'll get so steamy in here in the winter. Perhaps I'll get you one as a housewarming present.'
'You paid the god damn rent already!' he said expansively shrugging his shoulders.
'Yes but I'm going to get that back aren't I?' she breathed huskily. 'Besides they're for nothing in the supermarkets.'
They pulled the table out so that it was in the passageway between the bed and wardrobe then lifted one of the drop leaves over half the bed. There was just room for Sam to sit at one end of the table on his office chair and Jess to sit at the other in the bent wood chair. Sam had to walk along the bed to get to his place. Jess laughed as he wobbled along and took his hand

chivalrously as he dismounted.
'It is a bit intimate isn't it?' he puffed.
'I wouldn't have it any other way.'
After giving the potatoes a head start they balanced the steamer on the pan and opened the swordfish. Sam rummaged in a box for the frying pan and cooking oil.
'How long do you think this fish needs?'
'Five minutes tops, you don't want to overdo it.'
Jess found some plates and cutlery to set the table. She came across a large cylindrical candle and placed it in the middle. When the food was ready, Sam lit the candle and turned out the light. They sat for a moment in the soft wavering glow of the candle and held hands.
'This is perfect,' said Jess, 'I'm so happy that I've found you and we got this place and it's so lovely just being together and sharing our lives.'

After they had eaten and cleared away, they sat together on the bed with a coffee. Sam had some films on DVD and suggested playing one on his laptop but Jess was happy just to sit and talk. They left the candle burning and sat arm in arm in its lantern light.
'Did you manage to read much of the book?' asked Sam a little nervously.
'Yes, all three chapters.'
'And?'
'I don't really read thrillers, Sam. I don't feel qualified to comment.'
'You didn't like it did you?'
'It's not that; I think you write really well. It's just that it all seemed a bit flippant, as though you were taking the piss out of the genre, lampooning it. I'm just not sure how that will go down with the publisher.' She was anxious about offending him but at the same time wanted to be honest.
'Yeah, that's a very good point. What I'm trying to do is capture the mood of the Bond movies, particularly the early Connery ones. I think there was an element of pastiche in them that managed to steer clear of outright parody. It's the delightful

suave insouciance that I want to achieve.'
Jess thought for a moment. She was not sure if she had even seen any of the early Bond movies, they were all so ancient.
'Hmmm. I just worry that an editor will think you're being a bit disrespectful.'
'That's exactly what I want to be! It's the impudence that makes it so endearing.'
'I'm sure you know best; and I hope you don't think I'm being negative.'
'Not at all, I think your comments are very valid and you could well be right but there's no time to change it now. I have to get it printed and sent off tomorrow. I'm just hoping I can talk someone at work into doing it.'
'I'll do it at the office if you like. Write a covering letter and I'll post it as well.'

As Sam got up to pour more wine, he peeped through the crack in the curtains.
'Come and look at this!' he cried. It was a clear night and a full moon shone brilliantly in the sky. Jess came to his side and they knelt together on the floor staring out of the window.
'I love the moon, don't you?' she said.
'Yes. He's like a friend, the earth's travelling companion.'
'Do you think he's sad?'
'His expression reminds me of 'The Scream', you know, the painting? He's looking down at the earth, seeing us trash the place and it's a paradise compared to his barren landscape and he's just so horrified. He's trying to warn us, say 'look at what you're doing! If you don't stop you'll end up like me!''
'You could write a poem about that,' she said, resting her head on his shoulder as she gazed up at the troubled face.

Eleven

In the morning Jess lay on her back watching Sam sleep, trying not to disturb him. 'I wish I could lie like this for ever,' she thought.

Eventually he stirred and laid his arm rather heavily across her breasts. She wriggled onto her side and snuggled into him, pressing her nose up to his.

'What are you doing?' he asked sleepily.

'Giving you an Eskimo kiss.'

'I'd rather have a proper one.'

She propped herself up on one elbow and kissed him lingeringly on the lips.

'That better?'

'Not bad for an Eskimo.'

'Fancy a cup of tea babe?'

'Hmmm, please. Want me to go?'

'Well it's not exactly far is it?' she said, shuffling down the bed.

The room was not overlooked, so she opened the curtains and sunlight flooded onto her face, arms and chest. Sam lay watching her as she leaned back on the sink gazing out of the window waiting for the pan to boil, her shoulders gleaming in the brilliance.

'You're beautiful.' he murmured.

She looked round at him and smiled. 'Don't you think my tits are a bit small?' she asked, fanning her nipples with her fingers.

'They're the most perfect tits in the world.'

She lifted her arms and, placing her hands behind her head, arched her back smiling with pleasure. She looked wonderful then, the highlight on her long brown hair and soft smooth skin. Sam rose up and knelt before her, taking her in his arms and kissing her breasts hungrily, licking her nipples and sucking them into his mouth as she writhed with pleasure. He stood, lifting her in his arms, and clasping his shoulders she lowered herself onto him, wrapping her legs around his back. He leaned against the wardrobe as she thrust him deeply, deeply into her, plunging and writhing, as the water in the pan frenetically boiled itself away.

After breakfast they decided to go for a walk along the river. They crossed the busy Loughborough Road and a little cul-de-sac led them to the pedestrian suspension bridge spanning the Trent to Victoria Embankment.

'I've always loved this bridge,' said Jess, 'the river seems so wide and open here!'

They stood for a long time in the middle, leaning on the iron parapet. It was quiet and, apart from a few joggers, they had it more or less to themselves. The sun shone brightly on the white limestone of the war memorial.

'It's kind of ironic, having a gateway as a war memorial, don't you think?' asked Jess.

'Well, I guess it symbolises that the fallen have passed through to a place where they are forever young.'

'Forever dead.'

'Yeah. Doomed youth.'

'It's a fine monument and God knows they deserve it but don't you think it rather tends to sanitise all that carnage.'

'Yes, it's too lovely; more of a peace memorial'

'I remember peace!'

'Just think though, so many of them were just our age as they walked into those guns; all those young lives wasted.'

Jess turned to Sam and held him tight.

'We must live for them!' she cried. They kissed with a furious intensity and a middle-aged couple squeezed each other's hand a little tighter as they passed by.

Arm in arm they walked slowly upstream along a path where concrete steps descended into the water. They chatted about the events of the past week. Jess told Sam about her conversation with Lauren at the Poetry Café and they talked about Matt.

'How did you two meet?' she asked.

'I just answered an ad for a house share. He seemed ok and he wasn't asking too much for the room.'
'Will you miss him?'
'Yeah, I will I suppose. I mean he drove me mad but he was a laugh. We were kind of on a wavelength; you know, I would say something crazy and he would seize on it and run with it, like instantly, without hesitating.'
'What kind of thing?'
'Oh anything. It's like improvisation I suppose; one of us would go into character and the other would be right there with the other part and it would just take off. I can't describe it any better then that. Sometimes I still laugh out loud when I remember a thing we said.'
Jess felt a twinge of jealousy. She did not want Sam to have this special relationship with another person; she wanted him all to herself. It was irrational, but she was glad Matt had gone away. Then she felt guilty for being glad.
'So, do you think he'll get back in touch with you?'
'I should imagine so, I owe him two month's rent!'
'I don't get why he just vanished like that. How was that going to help exactly?'
'Maybe he has other debts I don't know about. In some ways our friendship was very superficial. We didn't often talk properly to each other, I mean really talk, like we do.'
Jess hugged his arm when he said that.
The conversation moved on to Jack.
'Are you planning to visit again today?' Sam asked.
'I don't think so. I might call home in a bit to see how things are going. Dad will probably be in the loop.'
Sam mentioned his meeting with Martin at the Hospital. Jess was shocked.
'How do you feel about it? I mean you and Gill were close once.'
'Obviously I wouldn't wish this on her, but after what she did to me I won't be shedding any tears.'
'Did she seem unstable when you were together?'
'With hindsight, I think she was depressed a lot of the time but I was too young, too inexperienced to understand. I would just

think it was something I had done or neglected to do that caused it.'
'Caused what?'
'She would literally shut down emotionally and I just couldn't reach her. The best way I can describe it, and this was how I used to think of it at the time, was that she had fallen down a well and though I could see her, no matter what I did I just could not reach her. There was a gap between us that I could not bridge.'
'What would happen?'
'It would be like that for days, like waiting for a huge thunderstorm to break. The tension was unbearable. I wanted to run away but I never did. Then suddenly, always in the early hours of the morning, she would snap, letting out this incredibly deep, unbelievably terrifying sob and then she'd weep violently for hours and I would hold her and it was like she was draining me, taking all my strength, all my life force and it would leave me utterly empty, like a squeezed out tube of toothpaste.'
'And was she ok after that?'
'She would sleep, sometimes for a whole day, and then she'd be fine, as if nothing had happened.'
'Didn't you ever say anything?'
'I know it seems ridiculous but it took me a long time to work out there was a pattern. When you're locked inside that roller coaster it's hard to be objective. I was always just so glad it was over and every time I thought it wouldn't happen again. We were only together for a year but it was a fucking long year.'
'So how did you dump her in the end?'
'I didn't,' he looked at her nervously, 'she dumped me for someone else and later I found out she had been seeing other people the whole time we were together. I know you must be wondering what I saw in her but she was, she is,' another anxious look, 'a very beautiful woman.'
'Great sex then?' asked Jess a little dispiritedly.
'No.'
'No?'
'No. I could never satisfy her; she always wanted more than I could provide.'

‘More what?’
‘More everything; longer, harder, oftener.’ They both laughed. Sam hadn’t meant it to be funny but it was, and it was a relief for them both to laugh.
‘God, I feel exhausted just listening to it!’
‘Well it’s obvious now isn’t it? She was using sex as an anti depressant.’
‘Don’t we all?’ They laughed again.
‘Not clinically, I hope. In the end I just felt she was using me like a tool, like ECT actually, to convulse the depression away.’
‘ECT? Remind me.’
‘Electro Convulsive Therapy.’
‘Yeah, yeah, yeah.’
‘They still use it you know, despite all the bad publicity about side effects. It does actually work, in that it does make people feel temporarily better.’
‘I wonder what made them think of passing a current through someone’s brain. It’s like Doctor Frankenstein.’
‘The story goes that this psychiatrist happened to notice epileptics never presented with depression, which he thought was a bit too much of a coincidence. Then, bizarrely, he went on a trip round an abattoir where they were killing pigs with electricity and he noticed how they convulsed after the shock. He put the two together and a wonderful new science was born.’
‘I think I’d rather do it the hard way.’
‘You certainly seem to like it, honey.’
‘Oh yeah!’ she said, doing a little dance, a kind of goal celebration, ‘no complaints from me in that department!’
‘Nor me!’ His mood changed and he looked at her seriously. ‘I mean it Jess, you’re the best thing that’s ever happened to me.’
‘So are you.’
They stopped for a moment and embraced, exchanging the tenderest of kisses.
‘So what became of that discarded tube of toothpaste?’ she asked as they walked on.
‘I had a few brief encounters in my final year at Uni, none of which were remotely satisfactory, and since I moved in with Matt, nothing at all. I seemed to have lost my confidence with

girls. You start to get like you can't even imagine yourself being intimate with someone ever again. I know you won't understand this, but it becomes almost inconceivable.'

'Oh I understand all right. Don't forget I've been living like a nun for the best part of a year. Well I suppose that's not strictly true; you should see my collection of burnt out vibrators.'

'I'd love to! A cert for the Turner Prize I would have thought! Especially a nun's collection, if such a thing exists.'

'I bet it does, and good luck to them.'

They talked for a bit about her sexual curriculum vitae. Her relationship, or rather non-relationship with Jack had not inhibited her at school but because she was nominally 'going out' with him it was all casual and spontaneous. She and Jack had never got beyond heavy petting. In her year at Leeds she had a series of partners but was not really interested in getting too involved with anyone.

'Here's the weird thing,' she said, 'and I'm not sure if I should tell you this, but just before I met you I was so desperate that I prayed. I prayed to this 'god' I don't actually believe in that I could meet someone special, and a week later you turn up in the middle of a field, like you'd, like you'd fallen from,' she hesitated, 'from the sky. How weird is that?' She turned to him and he was silent for a moment.

'So what do you think now? Coincidence, or irrefutable proof of the existence of the almighty?'

'It gets worse. I was so worried about Mum when she seemed to be fading away that I prayed again, prayed not for a 'take up thy bed and walk' kind of miracle, but just that she would get a bit better.'

'And she did.'

'Yep.'

'Well at least I'll know if I'm struck by a thunderbolt one morning that I must have done something to upset you.'

'Don't tease me Sam,' she said thumping him softly in the chest. 'You obviously think I'm hysterical.'

'All women are hysterical.'

'I wish I'd never told you now. Can't you take it even a bit seriously?'

'I'm sorry, Jess, I wish I could but I can't. God obviously doesn't exist.'
'Why obviously? You can't know something like that. It's just as much an expression of faith as belief is! Have you ever prayed?'
'I did once actually.'
'What about?'
'I couldn't find my passport.'
'Concentrating on the big issues, then.'
'It was important; I was off to Faliraki the following morning.'
'Oh, you should have said. And did you find it?'
'Yes, but that doesn't prove a thing!'
'Course not,' she grinned.

Peter and Theresa Spencer were at home together for the first time since Jack's overdose. They both accepted that for his sake it was important to try to return to something resembling normality, but it was no more than a ceasefire; too much damage had already been done. They were sitting on high stools at the breakfast bar drinking a glass of wine. Lunch was in a plastic dish in the microwave.
'Jack says he's planning to go back to Bristol as soon as he's fit. He wants to spend the whole summer there.'
'It might not be a bad idea,' said Peter, 'he could do with some breathing space.'
'But he'll be on his own in that house. All his friends will be off travelling. It could be very bad for him; very dangerous.'
Peter scratched his head. There was no point in continuing this discussion because it would only lead to an argument. He decided not to prevaricate.
'Theresa, I'm thinking of moving out,' he said as calmly as he could. She looked shocked but did not respond. 'If I do leave, do you not think it would be best for Jack to go to Bristol?'
'Where will you go?' she asked dully.
'I'm not saying it will be permanent, I just feel we need some time apart. I know we've had our ups and downs before and got through them but this is on a different scale. I can't live with you at the moment.'

'What's happened to you Peter? It's so unlike you to be proactive like this. What's changed? Have you met someone else?'
The microwave pinged and they both looked across to it, then back again.
'No, of course not.'
'Don't you think Jack will be upset?'
'Have you any idea how Jack sees our relationship? We may have tried to protect him from our vicissitudes but we've made a rotten job of it. I've stuck around here hating my life, hating myself to no-one's benefit for far too long.'
'Hating me too?'
'Yes Theresa, hating you too sometimes. The fact is I don't love you anymore. I stopped loving you a long time ago but I hung on, thinking it was all for Jack's sake. It's taken his attempt on his life to make me see I was wrong, that I have been actually making things worse.'
'But why go now if he's leaving home anyway? You can't go, Peter. What will happen to me?' She began quietly to cry. 'I know I've made mistakes, but in everything I have ever done I have tried to do the best for this home, for Jack and for you. You can't leave now. I couldn't bear it if the house had to be sold. What would people say?'
'What would people say?' Peter repeated in a dull voice, 'What would people say? Is that all you care about?'
'No, that's not what I meant.'
'It is what you meant! It's exactly what you meant! It's the reason why you wanted to get Jack discharged from hospital so early, in case people found out, in case they started to talk about it at the fucking bridge club! That's all that matters to you isn't it, appearance, appearance, appearance!'
Theresa put hear hands over her ears and yelled 'Stop it! Stop it! Stop it! You don't understand what it's like!'
'Anyway,' said Peter, trying to sound calm, 'we're not talking about selling the house, not at the moment. I just think we need some time apart, that's all.'
Theresa was silent for a while. She sat with her head in one hand staring hard at the worktop, as if trying to see through it.

'Very well then,' she said coldly, 'you don't love me, and if it's what you want you'd better go. Go on, pack your bags and go now, but I'm warning you, I shall be seeing a solicitor first thing on Monday. I'll take you for every penny I can get.'
'That's not how it works Theresa.'
'I've got plenty of friends who've been through this. I shan't be on my own.'
Peter knew that walking out was not the wisest of moves but he didn't care.
'What about visiting Jack?' he asked.
'Why don't you pack your stuff then go and see Jack and explain what you have done? I'll go over later.'
'That's not how I wanted it to happen. I wanted to wait until Jack was discharged.'
'You can't always get what you want,' she said icily.

As Sam and Jess returned from their walk they found Roland on the doorstep puffing away on another cigarette.
'Ah ha, the young lovers!' he cried. 'I'm glad I've seen you, I invited all the inmates down for a pre-prandial glass of sherry, would you care to imbibe?'
Sam looked at Jess and she smiled and nodded.
'Thanks Roland that would be great,' he said, and they agreed to meet in half an hour. They hurried upstairs trying to contain themselves, then dived into the room and fell about in hysterics.
'A pre-prandial glass of sherry!' mimicked Jess, helpless with laughter.
'He's so sweet, don't take the piss and it will be really good to meet all the other -'
'Inmates,' interrupted Jess with a giggle.
Since she had bought some smarter clothes, Jess decided to change. She rummaged around in her bag taking out hair straighteners and various bags of cosmetics.
'Whoa, the heavy artillery!' joked Sam. 'I wasn't planning to dress up, do you mind?'
'Well you're a bloke; there's no need to look smart is there?'
'Ouch! I'll comb my hair a bit then.'
While Jess was busy with the blusher and eyeliner, Sam fired up

his laptop to do the covering letter for his sample chapters.
'Hey, someone round here must have a wireless router, I've got Internet access!' he exclaimed.
'Brilliant! It's not password protected then?'
'Nope, I'm online now. That will be really useful. I hope they don't block me when they see I'm freeloading.'
'Perhaps it's an inmate. What's the name?'
'PollyG.'
'We'll have to ask at the imbibulation.'
Jess wore the new summer dress with her leather sandals.
'You look gorgeous,' said Sam admiringly.
'Thank you,' she said, 'you don't look so bad yourself, considering.'

Peter Spencer decided to call on the Beresford's before visiting Jack. Although he had briefly mentioned renting the flat, nothing had been agreed at the time. He badly needed an answer right away. As usual, he just tapped on the kitchen door and walked straight in. Mark and Christine were busy dishing up Sunday lunch.
'Peter!' smiled Christine, walking over and kissing him, 'how lovely to see you. How's Jack? Won't you join us, we've got far too much food.'
'Well I don't know; I didn't mean to gatecrash. I thought you'd be all done and dusted by now. Oh, and Jack's much better, thank you.'
'Grab yourself a beer, mate' called Mark who was energetically mashing a great pan of potatoes, 'we're a bit behind schedule I'm afraid.'
'It's made us appreciate just how much Jess does to help,' said Christine with a weary smile, 'Mark's done a great job but he's slightly over quota on the veg.'
'I've got enough spuds here to feed the whole bloody village!' laughed Mark.
Peter suspected that, despite their difficulties, they had really enjoyed themselves; the contrast with the kitchen he had just walked out of could not have been starker.
'Well in that case, I will join you if you really don't mind,' he

said, taking a can of lager from the fridge.
'Yes please, we need to shift this food mountain!' Mark lugged a sizzling leg of lamb out of the oven, 'do us a favour, nip upstairs and give Tommy a shout will you?'
Even though he was a frequent addition to the household, Peter felt a bit uncomfortable doing this. He walked into the rather drab, dingy hall and went half way up the stairs.
'Tom. Hello Tom. It's Peter,' he called awkwardly, 'your dad says to tell you lunch is ready.' There was no response. He tried again a little louder with the same result and went back down to the kitchen.
'Any luck?' asked Christine.
'I'm not sure really,' mumbled Peter apologetically.
Mark was busy carving the meat and Christine had just filled the vegetable tureens. Peter felt utterly useless.
'If you could carry these through to the dining room for me Peter, I'll soon get him moving!' Christine laughed.
'But you don't want to be trailing up and down stairs,' he protested.
'I won't have to!' There was a telephone mounted on the wall by the back door. She lifted the receiver and punched in a number.
'Are you up?' she shouted. 'Well get yourself down here in thirty seconds or there'll be no food!' She banged the receiver down and nodded to Peter, 'on his way, I think.' As she was saying this, the phone started ringing. They all laughed in surprise,
'The cheeky little,' said Christine reaching for the handset again. 'What?' she barked and her face immediately broke into a smile, 'Oh hello darling,' and to the others, ' its Jess!' She listened for a moment, 'no everything's fine, I just thought it was your brother playing silly buggers. How are you getting on? Good, good, how lovely! Look I'm going to have to go, we're just about to eat. I know, I was just saying we can't cope without you, but that's not to say; yes, yes we're fine really, I promise. Ok, that's nice; well don't be too late if you can bear to drag yourself away. Home for tea, that would be lovely. Ok darling, have fun, love you too. Bye!' She replaced the receiver

more gently this time.
'She's having a wonderful time; that's nice, that's very nice.'

When he had finished eating, Tom made the usual excuses and went back to his revision. This gave Peter the opportunity to tell Mark and Christine about the separation. Although they knew all about the troubled history of the relationship, they were still shocked and upset about it. They were also concerned about how Jack would react. After he had explained Jack's plan to move permanently to Bristol, Peter asked whether they had given any more thought to his request to rent the flat.
'I've got to be honest, we haven't discussed it at all,' apologised Mark, 'I had no idea things were going to happen so rapidly.'
'Neither had I,' Peter admitted. 'I just wanted to talk it over with Theresa today but I did it rather clumsily and she reacted very badly.'
'Could I talk to her?' asked Christine. ' Maybe I could get her to change her mind, if only for Jack's sake.'
'That's kind, but I couldn't go back there now, not after what's happened today.'
'You see the problem is mate we don't want to give the impression that we are taking sides,' explained Mark.
'On the other hand,' Christine added, 'if you really can't go back at the moment, you have to find somewhere and the flat would be the perfect solution.'
'Well obviously I have no objection,' agreed Mark, 'other than the fact that we should at the very least talk to Theresa first.'
'Thank you, I really appreciate this and I do understand your reservations.'
It was agreed that Peter would go to the hospital while Christine called Theresa. He would come back after seeing Jack, do all the washing up, he insisted, and they would make a final decision about the flat.
'I appreciate you supporting Peter like that,' Mark said after he had left.
'It's just common sense,' Christine shrugged, 'he needs a place to live, we have an empty flat, it's what Tom would call a no brainer.'

'Very appropriate,' chuckled Mark.

Jack seemed in good spirits when Peter arrived on the ward and his heart sank at the likelihood of reversing this improvement with the news he had to share.
'Where's Mum?' Jack asked immediately.
'She's coming later,' Peter explained. 'The thing is, I needed to see you on your own.' He went on to tell Jack everything that had happened earlier. To his amazement, Jack did not seem surprised.
'I think it might be best for both of you to separate, at least for a while. You need some time apart to cool down and evaluate how you really feel about each other.'
'But I told her I don't love her any more. There's no way back from that is there?'
'I think she knew that already, Dad!' groaned Jack in an idiot voice.
This was strange; he was not used to talking to Jack like that, as an equal, an adult with a contribution to make.
'Why haven't we talked like this before?' he asked.
'You tell me.'
'I'm sorry we've been such crap parents Jack. We've given you everything except what you really needed and now at this time of crisis, instead of being there for you, we just fall apart.'
'Don't you start! That's all I ever hear! Crisis, what crisis? So I OD'd, I didn't die, I'm better now, I'm over it. End of story.'
'Have they put you on any medication or anything?'
'No, to their credit they try other approaches first here. The downside is you get counselling all the time. I think drugs might be a softer option actually. Anyway I told them about going back to Bristol and they said that would be fine if I could continue with my care plan down there.'
They talked for a long time. It was as though the recent events had freed them and opened up a new level of communication. In the end, they clasped hands and hugged as Peter reminded him that Theresa would be visiting later.
'Don't worry Dad, I'll look after her,' he said.
Peter's elation at Jack's progress began to evaporate as he

drove up to the farm. He had no idea what he would do if it proved impossible to have the flat.
Mark was busy washing up when he walked in.
'I said I'd do that!' cried Peter.
'Well I thought I might as well make a start. Chris has just gone for a lie down.'
'Did she get through to Theresa?'
'Yes, she was fine about it. I think she liked the idea of you living in a place where you couldn't get up to too much mischief. Chris promised to give her regular bulletins!'
'Great. Is that settled then, do we have a deal?'
'Yes I think so.'
'When can I move in?'
'I'll go and chase the rats out now if you like.'
'Seriously?'
'About the rats?'
'No, idiot! I mean about moving straight in.'
'I suppose so. We keep it aired and tidy for all the guests we never have.'
'Yes please, then. I really don't fancy another night in a hotel.'
'I wouldn't mind a night in a hotel,' sighed Mark.

At the sherry party they did indeed discover the identity of PollyG. She was in fact Sam's next door neighbour, a middle aged divorcee who was busy trying to find a new man on the Internet. She had only just returned from a fruitless liaison with a gentleman in Runcorn.
'Why Runcorn?' asked Jess.
'Why not? I'll go wherever it takes to find Mr Right, darling.'
'Distance no object, then,' observed Sam.
'Absolutely! In some ways it's better because when you get a dud like I did last night, at least you're not likely to bump into them in Sainsburys.'
'So you just went off and spent a night in a complete stranger's house without any qualms?' asked Jess incredulously.
'I can look after myself sweetie, don't you worry. Take Mr Geriatric last night, there was no way he was going to try anything. People say women lie about their age but men are far

worse in my experience. He was claiming to be sixty, which is the absolute ceiling of my age range, and I bet we wasn't a day under eighty!'
'Eighty?' gasped Jess.
'Yep, and the rest!'
'But what's the point? I mean how can you initiate a relationship on the basis of such a transparent lie?' asked Sam.
'Ooh you're very articulate darling, you're not another bloody writer are you?'
'Well, an amateur, at the moment,' blushed Sam.
'They're all amateurs, trust me. Anyway, to answer your question, the point is they are all loaded and they seem to assume that you will be so blinded by conspicuous wealth you won't notice you're dating a cadaver!'
'Seriously, Polly,' said Jess earnestly, 'you should be careful. I've had a bad experience with on line dating.'
'What's a pretty little thing like you doing courting like that?'
'It's very popular with our age group, isn't it Sam?'
'Yes, and very unsuccessful in my case, though not especially scary.'
Sam mentioned about piggybacking on Polly's wireless router and she said that would be fine. She called over to Roland,
'Did you know we've got another scribe here, Roly?'
Roland wandered over with the sherry bottle,
'Anyone ready for a top up? So you're a fellow wordsmith are you lad? What sort of things do you do?'
'Well it's been mostly poetry and short stories up to now but, as I'm sure you know, there's no money in either, so I'm working on a thriller at the moment.'
'Splendid. Got an agent?'
They chatted for a bit about publishing. It turned out that Roland had been on the fringes of The Movement group of poets in the 1950's and, though never well known, had published a few pamphlets.
'I was a big chum of Philip Larkin, you know; often used to pop up to Hull for afternoon tea.'
Sam was seriously impressed. 'Wow, what was he like?'
'Absolute scream. Everyone says he was a miserable old git

don't they, but we always had a great laugh.'
Jess was right about the manual typewriter. Roland's room was lined with shelves of yellowing paperbacks and Sam had a browse.
'You really ought to get these valued, Roland. They're very collectable you know, the early Penguin books, especially these King Penguins.'
'Thanks for the tip, Sam. Maybe I should just flog 'em; it's hard to make ends meet on my pension these days.'
The other inmates were of less interest. There were two more rooms on the ground floor; one occupied by a postgraduate student at Nottingham Trent called Trevor, who was a biochemist, and the other by a mobile beautician called Sabrina, who had recently left her husband. She offered to let Jess have some sample jars of tanning cream, which she declined. The occupant of the remaining upstairs room was a contract worker for a financial services agency, who worked away most of the time.
'That sherry's gone straight to my head!' said Jess on the way back upstairs.
'Oh, I should have warned you about that,' said Polly, 'Roly gets this terrible stuff and decants it into a Harvey's bottle. Drink a pint of water as soon as you can to dilute it!' She laughed raucously. 'Well I'm feeling a bit depressed myself so I'll probably be playing Abba's greatest hits at full volume for an hour or so. Always cheers me up. Hope you don't mind.'
'Oh no, we love Abba don't we Sam?'
'Nothing better,' he agreed, with slightly less enthusiasm.

Lunch was a replica of the meal the night before, except for the background music. They sang along karaoke fashion to Dancing Queen and Waterloo, which somehow they seemed to know by heart, and when they had cleared away they sat together on the bed with mugs of coffee.
'This has been the best weekend ever, Sam, thank you so, so much.'
'Don't thank me; you made it all happen. Without you I'd be homeless and lonely and miserable, but here I am in my very

own, very cosy, very little room with the most special person in the world sitting right beside me!' He kissed her slobberingly on the cheek and she grimaced and rubbed at it exaggeratedly with the flat of her hand.

'Idiot,' she said playfully, nudging him so that he nearly spilled his drink.

He turned towards her and placed his hand gently against her face.

'I'm only being silly because I'm nervous about what I really want to say,' he murmured softly.

'Which was…'

'That I love you, Jess, I love you more than I could have ever imagined loving anyone.'

She looked at him with moist eyes.

'Well that's lucky then isn't it?' she croaked, 'because I love you too.'

Jess arrived home just after five o'clock. She was not particularly surprised to see Peter's car parked in the yard and walked into the house expecting to find him in the kitchen but there was nobody about. She took her bag up to her room and began unpacking. It seemed ages since she had been at work and it took her a while to adjust to the idea of going back in the morning. She was just deciding what to wear when she heard voices downstairs and hurried down to find her parents getting things ready for tea.

'Where's Peter?' she asked curiously.

Mark and Christine looked at each other anxiously.

'Sit down a minute, love,' Mark said to her, 'there's quite a lot been going off while you were away.' He explained about Peter and Theresa splitting up. 'Peter didn't have anywhere to go so we agreed to let him use Gran's flat for a bit while they sorted themselves out. It's just a trial separation, you see.'

Jess was shocked, not so much by break up as by Peter's arrival; it was completely unexpected and not especially welcome.

'I don't get a say in this, then?' she asked indignantly.

Christine looked horrified. It had never crossed her mind that Jess would not support the move.

'But you're so fond of Peter, darling. We didn't think - '
'Clearly!'
Christine became unsteady and had to grab the table for support.
'Oh Mum!' cried Jess, 'I'm sorry, I'm sorry it's just taken me by surprise.'
She helped her into a chair and exchanged an alarmed glance with Mark. On the verge of tears, she blurted out, 'I'm just going to check Darcy!' and rushed from the room.
Mark sat down next to Christine and placed a hand on hers,
'What have we done?' he asked in a wavering voice.
Tom drifted into the kitchen.
'Was that Jess I just heard? She sounded upset, did something go wrong at Sam's?'
'No, love' sighed Christine, 'that was all perfect, we're the ones who upset her.'
'Why? I thought you were fine about it.'
'We were, we are, it's just that, well you know we mentioned that Peter might be having the flat for a bit?' Tom nodded, 'well it's definite now, in fact he's moving in as we speak.'
'Yeah, and?'
'Well, Jess knew absolutely nothing about it and she's just arrived home to this fait accompli and she's not happy.'
'What's not to like?'
'Peter is her boss don't forget.'
'Hmmm,' ruminated Tom, 'I expect she's gone to discuss it with Darcy has she?' His parents nodded. 'Ok. Day thirteen in the Little Brother House, Tom is trying to talk sense into Jess,' he drawled in a Geordie accent as he headed for the door.
'Thanks mate,' Mark called as he walked out.

Jess looked up from stroking Darcy on the neck to see Tom stationed on the fence again.
'Are you going to make a habit of appearing on there like some kind of hobbit or something?' she rasped.
'I'm fine thanks, sis. How are you?'
She lifted her eyes to the heavens and growled in exasperation, then her expression suddenly changed. She walked slowly over to where Tom was sitting.

'Actually I'm fine too, thank you very much,' she sighed, 'it's just this business with Peter. I don't know why, but it really upset me.'
'Mum and Dad are mortified.'
'I know. I'm sorry, but it just feels as though the whole thing's been done behind my back.'
'Well if you're going to disappear on a fuck fest for the weekend what do you expect?'
'Tom!'
'Was it good then?' he grinned.
'None of your business!' she snapped, but her smile gave her away.
They walked together back up to the house and Jess hugged her mother and her father in turn. 'I'm sorry, I just feel a bit emotional at the moment,' she explained.
'Well we're sorry too,' said Christine, 'it was very thoughtless of us not to let you know.'
The three of them sat down together at the kitchen table.
'So tell us what you've been up to this weekend,' said Mark.
Tom, who was making his way back to his room, turned and made an arm flexing gesture behind his parents' backs. Jess looked up and narrowed her eyes at him and Tom used the door to make it look as though a hand was grabbing him by top of the head and dragging him into the hall.
As they were chatting, Peter walked in through the back door.
'You haven't got a spare extension lead have you Mark?' he asked, and then noticed Jess. 'Oh hi, you're back early. Everything ok?'
'Yes thank you. I'm sorry to hear about you and Theresa. How's Jack taken it?'
'Thanks, Jess. Jack has been amazing actually. We had a long chat this afternoon and, well, it wasn't a huge shock as you can imagine, but he was so mature about it and very supportive, very unselfish.'
'Yeah, he's changed. I felt that when I visited. It's as though he's no longer the centre of his own attention. Does that make sense?'
'Perfectly.'
'We're just about to have a bit of tea, do you want to join us?'

asked Mark.
'Well, I shouldn't but the fact is I've no food in at all. Can I scrounge some things for breakfast as well?'
'These bloody asylum seekers,' joked Mark.
'Do you find it odd, me moving into the flat, since nominally I'm your boss?' Peter asked Jess.
'Not at all,' she replied.

Theresa arrived at the hospital to find Jack chatting with Sanjay.
'Good evening Mrs Spencer,' he greeted her, 'we're very pleased with Jack. He's going to be ready to come home soon at this rate.'
Theresa looked around the ward with evident disdain.
'Thank you, we're very grateful for everything you've done.'
Sanjay left them to talk privately.
'Did Dad tell you what's happened?' she asked anxiously.
'Yes, we had a good chat, thanks Mum. I'm sorry it's come to this.'
'Well I'm glad he faced up to it and told you straight. I expected his usual waffle. Anyway I should imagine he'll come to his senses quite quickly living in that dreary old farm house.'
'Farmhouse?'
'Oh he didn't tell you that bit then?' Theresa sensed the opportunity to score points, 'he's moving into that poky little flat at the Beresford's.'
'Well, to be fair, I didn't ask him where he was going to live. I assumed he'd have to stop in a hotel for a bit.'
'Well, it'll do him good to see how the other half lives, like doing voluntary work in the third world or something.'
'You've always been jealous of his friendship with Mark haven't you?'
'Jealous? Hardly! I just feel the senior partner of a very successful firm of lawyers should be moving in much better circles socially. He's always had a low opinion of himself and his choice of friends reflects this. I've done my best with my extensive network of quality friends but I can't seem to drag him out of that dung heap.'

‘Maybe that’s because he measures quality with a different yardstick Mum; he values things like honesty, loyalty and generosity rather than the latest designer kitchen or garden makeover.’

‘He never objects when I initiate one though. I’ve transformed that house single-handedly; you know I have. If it wasn’t for me, it would be barely habitable.’

‘Mum, you’ve just steamrollered him into the ground, like a Tom and Jerry cartoon. He’s let you do exactly what you want because he can’t be bothered to argue. Maybe he’ll be happier where it doesn’t feel like living in a Vogue magazine PowerPoint.’

‘I’ve never heard you complain.’

‘Maybe you weren’t listening.’

‘Well you’ve certainly changed your tune. Is this the sort of thing they teach you in this place, in your counselling sessions?’

‘I’ve just seen through it all Mum, all the superficial decorative designer make over crap that you regard as mission critical and that Dad has secretly despised the whole time. All that clutter, all that junk, the whole lifestyle thing, that’s what’s suffocating your relationship and you’ll never get him back until you understand it.’

‘He doesn’t deserve me.’

‘Yeah right, Mum.’

‘What’s that supposed to mean?’

‘It means your relationship is poisonous and it nearly took me down with it. It’s that serious Mum; it’s that bloody serious.’

‘I didn’t expect you to side with your father like this.’

‘I’m not siding with him! I’m just trying to tell it like it is. It has to be said Mum. It has to be said.’ Suddenly Jack was sobbing, his whole body convulsing with anguish and rage. Theresa stepped away from the bed and waved to the desk where Sanjay was tapping away on a keyboard. He looked up and walked quickly towards them. Sitting by the bed, he gently took hold of Jack’s hand.

‘What happened?’ he asked, looking round at Theresa.

‘He was trying to explain something to me. He said I wasn’t taking him seriously and it upset him.’

'Will you start taking him seriously now?' asked Sanjay.
'Yes,' said Theresa falteringly, 'I had no idea; he's never said these kinds of things before.'

Later that evening, Jess called Sam.
'Hi babe!' he answered.
'Hi, how's it going?'
'All quiet on the Abba front, thank goodness. Maybe the cooking sherry's finally kicked in.'
'She's a case isn't she?'
'Yeah. It's a funny assortment of people really but they don't seem a bad crowd on the whole. I think we've been quite lucky.'
A little flurry of pleasure gusted through Jess at his use of the word 'we'.
'I think that Sabrina's after you.'
'God, I hope not; all that fake tan, it would be like being raped by a kipper!'
'And those nails!'
'Yes, you could scrape paint with them!'
'Anyway, make sure you keep your distance. I don't want her doing any freebies on you.'
'It's Roland I'm worried about.'
'Oh no! What makes you say that?'
'Well it's obvious isn't it?'
'Has he said something?'
'No, of course not and I'm sure he never will.'
'Perhaps he'll start writing Sonnets for you.'
'No. I wish I hadn't mentioned it now.'
'I think you're pretty safe with Polly though. I don't think you've got the financial clout to interest her.'
'Yeah. She's more likely to try and mother me, which could be almost as bad.'
Jess told Sam about Peter leaving Theresa and moving into the flat.
'Well I'm not surprised. You should have seen the body language when they walked into the hospital. Do you feel ok about it?'
'How do you mean?'

‘Well, does it bother you having your boss move in?’
‘Apart from him, you’re the only person to think of that.’
‘Is that bad?’
‘No. It’s good; it’s good. It did freak me out a bit at first but I’m fine with it now actually.’

They talked about all the things they had done together at the weekend and their plans for the week ahead.
‘I wish I was there with you now!’ whined Jess.
‘I wish you were too. It feels empty here without you; in so far as a room this size can ever feel empty!’
‘What have you been up to?’
‘Oh, just trying to tidy up a bit. I’ve got a couple of boxes of stories and poems that I don’t really want to leave in the shed. I’ve just been sorting through them.’
‘Don’t throw anything out! I want to read them.’
‘Well borrow them for a bit then; keep them safe for me.’
‘For when you’re famous.’
‘Yeah.’
‘Oh Sam, I’m really going to miss you this week. I just want to be with you all the time!’
‘I’m missing you already.’
‘Missing you already!’ she repeated in a shrill American accent. ‘I should go now,’ she continued reluctantly. ‘Sam, I really, really love you. I’ve never felt like this about anyone, ever.’
‘And I really, really love you too Jess.’
‘You hang up first’
‘No you!’
‘Oh ok then, love you, love you, love you,’ she cried as she pressed the end call button and watched as his number vanished from her screen. She sat holding the handset until the screen went dark and the last vestige of their contact was extinguished.

Twelve

The house seemed eerily quiet when Sam got up on Monday morning; clearly they were not early risers. That was good because it meant he would get a clear run at the bathroom. He decided to seize the opportunity and, finding some change for the shower, he grabbed his towel and wash bag and hurried out.

It was only when he returned that it dawned on him he had forgotten his key. He tried the door forlornly but the latch had been down; he was locked out. He stood there for a moment, still damp and wrapped in his towel, unable to think what to do. The house was still silent, the door strong and solid; he was stranded.

'Oh fuck, fuck, fuck,' he repeated under his breath as he banged on the door with his head.

Just then Polly's door opened and she appeared wrapped in a very elegant silk dressing gown.

'Ooh, a naked man outside my door, how lovely,' she chuckled.

'It's not funny, Polly, I've locked myself out,' Sam growled as politely as he could manage.

'Well I'd invite you in for a cup of tea but I'm not sure if your girlfriend would approve!'

Sam managed a grimacing sort of smile and struggled to stop himself telling her to piss off.

'It's ok, darling, I'm only teasing you.' She reached into her pocket and lifted out a Yale key, which she held dangling from her thumb and forefinger. The significance of this slowly dawned on him.

'You have a spare?'

'Yes. Maggie, your predecessor, was always doing it so she let me have this. I'd completely forgotten about it until I heard that string of expletives on the landing just now.'

‘Oh, sorry.’
‘It’s ok darling, I’ve heard worse.’ She unlocked the door and gently pushed it open a little. ‘Want me to hang onto this for a bit?’
‘I think you’d better, thank you very, very much,’ he accepted gratefully. ‘And I’m sorry you’ve had this to put up with so early in the morning.’
‘Not a bad way to start the day,’ she said, looking at Sam in a way that made him feel uncomfortable. He grinned weakly and hurried inside.

Despite this mishap, he still made it to work on time. Swiping himself in, he made his way over to Tech Support. Sam had a feeling that it was going to be a good week; things had all fallen into place for a change. He was just passing Martin Smith’s office when the door flew open.
‘Sam, just the person,’ he said, ‘mind if we have a quick word?’
‘How’s Gill?’
‘She’s going to be out of action for quite a while I’m afraid. She damaged the tendons in her right wrist and it will need surgery.’
‘Oh dear; how is she otherwise?’
‘Very down I’m afraid. They started her on Amitriptylene as soon as she was out of danger.’
‘Out of danger?’
‘Oh yes, she lost an awful lot of blood.’
‘I’m really sorry, Martin. If there’s anything I can do to help - ‘
‘I just wanted to make sure I could rely on you to be, you know, discrete.’
‘Oh, of course, of course.’
‘Senior management know but as far as everyone else is concerned she fell off her bike and broke a wrist.’
‘Her bike, ok,’ Sam nodded, ‘what about the colleague who found her?’
‘Senior management,’ said Martin.

Sam was a bit late by the time he got over to the office.
‘Sorry I’m late, I got collared by Martin Smith.’
‘What did he want?’ asked Raj.
‘Oh, you know, just catching up on my move to Tech Support.’

'There's a rumour going round that Gill tried to top herself again last week,' said Ricky.
Sam just managed to stop himself from saying 'Again?' and tried to sound offhand as he explained. 'He mentioned something about her falling off her bike. She broke a wrist or something I think.'
Raj and Ricky exchanged knowing glances but did not pursue it.
'Anyway, you haven't missed much. The first hour of Monday morning is always reserved for our team meeting.'
'Ok,' said Sam taking a seat, 'is there an agenda?'
'It's always the same,' explained Raj, 'we sit around and chat about what we've been up to over the weekend.'
Sam was introduced to the other team members, Ravi, Michael and Bavinda.
'As you can see,' smiled Ricky, 'we're a very multicultural team.'
'You've embarrassed him now,' said Ravi seeing Sam look uncomfortable.
'What did I say?' gasped Ricky pretending to look shocked, 'I didn't use the P word or anything.' The all laughed and it was clear they were all very relaxed in each other's company. 'Go on, Ravi do your Indian call centre impersonation.'
'Hello, my name is Patrick, how can I help you today?' gabbled Ravi.
Sam laughed nervously. Ricky's behaviour seemed rather inappropriate but he did not want to appear disapproving; white people did not have a monopoly on satirising themselves after all.
'And that reminds me,' Ricky said to Sam, 'you know how you're always told to say 'anything else I can help you with?' at the end of the call?' Sam nodded. 'Well we don't do pointless shit like that in this team. It's verboten, ja?'
Ricky had to go off to a line managers' meeting so Sam was left with Raj to start his support training.
'You mustn't worry about Ricky,' she said, 'he's got a heart of gold really.'
'He's a bit too much like David Brent for my liking,' Sam grimaced.

'Ha Ha! Did you hear that guys? Sam said Ricky reminds him of David Brent!'
'Oh, he's going to love that!' called Ravi, who was just logging on. 'We'll have to start calling him Gervaise.'
'You're not going to tell him?' asked Sam, aghast.
'What's it worth?' asked Raj, looking at him saucily.

In the end, Jess had been late to bed. After talking to Sam she chatted with her friends on-line for ages. They wanted a 'blow by blow' account of her weekend with Sam and, although happy to confirm they had slept together and it had been 'awesome' she was reticent about going into the kind of detail that her friends frequently did. They pressed her for the full story but she evaded them, saying they would have to wait until the weekend. Big plans were being made for this and she hoped they would all be too busy partying to interrogate her further.

It was busy in the Beresford kitchen that morning; Tom had a full day of exams and was munching his way through the obligatory plateful of scrambled eggs, and Christine was up early to cook it.
'You look a bit tired, love,' she said to Jess.
'Too much bed, not enough sleep!'
'Don't talk with your mouthful!' snapped Jess. 'In fact, don't talk at all. I'm fine Mum, just up a bit late internetting. How are you feeling?'
'I had a good night thanks. I'm going to do a bit more in the office this morning.'
'So what is it today Tom?'
Her brother pretended to tell her using sign language. Jess just sighed and dropped a slice of bread into the toaster.
'It's Business Studies this morning and Economics this afternoon,' Christine translated.
'And then just one more on Wednesday!' exclaimed Tom joyfully, then clapped his hand over his mouth and swivelled his eyes from side to side stupidly.

Jess gave Tom a lift to school. She noticed that Peter's car had gone; he was often first in to work.
'So, how are the plans for the Cornwall trip going?' she asked.

‘Not good, not good. The girls have all dropped out as you know and now it turns out that Adam is going away with his parents so we’re down to three.’
‘So? What’s the problem? You’ll meet loads of people in St Ives.’
‘Well that’s the other thing; apparently the locals are fed up with these droves of teenagers descending on them and they’re making life a bit difficult at the moment.’
‘Go somewhere else then.’
‘I thought I might have a few days off and then see if I can get some work at The Crown over the summer.’
‘The money’s terrible there but I suppose there might be some fringe benefits,’ Jess teased.
‘Yes, what we economists call intangibles,’ agreed Tom.

Christine went straight through to the office after clearing up in the kitchen. As soon as she sat down the phone rang. It was their business manager from the bank, Terry Watkins. He had been looking after them for years and was very supportive.
‘I’ve got some bad news,’ he said after enquiring after her health, ‘they’ve taken you off me. I’m not even supposed to be calling you so this conversation is strictly off the record.’
‘Why? What’s happened?’
‘Well, it’s all to do with this credit crunch business. They did a review of all the accounts the regularly exceed overdraft limits and flagged them up as high risk. I got my knuckles rapped for being too lenient with you and your account has been handed to a special circumstances manager.’
‘A what?’
‘I’m afraid it means that you are going to be very closely monitored and given no leeway at all. You’ll be getting a call from someone later today to make an appointment for an emergency meeting with you. Don’t put them off. Remember they can demand their money back without notice if they feel like it.’
‘But what can we do?’
‘Find some cash from somewhere and get your current account back below the overdraft limit as soon as you can. That will take

some of the heat off you but you'll still be in for a bit of an inquisition I'm afraid.'
'Oh Terry, that's awful. I really appreciate you tipping us off like this.'
'I have to go now. Remember, this call did not take place.'
'Thanks Terry, keep in touch won't you.'
'Good luck; say goodbye to Mark for me,' was all he said as he hung up.
Christine felt sick. They were cornered. Subsidies were paid annually in arrears and there was no money at all due in until the end of the month. She hurriedly downloaded a bank statement. They were almost two thousand over the limit; unauthorised borrowing they called it and it was probably being scrutinised at that very moment. There was nothing else for it, she picked up the phone and dialled Peter's mobile. He answered straight away.
'Mark? Is everything ok?'
'It's Christine, Peter. Yes, thanks we're all fine, well, apart from one thing.'
She went on to explain what had happened with the bank. 'The fact is, Peter, and I hate to have to ask this, but the rent money you offered could save us from ruin.'
'Of course, I can transfer it electronically on a same day payment if you like. We haven't even agreed a figure have we? How much were you thinking?'
'I have absolutely no idea Peter and I'm sure Mark isn't expecting anything.'
'Well let's leave him out of this shall we? How does five hundred a month sound?'
'It sounds far too much.'
'I can assure you it isn't. Give me your bank details and I'll transfer three thousand this morning.'

Jess arrived at work to discover Kerry had booked the week off. She was quite relieved, even though it meant she would have to cover her workload.
It occurred to her that she needed to check how much the staff knew about Jack's hospital admission. She hurriedly knocked

on Peter's door and walked in. He was in the middle of transferring the money into the farm account. He assumed Jess did not know the full extent of the problem and quickly minimised the screen.

'Morning Peter,' said Jess brightly, 'you set off very early this morning.'

'I've got a lot of catching up to do.'

'I was just wondering what the official line on Jack was in case I get into conversation with anyone.'

'Good point. If anyone asks, he had a fall and damaged his shoulder.

'Well that's all true.'

'A convenient truth,' smiled Peter grimly, 'or at least an economical one. We're just hoping the other thing doesn't make the local papers'

'Is that likely?'

'Well, Theresa places an awful lot of advertising with them so, shameful though it may seem, I think even if it has been reported, it will get the blue pencil.'

'Money talks.'

'Much, much louder than words, I'm afraid.'

'Ok, I'll stick to the budget version of events then. Any news of Jack this morning?'

'Oh, Theresa managed to upset him last night apparently. I got this long irate phone call from her when she got home. She made out it was all my fault as usual. Anyway, I mustn't bore you with all that. Jack is ok. He might even get discharged today. Thanks for visiting him on Saturday, it was kind of you and I think it helped.'

Jess smiled and turned to go.

'Oh, and on a business note, did you know Kerry is off all week? I wondered if you would work a full day tomorrow, Wednesday and Thursday? It would help us if you could.'

'If Mum stays as good as she has been recently that won't be a problem.'

Even though the partners all had direct dial numbers, the phone was still busy. Overflow calls from reception were diverted to Jess with Kerry being off and the morning passed quickly as she

fielded these. One was from Gary Swift.
'Is that Jess?' he asked nervously. 'Can you talk?'
'What about?'
'Jack.'
'What about Jack?'
'They were saying at the gym that he jumped out of a window.'
'He had a fall.'
'Ok. I know you have to say that but just hear me out. I've been to see my boss and we've torn up the contract. Tell his dad for me will you and if you see Jack, tell him I'm sorry.'
'Can you confirm that in writing? About the contract I mean.'
'No. You'll just have to trust me,' he said and hung up.
'That's a tall order,' Jess said to herself.

Christine felt exhausted after her conversation with Peter and decided to go for a lie down. She was just getting to her feet when the phone rang again.
She froze, like it was a fire alarm. She snatched up the receiver but could not utter a word.
'Hello?' a female voice enquired.
'Hello, this is Christine Beresford.'
'Oh Mrs Beresford, thank you. I don't know what happened there; the line went dead. My name is Lucy Baker. I've taken over from Terry Watkins as your business manager. I wondered if I could call in tomorrow to introduce myself? We need to review your overdraft facility and generally see how things are going. Will ten thirty be ok?'
'Has Terry moved away then?'
'I'll explain all that when I see you.'
'Ten thirty will be fine. Do you need to see Mark as well?'
'Yes please; it is an important meeting. Will that be possible?'
'I'm sure he can work round it. I'll look forward to seeing you tomorrow then.'
She replaced the handset. 'Not,' she added. 'Don't let me down, Peter, don't let me down,' she whispered through gritted teeth.

It was almost lunchtime when Jess remembered about printing out Sam's sample chapters. She decided to have a quick

word with Peter before knocking off.
'I had a call from Gary Swift this morning, Peter.' He looked puzzled. 'You know, Cuteprice?'
'Oh, how could I forget? What did he want?'
'He seemed to have picked up some gossip about Jack at the gym. I thought you should know.'
'What did he say?'
'Nothing specific and I stuck to our story so he just made it very clear that he knew there was more to it. He said they've torn up the contract Jack signed.'
'Well, he's clearly feeling guilty, and rightly so.'
'I asked him to confirm it in writing and he refused.'
'That's ok. I'll return our copy with a letter confirming cancellation.'
'I've got some stuff to order. I assume it's ok to give it to Geoff?'
'Yes of course. At least he'll be happy at any rate.'
'Is it ok if I knock off for lunch now?'
'Yes, I'll cover the phone for you.'
'I've got a short document to print out for Sam. Is it alright to run it off on the office laser?'
'That's fine,' he waved dismissively; 'just use my cost centre if you like.'
Jess had copied Sam's work onto her ipod. She plugged it in to the USB on her terminal, copied the files over and printed them off. Signing the letter with a quick scribble as they had agreed, she slid the document into a large window envelope and dropped it into the post tray. The firm could stand the postage cost. It was a relief to have done it and know Sam would hit his deadline but she was not confident he would be successful. She opened her sandwiches and turned back to her monitor. The screen had gone black. Assuming it was just the screen saver, she wiggled the mouse. A red box appeared and Jess felt a wave of panic as she read: 'VIRUS ALERT - A Trojan has been detected and quarantined. Close all active programmes.'
'Oh shit,' she gasped.
Just then Nick hurried into the office.
'The network's down,' he blurted out, 'I'm going to have to

restart the server. You'll lose any unsaved work. Ok?'
Jess nodded guiltily, her mouth still filled with unchewed sandwich. Peter wandered into the office. 'My screen's frozen, has yours?' he asked, without sounding too bothered about it.
Jess nodded again and gulped the soggy mouthful down whole.
'I think it might be me, Peter. It must have been that file I printed for Sam.'
'Just keep quiet about it. You asked my permission so it's my fault.'
'Well it isn't really is it Peter?' she said glumly.
Nick burst back in.
'The server booted up all right; just do control alt delete and restart your terminals. Are you likely to have lost anything important?'
Jess shook her head.
'I expect most people were at lunch, so with any luck they'll have saved what they were working on,' said Peter calmly.
'I should be able to track where that bug came from. Someone's in for the high jump,' Nick spluttered angrily.
'I think I can save you the trouble,' murmured Jess.

Sam was spending the whole day working through tutorials. Raj was on hand to guide him through these, but in the main he was just left sitting at a laptop going at his own pace. He enjoyed working alone like this. Mostly it was building on what he had already learned in the induction programme although much of it was aimed at dealing with 'Frequently Asked Questions.'
'Do you tend to get people asking the same thing over and over again?' he asked Raj, who was sitting nearby on her break.
'Well, there's an FAQ area on the website and people have to navigate through that before they get the support number, so a lot of obvious stuff gets sorted there. The really annoying thing is when people ring with a problem that is obviously hardware related, you know, 'my printer's not working' or something.'
'What do you say?'
'Chuck it away and buy a new one!'
Sam chatted with Raj during his lunch break. Her family had

been expelled from Uganda by the Amin regime, only coming to Nottingham because her Uncle was already there.
'This will probably sound awful,' said Sam, 'but you seem very European to me.'
'Hello? What do you expect? I was born in the QMC! Hey, isn't that a song?' She sang 'Born in the QMC,' and they both laughed.
'I'm sorry, I know it was a really stupid thing to say.'
'It's fine. I understand what you mean. English is our mother tongue and this country took us in; I'm just one of us!'

Later in the afternoon Raj came and sat by Sam to see how much he had done,
'Hey, that's really good! Are you sure you did all these thoroughly?'
She was sitting very close and leaned lightly on his arm, looking over his shoulder at the screen.
'Yeah, I think so. I don't feel as though I rushed it.'
'Well we'll soon see. Double click on assessment and do some of those tests. Don't bother cheating because it's only for your own use; so you can check your progress.' Her face was very close to his as he navigated through the options. She smiled at him and slid her hand under the hem of his shirt, gently stroking the base of his spine. It could have been perfectly innocent, no more than a pat on the back really. Sam did not react at all; he did not know what to say. In the end, he hitched himself up so that her hand slipped away.
'I'll leave you to it then,' she said, scooting off on her chair, 'let me know when you've finished.'

Peter's mobile rang during the afternoon. It was not a number he recognised but he took the call.
'Hi Dad!'
'Oh, hi Jack, how's it going?'
'Good. The head shrink did a ward round this morning and so long as the medics are happy with my guts I can leave. They fixed up so that I can continue my care plan in Bristol.'
'Great news! When will you find out?'
'They examined me this morning and there's no sign of serious

damage. They just want a consultant to take a look and if I get the all clear I'm on my way.'

'What do you want to do, go home for a bit?'

'No, I want to get straight back to Bristol'

'Is that a good idea? You won't be fit for any partying and you certainly won't be driving for a bit.'

'Don't worry, I'll take it steady. Thing is though, I want to take quite a bit of stuff and I wondered if you could give me a lift?'

'Tomorrow?' said Peter, scrolling through his diary, 'I could probably just about manage it but I'll need to know quite soon.'

'Ok if we just assume it's on and I'll call you to confirm?'

'Does your mother know about all this?'

'No, I'll call her in a minute. You're a star Dad, thanks,' Jack added as he hung up.

Peter was left with the uneasy feeling that he had been hustled into agreeing too readily. This was confirmed when his mobile rang again moments later. It was Theresa.

'Jack tells me that you're running him down to Bristol tomorrow,' she said acidly, 'is that right?'

'He did ask me but I told him to talk to you about it first, which is why he rang.'

'Oh I see. So it's up to me to be the one to say no as usual, is it?'

'Does anybody have to say no?'

'Oh come on Peter, don't be ridiculous, we can't have him running off down there in his condition.'

'If he gets discharged, bearing in mind that he's an adult, I don't see how we can stop him, Theresa.'

'Well that's just typical of you isn't it? Anything for a quiet life. Don't you think just for once it would be a good idea to act like a parent and put your foot down?'

'But I don't necessarily think it would be better for him to go home, given our situation. I think he would probably be better off in Bristol.'

'Well, why would I expect you to back me up? And how come you've got time to do all this ferrying around all of a sudden? Whenever I've wanted to do things you've never been able to spare a day off.'

‘Things are quieter; we hardly have any conveyancing with the house market being so dead.’
‘I don’t know why I’m asking, I really don’t care. Look, you do what you want then, and I hope you’ll be able to live with yourself if it all goes horribly wrong.’
Peter was tempted to remind Theresa what happened last time Jack went home from hospital, but he kept quiet.
‘Are you still there?’
‘Look, I really have to get on now.’
‘Oh, busy again are we?’
‘I’ll let you know what’s happening.’
‘Don’t bother!’ she spat, hanging up.

After having a lie down, Christine went back into the office to download a new bank statement. One transaction was showing for the day, a credit of three thousand. There was now over a grand between the current balance and the overdraft ceiling.
‘Yes!’ she hissed, making a fist in the air.

Jess felt a bit frazzled by the time she arrived home. Nick had been fairly decent about her crashing the network but she suspected it was mainly because Peter was having a bad time and he didn’t want to make a fuss. He just went on a bit about how catastrophic it could have been and that he hoped she would learn from it and respect the company system in future. When he had trudged off, she looked across at Peter and said how sorry she was but he just told her not to worry, the anti virus package had cost a fortune and it was nice to know it worked. Nevertheless she felt bad about it and very angry with Sam. She bustled into the kitchen laden with groceries.
‘It’s the bag lady!’ cried Tom who was looking relaxed, having now almost negotiated his exam minefield. Jess dropped the carriers heavily onto the floor,
‘Perhaps you’d like to do the shopping for a change,’ she said tetchily.
Christine was leaning with her back to the sink holding a mug of tea in both hands.

‘Thanks for doing all that love. There’s some tea in the pot if you fancy a cup,’ she said calmly. ‘Had a bad day?’
Jess sat down heavily. ‘Oh I just managed to crash the entire computer network at Spencer’s, that’s all.’
‘Nice one,’ said her brother.
‘You really are very irritating!’ she said menacingly. ‘Why don’t you make yourself useful for a change and put that shopping away instead of sitting around like a dork!’
‘Don’t suggest that, he’ll eat all the biscuits,’ said Christine trying to lighten the mood, ‘and don’t forget he has done two exams today.’
Tom pointed towards himself with both thumbs.
‘Yeah, check me out.’
‘Piece of piss?’ enquired Jess.
‘Piece of piss, sis,’ he confirmed.
‘So is the computer still down?’ asked Christine, returning to what appeared to be the source of her daughter’s petulance.
‘Oh no. It was fine really, but it made me feel a fool.’ She looked fiercely across at Tom, who wisely chose to remain silent.
Mark tramped wearily into the kitchen.
‘Any danger of getting a cup of tea?’ he asked hopefully.
Christine had started unpacking one of the bags. She turned towards him with a smile. ‘I think we might just squeeze one more out of the pot, but leave these biscuits please. I need them to sweeten the bank manager tomorrow.’
‘Oh, what time’s he coming?’
‘Ten-thirty, and it’s a she, Terry’s been replaced.’
‘Maybe he finally got promoted. I’m surprised he didn’t let us know though.’
‘Tell you in a bit,’ said Christine, nodding towards the children.

Later that evening Jess called Sam. She had calmed down a bit but she was still mad with him.
‘How was your day?’ he asked.
‘Well, not great,’ she began. ‘Remember I copied those files onto my ipod to take to work?’
‘Yeah, did you manage to get them printed?’

'I did, yeah and I also managed to infect the entire network with a virus. Don't you have any AV?'
'That can't be right. Of course I have Anti Virus, it's just a free one but it's good.'
'Well somehow my ipod appeared to introduce a virus into our network. It was quarantined immediately thank goodness but it still crashed the server and now I don't fancy connecting it to my laptop in case the same thing happens.'
'Hang on Jess; don't jump to conclusions. For a start your ipod isn't infected. Even if it's carrying a Word File with a virus it can't execute it; it's just a fancy memory stick. Just delete the file without opening it and your laptop will be fine. More importantly, I very much doubt if you caused this problem.'
'What makes you say that?'
'Well, we had loads of calls today about a new Trojan called Grotbot that's ripping through the Internet. I reckon one of your colleagues must have been surfing during lunch and introduced it into your network. You are probably completely innocent. It was just a coincidence.'
Jess was silent for a moment as she took this in.
'It did say on my screen it was a Trojan but I didn't see a name. Oh Sam I'm sorry if I've blamed you for something you were completely innocent of.'
'I'm just running an AV check on my whole C Drive. If it's in the clear, and I think it will be, then so are you.'
'Except I've just been vile to you and more importantly not trusted you. That's much, much worse than all the rest of it.'
'It was a plausible conclusion. I can understand how it must have seemed. Don't worry about it.'
'Can you forgive me?'
'There's nothing to forgive.'
'Oh Sam, I wish you could beam down on this mobile signal right now and give me a really big squeezy hug!'
'I'm not sure if I'm on the right tariff for that.'
'Well upgrade, I'll pay!'
'You've lobbed out quite enough on me already.'
'Oh no! I didn't mean it like that. Everything I say tonight is coming out wrong! Let's forget about me for a bit. Tell me how

your day went.'
Sam told her what he had been doing, carefully editing Raj out of the account.
'I'm glad it's working out, Sam. They sound like a nice team. Listen, I have to work three full days because Kerry's on holiday. I could call in and see you tomorrow after work!'
'Cool. I'll cook some food. Want to go out somewhere?'
'No, let's just stop in together.'
'Yeah, just us.'

'Are you worried about this new bank manager?' asked Mark as they cleared away after supper.
'I am a bit,' said Christine. 'You saw that letter didn't you?'
'Yes but I didn't take it seriously. We've banked with them for years, they would never pull the plug on us.'
'Terry never would have, sure, and that's why they took him off our account. The banks are all very jumpy at the moment. This new girl is coming to read the riot act. She won't be on our side like Terry was. It's just lucky Peter paid us some rent up front otherwise we wouldn't have had a leg to stand on.'
'Do I have to sit in on the meeting?'
'At least come and introduce yourself.'
'No. Tell her I'm busy. I don't want her to get the impression that we're scared of them.'
'Whatever,' sighed Christine. 'You're going to have to deal it all yourself sooner or later,' she thought grimly.

Thirteen

The following day Peter collected Jack from hospital and after calling at the house to pick up his things they drove non-stop down to Bristol and talked non-stop all the way.
'It's ironic really, just as you seem to have decided to sever your links with home, we finally manage to open up to each other.'
'Maybe the two are connected. Anyway, I'm not exactly leaving the planet am I?'
'You're leaving planet home by the sounds of it.'
'Yes, breaking out of Mum's force field, that's for sure.'
'You'll still be orbiting my bank account I take it.'
Jack went quiet for a moment.
'I was only joking,' said Peter, glancing across anxiously.
'I know but you're right, I will need some financial support. I could up my student loan to pay the tuition fees if you like.'
'Look, whatever happens with me and Mum, we will both make sure you have enough cash to get through Uni. That's one thing we do agree on.'
They talked for a bit about the separation and how things were going to work. Peter had plenty of experience of what tends to happen in these situations.
'Maybe all three of us just need to be by ourselves for a while,' concluded Jack .

Christine spent some time tidying the office before the bank manager arrived. She wanted to at least give the impression they were organised. Looking out of the window she could see a silver hatchback making its way hesitantly up the farm track; she was early. Christine quickly finished the spring clean, put the kettle on to boil and walked across the yard to meet the car as it pulled in.

‘Hi. I’m Christine Beresford, nice to meet you,’ she said as they shook hands. ‘I thought I’d better intercept you here because it’s not obvious where the office is.’

‘Lucy Baker; good to meet you too.’

She was petite and very attractive with black hair styled fashionably in a fringe with a bob cut straight across at the back. She wore a black suit with a silky maroon and green floral pattern shirt.

‘What a lovely blouse,’ said Christine.

‘Well, thanks, but it’s only from Primark,’ smiled Lucy.

‘Goodness, you’d never have guessed. My daughter swears by them.’

Christine looked down at her smart, very pointy shoes. ‘I’m not sure how you’re going to get across the yard in those. It’s still a bit muddy after all that rain the other week.’

‘Is Mr Beresford going to be able to join us?’ Lucy asked as she tiptoed through the slime.

‘I’m afraid not. The winter wheat needs spraying and he wants to get it done before the weather breaks again. I tend to look after the accounts anyway to be honest.’

‘It’s just that I’m afraid we do have some serious issues to discuss today.’

Christine made coffee and put some biscuits out. ‘Help your self to these.’

‘Ooh thanks. I love these chocolate chip ones,’ said Lucy, munching a cookie the size of a dinner plate.

‘Well,’ sighed Christine, ‘I suppose we’d better get down to business. I take it they’ve sent you to give us an ultimatum?’

‘You do understand why the bank is so concerned about your overdraft?’ Christine nodded nervously. Lucy took a spreadsheet from her folder and placed it sideways on the desk so they could both read it.

‘The columns are really self explanatory,’ she began, ‘so this one is the highest overdraft level each month, this one is the lowest and the one on the end here is the average. Obviously your overdraft will fluctuate, that’s what it’s for, but these numbers are worrying. For instance, you have hardly been below your limit all year. Your average balance is way over

20k, which means you are almost permanently into unauthorised borrowing. In other words, you are using the facility as working capital, which is not an appropriate use of the provision.'
'I'm afraid we have let things slip recently because of my illness. Mark can't do everything.'
'Your illness?' asked Lucy looking puzzled. As Christine explained, Lucy's face fell and she turned very pale. 'They never said anything about that. I'm so, so sorry.'
'Would you like a tissue?' asked Christine, passing a box across the desk.

Peter did not feel like driving straight home after he had dropped Jack off at the house he so he went down to the floating harbour and bought a ticket for the SS Great Britain. It was something that he and Theresa had always been meaning to do; visit Jack and stop for a long weekend looking round the city. He walked quickly through the old warehouse that housed the museum and boarded the ship itself. This was what he most wanted to do, stand on the deck of the world's first modern ship in the very dock where it was built, look round the harbour with its pastel terraces piled on the surrounding hills and take it all in, all that marvellous tangible history. It was thrilling, plugging in to the current that seemed to flow through the whole vessel. He walked below decks and looked at the replica engine and all the various cabins and rooms, then back outside and below the hull itself. It was such an incredible story, the way it had survived for so long beached in the Falklands, waiting for this rescue and renovation. It thrilled him, but at the same time he felt bad because he and Theresa could have, should have found the time to do this together but never did, and never would now. Maybe she was right, perhaps it was his fault that they had never done the things they planned, never managed to make the effort to spend time together like this. Was it too late now to put that right? He tried to imagine standing beside her, looking up at the corroding flanks of the great iron hull, but he could not. He could not picture them together any more.

Christine made another coffee while Lucy composed herself.

'Sorry about that, it was very unprofessional.'
'It was very human,' said Christine, pressing her hand gently.
'That's the trouble with banking,' Lucy sighed, 'so many people just can't see beyond the bottom line. There's so much more to take into account than just a balance sheet.'
'Yes but the fact is our accounts don't make pleasant reading. I think technically we're insolvent aren't we?' Christine was acutely aware that this was probably the last thing you should say to your bank manager.
'It depends on your assets. We'd need to do some work on the numbers but I don't really see why we shouldn't be able to give you a loan over a fairly long term so the monthly repayment would be manageable.'
'I thought the banks didn't have any cash because of all this 'credit crunch' business.'
'Well that's not strictly true. It's all much tighter of course but we've done just as much commercial lending as last year. Don't forget there will always be demand for what you produce. Food don't go out of fashion!'
'So what do you suggest?' asked Christine hopefully.
'It would be better to take out a commercial loan for say 20k to use as working capital and reduce your overdraft facility right down to maybe 10k. That would be cheaper for you in terms of both arrangement fees and interest.'
'Would you be prepared to do that?'
'We'll have to see. I need to take some figures from you so that we can make an informed decision.'
She carefully studied the annual accounts from the previous year and took a lot of detailed information from Christine about the farm, crops, stock, plant and machinery, debts and assets.
'I noticed this morning before I left that you managed to just sneak under your limit yesterday. Was that for my benefit?'
'I suppose it was a bit,' smiled Christine, 'the fact is we just let our empty granny flat and the tenant gave us an up front payment.'
'That's excellent,' grinned Lucy, 'a perfect example of a hidden asset which you have now turned into a very useful revenue stream.'

‘So you really think things aren’t as bad as they seem?’
‘It looked to us as though you were just burying you heads in the sand and waiting to run out of money. Exceeding your overdraft limit is a very expensive way to borrow and it sets alarm bells ringing in high places. I’ll have to run it by my boss, but I’m sure we can offer you a more structured finance package at significantly lower cost.’
‘This is such a relief,’ breathed Christine, ‘I honestly thought you were coming to ask for your money back this morning.’
‘The brutal truth is that we can do that but it’s very much a last resort. It goes without saying that it’s in everyone’s interest for your business to be successful and it’s up to us to help make that happen.’
As they walked back to the car, Lucy handed Christine her business card.
‘Just call me on my mobile any time you need help or advice. It will take a week or two to sort out the proposal and if you can keep within your borrowing limit in the meantime it would help a lot.’
‘Thank you for being so understanding,’ said Christine, placing her hand on Lucy’s arm.
‘Take care,’ said Lucy, and took her hand, ‘I’ll be thinking of you.’

As Lucy drove away, Christine walked slowly down the hill to let Darcy out. She leaned on the fence for a moment and sighed heavily with relief. She could never have expected that meeting to have such a positive outcome. By this time tomorrow Tom would have finished his exams and the thought of that, together with this discovery that the farm was not about to slip into oblivion, made her feel quite giddy with elation. She badly needed someone to hug and since he was the most accessible member of the family at that moment, Darcy caught the full force of it.
‘We’re not dead yet old buddy!’ she cried as she clung tightly to his neck, ‘we’re not dead yet.’

Jess arrived at Sam’s earlier than he was expecting and he had only just emerged from the shower. He answered the front

door in his dressing gown with his hair still wet. Jess kissed him and sniffed his hair,
'You smell all woolly, like a hand washed jumper!' she laughed.
'Must be that own label shampoo from the supermarket, essence of ewe.'
'Or maybe ram,' she snarled, slipping her hand inside his wrap.
'Please, not on the doorstep if you don't mind!'
'I like to linger on the threshold with my hand on the knob.'
'I thought you'd be tired after a full day at work,' he said as they ascended the stairs.
'I've spent most of it deciding how I want you,' she whispered in his ear.
Sam poured some wine and they sat together on the bed. Jess knelt behind him with her arms round his chest leaning her head on his shoulder.
'You're not mad with me then about that virus thing?' she asked.
'Course not. Did you find out if it was Grotbot?'
'No. I couldn't face mentioning it. Everything was back to normal and Peter was out for the day taking Jack to Bristol so I just left it. I'm sure you're right though.'
'Jack's ok then?'
'It'll take a while for his shoulder to heal but psychologically he's in much better shape now.'
'That's good. You hungry?'
'Only for you,' she said sliding her hands across his chest. 'It's lovely being met by a naked man.' She moved her hands further down his torso, 'Ooh what's going on down here then? Hello young man.' Sam groaned with pleasure as she gently stroked him. 'I think I'm ready for my starter,' she murmured, undoing the belt of his dressing gown.

Sam made a simple pasta meal. While he was doing this Jess looked round the room. He had put a row of books along the top of the chest of drawers and blutacked some posters to the walls. It all looked much more homely.
'Are these all your favourites?' asked Jess looking along the

improvised bookshelf.

'Yes, my desert island books,' he replied.

'Hmmm,' she hummed absent-mindedly. 'Oh this is interesting.' She picked out a copy of 'Lady Chatterley's Lover' in the original orange and white Penguin sleeve. 'Printed in 1960, so it's one from the first print run after the trial?'

'I suppose it must be. I found it in a charity shop.'

'Complete and unabridged, three shillings and sixpence,' Jess quoted from the front cover in a BBC voice.

'Do you like Lawrence?' asked Sam.

'He's a brilliant writer of course but I don't think he's a great novelist in the sense of being a really good storyteller.'

'It's interesting; I've met very few girls who are really enthusiastic about him. It's always blokes who rave about him. He must be whatever the opposite of chick lit is.'

'Cock lit?' smiled Jess, and they both laughed.

'Read the quote from Lawrence on the inside cover,' asked Sam.

Jess opened the book.

'I always labour at the same thing, to make the sex relation valid and precious instead of shameful. And this novel is the furthest I've gone. To me it is beautiful and tender as the naked self...'

'Beautiful and tender as the naked self,' repeated Sam. 'Isn't that wonderful?' Jess nodded. 'You know there are three versions of this book?' Jess nodded again. 'Well he wanted to call this final version 'John Thomas and Lady Jane' but his private publisher advised against it.' 'Wisely, I think,' Jess remarked. 'Maybe so, but after settling on 'Lady Chatterley', he changed his mind again and wanted to call it 'Tenderness,' but it was too late, the book had gone to press.'

'Fascinating,' Jess agreed, 'and do you think that would have been a better title?'

'Not commercially, no but it would have been a truer title, closer to what Lawrence was trying to achieve.'

'Tenderness,' repeated Jess, 'yes, it's perfect; it really captures the intimacy.' She put the book down on the bed, 'yet when you read it there is really nothing in it which is at all shocking. It

seems quite tame don't you think? Is that just because standards have changed?'
'I don't think that's it at all. The main reason the book was banned is that she is shagging a servant. That's what made it absolutely unacceptable at the time and it's where attitudes have changed most significantly since.'
'Do you really think so?'
'Oh yes, there's no doubt. In those days it was considered as unthinkable as, say doing it with the alsatian would be today. Lawrence knew that. He tried to make Mellors more socially kosher in this final version by having him rise through the ranks in the army so that he was almost an officer, almost acceptable.'
'So really the whole obscenity thing completely missed the point, the issue was one of class rather than fucking?'
'Yes, if the book is about anything, it's about how two people could transcend those social divisions and achieve their ultimate union, despite everything. And that is what was considered so despicable.'
They were silent for a moment, then Jess replaced the book and walked slowly over to Sam.
'And have we achieved an ultimate union?' she asked softly.
'Yes,' he said, taking her in his arms, 'yes I believe we have.'

Jess did not stop late at Sam's, even though she would have liked to. She knew Christine had been meeting the bank manager and, having seen the letter in the office, was anxious to find out how things went.

As soon as she walked into the kitchen, it was obvious that morale had been given a boost. A bottle of sparkling wine stood open on the table and Christine was a bit tipsy.
'Oh hello darling,' she slurred rather too loudly, 'you've had a long day. Come and have a glass of bubbly!'
'Mum's pissed,' grinned Tom.
'I'm not pissed you cheeky monkey, it's just rather a long time since I had a drink, that's all.'
'Yeah, and check this out, sis, I wasn't even allowed one glass. How sad is that?'
'Well you have got an exam in the morning,' said Jess

parentally, 'and it wouldn't look good if you showed up with a hang over.' Tom pulled a face as Jess turned to her parents. 'I take it the lady from the bank turned out not to be Cruella Deville, then?'
'I left her to your mother,' said Mark, who had drunk a couple of beers after the wine and was equally mellow. 'She wrapped her round her little finger.'
'Well that's right Dad, you wouldn't want a girl telling you how to run the farm would you?'
'It was a very constructive meeting,' said Christine, and she explained what had been discussed.
'Well that is good news,' said Jess, 'I might have a drop of this myself.' She poured a glass and took a sip, then pulled a face. 'You're really not missing anything, Tommy,' she laughed.

It was decided that they would have a bit of a party the following evening to celebrate both Tom finishing his exams and the stay of execution from the bank.
'Do you think Sam would like to come?' asked Christine.
'Yes I'm sure. I have to work a full day again tomorrow so I could pick him up. The only trouble is I won't be around to help in the kitchen.'
'That's ok. There's a big moussaka in the freezer that needs eating. We can just do a salad with it.'
'That won't be any good for Sam, he doesn't eat meat.'
'Oh for goodness sake!' cried Mark, 'the daughter of a farmer going out with a bloody veggie. I'll be black balled by the hunt committee you know.'
'We don't want to know what you get up to at the hunt committee, thank you Father. Anyway it's no problem, I can pick up a lentil one at M&S on the way to Sam's and we can micro it.'
'Not just ordinary moussaka,' said Tom, mimicking the voice on the advert.

Sam decided to do some more work on the novel after Jess left. He had opened up a second plot line which was taking place in Germany. His dad had been stationed there for a while so he knew some areas quite well. He was working on a car chase and finding it particularly difficult because he did not drive and knew very little about fast cars. As with all the gadgetry that it was essential to introduce into the story, every last detail would have to be described with total accuracy. He decided to do some research on the Internet but when he turned to his laptop the screen had gone black. He tried switching off and restarting but it was completely dead.

'I must have had that bloody virus after all,' he said to himself. He had just decided that his only option was to take into work in the morning and ask for help when there was a knock on the door and Polly walked in.

'Sorry to disturb you, darling, I just wondered if I could leave my key with you. I'm expecting a case of wine to be delivered tomorrow and as it's turned out I'll be away.'

'Not another octogenarian?'

'No thank god. This is the lovely Miles, who I have been after for ages. He's just been dumped by his latest teenager and he needs someone to kiss him better.'

'Well, I hope it works out for you Polly and of course I'll put the wine away.'

'Thanks so much, do help yourself to a bottle for your trouble!'

'I could do with one now,' Sam sighed.

'What's the matter darling? I thought you were looking a bit miz. Not had a tiff with little Jess I hope?'

'No, no, that's all fine thanks Polly; it's my laptop, I think I've picked up a virus.'

'Oh no, not Grotbot, it's a devil.'

'Why have you had it?'

'Not me! When you go on some of the sites I visit you have to have the best anti virus in the business! I can download you a patch if you like, got your recovery disk handy?'

Sam was rather taken aback.

'Yes, I think I can find it,' he said reaching a box down from the top of the wardrobe.

'Good. I'll go and pop it on a flash drive for you.'

As Polly bustled out, Sam shook his head in amazement. He inserted the recovery CD and restarted the laptop in safe mode. Polly came back a few minutes later brandishing a memory

stick.
'Here we are. Thank goodness for broadband. That would have taken ages to download with dial up. Shall I leave you to it?'
'Yes, I think I can manage Polly, thanks.'
'It's called Fixgrot. Sounds like something you should use in the bathroom doesn't it? Just pop the stick back in the room with the wine if you like.'
'Thanks ever so Polly, and good luck with Miles.'
'Oh I daresay he'll get bored with me after a couple of days. I could do with being about forty years younger really.'
'What, back in the womb?'
'Ha ha! Flattery will get you everywhere darling!'

Peter Spencer stayed in Bristol until early evening to miss the worst of the traffic on the motorway. As he reached the turn off for the M42 he decided to pull off at the service station and call Theresa.
'Just ringing to let you know I got Jack settled back in ok.'
'I know thank you. I've just been talking to him for the last hour.'
'Good. What did he have to say?'
'Nothing you need to know.'
Peter's heart sank. He had seen this happen with clients so many times. Information is a scarce resource at the best of times with teenage and young adult children. When a marriage breaks down, it becomes priceless and its retention can be used as a weapon.
'Look Theresa, whatever happens between us, we must remember that Jack is and will always be our child. I think it is very important that we share any news from him. He needs as much support as he can get at the moment.'
'You should have thought of that before you walked out,' she snarled.
'I left because life together had become intolerable. We both agreed we needed some time apart but it's essential that we communicate openly during this period.'
'You have treated me very, very badly Peter. The more I think about it the angrier I get. I'm so furious with you I can't sleep at

night. The way you dumped me in that lay-by, your violence, it was unforgivable.'
'Violence?'
'Yes violence. I'm covered in bruises. Tasha said I should go to the Police about it.'
'I honestly don't think they would be very interested.'
'You're wrong there, Mr matrimonial expert.'
'You've reported it?'
'You'll just have to wait and see won't you?'
'Theresa?' shouted Peter as the line went dead.

Jess decided to give Sam a call about the invitation to their meal. He had just managed to zap the virus when she rang.
'I was just about to call you,' he said. It had occurred to him that the infected Word file would still be lurking on her ipod.
'Oh that's nice!' she said, and went on to pass on the good news about the bank manager and their invitation, which he accepted.
'The reason I was about to ring you was to eat humble pie actually.'
'Is that suitable for vegetarians then?'
'Yes. The fact is my laptop just crashed and it seems I did have that virus after all.'
'Is it salvageable?'
'Yes, Polly fixed it for me.'
'Polly?'
'Yes, she's a bit of an expert on Trojans.'
'I bet she is.'
'Anyway, this means it probably was you that infected the server at work. Have you still got the file on your ipod?'
'I just copied it onto my laptop.'
'Oh god. Have you opened it?'
'No.'
'Ok. Is it switched on now?'
'Yes.'
'Right, find the file but do not open it. Highlight it and press shift and delete at the same time. That will permanently eradicate it.'
'Ok. Done that.'

‘Now plug in your ipod and open it and do the same with that.’
Jess did as directed. ‘I’m really, really sorry about all this. I feel such a fool.’
‘Don’t worry about it. No harm done, apart from than all that unnecessary grovelling I did earlier this evening.’
‘Well I’ll grovel back.’
‘Ooh, can’t wait,’
Jess arranged to pick him up at the same time the following day.
‘Try not to be naked this time,’ she said, ‘or I’ll have to shag you before we leave.’

Fourteen

The following evening Jess arrived a little later, having done her shopping on the way, and Sam was all dressed and ready. He was wearing a smart Ben Sherman shirt and a pair of cream chinos.

'You look nice,' she said, giving him a kiss, 'had a good day at work?'

'Not bad thanks; I'm still just ploughing my way through tutorials. It's a bit mind numbing but I don't mind it. Do you want to come up for a sec? I just want to save what I've written to a stick. It turned out that I'd lost quite a bit last night.'

'Oh no, how awful. Have you managed to reconstruct it?'

'I got up early and rewrote most of it. There were a couple of bits that I remembered during the day so I just added them.'

While Sam was doing this, Jess noticed something in the cardboard box, which was still on the floor.

'What's this?'

'Oh it's a magnetic poetry writing kit, just a load of random words really. You're supposed to just grab a handful and write something really quickly without thinking.'

'Sounds like my kind of poetry! Oh and you've got a magnetic alphabet too.' She picked out a tub of brightly coloured plastic letters. While Sam was hiding his laptop away, she knelt on the floor by the fridge and quickly wrote 'i love samuel taylor' rather wonkily on the door. Beneath the 'y' she slid Sam's copy of the booth photo from the supermarket, which had been lying on the windowsill. Before he could turn to look at what she had done, she hurried him out of the room.

The mood was still buoyant in the Beresford camp. Tom's final exam had registered suitably high on the urine scale and he

had already been at the lager. Jess gave him a hug as she walked in.
'Well done, Tommy. It's a great feeling isn't it?'
'I don't feel anything really, but most of my friends haven't finished yet so it might kick in when they start celebrating.'
Tom latched on to Sam while Jess helped in the kitchen.
'How are you feeling Mum?'
'Oh, I don't know, a mixture of relief and exhaustion really. I feel as though I could sleep for a week! This isn't going to be much of a meal I'm afraid, this iceberg lettuce has had it.'
Luckily Jess had bought some fresh salad stuff when she picked up the moussaka. 'Look, I got some tzaziki and stuffed vine leaves,' she said unpacking various plastic boxes.
'How clever of you,' said Christine, 'what would I do without you?'
'And I got some sticky toffee puddings too as a treat for Tom.'
'Very Greek,' smiled Christine.

Unlike the previous time they had eaten together, Sam was welcomed as an accepted addition to the family. Mark and Christine showed far more interest in him and asked him all about his job and the new flat. Tom tried to monopolise him again but Jess had arranged the seating to make that less likely. Mark listened politely to his reasons for not eating meat.
'So you don't claim to be a vegetarian?' he asked.
'No, I eat fish and some seafood,' explained Sam.
'Where do you draw the line then? How do you decide which living creatures you can consume?'
'Well my main criterion is that I don't eat mammals. I feel less strongly about birds and of course I do eat eggs.'
'So what is it about mammals?' Mark persisted.
'I just feel too closely related to them to regard them as food.'
Apart from Jess, the rest of the family roared with laughter at this.
'So you feel closely related to a pig?' asked Tom incredulously.
'Yes. Our DNA is over ninety nine percent identical. I am a mammal, part of a family of mammals and I don't want to eat my family.'
'So what do you think about people who do eat them?' asked

Christine.
'And about people who farm them?' added Mark.
'I don't have any issues with either,' replied Sam, 'my decision is purely personal and I don't seek to influence or pass judgement on others under any circumstances.'
'Well I think you are being totally inconsistent,' snorted Mark. 'You just eat what suits you and you don't even feel strongly enough about what principles you do have to stick up for them.'
'I'm quite happy to stick up for them; I just don't impose them on others. And as for inconsistency, you are in no position to complain about me. I daresay you wouldn't want to eat a dog or a horse for instance.'
Again Jess was uncomfortably silent as the rest of the family laughed at the very idea.
'What's inconsistent about that?' asked Tom.
'You would happily butcher and eat some mammals but react with horror at the thought of doing it to others. I won't eat them at all so I am more consistent.'
'Well, I think we've just about exhausted that one,' said Jess nervously, 'who's ready for sticky toffee pudding?'
'It was a good effort, Sam' said Tom, 'but you'll never convince Dad. He said he'd get black balled by the hunt committee for entertaining a veggie!'
'The hunt?' asked Sam, looking puzzled, 'I thought that had all been banned ages ago.'
'Here we go,' said Mark, 'are we going to have to endure some more of your stupid, misguided townie prejudices?'
'Pudding anyone?' offered Jess forlornly.
'Hunting and killing foxes with hounds has been banned but it's still legal ride with them and follow a prepared trail of a fox based scent. We call it trail hunting,' explained Christine.
'So it all still exists?' asked Sam, 'the infrastructure of hunting is all still intact?'
'Damn right it is,' said Mark aggressively, 'and a bloody good job too. It's a fundamental part of our way of life here, part of a culture you'll never even begin to understand.'
'Dad, please!' cried Jess. 'You started this argument, there's no need to be horrible to Sam.'

'You're in no position to side with him young lady,' said Mark, 'you spent enough years in the pony club.'
'You've ridden with the hunt?' asked Sam, looking at Jess in disbelief.
'We followed sometimes when I was younger, everyone did. If you don't live in the country you can't possibly understand the part it plays in the community.'
'So you support the Countryside Alliance?'
'I don't support them but I can see where they are coming from,' said Jess desperately trying to find some middle ground.
'Don't bother trying to reason with him,' snarled Mark, 'he just regards the countryside a playground, a pretty place for him to trespass in.'
'Ok, so let me get this right,' persisted Sam, 'you lay this trail right through their habitat and set the hounds off after it. Isn't it inevitable they will eventually flush out a fox?'
'It happens,' said Mark indifferently, 'but that's perfectly legal. So long as you can prove there was no intent to injure a fox, they can't touch you.'
'So nothing's changed really?' asked Sam, incredulous, 'all that vicious, barbaric cruelty is still going on.'
'It's part of our heritage,' snapped Mark angrily. 'I'm proud to be Joint Master of Hounds and although it's not easy we intend to carry on until we get that blasted law repealed and we don't need ignorant people like you telling us how to live our lives!'
'Dad, stop being such a nob!' shouted Jess. 'Sam didn't come here to have an argument. Why are you being so confrontational?'
'Oh please don't cry love,' said Christine. 'Mark look what you've done now, it's just too bad.' Christine got up to comfort Jess but she shook her away.
'The evening's ruined now,' she said bitterly. 'Come on Sam, let's go.'
'I'm sorry if I've offended you,' said Sam as he got up to leave.
'It's not your fault,' said Christine, 'please don't go.' But Jess grabbed his hand and pulled him out of the room.
'There was no need for that,' said Christine to Mark.
'Nice one Dad,' said Tom as the back door slammed.

'Well, they get on my nerves, imposing their city views on us,' muttered Mark.
'Can I have his pudding?' asked Tom.

'Why don't we go somewhere for a drink?' suggested Sam as they drove back into town. 'I think you need to calm down a bit.'
'I can't believe my dad did that. It was like he was trying to find a way to drive us apart.'
'I'm not sure, I think he just feels a bit threatened by urban attitudes and I happened to be in his line of fire.'
'You're not mad then?'
'No, I thought it was funny.'
'It was not funny! What did you think about me being involved in hunting?'
'Do you still support it?'
'Not actively, but I am sympathetic. It's a rural tradition, a sort of religion really. In a city the equivalent would be banning football. Does that put it in perspective?'
'Yes but it doesn't alter the fact that it's a barbaric thing to do and it has no place in a civilised world.'
'You mean it reveals an aspect of the human psyche that you would rather not recognise so you prefer it to be suppressed, persecuted out of existence like the opposition in a one party state.'
'Well fine, we're all still hunter gatherers under the surface but surely things like sport have developed to allow us to sublimate those urges.'
'So what about shooting and fishing? Would you ban them too? Oh no, of course, that's not being cruel to your precious little mammals is it?'
'Jess, I'm not banning anything. Why am I suddenly personally responsible for all this?'
'I'm sorry,' Jess sighed. 'I'm starting to sound like my dad now. It's so stupid isn't it.'

Tom disappeared upstairs after eating most of the puddings, leaving his parents to clear away.

'Did you hear what she called me?' said Mark, shaking his head in disbelief.
'Well I don't blame her. Why did you pick on Sam like that just because he doesn't eat meat? You wrecked what should have been a lovely evening. Jess will probably never forgive us.'
'Yes and I'm sorry. I really don't know how it happened. It was just the look on his face when Tom mentioned hunting; it just triggered something in me. I suppose I was being a bit obnoxious, but fancy calling your own father that.'
'Well I get called worse; or at least I think it's worse. Sometimes I'm not entirely sure whether I'm actually being insulted. Tom called me a spoon the other day.'
'God, they seem to be developing an entirely different language, these kids. A spoon? What context was it used in?'
'Oh I don't know, I was probably trying to introduce a trace element of common sense into an argument. I got the impression it was to do with being slow on the uptake.'
'As opposed to being sharp as a knife?'
'Oh yes, I suppose so. That's quite clever actually.'
'Was I being a spoon tonight?'
'No I don't think we can measure it by household cutlery.'
'More household cavalry?'
'The charge of the heavy brigade, no, in terms of implements, I would say lump hammer springs to mind.'
'A bit of a nob then?'
'Quite a lot of one.'
'Are you mad with me?'
'I don't know; I'm too tired to be angry. I think we've all been under so much pressure recently it was bound to end in tears somehow. It's just a shame poor Sam took the brunt of it. I do hope he can forgive us.'
Christine decided to get off to bed, leaving Mark to serve time in the kitchen and reflect on what he might do to win back the affections of his wounded daughter.

In the end Sam and Jess decided not to go to the pub. She pulled up outside the flat and they sat talking in the car. Neither of them seemed keen to go inside and spoil the magic of their

little room with this dismal mood. They held hands and she rested her head on his shoulder.
'I don't want you to go, but I think it would be best if you went home and talked this through with your dad. It's not a good idea to let these things fester.'
'I'm not going to apologise,' Jess snapped.
'I think you'll find he'll be the one doing that.'
'I don't know; he can be very stubborn.'
'Oh come on. It's a storm in a teacup. We'll all be laughing about it tomorrow.'
'It's a bit more serious than that, Sam.'
'Storm in a teapot then.'
'Yes, that's more like it,' she said squeezing him tight. She pressed his nose with her finger like it was a button.
'Hey, what are you doing?'
'Trying to turn you off.'
'How do you know that isn't turning me on?' he drawled amorously.
'Everything turns you on.'
'Yes, you'd better go before I take you by force on the back seat.'
'You'll have a job, there's an old horse blanket on it.'
'How romantic.'
She walked him to the front door and as they kissed on the doorstep they both felt something mending between them and a growing realisation that everything would be fine. Sam was just about to unlock the door when it opened and Roland walked out, cigarette in hand.
'The lovebirds!' he cried, 'How perfect, I have something to ask you dear boy.'
Jess winked at Sam and grinned as she turned to walk back to the car.

As she walked into the kitchen, Jess was surprised to see Mark sitting at the far end of the table, turning a whisky glass in his hand. He looked up and as their eyes met, Jess narrowed hers.
'Ouch!' he said.

She walked slowly towards her end of the table. There was a small blob of mayonnaise in the middle of it.
'This needs a wipe,' she said indifferently.
'Is Sam ok?' asked Mark tentatively.
Jess leaned on the table with both hands, as if about to address a meeting. She paused, drawing out the moment a little to make him suffer.
'Yeah he's fine. He thought it was quite funny actually,' she paused again and looked Mark straight in the eye, 'I didn't though.'
'What I did, what I said, was unforgivable. I can't understand how it happened. Your mum thinks it's because we've all been so stressed recently and relaxing tonight kind of lifted the lid on feelings I'd been repressing for ages.'
'Like anger?'
'Yes anger; I am angry that my lovely, beautiful wife is about to have her life snatched away when we still had so much left to do together. I feel cheated and bitter and I've been bottling it all up inside me like toxic waste.'
Jess's severity evaporated and her face crumpled as she lifted her hand to her mouth. 'Oh Christ Dad!' She ran the length of the table as Mark got to his feet and flung herself into his arms. 'I was determined to stay cross with you for quite a long time,' she sobbed. 'I'm so glad you waited up to-'
'Apologise,' interrupted Mark, 'I haven't said it yet and I am truly, deeply sorry for what I did, my darling. I know you probably think I was trying to drive Sam away because I don't approve or in some perverted way we want to keep you for ourselves, but nothing could be further from the truth. Mum and I are delighted that you have found someone special. I still can't believe what happened.'
'Forget it, right?' Jess gasped through tears, her face pressed into his shoulder. 'Sam's fine, really. He said we'd probably all laugh about in the morning. We're fine; I'm fine. I was mad that what should have been a lovely evening was ruined but there's no harm done and maybe it's a good thing that you were able to express some of that rage. What did Tom have to say about it all?'

'Oh he seemed oblivious to it all.'
'No change there then.'
'He ate all the puddings, he was quite happy.'
'Pig.'
'Can we ring Sam? I'd like to apologise to him as soon as I can.'
Jess took out her mobile and selected his number.
'Hi. Yeah, yeah, yeah, everything's fine. It was just a storm in a teapot like you said. Dad thinks it was just because we all relaxed for the first time in like ages and it let some demons out. He wants a quick word. I'll just put him on.'
She passed the phone to Mark, who held it like it was a hand grenade for a moment, then repeated his apology. He listened for a while, nodding as Sam spoke, then burst out laughing.
'I might just take you up on that. Thanks for being so understanding, Sam. You must come up again soon and I'll try to behave a bit better. Yes, Round Two!' he laughed again. 'I'll put you back on to Jess then, goodbye Sam and sorry again.'
After a brief chat, they said their goodbyes and Jess hung up.
'What did he say to make you laugh?' she asked.
'Oh, he said I could call him any time I felt like raving at someone. He's a case isn't he?'
'Oh yeah, he's a case all right,' nodded Jess.

Roland asked Sam about selling his books. It transpired that he was falling into dept with no realistic prospect of increasing his income and was keen to turn them into cash.
'When I said they were valuable I wasn't suggesting you should sell them,' Sam protested.
'I never look at them,' said Roland, 'they may as well go to someone who will appreciate them.'
Sam picked a slim hardback from the shelf. It was a limited edition poetry book published in 1937. Beautifully produced, it was printed on a thick alabaster wove paper, which had turned creamy now but still felt luxurious to the touch. He sniffed the slightly musty pages as if it could transport him back to a world on the brink of catastrophe.
'It's like a passport to the past,' he murmured.

'It's terrible poetry,' said Roland, 'I was talking to Polly about it and she said she could sell them on the Internet for me but she doesn't value books like you do and I don't want them jobbing off on Ebay.'
'Well you could use Ebay but it might be better to approach rare booksellers. I'll have a look for you and see what sort of prices they're fetching.'
'Would you dear boy? I'd be ever so grateful.'
'I don't suppose you've a list of what you've got here?'
Roland shook his head. Sam picked a small red hard back off the shelf called 'The Battle for Peace' and at the foot of the cover was printed in bold capitals 'Left Book Club Edition. Not for sale to the public.'
'Fascinating,' said Sam, 'some of these are probably very collectable. Could you make me a list of the ones you would like to sell: title, author, publisher and date of publication, condition and whether they have a dust jacket?'
'I'll do it tomorrow,' said Roland, 'I could get rid of most of these, really.'
'It does seem a shame though,' sighed Sam.
'I know, and I'm glad you appreciate that. Polly's been on at me to take them to Oxfam for years!'
'Oh no! I'm sure we can get a good price for some of these,' said Sam, lovingly replacing the Left Book on the shelf.'
'You must keep any you want for your trouble,' said Roland, placing his hand on Sam's arm.
'Don't say that, I'd want them all!' laughed Sam. 'If Polly's left her Internet switched on I'll have a look tonight. I could be completely wrong. Just because I think they're valuable, it doesn't mean a thing.'
'No, but it's nice that you do. I can't tell you how wonderful it is to have a fellow aesthete under the same roof.'
'I'll let you know tomorrow if you're sitting on a goldmine,' said Sam.
'Fingers crossed!' smiled Roland.

After Sam had spoken to Jess and Mark on the phone he searched for books on the Internet. He tried a rare books site

first in the hope that the prices would be better. He keyed the title of the book he had just looked at into the search and it came up straight away.
'There it is!' he cried, 'The Battle For Peace.' There was even a picture, the exact same red cover that he had just been holding. This moment of elation passed quickly when he looked at the price, 'Oh no,' he groaned, 'three pounds ninety five, that's ridiculous. What am I going to tell Roland?'
There were several copies listed, all around the same figure. He tried Amazon, where there were plenty of copies, a few of them priced higher, and Ebay where some were priced even lower.
'It clearly isn't scarce so it's probably just a bad example,' he muttered to himself. Then he thought for a moment; Roland had literally hundreds of books, if he could average four pounds a copy it would still be worth doing but who was going to do all the legwork? It would be incredibly time consuming and there was no way he could take it on. He decided it would be best not to mention it again in the hope that Roland might forget all about it.

Sam was just opening his story on the laptop when there was a loud banging on the front door. He jumped up quickly and hurried downstairs. It was dark and he didn't want Roland answering in case it was trouble.
He opened the door warily and peered round it to discover a burly, bearded man with wild hair. He had no idea who this person was until he spoke, and then he knew straight away; it was Matt.

Jess went to lie on her bed for a while. She felt exhausted but relieved that she had made her peace with her father. Eventually, there was a tap on the door and Tom drifted in, looking very glum.
'Are you really mad with us?' he asked pathetically.
'Well I was really, really, really mad with Dad,' she said sternly, 'but it's all sorted now. We just had a chat and put it all into perspective and it's fine, no harm done.'
'I wasn't much help though,'
'No, in fact you mentioned the H word, but I suppose it was an

issue we would have had to face eventually, so it's all good. How's life in the post-exam world?'
'Rubbish.'
'I'm sorry Tom, I know it was supposed to be your special meal and I wrecked it by flouncing out but you have to agree I was provoked.'
'Oh I'm not bothered about that,' he sighed, 'it's the Cornwall trip, we finally had to abandon it.'
'That is a shame, you've been looking forward to it for ages haven't you?'
'Yeah, but I had a feeling it was dead in the water when the girls pulled out.'
'Yes, I can see that would have reduced its attraction somewhat. So is there a plan B?'
'Well not exactly, but I was wondering whether to get that job at the Crown.' Jess looked at him knowingly. 'What?' he asked angrily, blushing a little.
'Well, it won't be the job, 'cause it's crap and it can't be the money, 'cause it's rubbish so what other attraction would there be?' asked Jess mischievously.
'Ok,' sighed Tom, 'and I don't really care if she does ignore me, it will just be nice to be around her sometimes.'
'Oh that's so sweet, no seriously, I mean it and if it's any consolation I think you're way nicer than the losers she chooses to hang around with most of the time.'
'Yeah, but nice is boring isn't it.'
'Well I suppose if you don't have an Asbo, an illegal motorbike or a sawn off shotgun it is kind of hard to compete but she seemed pretty friendly when we saw her there the other night.'
'I know but I'm worried she'll think I'm stalking her.'
'I thought she was barely aware of your existence most of the time?'
'You're not really helping Jess.'
'I'm just saying, I think you should do it. Work there for the summer and if nothing happens, well at least you'll have earned some cash.'
Tom seemed reassured by this advice and wandered back to his computer games, which suddenly seemed so much less

enthralling now he had all the time in the world to play them. He had begun to look elsewhere for alternatives and had found one in a multiplayer online combat game.

'Matt!' whispered Sam, 'God, you look like the wild man of Borneo! What have you been up to?'

'Can I come in, mate?'

'Yes, of course, come up to my room before we wake people up.'

'I was wondering if I could crash on your floor for a few nights.'

'Of course mate. The only problem is I haven't got much floor to crash on.' He opened his door and ushered Matt in.

'Bloody hell! You're not kidding are you.' exclaimed Matt.

'My neighbours call it the broom cupboard. How did you manage to track me down by the way?'

'Oh I went to the house and Wayne was there doing some decorating. He told me what had happened.'

'Oh dear, was that a bit embarrassing?'

'No he was okay about it actually. He's got a tenant lined up at a much higher rent so he's well happy. He's agreed to take half what I owe him, call it quits at that and give me time to pay, which is pretty reasonable so you did me a favour there mate.'

'I still owe you though.'

'I know but if I can doss here for a few nights, I'll settle for a hundred. How does that sound?'

'Far too generous, what about the gas and electric?'

'Fine. Wayne gave me letters that had just arrived from them. I'd been paying monthly so I'm almost back in credit.'

Sam made coffees and they sat on the bed catching up with each other. Matt noticed the little message Jess had written on the fridge.

'Romance still prospering then?' he remarked, nodding towards it.

'Oh yeah, it's really lovely thanks.'

'Very cosy in here I expect.'

'She just loves this room! It's a sort of doll's house thing I think. I wasn't sure at first but she insisted'

'You don't want to be setting precedents like that mate.'

'I didn't have much choice, she paid the first month's rent.'

'See, I told you she'd be loaded.'
'I don't think so and anyway it's only a loan. I'll pay her back as soon as I can.'

They talked about Sam's job for a bit and then Matt finally began to tell him what had been going on in his life for the past couple of weeks. It turned out that he had planned to stay with a former colleague who had set up a driving school in Rochdale. They had never discussed pay or rent or anything; it was something they had talked about for years but in the end it was all done on the spur of the moment. It soon became clear that they had wildly differing expectations about these financial matters. With rocketing petrol prices and a collapse in demand for lessons, Matt had chosen the worst possible time to take the plunge. In the end they quarrelled and Matt walked out, ending up in a bed and breakfast in Hebden Bridge with no job, no money and no friends. When he was thrown out of that because his cheque bounced, he slept in the car for a few days and in the end had to admit defeat and head for home.
'Did you just assume I would still be in the house then?' asked Sam.
'I don't know. They cut my phone off and then the battery went so I couldn't even get your number to call you from a phone box, so I just kind of showed up.'
'I don't get it though, Matt. Why all the secrecy and the sudden disappearance? What did you need to run away for?'
'It's not particularly sinister,' said Matt, wearily putting his head in his hands, 'I've got massive credit card debt. I used to manage by moving it around all the time so that I was always on interest free but they suddenly stopped letting you do that and I can't even begin to pay the interest.'
'Go bankrupt then, everyone's doing it.'
'I just panicked. I thought I could disappear for a while and go and work for Jimmy for pound notes and in the end they would give up looking for me and write off the debt. That's why I had to do a runner; I didn't want to involve anyone down here and burden them with having to keep schtum about it.'
'They just sell the debt mate. People will be on your case for years.'

Matt had cancelled his holiday and lost all that money and had not even handed his notice in at work.
'So Pass Masters just think you've been in Xante for the last couple of weeks?'
'Yes, and that's the saving grace. I can just turn up on Monday and get back to work!'
'That's incredible! And you're really going to do it?'
'Why not? I'll do what you say and contact one of these debt-counselling agencies and go bust if I have to. Just to have the thing out in the open and being sorted with will be such a huge weight off my mind.'
'Not being funny, mate but this isn't really going to work on a permanent basis,' said Sam, gesturing round the room. 'I'm away for the weekend so that's no problem but after that, well, I'm not so sure.'
'No, of course, I understand. If I can stop till Monday and you can find me a hundred quid, I'll charge my mobile up, buy a pay as you go sim and get something else sorted.'
Sam's heart sank. He was still on weekly pay so should have the money in the morning but that would leave him with hardly any cash to spend in Leeds. He had no choice though; he owed Matt that and much more, and his need was undeniably greater. He took out his wallet and handed Matt ten pounds.
'That's all I've got on me but I'll give you the rest after work tomorrow.'
'You're a star mate. I knew I could count on you.'
'I'm going to have to turn in now Matt. Do you want a sandwich or anything?'
'Yeah, whatever you've got. I'm starving!'
Matt settled on a bowl of cereal and sat on the bed eating it while Sam reached his sleeping bag down from the top of the wardrobe.
'I couldn't interest you in having a shower could I?' he asked as tactfully as possible.
'I'm just so exhausted. I haven't slept properly for over a week. Is it that bad?'
'It's pretty bad, but don't worry. The main problem is whether you're actually going to fit on this floor,' said Sam, looking

down dubiously. It was then that he noticed Polly's key on the chest of drawers.

Matt finished his cereal and tried lying down beside the bed. 'God, it'll be like sleeping in a bloody coffin!' he laughed. 'Still it will have to do. I can't stand another night in that car.'

'There is another option,' said Sam hesitantly, acutely aware that he was probably about to make a huge mistake.

Sam gingerly opened the door of Polly's room. He had never set foot inside it before. Turning on the light, he was surprised by how spacious it seemed compared to his. There was a fireplace with an old metal gas fire and a small sofa facing it. The room was spotlessly clean and tidy and all the surfaces were covered with little porcelain ornaments. Matt picked one up off the mantle piece. It was a figurine of a little beggar girl in a shawl with bare feet, carrying a basket of violets.

'Very tasteful,' said Matt.

'Put that down!' hissed Sam. 'Don't touch anything! I knew this was going to be a mistake.'

'I'll be fine in here,' said Matt, 'look I can put these cushions from the sofa on the floor here and I promise I'll be spark out for hours.'

'Ok then, I'll give you a knock when I go to work and you can move onto my bed in case she comes back in the morning.'

Sam went to bed full of misgiving. Matt was not the most reliable of people. He was bound to wake up in the night and raid Polly's larder. In the end he fell deeply asleep and was disturbed neither by the noise of a car in the street, nor by the sound of footsteps on the stairs; it was the scream that woke him.

Jess was just getting ready for bed when her mobile rang.

'Hi this is Leeds calling,' a very drunken voice echoed in her ear.

'Alice! Hi!' exclaimed Jess. She could hear a heavy, repetitive beat thumping in the background. 'Where are you?'

'Devolution!' shouted Alice. 'They've got this wicked trance disco and shots are half price so we're all totally wasted already.' Jess glanced at her clock at this use of the word

'already' and noticed it was way past midnight. It crossed her mind that she was going to struggle to keep up at the weekend.
'Sounds like a perfect way to kick off the celebrations,' said Jess, acutely aware that this was a rather lame response.
'Anyway, I called because we just realised that on Friday we've got tickets for the Futurists gig at the Union. Do you want me to see if I can pick a couple up from somewhere?'
'The Futurists! God that would be incredible if you could!'
'Well I can't promise, they're like gold obviously but I'll see what I can do.'
'Cool,' said Jess, 'and don't worry if you can't, I'll just take Sam into town.' The noise in the bar ratcheted up and it was getting harder to hear so they just shouted their goodbyes. Jess lay in bed thinking for ages before she drifted off to sleep.

Sam sat bolt upright in bed. There was a loud hammering on his door.
'Is this vagrant in my room anything to do with you?' yelled Polly.
He leapt up and flung himself into his dressing gown, opening the door in the same movement. Polly was right there facing him as he emerged.
'We can't go on meeting like this,' she said dryly.
'Oh Polly, I don't know what to say, this is just too awful.'
'How about sorry, assuming that tramp on my floor is an associate of yours.'
'Yes, of course, I am most massively sorry, Polly. That is Matt, my former flat mate who is now homeless. He turned up unexpectedly late last night asking if he could crash on my floor for a few nights and there isn't really enough floor to crash on.'
'So you diverted him to mine for his emergency landing.'
'Yes, it was an unforgivable breach of trust and I'm mortified that…'
'That I turned up and rumbled your little operation,' interrupted Polly.
'I promise I did not invite him here, Polly,' stammered an increasingly distressed Sam.
To his utter amazement, Polly began to laugh.

'Don't look so distraught, darling; it's not the end of the world. At least you had the decency to put him on the floor in a sleeping bag. Now if he'd been in, or even on my bed that would have been a whole different ball game I assure you.' Polly emphasised the word 'ball' in a way that made Sam wince.
Just then they heard a shuffling noise downstairs. Polly peered into the darkness of the hall.
'I think we've disturbed Roly,' she whispered, 'I'll go and get him back to bed.' She began to descend the stairs calling softly, 'Did I wake you darling? I'm so sorry.'
Sam walked hesitantly over to Polly's threshold and looked into the room. Matt had slept blissfully through all the pandemonium and was sprawled lavishly across Polly's floor like some kind of live art installation, looking every inch a hobo. Sam stepped forward and roughly shook him awake.
'Is it time to get up already?' he murmured sleepily as he swam into consciousness.
'The unthinkable has happened,' snapped Sam, 'Polly has just arrived home and walked in to find you here on her floor.'
'Where is she then?' asked Matt looking round, trying to make sense of the situation.
'She'll be back in a minute. In the meantime let's get you out of here!'
Matt took a few moments to collect himself and was just hopping along the landing, sack race fashion in the sleeping bag when Polly reappeared on the stairs.
'Where are you two sneaking off to?' she hissed.
'Back to my room of course,' replied a puzzled Sam. 'I assumed you would want us to make ourselves scarce.'
'No, you can keep me company for a bit now you're up. I'm feeling very depressed and I hate drinking alone. Anyone fancy a brandy?'
The boys looked at each other with a mixture of terror and disbelief. After what they had done, they didn't have much choice.
'It's four in the morning, Polly,' Sam protested lamely.
'Oh come on, what's the matter with you? I thought you young

things were always clubbing into the early hours.'
With a doomed look on their faces, the boys turned and Sam helped his friend hop back into Polly's room. He had already replaced the cushions on the sofa so they cautiously installed themselves there. Polly was busy pouring three large tumblers of supermarket brandy, crooning the 'it's four in the morning, da da da, dee dee dee.'
'I love that song,' she sighed handing the glasses round and sitting on one of the dining chairs with her back to the table. 'Who was it by now?'
'I'm not sure,' said Sam hesitantly, 'I don't know an awful lot about Country and Western.' He looked across at Matt for assistance.
'Tammy Wynette?' suggested Matt randomly.
There was an awkward pause as they sipped the terrible firewater.
'It didn't work out with Miles, then?' asked Sam tentatively.
'That man!' exclaimed Polly, 'he does not deserve a friend like me.' She concentrated for a moment as if trying to rein in powerful emotions. 'Everything was going beautifully,' she continued, 'we had a fantastic meal at this phenomenal restaurant he virtually owns, one of those young chefs who's just coming through on the telly, then we get back to his place to a tearful message on the answering machine from that pathetic little bimbo. He played it in front of me. Can you believe it? All stuff about how good they are together; too much information! Anyway when the tape finally ran out I just said 'dump the bitch she's only after your money!' He completely ignored me. It was as if I wasn't there. He called her and they began this sickening reconciliation. In the end I just grabbed my suitcase, turned tail and walked out on him. I daresay he'll be bombarding me with repentant calls all day but I shall not be answering my phone!'
'And then you had this to greet you on your return. I'm so sorry Polly,' said Sam remorsefully.
'Oh don't worry about that. I'd probably have done the same myself in your situation,' she shrugged. 'It's not as if you threw a party in here or anything and it's very nice to have someone

talk to and get all this off my chest.'

After an hour and several more glasses of brandy Polly finally released the exhausted boys from custody. They had to sit through a blow-by-blow account of her turbulent relationship with Miles, which had lasted spasmodically for a number of years. Even after this latest disaster she still nurtured the delusion that it would only be a matter of time before he finally saw the light and invited her into his life forever. It was after five when they staggered back to his room and Sam did not dare risk trying to sleep so he let Matt have the bed, showered and got ready for work. Matt was fortunate to be such a heavy sleeper because as Sam sat watching the night sky fade, the opening chords of 'Super Trooper' abruptly filled the air as if Abba were broadcasting to the whole planet from outer space.

Fifteen

Sam worked lunch on Thursday and Friday so he could leave early for the trip to Leeds. Jess took her case to work and went straight round to pick him up as soon as she finished. He had already told her on the phone the previous evening about the business with Polly and Matt and she had been expecting to finally meet him but he was not around and there was no time to wait; they wanted to miss the worst of the motorway traffic.

As they sped up the hill towards the A52 they could see for miles; the whole of Nottingham was spread out to their right and ahead they could see into Leicestershire.

'That awful power station is such a blot on the landscape,' complained Jess.

'Oh I don't know, I think it's rather fine.'

'I don't believe it! You are such a freak. What's good about that monstrosity?'

'Cooling towers are structurally beautiful. They are only dismissed because they're so functional. If we didn't know what they were for we'd think them marvellous.'

'You're having a laugh aren't you?'

'No, I really do think they are superb. Look at them now in the distance, like a giant tray of steaming coffee cups.'

'What about all the CO_2 emissions? That's not so fantastic is it?'

'Well that's nothing to do with the visual aesthetics and anyway there's only steam puffing out of them. Look at them now, like the funnels of a transatlantic liner slipping down over the horizon.'

'The Titanic?'

'Stop being so cynical!'

'I'm sorry, but you're just unbelievable. You managed to get me to appreciate the jet planes constantly droning over my head but

I really must draw the line at power stations. Next thing you'll be telling me you like electricity pylons.'
'They do have a kind of savage beauty.'
'Beam me up Scotty! Now you are taking the piss.'
'You've got to remember that the pyramids, Stonehenge, cathedrals are all functional constructs; they all have or did have a job to do. You should never dismiss something purely on the grounds of its functionality.'
'Like that urinal you mean?'
'Yes, Duchamp's fountain, exactly.'
'He wasn't taking the piss then?'

Despite their early departure, the motorway was busy and it was after six by the time they peeled off the M1 and began descending the long incline towards the city.
'Hello Leeds!' cried Jess as the metropolis spread itself out before them. It was almost a year since she had been there and already the skyline was noticeably changed. Some of the new towers that had been under construction were finished and several more were beginning to sprout. 'It's such a dynamic place!' she exclaimed, 'masses of new buildings going up all the time.'
'I'll probably hate most of them,' said Sam.
'Well, obviously they wouldn't compare favourably to a power station.'

The commuter traffic had subsided and they quickly drove straight through town, past the station, City Square and the town hall. Sam had never been to Leeds before and he looked this way and that trying to take it all in.
'I'll show you round town tomorrow,' said Jess, 'it's brilliant for shopping, especially the Victoria Quarter with all the lovely old arcades.'
'Yes, I think I've seen photographs of them,' Sam nodded.
'You can buy me lunch in Harvey Nicks darling!'
'Absolutely fabulous,' laughed Sam, hoping it would not be too expensive. He had given Matt the rest of the money the previous evening and it had left him perilously close to his overdraft limit again.

As they turned up the steep hill of Woodhouse Lane, the distinctive University tower came into view.
'Hello Brotherton!' called Jess. 'Oh it's so lovely to come back. I can't believe I've left it a year. I expect you hate that do you?' she asked, nodding towards the tower.
'It's a bit clumsy but I don't dislike it. Is it art deco?'
'I don't know. It's just a great big beacon that says 'welcome home' to me.'
They drove by the university and up to Hyde Park. The girls shared a little three bed roomed back-to-back terrace in John Street. The original intention was that Jess would have the third room. She had been involved in choosing the place and knew where it was but because of the rather random street plan in the area it took a while to find. Eventually they pulled up outside and the girls, who had been kneeling on the sofa looking out of the window like children, dashed out into the street to greet them. After a great deal of jumping up and down and hugging, which left out Sam for a moment, Kat's head emerged from the scrum of tangled limbs.
'Oh hi. You must be Sam.'
'I must,' he replied.
'Hi. I'm Kat and this is Alice,' she said disengaging an arm and pointing with her finger and thumb like a six-gun.
The two girls might have been sisters. They were both of a similar slight build with long straight blond hair cut in the same style and both wore ragged jeans with bright flowery smock tops and an abundance of bangles and necklaces. Sam noticed then that Jess had dressed differently. She wore a short black skirt with black tights and slip on pumps, a white blouse and a very long black cardigan with similar bracelets and necklaces and a bulky handbag slung diagonally across her chest. She had come straight from work and the absence of colour reflected this but the overall look curiously mirrored the other two.

They went inside and sat in the living room with a bottle of lager each. The house had clearly once been the deluxe version of back-to-back housing; there was a moulded cornice on the ceiling and a stained glass panel above the front door with leaded rectangles in red and blue. Sam looked around with interest while the girls conducted a rapid exchange of gossip punctuated with cries of 'No!' and 'Oh my god!' The decoration was eccentric, no carpet and the floorboards, walls, doors and ceiling all rag roll painted in a peculiar khaki colour. Apart from the armchair and sofa, there was just a small Formica table in the corner with a TV on it. On the walls there was just a solitary poster, a reproduction of a 1950's advert, which was a mostly orange and yellow aerial painting of a crowded beach and a title white out of a black box saying 'Filey for the family.'

'Curious décor isn't it?' said Kat noticing Sam's observation.

He nodded and smiled. 'Eccentric,' he agreed. 'I don't dislike it but it's not very homely.'

'Yeah, the previous tenant must have had buckets of this paint to get rid of, it's all over the place. Come on I'll show you round.'

Sam looked across at Jess and Alice but they were deep in conversation so he followed Kat into the kitchen.

'This is compact,' he said standing beside her at a sink full of dishes.

'Yes you could say that. The scullery would have been downstairs though.'

'Downstairs?'

'Yes, there's a basement, come on.' She opened a narrow door at the far end of the room and descended a curving flight of shallow stone steps which led into a single room the width of the house lit by a small pavement level window. It was dusty and full of broken furniture and smelt rather fusty. There were some stained wood shelves on the opposite wall and a shallow ceramic sink in the far corner.

'So this would have been a kind of pantry and back kitchen?'

'I suppose so. In some houses it's been converted into a bedroom. I wouldn't fancy it though,' shivered Kat.

They made their way back up to find the others still engrossed in their discussion so Kat just pointed to indicate that she was showing Sam round and opened the door to the stairs. From floor to ceiling the staircase was plastered with the same scumble of green murk. On the first floor there was a narrow corridor of a bathroom that somehow managed to accommodate a toilet and washbasin as well, and two small bedrooms for Alice and Kat. Sam was beginning to feel that his bed-sit was relatively spacious when he noticed a further, narrower flight of stairs curving up from the landing. The army surplus paint must have mercifully run out by then because the walls were painted deep maroon.

'Where does that go?' he asked indicating with his thumb.

'Your room,' answered Kat.

Sam was about to seek clarification when they heard the naked soles of Alice and Jess slapping up the steps.

'Sorry about that guys,' sang Alice, 'important stuff to catch up on.'

'Oh yeah, like you've not been in touch with each other for months!' scoffed Kat.

'We've got the loft apartment it seems,' said Sam, indicating the stairs with his eyes.

'Oh that's so sweet!' enthused Jess, embracing each girl in turn. 'When we got this house we drew lots for that room and I won,' she explained to Sam, 'but of course I never got to move in.'

'We kept it free for weeks in case she came back,' continued Alice 'and by the time we started looking for someone else we were kind of settled in down here so Helen had that room.'

'Is she ok about us using it?' asked Sam.

'She's gone. She was in her final year and she cleared out straight after her exams,' explained Kat.

'Probably couldn't stand you two nutters any longer,' teased Jess, 'so have you found a new tenant yet?'

'We've got someone pencilled in,' Kat continued and the two girls exchanged conspiratorial glances.

'What?' questioned Jess, intrigued, 'is it someone I know?'

'You could say that,' said Alice mysteriously.

'Well who then?' demanded Jess impatiently.

'You!' they exclaimed in unison.

'That is the sweetest, most lovely thing,' stammered Jess, tears welling up in her eyes.

'Oh my god she's getting all emotional!' teased Alice.

'Seriously,' said Kat earnestly, 'you need to think about this

right now. The department's open in the morning. Go in and talk to them about it. We want you back Jessie my love. We want you back.'
They embraced again. 'But then you'll both leave next year and I'll be all on my own,' she sobbed indistinctly into Kat's shoulder.
'No you won't, silly,' her friend reassured, 'I'm applying to do an MA and Alice can't leave, Morrisons would have to close down.'
'Yeah, that's right,' confirmed Alice, 'no one stacks shelves like I do!'
Jess looked anxiously across at Sam. 'There's a lot to consider,' she hesitated, 'I have to talk to Mum and Dad and Sam, obviously.'
'Yes, fine, of course but you should still get your name down. Tell the faculty you're coming back, you can always change your mind,' insisted Kat.
'You're probably right but I can't think at the moment; it's all so sudden and that lager's gone straight to my head.'
'No change there then,' grinned Alice.

It transpired that there were no spare tickets to be had for The Futurists so Jess decided to take Sam into town for some food and to show him the Leeds nightlife. They sat together on the bed in the loft after the girls had left for the concert. It was a beautiful room. There were two windows let into the sloping ceiling and the bright June evening light flooded in. Apart from the stairwell it was the full floor area of the house, which gave ample space for a double bed, built in wardrobe, already filling with the girls' stuff, and a desk in the alcove by the door.
'I can't believe one of them didn't take this when that girl moved out,' muttered Sam.
'It gets pretty freezing up here in the winter apparently.'
'Even so, did you see how tiny those two bedrooms are?'
'I know but they spend quite a bit of time at Dan and Henry's.'
Sam had very briefly met the two boyfriends earlier when they came to pick the girls up. The plan had been to get to the Union early to avoid the crush but predictably they were running late.

Jess knew them from the first year and the word on the net was that they were both very settled couples. The boys lived in a larger house nearby with two other lads.
'Why didn't they all move in together for the third year,' wondered Sam.
'What?' laughed Jess, 'you expect boys to show that kind of commitment?'
'I know, and actually it's probably sensible in some ways to stay as they are for another year but can you see them carrying on like this after that?'
Jess understood what Sam meant. There were all sorts of issues to consider about returning, not least their relationship.
'What do you think about me coming back?' she asked looking deep into his eyes. Sam thought for a moment.
'You'd be crazy not to,' he said eventually. Jess squeezed his hand.
'What about us though?' she asked anxiously.

They caught the bus into town and walked along The Headrow to a small vegetarian restaurant Jess knew called Eggs & Co. It was in one of the smaller arcades off King Charles Street that ran down to the main pedestrianised shopping area of the Victoria Quarter. Jess knew one of the waitresses and a quick text had secured them a table for two.
The restaurant was packed and though Jess was able to introduce Sam to her friend Ellie, there was no time to talk.
'I would order as soon as you can,' she said handing them menus, 'it's a forty-minute wait at the moment. Do you want a bottle of house white to start off with?'
'Please love, and could we have some garlic bread or something?'
'I'll see what I can do,' grimaced her friend, drawing a finger across her throat.
The décor in Eggs & Co was fairly spartan, whitewashed walls, sanded floorboards and a random assortment of stripped Utility dining tables with bent wood chairs; charity shop chic.
'My Gran used to have a dining table just like this,' said Jess, tracing the grooved rectangular detail with her finger.

'I bet it was stained walnut brown and polished till it gleamed,' smiled Sam.
'Yes,' nodded Jess, 'it looks strange stripped like this but I don't dislike it.'
Ellie arrived with the wine and a large plate of garlic bread.
'You owe me big time,' she hissed as the people on the next table asked when they might be getting their starter, implying that Sam and Jess had pushed in. Ellie explained that the garlic bread had been pre-ordered and hurried away to chase up theirs.
Jess poured a generous measure of wine for each of them and they clinked glasses and drank thirstily. She was glad in a way that they had not been able to get tickets for the concert. It meant she could spend more time with Sam and show him her adopted home city. It was great to be back and for the first time in ages she felt completely relaxed, despite the dilemma about resuming her studies running constantly in the back of her mind.
'Seen anything you fancy?' she asked, chewing on a savoury honeycomb of garlic bread.
'The vegetable green curry looks good to me,' said Sam, hoping Jess had not noticed that it was the cheapest main on the menu.
'Do you like Thai food?' she asked. Sam nodded, trying to disguise the fact that he had no idea it was a Thai recipe.
'I'm not keen on lemongrass; I think it has a funny flavour and I can't stand that rubbery bean curd stuff or Tofu I think it is.'
'Oh yeah, I never cook with it, or Quorn. If you're that desperate to eat meat, eat meat I say.'
'So why did you choose it?'
'Dunno; I guess I was rushing,' he fudged.
'Did you give Matt some money?' Sam nodded. 'So you're skint, right?' Another nod. 'Why didn't you tell me?' A shrug. 'Just order what you really want. This is my treat. I'm feeling blissfully chilled and happy and I want you to feel the same.'
'But,' she held up her hand decisively to silence him so he just gave in and returned to the menu.
'I'm going to have the lentil lasagne with a green salad,' said Jess.
'I'll have the same then. Shall we share a portion of fries?'
Ellie arrived back and they ordered. As Sam handed the menus

over, he said he liked the name of the restaurant.
'Well that's a shame because Robbie's just decided to change it.'
'Oh, why's that then?' asked Sam.
'Vegans!'
'But most of your food is suitable for Vegans,' laughed Jess incredulously.
'Oh yeah but is that good enough? They said we might as well call the place Steak and Co and threatened a boycott.'
'Unbelievable. So what's the new name going to be?' asked Sam.
'I'm not supposed to say.'
'How about Shoots and Leaves?' he suggested.
'Sounds like a garden centre,' giggled Jess as Ellie was called away by another impatient customer.

'I'll take you to my favourite bar now,' said Jess as they left the restaurant.
They walked back up to The Headrow and through a tall glass roofed shopping mall called The Light.
'This is impressive,' said Sam looking around, 'a sort of contemporary version of the Victorian arcades I suppose.'
'Yeah, the Modern Quarter! They're building so much new stuff up this side of town, it's like Shanghai or something.'
'The Yorkshire Tiger!'
'Kind of.'
Jess led the way into a very crowded Vodka bar called Bar Acuda. Dance music was pounding from floor and the atmosphere was vibrant. Sam began to shoulder his way to the bar.
'What do you want?' he called.
'Get the two for one on a stick of shots. I'll wait over in the chill zone,' said Jess pointing the way.
This was the first time they had been on a proper night out together. In truth it was a long time since either of them been out drinking shots. Sam arrived eventually with two sticks of shot glasses. They chinked the first two and downed them.
'Woo!' cried Jess, 'mine was peppermint, what was yours?'

'Same I suppose. Tasted like toothpaste!'
They downed the next one.
'Apricot!' cried Sam, 'I liked that one.'
'This is brilliant!' laughed Jess, 'I have so missed this kind of thing! Let's get totally wasted!'
They wanted to dance but it was not a good idea to leave drinks lying around so they tossed off the rest of the shots and barged their way onto the floor.
'I love this trance music,' said Jess, who stood still and swayed to the thumping electronic beat waving her arms above her head. The alcohol was hitting her now and she felt a sudden rush of euphoria. She leapt at Sam and clung to his shoulders.
'I love you so much!' she shouted in his ear. 'I'm so, so happy!'

After they had danced for a while the first flush of the vodka began to wear off and Jess began to look very unsteady. Sam steered her off the floor and back into the chill zone.
'I'm so dizzy,' she moaned. 'I don't think I can stand up.'
'I'm taking you outside for some air,' said Sam. He noticed an exit at the side of the room and half carried her through it. They emerged into a large courtyard.
'Is there anywhere we can sit for a moment mate?' he asked one of the burly overcoated doormen.
'Some benches over there pal,' he muttered, pointing to the opposite end of the square.
In the end Sam took Jess in his arms like a child and carried her over to the seating. He lay her on a bench and put his jacket over her but she immediately sat up with her hand over her mouth.
'Gonna throw up!' she slurred and before he could do anything, she puked copiously all over his coat.
'Oh god, I'm so sorry,' she groaned.
'It's ok,' said Sam who was also starting to feel the effect of the alcohol now.
'Do you want me to get you some water?' Jess was now kneeling on the bench retching over the back of it, but there was nothing left to come out. She nodded, so he hung his jacket over the end of the backrest to drip and weaved his way back to the bar.

'You're not coming back in here pal,' growled the bouncer, 'not in that state.'
'I just need to get some water for my friend,' said Sam as carefully as he could, 'she's been ill.'
'Well get it somewhere else. You're not going back in.'
'I'll only be a minute,' said Sam trying to push past him. He grabbed Sam's arm roughly and bundled him to the side of the entrance.
'You are going to get hurt in a minute sonny,' he snarled, pushing his face right up to Sam's.
'Ok, ok,' said Sam trying to back away as a rowdy group of girls spilled out of the bar. One of them looked across at Sam.
'You couldn't just go back inside and get some water for my friend?' he asked hopefully. She opened her bag and handed him a half full bottle of mineral water and walked off without saying a word. 'Thanks!' he called after her. The bouncer released him and he weaved his way unsteadily back over to the benches. His coat was still hanging where he had left it, but Jess was nowhere to be seen.

Matt was sitting at Sam's laptop looking at debt counselling websites. He had three credit card accounts each with a balance exceeding ten thousand pounds. They were all coming to the end of their interest free periods and suddenly all those enticing offers to move his debt had dried up. One thing was certain, he would not be able manage when the interest kicked in. He had chosen a site that claimed to be a charity and to have the lowest arrangement fees. He emailed an enquiry form over and rapidly received a response from an advisor called Alan. He was not pushy and his advice seemed sensible, pointing out that Matt had not defaulted on anything yet apart from his tenancy, which he had managed to resolve anyway. The first thing to do was contact each of the credit card providers and explain that he was not going to be able to afford the interest when it fell due. In the short term as long as he could come up with the minimum monthly repayment he would stay out of trouble but his debt would begin to grow alarmingly. As Alan rightly said, there were options and he still had time to explore them; there was no need to panic, yet. And panic was exactly what he had done.

Matt felt better for this advice and for being able to share his problem with someone who appeared to know what they were talking about, someone who was batting for him rather than protecting the interests of a massive financial corporation. For the first time, he calmly took stock of his situation. Having already sold his TV, DVD and stereo in Rochdale, his only real asset now was the car. He wondered what would happen if he tried to sell the car immediately and settle the finance. He had no idea and decided to ask Alan. He was just typing this into an email when there was a knock on the door. Matt was startled and before he could get up to answer it, Polly walked in.

'Are you decent?' she asked. She knew he was staying there because Sam had borrowed the spare key and explained what was happening over the weekend. Matt did not reply. 'Well you've scrubbed up quite well I must say,' she continued.

'Yeah, sorry I was a bit of a fright the other night,' he mumbled, wondering what the hell she wanted.

'I was just wondering if you could log off tinter for a bit darling. I want to download a movie and I'm going to need all my bandwidth. The contention ratio round here is terrible at the weekend.'

'Of course, it's your router after all. Do you mind if I just quickly finish this email?' he asked, amazed at the techno vocab of this antique lady.

'No that's fine, you hungry?'

'Um, I am actually,' Matt had not eaten since foraging an unappetising brunch from Sam's limited supplies and it was now early evening.

'I've got a lasagne in the oven that's far too big for me. I can't share it with Roly because he's a bit of a veggie like your chum. Come round when you've finished and I'll dish up.'

'I'll do that, Polly, thank you, you're a star.'

'More of a black hole at the moment I'm afraid,' she sighed, letting herself out.

What Matt had neglected to tell Alan was that he was homeless, which was in reality his most pressing need. He had been in touch with a string of acquaintances during the day but had only managed to arrange a few offers of a week or so here and there. It would tide him over and keep a roof over his head, but to sort out his finances he was going to need an address for correspondence. He had already filled in some online forms giving Sam's address; it was going to have to be his post restante for the foreseeable future. He quickly finished his email and logged off. Presumably Alan would have gone home anyway, if he existed at all.

Matt tapped on Polly's door and walked in. 'Ok, I'm out of contention,' he said.

'You don't like it do you?' smiled Polly as she clicked the 'download now' button and opened the oven door in one swift movement.

'What?'

'An old biddy like me trespassing into your virtual world.'

'I think it's brilliant. My parents are totally clueless. They even find SMS an insurmountable challenge.'

'I'd be lost without my mobile,' reflected Polly as she carefully lifted a spatula of bubbling lasagne out of the foil tray and lowered it onto a plate. 'Truly irresistible; at least that's what it says on the box. Help yourself to salad.'

Matt had also helped himself to the bottle of dry white that remained in Sam's fridge.

'Fancy a glass of chenin blanc?' he asked, unscrewing the lid.

They chatted easily with each other as they ate and Matt was very frank about his financial plight.

'Can't your parents help you out a bit?' asked Polly.

'They don't know anything about all this and I don't want them to. My dad took early retirement on health grounds and they really don't have the cash to be baling me out.'

'Can't you at least stay with them for a while?'

'They moved up to Sunderland to be near Mum's family so it would mean giving up work and that would just make things worse.'

Polly told Matt about her history, a catalogue of failed relationships which always seemed to leave her out of pocket.

'Men have always treated me so badly,' she sighed, 'I honestly don't know why I'm trying so hard to find one now.'

'Is that why you first got into the World Wide Web?'
'Yes,' sighed Polly, 'I'm still registered with a string of dating agencies but I only seem to attract the attention the living dead these days.'
They finished the wine and Polly lifted a cheesecake out of the fridge.
'Fancy some pud?' she asked.
Matt nodded eagerly. Despite having consumed the lion's share of the lasagne he was still starving.
'Help yourself then, have as much as you like, I don't want any. Fancy a glass of brandy?' She poured two large tumblers and carried one over to the sofa.
'I'd better not drink too much thanks Polly, I'm working tomorrow.'
Matt often did not worked weekends but he had called the office and asked them to put him on the rota immediately. He was planning to do every shift that was going to maximise his income.
'Come and sit with me if you like,' said Polly, patting the cushion beside her on the sofa. 'It's nice having a fit young man about the place. You could always come and stay here if you get really desperate. I wouldn't charge you any rent so long as you don't mind doing one or two little odd jobs for me.'
'I might just take you up on that, Polly,' said Matt as he finished off the cheesecake.

Sam looked all round the courtyard for a sign of Jess. The shock of her disappearance had jolted him into sobriety. He picked up his jacket, carefully folded it inside out, rolled it up and stuffed it under his arm. He noticed a narrow alley leading out of the courtyard nearby and instinctively headed that way. It turned a right angle and opened out onto a wide, busy well-lit street, which was full of groups of young people; mostly raucous scantily clad girls in various states of intoxication. Suddenly, out of the corner of his eye, Sam noticed someone waving. It was Jess. She had staggered into the street and hailed a cab and was trying to call Sam on her mobile. He waved back and hurried over to where she was standing, clinging to the open

back door as if trying to prevent it from driving away. Sam ducked his head into the open passenger window.
'Do you know this lady?' asked the rather flustered driver. 'I think she is too drunk to carry.'
'She's been a little unwell,' Sam explained calmly, 'I just need to get her home as quickly as possible if you don't mind.'
The driver seemed reassured by Sam's demeanour although he did eye the parcel under his arm with a certain amount of suspicion.
'Where do you want to go?' he asked cautiously.
Sam panicked. What was the area called? Like somewhere in London. He looked across to Jess but she was resting her forehead on the roof of the car as if trying to soothe it. Suddenly he remembered. 'Hyde Park!' he cried.
The cabby decided it would be quicker to take them rather than argue about it.
'All right, get in. Quickly please!' he shouted.
Sam pushed Jess down into the back seat like a detective with a suspect, got in beside her and the taxi sped away.
'What is the address please?' asked the driver.
Sam looked across at Jess. Her pupils were wildly dilated; she was completely out of it. 'Can you drop us near that little Sainsburys?' he asked hopefully. It was the only landmark he could remember noticing as they walked up to the bus stop.
'Ok. I know where you mean,' called the driver.
The traffic heading out of town was light and the car sped up by the university and soon reached Hyde Park Corner. The driver took a left and asked whether it was second or third on the right.
'Third!' Sam guessed wildly. The driver turned off the main road and nosed carefully down a narrow terraced street between rows of parked cars, pulling up outside the brightly lit convenience store. Sam sighed with relief. The next problem was going to be finding enough cash to pay the fare.
'Eight pounds fifty please.'
Sam took a crumpled ten-pound note out of his trouser pocket. 'Thanks for your trouble mate, keep the change!' he called. He helped Jess out onto the pavement, slammed the door and banged twice on the roof. It sped away, turning right by the

entrance to the store. The weekend had hardly begun and Sam was already totally skint. Jess was slumped against him, barely conscious. He knew roughly the direction they must go and slung his arm around her, half carrying her down the street like a wounded comrade.

Sixteen

Despite the excesses of the night, the vodka did not give Jess a bad head in the morning. She could remember the meal and going to Bar Acuda but she had absolutely no idea how she had managed to get home and into bed. Sam was deeply asleep with his back to her. She turned towards him and wrapped her arm across his chest, gently hugging his back. He instinctively turned towards her in his sleep, folding her tightly into him. This was bliss. She lay there looking out through the Velux window as the dawn sky turned from light grey to a wash of pale pink. Jess still could not believe she was in this room, the very one she had found and lost without ever moving into. It was incredible that this opportunity had arisen and that, if her parents could manage, she would be able to restart her life from the very point at which it was interrupted one year previously, with the same dear, dear friends as flatmates. Winning the lottery could not feel as good as this.

Sam moved in his sleep muttering something incomprehensible. It reminded her that returning to Leeds would have serious implications for their relationship. Yes, it was only about an hour on the motorway to Nottingham but she would be immersed in the rich, enthralling pick and mix of student life while he was stuck in a much less appetizing and poorly paid job with very limited prospects. She had seen it happen so many times; the partner left at home falling behind, losing touch, left out by the fast moving events of the undergraduate world. She made a promise to herself that she would never ever let that happen even if it meant getting the bus home every weekend, she would not become estranged from Sam!

Suddenly his eyes flicked open. They looked at each other and smiled.

'Hello sleepyhead,' she laughed, kissing him softly on the forehead.
'You made it through the night then?' he teased.
'What do you mean?'
'Don't remember the vodka shots then?'
'I can remember going into Sharky's but everything after that is a complete blank.'
'Sharky's?'
'Bar Acuda; Barracuda!' she explained, 'see what they did there?'
'That's stupid, the vowel lengths are different.'
'Don't be so pedantic. Anyway, enlighten me, how did I get home.'
'Well, shall we start from where you threw up all over my jacket?'
'Oh no, that's awful. I'll get banned.'
'Barred from Bar Acuda? I doubt it, that all happened outside.'
'I think I vaguely remember lying on one of those benches.'
Sam ran through the sequence of events up to their arrival back at the house.
'Oh dear, I'm really sorry. I'm obviously a bit out of practice. And all that lovely food from gone to waste.'
'I can scrape it off my jacket and microwave it if you like.'
'Oh please!' cried Jess, clamping her hand over her mouth. 'What happened to it anyway?'
'I put it in a plastic bag and left it in the bathroom. I think it's probably beyond redemption now.'
'I'm so sorry. I have absolutely no recollection of it happening. How can something just be wiped from your memory like that?'
'Maybe it never got in there in the first place. Do you remember flagging down that taxi?' Jess concentrated for a moment then shook her head. They both laughed.
'Oh well, no harm done I suppose, except to your poor jacket,' said Jess giving him a conciliatory hug. 'Do you know if it's machine washable?'
'Haven't a clue,' said Sam. 'I can however confirm that it has never been near a washing machine.'
'Right!' said Jess leaping out of bed. 'You stay there and have a

snooze. I'm going to make you a nice cup of tea and see if I can de-puke your jacket.'
She took a very brief silky wrap out of her case and slipped it over her shoulders.
'Sexy!' growled Sam.
'La Senza!' Jess enunciated, stressing each syllable.
'Expensive!' said Sam with the same intonation.
Jess knelt on the bed and slid a shoulder provocatively out of the wrap. Sam sat up and pulled her towards him, kissing her hungrily as the silky material rippled elegantly to the floor. His jacket would have to wait a while for the non-bio.

Since finishing his exams Tom had continued to spend most of the time in his bedroom. At first Mark and Christine were not over concerned about this; they just assumed he was relaxing after working so hard. In fact Tom had become completely immersed in the virtual world of a multiplayer online game called Ultimate Pursuit. It was a mixture of combat and vehicle racing that took place in the post apocalyptic world of a fantasy desert state called Samira. Most land masses had been devastated by an immense earthquake and tidal wave but Samira was mountainous, with settlements in high plateau areas and had survived despite massive structural damage. Participants teamed up to build their own customised vehicles either through barter or victory in combat. Tom had grown bored with his gothic fantasy combat games with their monsters and auks. The appeal of this game was that it took place in a recognizable world populated with familiar if somewhat eccentric human characters. He had taken on a persona called Ethan, teamed up with three other players to form a chapter called Roadkillers and between them they had built two heavily armed and well-equipped high performance vehicles. The problem with this game was that if you got killed, you stayed dead. You could rejoin the game as a new personality of course but there was no restart button for your old character. Tom had become very attached to Ethan and was desperate not to lose him but things were going badly; the Killers had antagonised a very powerful group called ButcherBoyz who were out to destroy them. This meant you could not relax for a minute. Two of Tom's chapter were from the States, which was good in a way because much of the action took place in North American time but in reality it meant that players in the UK got very little sleep. Without realising it, Tom had allowed this parallel existence to become more important to him than the real world; he had become addicted to the game.

ButcherBoyz were a bigger and better equipped group but they lacked the quickness and dexterity of Roadkillers. Ethan was racing along a desert road with a BB vehicle in hot pursuit. It was gaining on them and his co-driver Ramirez was blasting them with the high calibre canon mounted in the rear of their pick up truck. The chasing vehicle was swerving all over the road to avoid this deadly fusillade and in the back of the truck one of the crew was poised with a rocket launcher. In a matter of seconds they would be within range. Ramirez was pounding them but they were heavily armoured and could withstand his barrage. Suddenly the BB gunner got to his feet and put the launcher to his shoulder. Ramirez hammered on the roof of the cab yelling 'incoming!' and Ethan tried to take evasive action but it was too late; the missile piled into the back of the vehicle and the explosion blew Ramirez to bits. Ethan still had some control and he swerved off the road into a rocky area where the enemy truck would not be able to follow. Grabbing a heavy machine gun and a sack of ammo he raced into the boulder-strewn landscape and found a sheltered area with a good field of fire. One thing was certain; they were not going to take him alive and he would take at least one of them with him. If it was the last thing he did, he would avenge the death of his buddy Ramirez.

With his jacket happily gyrating away on mixed synthetics, Sam and Jess sat down to breakfast in the living room. The girls' rooms were empty. If they had made it to bed at all, it must have been at the boys' place. The plan was to get out early and head for the English Department.

'Are you ok with this?' asked Jess anxiously, 'I was lying in bed thinking about it this morning. It doesn't always work, you

know, being apart like that even if the distances aren't vast.'
'Look, silly,' said Sam, placing his hand over hers, 'this is your golden chance. It's like rewinding a video; pressing the replay button. It's the only chance you'll ever get to pick up where you left off. You have to take it, you know you do.'
'Oh Sam,' she sighed, 'I do know it, but I'm so happy with you and I don't want to jeopardize that either. Are you sure it will work out?'
'Look,' he said softly, placing his forehead against hers, 'there's nothing tying me to Nottingham. I can hand in my notice, give up the room and be out of there in a couple of weeks if necessary. I'm sure I could find a job up here easily enough.'
'Would you really do that for me?'
'I'd do anything for you, my love,' he whispered into her ear. And as they clung together a wave of emotion surged through them, a feeling they had never experienced before, a feeling that left them both breathless.

It was a lovely morning and they decided to walk through the park to campus. Spring had segued into early summer now but the leaves on the lime trees were still young and tender, almost translucent in the bright sunlight. They walked arm in arm and in step so their thighs pressed tightly together, as lovers do. Jess said she should ring Alice and Kat to arrange to meet later but neither of them really wanted to. They were greedy with each other's time, hungry for each other's company. It was as though they were in a cocoon, a bubble of love, and an aura seemed to glow around them, so much so that people walking by would smile, basking in this radiance.

The English Department consisted of two spacious adjoining Victorian town houses which were largely unmodernised, retaining even their gardens. It was little oasis in the chaotic jumble of architecture that the expanding university had thrown at the landscape. Jess led the way up the front steps and through the main entrance into reception. Something reminded her of the very first time she walked into this building on the day of her interview; the sense of excitement tinged with fear, the newness of it all combined with the tasteful elegance of the beautiful old building. Sam looked around in wonder at the superb panelling on the walls and the painted plasterwork of the ceiling; the way it retained the character of an elegant residence was pleasing.

A middle-aged woman walked through carrying an armful for folders.

'Hello stranger!' she cried. It was Veronica, the head of administration. Jess was surprised to be instantly recognized in this way. She walked up to Jess squeezed her arm. 'How's Mum?' she asked confidentially.

'She's rallied a little thanks,' Jess answered, 'a few weeks ago we thought we were losing her but they changed the medication and it worked a minor miracle.'

'That's good,' smiled Veronica.

'Oh, this is Sam by the way; friend from Nottingham.' Jess explained.

After briefly exchanged greetings Veronica turned back to Jess.

'I had a tip off you might be calling in this morning. It's good timing actually, Prof. Jenkins is in and it would be a good idea to have a word with her if you are thinking of coming back in October. I take it that's why you came?' Jess nodded. Veronica picked up the phone on the reception desk and punched three keys. After a brief conversation she replaced the handset.

'She can see you right away if you'd care to follow me. You make yourself at home in the common room, Sam,' she smiled pointing through an archway into a decoratively tiled and panelled chapel-like room with fine stained glass windows.

'See you in a bit,' waved Jess.

Sam had spotted a cash machine outside the Union as they walked to the department. He decided to run back and do a balance enquiry, which revealed he was even closer to his overdraft limit than he had feared. If he spent more than twenty pounds it would trigger a thirty-five pound penalty. He grimly resigned himself to the near certainty of incurring this charge and three days of virtual starvation until payday. It was a depressing prospect. He wandered slowly back to the department to find Jess sitting on the steps waiting for him.

'Thought you'd done a runner!' she laughed.

'I assumed you'd be way longer than that. Was everything ok?'

'Yep. I just need to confirm in writing by the end of the month and restart my student loan and I'm good to go.'
'Cool.'
'Yeah. Let's go celebrate. Where did you go just then by the way?'
Sam decided to own up. It was pointless trying to conceal his personal credit crunch.
'I just did a balance enquiry.'
'And?'
'Close to the edge,' he grimaced.
'Ok. Looks like lunch is on me then!'
'No Jess, that's not fair.'
'It's absolutely fine. You can treat me when 'Thine is the Kingdom' wins the Man Booker.'
'I wouldn't hold your breath,' muttered Sam.

There was a knock on Tom's door and Mark walked in.
'Your Mother and I think you've played quite enough on this game now,' he said firmly.
'Not now Dad, please,' Tom cried anxiously.
'No, I'm sorry Tom but it's taking over your life and it's got to stop. You've had a break after your exams and that's fair enough but it's time to do something else now so just log off or whatever you do and leave it alone for a bit.'
Tom was clearly not listening as he furiously manipulated his handset.
'Tom, listen to me please. I've tried to reason with you and it's clearly a waste of time so I am going down stairs to turn the router off now.'
'No. Dad you don't understand I have to finish this!'
Without another word, Mark turned and grimly left the room heading towards the stairs. Tom looked round to call after his father but this moment of distraction proved fatal. Ethan was exposed for a second and one of the BB gunners got a clear shot at him. His chest was ripped apart by a hail of automatic fire. No one could survive that kind of punishment. The screen froze as the connection was lost with the image of him flung backwards onto the rock face by the force of the impact. Tom

put his head in his hands and wept; Ethan was dead.

'I wish Jess was here,' Mark said to Christine as they sat together in the kitchen, 'she'd know how to get through to him and talk him round.'

'I can't understand why he hasn't come down,' said Christine, 'are you sure you turned the router off?'

'Certain,' he replied, ' I pulled the plug out.'

'I suppose I'd better go up and have a word with him,' she sighed. 'I do hope he hasn't been playing that bloody game all the time instead of doing his revision.'

'It never seemed to be on when I looked in.'

'They just minimise the screen when they hear you coming though. You have to check the icons along the bottom apparently.'

'Oh well, it's too late now,' sighed Mark.

Christine got wearily to her feet and headed for the hall.

'This really is not fair,' hissed Mark angrily, 'we've got enough on without having to worry about him. He's a selfish, spoiled little brat, that's what he is.'

'You stay down here please love; you'll only antagonise him. Let me handle it,' said Christine as she left the room.

She tapped on Tom's door and walked in. He was still hunched over his desk sobbing uncontrollably. She walked towards him and touched him on the shoulder.

'What is it Tommy?' she asked softly, then gasped as he turned towards her. She hurried to the door.

'Mark! Mark! Come quickly please, come now!' she shouted urgently.

Sam and Jess were sitting at a balcony table on the top floor restaurant of Harvey Nicks looking out over a crowded street. As Jess was still feeling a bit delicate she just ordered a bowl of soup and a mineral water.

'This is the life,' she smiled as they clinked glasses.

'Have you eaten here before?' asked Sam.

'God no!' laughed Jess, 'though these prices seem quite reasonable really; a cunning plan to lure you into the store I expect.'

Her phone rang; it was Alice.
'Hi babe,' she sang lifting it to her ear. 'Don't apologize, we're fine thanks, except I got totally battered at Sharky's last night. Yeah, lost the tolerance for that surgical spirit they serve up as vodka I expect! How were The Futurists? Oh wicked, I'm so jealous! No, don't worry, we had a lovely meal at Eggs & Co.' She grinned at Sam and recounted the episode with his jacket, then listened for a moment. 'Yeah, I saw Prof Jenkins this morning and its all good. They said a little bird had told them I would be calling in. Now who might that have been, then? I just need to run it by Mum and Dad and confirm it in writing, so hold the room please! I know! I can't believe it either. It's just so perfect. You really are the most lovely, wonderful person Allie.' She listened again for a few moments. 'They want to cook a meal at their place for us all rather than hitting town tonight. Does that sound ok to you?' she asked Sam. He nodded and gave a thumbs-up sign. 'Yeah, that's fine with us darling. Do you need any shopping? Sure? Ok, we'll get some beer and wine and choccies then. We'll be back about tea time probably, that ok? Yeah, yeah, great ok then darling, love you loads, bye, bye, bye.'
She placed her phone on the table and stretched luxuriously in the sunshine. 'I'm so happy!' she laughed. 'You ok with that?'
'Yes, it's really kind of them. Are you sure they don't mind. I thought they had this massive bender planned.'
'I think last night exceeded expectations by the sound of it. They never got to bed at all. Al has only just woken up and the others are still spark out. That means we can have a nice afternoon shopping together!'
Sam smiled. As long as he didn't actually have to spend any money, that suited him fine.

They arrived back at the house just before six, having spent the afternoon wandering round the arcades of the Victoria Quarter. Jess had tried on a few things in some of the classy boutiques but had not bought anything.

The living room had been transformed. A table and four chairs had been borrowed from somewhere and butted up to the

girls' little drop leaf. A relatively clean double bed sheet had been commandeered as a cloth and balloons and streamers hung from the light fitting. Blu-tacked to the wall was a hastily written poster saying, 'Welcome Home Jess!' The latest Futurists album was blasting out from the ipod docking station. Jess ran to the little kitchen, her eyes filling with tears.
'Oh guys, this is lovely!' she cried, 'you are so, so kind.'
The two girls turned from their chopping boards and they all embraced in a big three-way hug. Sam tried to enter with two bulging carrier bags but there was no space.
'Hi Sam,' said Kat, 'what have you got there?'
'Mostly wine and beer and some cheese, oh and this needs to go in the fridge.' He pulled out a bottle of champagne and handed it to her.
'Oh that's really sweet. Look Al, Sam's bought some bubbly!'
'You two look busy,' said Jess, 'what are you making.'
'We've got the easy bit really,' said Alice, 'the boys are doing starters and sweets at their place and bringing it with them so all we have to do is make a load of salad.'
'And this!' cried Kat lifting a large white plastic bag out of the fridge after depositing the champagne.
'Steak night!' cheered the two girls in unison.

Mark raced up the stairs two at a time and burst into Tom's room to find Christine kneeling on the floor pressing a damp flannel to his forearm.
'Look what he's done,' she shrieked peeling back the flannel to reveal a bloody mess where Tom had punched the word ETHAN into his skin by jabbing it with the point of a pair of compasses. There was blood all over his desk and he looked faint.
'Who the hell is Ethan?' asked Mark.
'Never mind about that now!' cried Christine, 'go and fetch the car, we have to get him to casualty. I'm not sure if his tetanus is up to date.'
'Shouldn't we call an ambulance?' asked Mark.
'Just get the car!' screamed Christine.
She wanted to go with them to casualty but Mark persuaded her

to stay. They might be gone for hours and it would all be too much for her. Mark quickly made her a cup of strong tea and helped her into bed. She was shaking uncontrollably with a mixture of shock and exhaustion.

'Will Mum be ok?' asked Tom sullenly as they sped towards Nottingham. Mark somehow managed to restrain himself from venting the intense anger he felt towards his son. 'We'll all be ok,' he said straining to keep his voice even. The effort showed through and Tom sensed his mood.

'You're really mad at me aren't you Dad?' he said in a dull monotone.

'Whatever I feel will have to wait. We have things to do now and it would be best to just get them done and get home as fast as we can. We'll talk about it later, ok?'

'I need to talk now,' said Tom, 'I wish Jess was here, she'd know what to do.'

'We all wish Jess was here but she is taking a break that she thoroughly deserves. I don't know what she's going to think when she gets home.'

'Can't turn my back for five minutes,' said Tom in a silly voice.

Mark had never found it easy to talk to Tom and despite his best efforts to be impartial, he had always been closer to Jess. She seemed to have inherited more of his characteristics, not all of which she was grateful for, and a sort of genetic empathy had developed between them. Tom was much more like his mother and they had a much easier relationship.

'What is it you want to say then?' asked Mark after a lengthy pause.

'Well, sorry obviously, for mutilating myself and more importantly for upsetting Mum.'

'Well that's a start,' grunted Mark.

'You've never really liked me have you Dad?'

'What on earth makes you say that?' asked Mark incredulously.

'It's ok you know; you don't have to like your kids, I don't mind. Well I mind a bit but I can handle it.'

'But it isn't true.'

'I'm not saying you hate me or anything; it's just that you're disappointed because I haven't shown any interest in the farm or

hunting and stuff. I'm not the son you ordered.'
'That doesn't worry me in the least; there's no future in it anyway. And just because I haven't tried to influence you it doesn't mean I don't care or that I'm disappointed in you.'
'Mum thinks you are.'
Since they were already on the slip road for the QMC, there was no time to take this any further. As he drove carefully towards A&E, Mark looked across at his son.
'To be continued, right?' he said pointedly but Tom did not reply. Mark pulled up in a hatched area that was reserved for emergency vehicles. 'I'll go in with you while they take your details then I'll find a place to park,' he said. Tom shrugged indifferently.

After he had moved the car, Mark caught up with Tom in one of the curtained cubicles that lined a corridor beyond the waiting room. The curtain parted and a young nurse walked in carrying a medical record folder.
'Hi,' he said, 'my name is Ross; I'm a triage nurse. That means I do some initial treatment and assess the damage, ok?' Tom and Mark nodded. 'Good, so you are?'
'Tom Beresford.'
'Good, thank you, and you must be dad?' Mark nodded again.
Ross looked at the wound and without making any comment or judgement reached for a pack in a mobile cabinet next to the bed. He tore it open and pulled out a piece of gauze.
'This is just an antiseptic wipe to clean you up a bit,' he explained, 'I'm afraid it's going to sting.'
Tom winced as he gently dabbed his forearm, which was already looking bruised and swollen.
'We really need to let the air get to this and dry it up so it can start to heal,' he explained. He applied a very light, breathable dressing. 'Someone will be along in a minute to give you a tetanus jab and then I think we'll let you go. We'll send a report to your GP and you need to see them in a few days to make sure it's on the mend.' He paused, 'there's a few questions I have to ask about how and why this happened though.'

To compound the problem with the menu, the boys turned up with a massive pan of minestrone soup, complete with large chunks of ham hock floating around in it. Jess was mortified.
'I'm so sorry,' she groaned, 'I can't believe I never told you Sam doesn't eat meat!'
'Well I suppose we should have figured out he was a veggie when you said you'd been to Eggs & Co,' said Alice generously.
'And it's not as if we said we were going to cook a meal for you,' added Kat.
'I know but I feel such a prat,' whined Jess.
'I'll be fine with that salad and some cheese or something. I promise it won't bother me at all if you're tucking into steaks,' Sam reassured them.
'Oh dear,' said Dan, rubbing his chin thoughtfully, 'what on earth are we going to do with Sam's piece?'
'I can think of a couple of pigs who might be persuaded to stick their fat snouts in the trough,' said Alice, playfully thumping him in the shoulder.
'Moi?' said Dan innocently, 'well we wouldn't want to see it go to waste would we Henry old man?'
'Indeed no, Daniel; that would be nothing short of a crime.'
A portion of golden vegetable cup a soup was rustled up for Sam and Kat found a tin of tuna to go with the salad.
'That's not fair, he's got croutons!' wailed Henry.
'The Croutons,' announced Dan, 'that would be a good name for our band don't you think?'
'Yes,' said Kat, 'stale and crusty,' and she winked at Sam.
'Actually I'm not sure whether these are croutons or granite chippings,' said Sam biting gingerly on one.
'Typical!' cried Henry, striking an affronted pose, 'he ruins our beautifully crafted menu then has the cheek to complain about the vegetarian alternative!'
'No, no, it's lovely I assure you,' said Sam, 'it just appears to have bullets in it.'
'Bullets innit,' said Alice.
Jess popped the bubbly, poured into a random assortment of glasses and tumblers and her return to the fold was toasted with

gusto.

The boys had thrown all their creative energies into the soup and were forced to resort to microwave golden syrup puddings for the sweet.

'This might have beef suet in it, Sam' said Henry solicitously as he passed them round. 'We won't be offended if you'd rather not take the chance.'

'I'll risk it, thanks,' smiled Sam.

'There's a party on Henrietta Street and we're all invited if you fancy going on there,' said Dan as they drank coffee.

'Cool,' said Alice, 'I'm up for it, how about you guys?' she asked looking over to Sam and Jess.

'I'm bushed,' she said, 'how about you Sam?'

'Why don't you lot go and leave us to wash up?' suggested Sam. 'I think we're a bit off the pace at the moment.'

'We'll soon change that,' grinned Kat.

'Don't let any strange people in,' said Alice as the four set out to continue their evening.

'They all just left the building,' said Jess as she waved them off.

Seventeen

'We never did stuff like that when we were kids did we?' asked Mark, who was having a Sunday lunchtime beer in the kitchen with Peter Spencer.

Christine was in bed, exhausted by the events of the previous day. Mark had looked in on Tom a couple of times and decided to leave him to sleep, or pretend to sleep.

'Like self harm you mean?' asked Peter.

'Yes, if that's what you want to call it.'

'I'm not saying it never happened but I really can't remember coming across it.'

'I'll be glad when Jess is back, I just don't know what to say to him.'

'What time is she due?'

'The plan is to have Sunday lunch about six. She's going to ring me when they set off.'

'Is Sam coming?'

'No. That's another thing I've messed up I'm afraid,' sighed Mark as he told Peter about his outburst the previous week. 'He's fine about it but I think Jess decided to give it a bit longer before letting me loose on him again.'

'Don't be so hard on yourself,' said Peter. 'I don't have anything like the challenges you have to face but I've still managed to allow my son to get into such a state that he's tried to take his own life twice.'

'Oh dear, what a pair of no-hopers we are; we'll have to start a support group.'

'Yeah, the Crap Father's Club,' agreed Peter with a grim smile.

'I'll be president,' said Mark ruefully.

'You're not blaming yourself for what Tom did are you?'

'Well, I pulled the plug didn't I? He was on the edge and I

pushed him over. I jumped in with both feet and got it all wrong as usual.'
'Is that what Chris feels?'
'She hasn't said as much but yes, I think she does.'
'You can't be expected to understand the implications of playing these multiplayer online games.'
'You've lost me there already, mate.'
'Believe it or not, I come across it quite a lot on the matrimonial side. Young, mostly male, gamers are getting so immersed in their virtual personality and the alternative reality of the game that they neglect their partner to the point of marital break down.'
'Is that who this Ethan person was then, Tom's alter ego?'
'I expect so. This artificial world becomes more real than their own lives to some people.'
'You're a mine of bloody information today aren't you?' joked Mark. Peter had just been advising him to fit a decent padlock to his diesel storage tank because fuel prices had risen so much that thieves were going round draining them into containers in the back of transit vans.
'Your friendly neighbourhood lawyer,' smiled Peter.
The phone rang and Mark jumped to his feet to answer it.
'Hello darling, have you had a lovely time? Good. Yes we're all fine thanks; well we had a bit of bother with Tommy but I'll tell you about it when you get home. About six, that's perfect, drive safely, love you too, bye.'

Sam and Jess had woken to an empty house again.
'I'm beginning to wonder if you're going to be a bit lonely living here,' Sam reflected.
'Oh I wouldn't worry, it's just end of year excess. Things will settle down next term,' Jess reassured him. 'Perhaps they just want to give us some time on our own together anyway.'
'It has been nice,' said Sam, walking up behind her and wrapping her tightly in his arms.
'You're squashing me!' she squealed making no attempt to wriggle away.
'Have you enjoyed it?' he asked.

'Oh yes, but I am still worried about what will happen to us when I move up here.'
'We'll be fine, trust me,' he reassured her.
It was too early to think of ringing one of the girls so they packed their bags, tidied the room and set off for a walk in the park. Eventually they came to an old fashioned playground with a brightly painted wooden roundabout.
'Look,' said Sam, 'I used to love these. You never see them these days.'
'Probably failed the risk assessment. Far too much fun for the modern child.'
Jess sat on it and Sam pushed her gently round. He stood back watching her slowly rotating and she waved to him, a little girl wave. She jumped off while it was still moving and skidded into his arms. There were some swings too but only a couple of them still had seats on. They sat side-by-side and chatted as they lazily rocked backwards and forwards.
'This is fun,' laughed Sam, 'they should have playgrounds for grown ups!'
'Almost grown ups,' smiled Jess. 'This will all be gone soon though, they built a sensible new play area down the road; all bark chippings and safe apparatus. Look you can see where the slide and see-saw used to be.'
Her phone rang, 'it's Alice,' she cried and answered while still swinging.
'Hi babe, you're up early. Well, awake then. Full English! It's not really Sam's cup of tea and anyway we already liberated some of your Coco Pops. The Orient? Ok, well we'll wander over and meet you there. What time are you likely to have roused the others by? Ok, see you then, ciao.'

'Do you want any lunch love?' asked Mark as he handed Christine a cup of tea.
She shook her head. 'No thanks, have you had anything?'
'Just a sandwich. Jess rang, she's fine, had a great time and should be home by six so I'll put that piece of topside in at about four.'
'Thanks love. Has Tommy surfaced yet?'

‘No. I’ve looked in on him but he’s dead to the world. It’s probably the best thing for him.’
‘All the same, I think we should wake him. The dressing might need changing. I’ll get up and do it now.’
‘Are you sure you’re up to it?’
‘Yes, I’ll be fine. Can you bring the all the stuff up and some boiled water?’
Christine put on her dressing gown and walked unsteadily over to Tom’s room. She tapped on the door and went in. He was awake, lying staring at the ceiling. She sat on the edge of the bed and gently placed her hand on his forehead.
‘How are you feeling love?’ she asked softly.
‘Sorry,’ he said miserably.
‘How do you mean?’
‘I’m sorry for making you bad again.’
‘I’ll be fine,’ she whispered, ‘I meant how is your arm. Is it hurting?’
‘It’s throbbing a bit,’ he said looking down to where it lay on top of the covers.
‘Shall we take a look at it now?’ she asked gently.
He nodded like a child and it took Christine back to the times when he had been poorly and off school and she had nursed him back to health. She suddenly felt she was going to weep but fought it back. She leant forward and kissed him on the forehead.
‘I love you, you know,’ she whispered.
‘Love you too Mum,’ he mumbled.
Mark tapped on the door and walked in with a bowl of water, cotton wool and various dressings.
‘How’s it looking?’ he asked anxiously.
‘We’re about to find out,’ said Christine gently peeling back the micropore tape that held the dressing in place. The wound still looked very sore and bruised but it was dry and starting to heal already. ‘That’s not too bad,’ she breathed. ‘I don’t think we need to wash it this morning. Can you have a bath instead of a shower and keep it out of the water?’ Tom nodded. He looked over to Mark.
‘I’m sorry about those things I said at the hospital, Dad.’

‘What things?’ asked Christine.
‘Oh nothing,’ said Mark hastily, ‘let’s just forget about it shall we? Peter, who seems to know all about these things, has been explaining that I probably killed your character in the game when I turned the router off and that’s what made you so upset.’
‘He was as good as dead by then and to be honest he’d been cornered by the ButcherBoyz and didn’t have a hope in hell anyway,’ Tom conceded.
‘Is that good?’ asked Mark, looking helplessly across to Christine.

The evocative motion of the swings seemed to trigger a juvenile mood in Sam and Jess. When they had finished in the playground, they raced each other to the bandstand, played a game of dobby off ground, which is tricky with only two people, followed by hide and seek, then rolled down a steep grassy bank until they were dizzy. Sam pretended to be a robot and made his eyes go funny but Jess wasn’t scared. They walked arm in arm as fast as they could and passers by gave them a wide berth, assuming they were still drunk from Saturday night. They arrived at the Orient Café looking breathless and dishevelled.
‘What on earth have you two been up to?’ asked Kat and she bit into a sausage, skewered whole on her fork.
‘We’ve been playing in the park!’ laughed Jess.
‘Ooh I bet you have!’ said Alice.
‘You could get banged up for that sort of thing you know,’ said Henry with his mouth full of bacon.
Sam ordered a pot of tea for two and just managed to round up enough change in his pockets to pay for it.
‘Look guys,’ said Jess, ‘we’re going to head home pretty soon.’
‘But we’ve hardly seen you,’ wailed Alice.
‘Well you’ll be seeing plenty of me soon, hopefully. Are you all still planning to hitch to Morocco in July?’
‘Yeah but we’ll be back here in August; got to work full time for the rest of the hols to get some cash together. When do you think you’ll be coming up?’
‘I really can’t say at the moment. I’ll have to talk to Mum and

Dad and hand my notice in at work but I'll want to spend some time in the library before term starts to get back into it.'
'Which options are you going to do next year?' asked Kat.
'God, I haven't even begun to think of that. Have they changed since the first year?'
'No, it's pretty much the same. You can choose them online.'
'Yeah, I'll have to get on to that.' The reality of returning to student life was both daunting and exciting but Jess was now absolutely certain it was the right thing to do.
They walked back to the house and sat chatting for a bit while the boys returned the borrowed table and chairs to their rightful owners.
'It's been a brilliant weekend,' said Jess, 'and thank you so, so much for saving that room for me. You're the best friends in the whole world.'
'It'll be great to have the Leodis Angels back together,' said Alice and the three of them grouped together making pistol shapes with one hand.
'Scary,' said Sam, 'I wouldn't mess with you if I was a baddie.'
'You betta not!' said Kat making kick boxing moves.
They loaded up the car and the girls all embraced in a final huddle. Alice and Kat both gave Sam a big hug and kiss.
'I hope we'll be seeing plenty of you too,' said Kat.
'Don't worry, you will,' said Sam.
Jess could hardly drive as they headed back up to Hyde Park Corner; her eyes were filled with tears.

They arrived back at the bed-sit to a note from Matt thanking Sam for the bed and explaining he had gone to work and would be moving straight in with some friends for a week or so.
'He must mean business if he's working Sundays,' whistled Sam.
They had made good time on the motorway and Jess had a couple of hours before she needed to head home.
'There's a bottle of wine left in the fridge, do you fancy a glass?' he asked. Jess smiled and nodded. She was fighting that sinking feeling of the weekend declining to its nadir, the spectre of work lurking horribly just below the horizon. Sam opened the

fridge.
'Why am I not surprised?' he snarled, 'the bugger's only gone and swilled it.'
'I'll be fine with a cup of tea,' said Jess quietly.
Sam put the pan on to boil and sniffed the milk suspiciously.
'At least he left me a morsel o' bread and cheese for tomorrow!' he drawled in Dickensian mockney. Jess smiled wanly as she sat on the bed.
'Are you ok?' he asked. Jess nodded, but a single tear welled up in her eye and ran rapidly down her cheek. She swiped it away with a clumsy movement of her hand. Sam hurried to her side and put his arm round her.
'What is it?'
'I'm fine, really. Just hold me for a minute,' she whispered. He folded her in his arms and she pressed her forehead into his shoulder. 'That's better,' she sighed, 'wish I could stop with you tonight.'
'I'm so insensitive,' muttered Sam.
'Don't be silly. I just feel a bit emotional, that's all.'
The pan began to boil.
'Ok if I just make some tea?' he asked and she nodded, lifting her head away. She fumbled in her handbag for a tissue as Sam mashed teabags in mugs.
'It's all come as a bit of a shock hasn't it?' he said as he set the drinks down on the chest of drawers.
'Yes. I suppose I'd never really told Alice and Kat I wasn't planning to come back and they just assumed that I would.'
'Which was nice.'
'It was brilliant, but I'm not sure how Mum and Dad are going to react.'
'They won't try to stand in your way, surely?'
'No, but I've been doing a lot for them recently and I think they've rather come to depend on me.'
'Well you've got a month or two to work something out; there's time.'
'Yeah,' Jess nodded, 'but what about us? How's that going to work?'
'It'll be fine. I bet it's only a couple of hours on the bus to

Leeds and like I said, if it's not working, I can always move up there.'
'If it wasn't working, I'd come back home,' said Jess fiercely.
'No you would not,' said Sam firmly, 'I'll get you through that degree if it it's the last thing I do.'
'Degree of separation.'
'What?'
'Nothing.'
They were silent for a moment then she suddenly turned to him and looked deep into his eyes.
'Tell me you'll never leave me!' she said urgently.
'I'll never leave you,' he said in a robotic monotone.
'Fool!' she laughed, slapping him on the arm.

As Jess drove back up the track to the farm she could see the cab of the tractor above the hedgerow making its way slowly down the hill towards the yard.
'Goodness,' she thought, 'Dad's cooking Sunday lunch and working the farm; I thought men couldn't do multi tasking.'
The two vehicles arrived in the yard almost simultaneously but Jess was puzzled when she saw the person jumping out of the John Deere was clearly not her father. He turned and looked towards her as she drew up, then smiled and waved. To her amazement, she suddenly realised it was Peter Spencer. He walked over as she lifted her bag out of the boot.
'That surprised you didn't it?' he laughed.
'Well, I wouldn't say you were the last person on earth I expected to drive up in our tractor, but you'd have come pretty close,' smiled Jess.
'You're forgetting I used to help your dad here when we were younger.'
'What have you been up to then?'
'Just checking the ewes have got plenty of water; it's been so dry lately.'
'Why didn't you take the quad bike?'
'Didn't know you had one.'
'Would you mind dropping my bag in the porch if you're going inside? I just want to run down and check Darcy.'

As Jess hurried down to the stable she tried hard to be rational about Peter's presence on the farm. He was obviously contributing financially and if he could help Mark out practically as well it was a real bonus. There was something about it that made her feel uncomfortable though, and she was acutely aware that she had just made that very clear to Peter.
'Your daughter's home,' said Peter as he walked into the kitchen.
'Oh good, perfect timing. She ok?' said Mark amid great clouds of steam as he drained the vegetables.
'I think so. She seemed a bit unenthusiastic about me helping out.'
'I can't imagine why. Are you eating with us?'
'I'm not sure,' said Peter hesitantly, 'I might go to the gym.'
'What did Jess say?'
'Nothing. Really, nothing at all. She just seemed a bit put out, that's all, probably my imagination. Besides you'll want to talk about what happened with Tom.'
Mark was unable to persuade Peter to stay and when Jess eventually came in, he decided not to mention it, having caused quite enough upset for one weekend. She briskly laid the table for the meal and helped Mark dish up.
'Sorry, I should have got here a bit sooner but I just wanted to check on Darcy. It all seems very shipshape down there, have you been tidying up?'
Before Mark could explain, Tom and Christine walked into the kitchen.
'What have you been up to then?' asked Jess looking at his bandaged wrist.
The three of them looked at each other sheepishly.
'It's a long story,' sighed Mark.

Mysteriously the whole episode seemed far less traumatic than it had felt at the time as they recounted it to Jess.
'My God,' she laughed, 'we shall need a season ticket for that QMC car park at this rate.'
Once they had confessed, the mood of guilt and despondency that had pervaded the household all weekend suddenly evaporated and for the rest of the meal the atmosphere was

cheerful. Jess told them all about the events in Leeds, carefully editing out her visit to the English Department. She had not decided quite how to broach this.
'So is Sam's jacket ok?' asked Christine once they had all finished laughing about the episode at Bar Acuda.
'Think so, we put it in the automatic at John Street and I've brought it home in a carrier to tumble dry; don't let me forget.'
It had clearly not occurred to any of them that Jess might have considered resuming her studies at Leeds while she was up there. She was not sure whether to just come out with it or somehow drip-feed them with the idea in instalments.
'So how did you find the time to tidy up the stable so nicely while I was away?' she asked. It had occurred to her that Darcy was going to be a serious problem when she left home this time.
Again Mark and Christine looked uncomfortable for a moment.
'Well, as you can imagine, we had our hands full with what went off with your brother,' said Mark, hesitantly, as though choosing his words with care, 'so Peter got Theresa to come over and look after him for us.'
'Theresa?' cried Jess incredulously.
'Yes,' continued Mark, looking even more nervous now, 'she used to be a very keen rider and apparently she's been looking round for quite a while for a horse with stabling,' Mark paused as if bracing himself for an onslaught, but none came, 'she actually took him out for a bit of exercise, just a short walk along the bridle path, I hope you don't mind.'
'No,' said Jess quietly, 'I don't mind at all, that was very kind of her.'
Mark and Christine looked at each other with disbelief and relief in equal measure.
'We thought you'd be absolutely livid,' admitted Christine. 'We never said she could ride him but you know what she's like.'
'Not at all, it was exactly what he needed; she's looked after him beautifully.'
'Would you mind if she rode him occasionally?' asked Mark diffidently as if he had reached the critical moment defusing an unexploded bomb.
'She can buy him if she likes,' said Jess calmly.

‘But why would you want to sell him?’ asked Christine in disbelief.
‘It’s the perfect solution. We all know we can’t afford to keep him much longer and this way he’ll still be around but Theresa will pick up all the overheads, including paying us for stabling.’
‘You are really the most contrary person!’ exclaimed Mark.
‘Why?’ laughed Jess.
‘I was absolutely dreading telling you about this,’ he continued, ‘but you’ve just taken it in your stride as though you’d been planning it all along.’
‘I couldn’t have planned it that well,’ smiled Jess.
‘But I don’t understand,’ persisted Christine, ‘you love Darcy so much, why would you want to sell him now?’
‘Because I do love him,’ whispered Jess hoarsely, and for the first time a spasm of emotion flickered across her face. ‘I want him to be properly looked after and this is the perfect solution; he gets to stay here in familiar surroundings and his future will be secure.’ Suddenly she was crying. ‘Oh,’ she sobbed angrily, ‘I was so determined not to cry. There’s something I have to tell you.’

After Jess had gone home, Sam started up the laptop to check his email. He dropped down the recent history from the address bar to save typing in the URL of his web mail and was confronted with a string of debt counselling sites. Matt had clearly been busy while he was away.

There was an email from his agent, sent late on Friday. He quickly opened it and his heart sank as he read that the publisher had rejected his sample chapters. Jess had been exactly right; they found it too flippant for their readership and whilst they accepted that the writer had talent, it was not a style they were looking for and would be better placed elsewhere. Sam was shocked, not so much because of the rejection, but at the speed with which it had taken place.
‘They must have really hated it,’ he thought to himself grimly.
The agent had tried to put a positive spin on it, emphasising that just because it was not suitable for this publisher, there were plenty of others they could try. In a way they had paid him the

compliment of recognising the integrity of his work rather than suggesting a rewrite. Sam shrugged and shook his head. For the sake of a book deal he would have rewritten every single word if necessary but it was too late now; he had blown it and would probably never get a chance like that again. The agent had urged him to carry on with it because he was certain he could place the work eventually but Sam replied thanking him for his trouble and declining the offer. He had never really considered himself a thriller writer and this outcome was all the proof he needed. He had given writing his best shot for long enough and it had got him nowhere. He had no savings, no property and no prospects and the time had come to face up to the fact that he would never make it now. He could draw some comfort from the fact that he had at least been brave enough to try but now he needed to have the courage to give up. He didn't want to be a wannabe any more.

Sam did not want to disturb Jess. He decided to go down and have a word with Roland, who would no doubt be sympathetic. He had in any case still to get back to him about the valuations on the Internet for his books, more bad news. Sam tapped on the door and was surprised when Polly answered it.

'Hi darling!' she gushed, 'had a lovely time in Leeds?'

'Brilliant Polly thank you, did Matt behave himself?'

'In a manner of speaking; deep down he's a lovely lad really isn't he?'

'He has a certain charm I suppose, yes,' Sam conceded warily.

'Don't leave the poor boy standing on the doorstep,' shouted Roland, 'bring him in!'

Polly stepped aside and gestured for Sam to enter.

'Hello Roland,' said Sam quietly, 'I'm sorry I never got back to you about your book collection, but unfortunately Polly's valuation seems to be more realistic than mine.'

'That's because Polly's always right about everything, aren't you my dear?'

'I just know the price of everything and the value of nothing darling,' said Polly sadly.

'Would you care to partake of a small sherry with us young man?' asked Roland cheerily. They had clearly been knocking

them back for quite a while. Polly often cooked enough for two and took a meal down for Roland. She also did most of his shopping and seldom took enough money for it. In return, he was always there to cheer her up when she was lonely.
Sam was handed a glass of dark brown liquor, which he sipped tentatively.
'What can I do for you then, apart from not entrust you with my priceless book collection?' asked Roland.
'Oh, I've had some bad news,' sighed Sam, 'I just needed a shoulder to cry on.'
'Not about Jess I hope,' said Polly anxiously.
'No, no we're just fine thanks, really. No I had an email from my agent, the publisher rejected my book.'
'Ah, I do feel for you my boy,' sympathised Roland, 'I know only too well the bitter taste of rejection.'
'I think I'm going to leave you two failures to it,' said Polly getting unsteadily to her feet, 'it's not the end of the world you know, darling.'
'I know Polly but it is the end of my writing world. I'm going to call it a day, finish it now, burn all my notes in the garden like Jude Fawley.'
'Oh I love his films, is he still married to that what's her name?'
'Off you go now Polly, this boy needs counselling,' said Roland, 'you have no idea what it's like to be rejected.'
'Believe me, I do,' she slurred as she swayed out of the room, 'believe me I do.'

Jess was relieved to discover that her family all approved of her decision to return to Leeds. They all agreed that moving in with Alice and Kat was the perfect opportunity for her to get back into it and she would be crazy not to take it.
'Are you sure you'll manage ok, though?' she asked her parents anxiously.
'Having Peter around has made a massive difference,' said Mark. 'We cut and bagged the whole of Jericho for silage this weekend. He was in his element!'
'Oh dear, I'm afraid I was a bit off with him when I got home,' said Jess guiltily.

‘Yes, he mentioned,’ said Mark with a wry smile, ‘but don’t worry, he was fine about it.’
‘But surely he and Theresa might get back together, and he works all hours at the office.’
‘I know, but just between us, he wants to start scaling things back at work and even if things do work out with Theresa they will probably still keep the flat, especially if she takes Darcy on.’
‘Are things any better between them?’
‘They sat together on the fence at the stables this morning and had a good long chat,’ said Christine.
Jess caught Tommy’s eye and they smiled.
‘I think you should have the final say on this Mum. If you’re not completely happy with it, I won’t go. Have a think about it before you decide,’ suggested Jess.
‘I don’t need to think about it, it’s a wonderful idea. Don’t you agree Mark?’
‘Absolutely,’ he confirmed.

As usual, Mark had made far too much food, so as she and Tom cleared away and washed up, Jess plated up a meal for Peter as a peace offering. When she saw the beam of his headlights bouncing up the farm track, she slipped out of the kitchen and waited in the yard as he drew up.
‘Hi,’ she said.
‘Everything ok?’ asked Peter cautiously.
‘Yeah, um, I just wanted to say sorry for being a bit short with you earlier and are you hungry? There’s loads left if you are.’
‘You don’t have to apologise Jess, and yes I’m starving if you have a spare meal!’
‘Good,’ she smiled, ‘do you want to come over now?’
‘I just have to send a few emails,’ hesitated Peter.
‘Ok, I’ll nuke it and bring it over to the flat for you!’
‘Thanks,’ a slightly bemused Peter called after Jess as she hurried away.

Tom was sitting at the kitchen table with a cup of tea when Jess returned; he clearly wanted to talk.
‘So how long have you been doing this online thing?’ asked Jess as she set the food off in the microwave.

'Longer than Mum and Dad know,' said Tom dismally.
'You mean it affected your revision?'
'It took over my revision; it took over my life.'
'Yeah, I've heard how addictive these second life games can be. It's never really appealed to me.'
'I still feel terrible about it, but in a way I'm glad the spell has been broken. I'm not going back in.'
'Can you do that?'
'Yeah, as a new character. The guys in my chapter keep emailing me. They say I was a hero and they want me back but I haven't replied.'
'Good,' said Jess firmly, 'make sure you don't. Cancel your subscription and get on with your own life. Did you get fixed up at the Crown?'
'I haven't had time,' said Tom lamely.
Jess looked up at the clock. There was no point ringing now, the place would be heaving. The microwave dinged and she snatched up the plate and headed for the door.
'First thing tomorrow, right?' she barked, looking at him pointedly.
'Yes sir Yes!' he shouted with a grin.

Jess decided to tell Peter straight away about her decision to return to Leeds.
'I'm very pleased for you Jess,' he said, 'but we'll certainly miss you at the office. When will you be finishing?'
'I don't know exactly, not until the end of July probably.'
'Do you think Kerry would be able to handle the Purchase Ledger?'
'I don't see why not. Will she have time though?'
'She will while the housing market stays this flat. We'll set someone on when it picks up and she can train her.'
'Or him,' said Jess.
'He, she or it,' smiled Peter. 'I'll have a word with her in the morning if you don't mind and if she's interested you can begin straight away.'
'Fine with me,' said Jess, 'I think she'll be pleased.'
'Mum and Dad will miss you,' said Peter carefully.

‘I know,’ sighed Jess, ‘but Dad said Theresa might be interested in riding Darcy and if you two were around more I’d feel much happier about being away.’
‘You don’t mind about Darcy then?’
‘No, it’s the perfect solution. We could never have kept him otherwise.’
‘Everything seems to be falling into place then,’ smiled Peter.
‘It does,’ she agreed.

Jess hurried back to the house, pleased to have made her peace with Peter. Remembering she had turned off her mobile before the meal, she switched it back on and carried her bag up to her room. A text arrived as she was unpacking. It was from Sam and simply said ‘Bad news. Call me when you can.’ She immediately pressed call and sat on her bed as it rang, wondering what could have gone wrong.
‘Hi babe, what is it?’ she blurted out as soon as he picked up.
‘The book got rejected,’ he said simply.
‘No! How come, what reasons did they give?’
‘Exactly what you said; not taking the genre seriously enough.’
‘No second chance?’
‘Nope. It wasn’t what they were looking for so it’s going straight in the trash.’
‘No Sam, please don’t say that. You know you’ve got talent; sooner or later you’ll get your break. What did your agent say?’
‘Exactly that, but he would wouldn’t he.’
‘I don’t see why. It’s not going to benefit him spending time and money on a no hoper.’
‘Well he won’t have to with this one.’
‘You haven’t fired him?’
‘No of course not. He can carry on touting my synopsis and sample chapters if he wants to but I’ve told him I’m not writing any more.’
‘Unless you get an advance.’
‘Well obviously I would in that unlikely eventuality.’
‘So you haven’t given up completely.’
‘It’s about as likely as winning the lottery.’
‘You don’t do the lottery.’
‘I do literary lottery, or rather I did.’

'Do you want me to come over?'
'That's really sweet of you, but no, there's no need thanks. I feel better already for talking to you, and Roland has been very kind.'
'Bless.'
'Yeah, he was really sympathetic.'
They agreed to meet after work the following evening.
'Thanks for being so supportive, love you,' said Sam.
'Love you, love you, love you,' gushed Jess as he hung up.

Sam turned back to his email. His agent had a habit of working all hours and he half expected to find a reply. There was new mail waiting in his inbox but it was from a very different source and it contained news that was worse, far, far worse.

Eighteen

On Monday Jess stopped late at work even though Kerry was back. It suited her to stay until Sam finished, and in any case Kerry had been so excited about taking over her duties she couldn't wait to get started.

Jess had spent her lunch break writing a letter to the faculty confirming that she would be resuming her studies in October and promising to select her options online by the end of the week. As she dropped the envelope in the post tray a wave of euphoria swept through her; suddenly it was a real, she was going back to Leeds! She emailed Alice to confirm that it was on and she would be taking the room. The girls paid their rent individually to the landlord so she would need to set up a standing order. Alice replied with an ecstatic email saying how much they were looking forward to having her back and how everyone thought Sam was lovely. The previous occupant of the room had paid until the end of June so Jess did not need to make a payment until mid July. She enclosed all the relevant details and said she would tell the landlord that the room was let.

It turned out that Jess had to contact the County Council to reactivate her student loan. By the end of the day that too was done and lying in the post tray next to her letter to Leeds. She even had time to give Peter written notice that she would be leaving at the end of July. Because she had accrued a fair amount of holiday and bonus, he generously agreed to pay her until the end of September, timed perfectly for her student loan to kick in.

Jess noticed as she switched on her mobile after finally getting away that Sam had tried to ring her a couple of times. She did not bother calling him and headed straight over to the house to wait in the car until he arrived home. Roland appeared

on the doorstep for a cigarette so she wandered over to say hello.
'Hello my dear,' he said, 'terrible news about Sam isn't it?'
'I know but I'm sure he'll find a publisher eventually,' she said calmly.
'Oh dear, you haven't heard then?'
'He hasn't been dumped by his agent?'
'No, no it's nothing to do with the book. I'm sorry I wish I'd never mentioned it now. Why don't you go up and see him, he's been home for a while.'
Jess was desperate to know what had happened but it was not fair to press Roland for information so she hurried upstairs and tapped on Sam's door but there was no reply.
'Hello, it's me; are you there?' she called softly but there was no response. She was just wondering whether to run back downstairs and find out what Roland knew when she heard the shower. It seemed pointless knocking on the bathroom door so she sat impatiently at the top of the stairs frantically trying to figure out what this awful news could possibly be.

Tom rose early for once, determined to start the week in a positive and constructive frame of mind. His arm was healing nicely and the trip to the doctor was looking increasingly unnecessary. Christine was also feeling much brighter, so they breakfasted together in the kitchen.
'What have you got planned for today then?' she asked.
'First job is to call The Crown to see if they have any vacancies,' he said briskly.
'I wonder whether you might have left that a bit late.'
'Don't you think a lot of staff will be booking holidays now?'
'Well there's certainly no harm in asking!'

Tom rang The Crown and was put through to the restaurant manager. This was the lady who had been bothering Amy last time they ate there. She was very offhand at first but thawed a little when he gave his name and address; Mark and Christine had been good customers for years.
'Do you have any experience?' she asked.
Tom hadn't but was willing to consider anything.

'Well, we always need help in the kitchen at weekends and some evenings too. It's not very glamorous I'm afraid and it's minimum wage with no share of the tips.'
As Tom would not be eighteen until August, he would start on £3.40 an hour, rising to £4.60 on his birthday. His heart sank at the thought of spending the summer slaving in a boiling hot kitchen being treated like a piece of shit for that kind of money.
'Do you think there would be a chance to move into the restaurant after a bit?' he asked hopefully.
'There might be, it all depends. Why don't you call in this morning and have a look round before you decide?'
Tom agreed to this. It did not matter how rubbish the job was, or how bad the pay, as long he got the chance to see Amy once in a while it would all be worth it. He changed into some smarter clothes, jumped on his bike and pedalled off down the track to The Crown.

Mondays were always quiet at the restaurant and a lot of staff had the day off. Nevertheless there was plenty to do in the kitchen, which often had the appearance of a scrap yard after the weekend. When Tom arrived only one assistant had shown up, a girl called Vicky who he knew from school. She was working her way through a great pile of dirty roasting tins caked with burnt on fat, scrubbing them in a huge sink with a scourer.
'How long have you been working here?' he asked indifferently.
'Couple of weeks. It's really crap but what else can we do stuck out here in the middle of nowhere?'
Just then the restaurant manager burst in through the swing doors like a Wild West baddie.
'This is rather good timing as it happens, young man. We've been let down badly this morning by a very unreliable employee and his job's yours if you want it.'
'Cool, when do I start?' asked Tom.
'Right now!' she cried throwing him an industrial sized roll of kitchen paper.
'Dry those for Vicky and try to wipe off some of the grot she will have undoubtedly left behind. Vicky, when you've done that scrub down all the hobs and work tops and make sure they're spotless. Tom when you've finished mop the floor right

through please.'
When she had gone, Tom and Vicky looked at each other dumbfounded.
'You'll ruin that nice shirt if you're not careful,' said Vicky, 'there's some aprons hanging up by those lockers, put one of them on.'
As he rolled his selves up she noticed his bandage.
'What did you do to your arm?' she asked.
Tom tried to just pass it off as a graze but somehow she managed to wheedle the whole story out of him.
'Wicked!' she cried. 'Let's see it!'
He reluctantly peeled back the dressing to reveal the wound, which was still bruised and swollen. The scabs where the name had been punched in made it clearly readable.
'Will you have a scar?'
'I hope not.'
'Why did you do it then?'
'I just went a bit crazy.'
'Yeah,' said Vicky, clearly impressed, 'I know exactly what you mean.'

When it was time for their break, they went and stood in the sun near the bins by the kitchen door. They were chatting about mutual acquaintances and what they were up to when an open topped Z3 convertible swept into the car park. Tom was dismayed to see the passenger was Amy. She kissed the smartly dressed owner of the car, ruffled his hair and hopped out. She waved as he sped away then ran into the main entrance, completely ignoring Tom and Vicky.
'Who was that, then?' asked Tom, trying to hide his disappointment.
'Didn't you know? It's Lucas Jensen, the footballer. Amy's just moved in with him; she's a proper WAG,' said Vicky enviously.
Tom felt a complete fool. He had taken on this terrible job just to see her and all it would result in was a daily reminder that she was in a completely different league to him with her First Division friend.
'You doing anything tonight?' Vicky asked casually.

'Um, no I don't think so.'
'It's just that Robbie's parents are away and he's having an open house, fancy going?'
'Yeah, great.'
'Ok. Shall we meet by the war memorial at about eight thirty then?'

Sam emerged from the bathroom, making Jess jump.
'Oh, hi. I've been trying to ring you,' he said stooping to exchange a kiss.
'What's happened?' asked Jess anxiously.
'Come in,' said Sam, as he fished the key out of his dressing gown pocket. 'It's my Dad,' he explained as they walked in, 'he's had a heart attack.'
'Oh no!' cried Jess, 'that's terrible. How bad was it?' she asked hugging him tightly.
'Well, he's out of danger but they're keeping him in for observation. My brother emailed me last night and then rang me first thing this morning, which is like early evening over there.'
'Have you spoken to your mum? Is she ok?'
'Yeah, she's just shocked. We're all shocked; it's completely out of the blue, and I think it's made Dad feel very mortal, if you know what I mean. They want me to go over.'
'How can you possibly afford that?'
'The flight is all booked and paid for. I leave from Heathrow on Friday.'
'God, so soon! But that's right, of course. I'll take the day off work and run you down there.'
'I'd really like that but I can get the bus if it's not convenient.'
'I'll make damn sure it's convenient. What about your work?'
Sam had gone in to work at the normal time and explained the problem to Ricky who had been brilliant and got straight on to HR to see what they could do for him. He hadn't earned any holiday so the only option was to take unpaid leave. Due to the exceptional circumstances, they had agreed to pay him until the end of the month then keep him on the books for up to eight weeks unpaid. They had also given him the rest of the week off to get things sorted out and the guys in the team had a whip

round and gave him fifty pounds.
'Everybody's been really great about it, to say I've hardly been there five minutes,' he concluded.
Jess was struggling to take it all in. They had not particularly made any plans for the summer but she had just assumed they would be spending a lot of time together. Suddenly that had been snatched away from her and though she tried very hard not to show it, she was bitterly disappointed.
'Any idea how long you'll be away for?' she asked tentatively.
'It will all depend on whether Dad makes a full recovery. If he bounces straight back I'll probably just stop for a fortnight or so.'
'It seems a shame to go all that way just for a couple of weeks,' said Jess, fervently hoping he would disagree.
'I know but Dave's really busy at work, they've got the baby and with Dad being ill on top of that they're not going to want to be showing me round all the time.'
'What if he doesn't get better?'
'I'd rather not think about that but if he does deteriorate, the expectation is that I'll stop until, well, you know.'
Jess suddenly noticed that Sam looked exhausted.
'Are you ok?' she asked anxiously.
'I feel terrible actually, I hardly slept last night.'
'Do you want to get your head down for a bit?'
'I don't know what I want, I can't think straight at the moment. It's all happened so quickly. Dad's just never ever ill, I can't get my head round it.'
Jess sat him down on the bed and put the pan on to boil. She went to the fridge for milk and was pleased to see her magnetic message still there on the door. It was hard to believe only a week had elapsed since she wrote those words. In that brief time she had completely turned her life around, but just as she was heading back into the mainstream her pilot was leaving and there was no guarantee that he would ever come back.

The fridge was empty apart from a small box of soft marg and a piece of unwrapped cheddar that had gone all crusty.
'I think I'll just nip down to the Co-op for a few things,' she said, 'what would you like to eat?' There was no reply and

when she stood up she could see why; Sam was already deeply asleep. She left his door on the latch and went down to Roland's room to ask him to let her back in.
'How is he?' asked Roland solicitously.
'Dead to the world at the moment, I don't think he slept last night.'
'It is a shame,' he sighed.
'People recover from heart attacks Roland, don't write him off yet,' she said impatiently.
Sam was still fast asleep when Jess got back. She put some cheese and salad in the fridge and waited a while. When he still did not stir, she left a note saying to call later if he woke up in time, and went home.

As Jess drove back up to the farm she could see Darcy was out in the paddock with someone. When she got closer she realised it was Theresa, who waved enthusiastically.
'Those bloody Spencers,' she growled, 'they're taking over!'
She pulled up by the stable and took a deep breath. She was really not in the mood for a conversation with Theresa Spencer but it would have been rude to just drive by.
'Thank you for taking care of Darcy at the weekend,' she said, forcing herself to smile.
'Thank you for letting me,' gushed Theresa.
Jess suppressed the thought that she had not actually been consulted about the matter.
'Did Peter tell you I'm going back to Leeds in October?'
'He did, darling and he said you might be interested in selling.'
'That's right, on the condition that he remains here though.'
'Well that would suit me, what do you think he's worth?'
'Well, he's in pretty good nick for a ten year old, but I would have thought no more than a couple of thousand.'
'I'll give you two and a half.'
'I think that's very fair. Do you mind if I just run it by Mum and Dad first.'
'Of course not, there's no rush.'
Theresa turned away as if Jess was dismissed now that their business was concluded.

‘How’s Jack?’ she called after her.

Theresa turned round and looked at her superciliously. ‘Oh he’s much better thanks. I think he was so sensible to make a clean break from all this, don’t you?’

Jess wanted to say ‘all what?’ but she resisted the urge.

‘Give him my best wishes,’ she called, but Theresa just walked away as though she had not heard.

Jess entered the kitchen as Christine was dishing up a microwave meal for two while Mark sat at the table reading the paper.

‘Hello, I thought you were eating with Sam tonight,’ she said, surprised.

‘Change of plan,’ said Jess laconically.

‘Everything ok?’

Jess explained about Sam’s dad and the emergency trip to Australia.

‘How bad is it?’ asked Mark.

‘We don’t really know. I can’t help wondering if they’ve panicked a bit.’

‘I thought you and Sam must have had a row, walking in like that with a face like thunder,’ smiled Christine.

‘Oh no, it’s that bloody Spencer woman!’ cried Jess.

‘What’s she done now?’ asked Mark looking anxiously across to Christine.

‘She’s just so arrogant, though to be fair she has just offered me two and a half for Darcy.’

‘That’s a good offer, have you accepted?’ asked Mark, who knew this generosity was all Peter’s doing.

‘More or less, I just said I ought to run it by you two first and that it was on the condition that she keeps him here. Do you think I could stipulate that I can still ride him occasionally?’

‘Peter’s the best person to ask about all that. He’ll be back from the gym soon I expect,’ said Mark.

Christine brought two plates of sloppy looking cottage pie and a dish of garden peas to the table.

‘I’m afraid we haven’t catered for you, love and Tommy’s off out tonight as well,’ she apologised.

‘That’s ok, I’ll make myself an omelette or something later. Did

Tom get in touch with the Crown then?'
'Yes, and they've taken him on to work in the kitchen. It's not full time but it's a start,' said Christine.
Just then Tom walked in looking very smart in his next best shirt, with his hair gelled into spikes.
'You look a bit overdressed for pot washing!' laughed Jess.
'I'm not working tonight,' he mumbled, looking evasive.
'He's got a date,' said Christine confidentially.
'Mum!' he cried looking mortified.
'What, with Amy? You don't mess around do you?'
'Not with that slag!' he grunted.
'She's a footballer's wife now apparently,' smiled Mark, 'none other than Lucas Jensen.'
'Yeah right!' snorted Jess, 'if that lasts more than a fortnight she'll be in the Guinness Book of records. So who's the lucky girl then Tom?'
Her brother ignored her, hurrying head down and red faced towards the back door.
'It's Vicky Butler,' whispered Christine.
'At last!' cried Jess.
Tom turned in the doorway and looked at his sister, eyes narrowed. 'What do you mean 'at last'?' he asked menacingly.
'She's fancied you for years!' exclaimed Jess, 'don't tell me you didn't know. And for what it's worth, I think she's a lovely girl. You could do a lot worse than Vicky Butler.'
'God, you're worse than Mum!' he scowled, slamming the door as he departed, leaving his infuriatingly patronising family to their collective mirth.

After Jess had made a snack, she cleared up in the kitchen and went up to her room. She lay on the bed for a while trying to get to grips with this massive disruption to her plans. Sam's brother had bought him a one-way ticket, which was understandable under the circumstances, but what if he really liked it there; what if he decided to stay? He had already said there was nothing to keep him in Nottingham, if he could up sticks and move to Leeds, why not Canberra? His family was there after all. Everything seemed to have fallen into place so perfectly and now the vital component in her newfound happiness was about to disappear. She knew none of this could be helped and felt very selfish for being so disappointed but it was all so unfair. Sam's impromptu trip would be a waste because he would not have had time to prepare himself and his family would be too distracted for him to make the most of it. She had this awful feeling that even if he did come back, things would not be the same between them.

It was gone nine by the time Sam woke up and called her.
'How are you feeling?' she asked.
'Rough,' he groaned, 'I hate going to sleep in the evening. I probably won't sleep tonight now. I wish you'd stayed and woken me up.'
'Oh, I'm sorry. I didn't know what to do for the best.'
'Never mind. Thanks for the food by the way, I'm starving.'
'Do you want me to come back over?'
'No, it's too far and I have to ring my brother soon before he goes to work. This has really messed things up hasn't it?'
'It can't be helped. It's not the end of the world.'
'I know, but it's spoiled things and I'm sorry. Look, were you serious about running me down to Heathrow?'
'Of course!'
'The flight's at twelve fifteen and you're supposed to check in three hours before so we'll have to leave pretty early. Will that be ok?'
'Yes, that's fine. I'll stop with you Thursday night. We'll have to set off at about six I should think; try to miss the worst of the traffic on the M25.'
'Oh, thanks. That's really kind of you.'
'Don't be silly. It's what I want. I'm going to miss you so much you know.'
'I'm going to miss you too but we can talk every day. Are you set up for Skype?'
'Oh, that voice over internet thing? No, but I can. It's like free isn't it?'
'Yeah, totally.'
'It won't be the same though.'

'I know but I'll be back sooner than you know it.'
'Promise?'
'Of course! Why, did you think I was planning to stay?'
'I wondered.'
'Don't worry. If Dad does get better like you say we'll be at each other's throats in a matter of days. They'll soon be sending me back.'
'Good!' cried Jess; though this hadn't been exactly the answer she was hoping for.

After speaking to Sam, Jess hurried down to the paddock to see if Theresa was still around. Her car was still there but Jess could not find her in the stable. Peter was back from the gym so Theresa must have gone up to the flat to see him. Jess was not sure whether to disturb them but as she walked back up, Peter opened the flat door and waved her over.
'I gather we have a bit of business to conclude,' he called.
She followed him into the kitchen, where Theresa was at the sink washing some salad. She turned and smiled frostily.
'You're happy with that price then?' asked Peter.
'Yes, it's very fair and it will be so lovely to have him around still. I was wondering if I might include in the agreement that I could still ride him occasionally?' she asked tentatively.
'Of course you can still ride him,' said Theresa 'but we don't need to put it all in writing do we? I mean we've all known each other long enough.'
'Yes but I should be very sad if you did change your mind and take him away,' explained Jess.
'Well I think you can trust me to keep my word can't you dear?' said Theresa acidly.
'Yes,' agreed Jess miserably.
'Are you quite sure you want to go ahead?' asked Peter, sensing her apprehension.
'It's the best outcome I could have hoped for,' Jess confirmed.
'Want us to pay now?' he asked, reaching for his briefcase.
'If you like.'
He carefully filled out a cheque with his fat silver fountain pen, blew on it, tore it out and handed it across to Jess.

‘Would you like me to draw up a bill of sale for you?’
‘Um, yes, if you don’t mind. I’ll sort out all his documentation for you and let you have it tomorrow.’
‘Thanks. I’ll speak to your dad about paying for his fodder and stabling. Any idea how much that’s likely to come to?’
‘It might be best to ask Mum about it. She’ll have a much better idea than Dad,’ said Jess who knew perfectly well that Mark would not ask nearly enough. She wafted the cheque a little then carefully folded it in half and slipped it into the back pocket of her jeans.

Before going back up to the house Jess walked back down to the stable. She suddenly felt overwhelmed by grief. She walked in and placed her arms around Darcy’s neck and her eyes filled with tears. Throughout all the troubles and difficulties of the last few years, he had been her best and most reliable friend. Like so many things in the past few weeks, his sale had happened suddenly and unexpectedly and she was not at all prepared for the awful reality of it.
‘I’ve just done the most terrible thing,’ she sobbed, ‘but it’s for the best, darling, it really is for the best.’

Nineteen

Sam decided to let Matt move into his room while he was away. It was the perfect solution, giving Matt a base of his own while he tried to sort his life out whilst taking care of the rent for Sam, though because it was so tiny, he would have to move his things out for the duration. Jess arrived on Thursday evening with a large suitcase from home to use for storage and a smaller one of hers for him to use on the journey, which though just the right size, was bright pink with black leopard spots all over it.
'Nice case,' said Sam, picking it up to try out, 'just my colour.'
'Yes, it is rather lovely isn't it?'
'Certainly won't have any difficulty spotting this on the carousel. Not sure what the Aussies will make of it, though.'
'They'll probably give you a very wide berth.'
Polly had kindly agreed to look after the big case while Sam was away.
'I hope you don't mind Matt moving in for a bit,' said Sam as he struggled into her room with it, 'I know your first meeting was a bit traumatic.'
'Oh, we're best of friends now, darling, don't you worry about that. I'll keep him under my wing while you're down under.'
'Thanks Polly. Make sure he behaves himself.'
'I'll do my level best,' she smiled.
'Can you believe I still haven't met this man?' said Jess.
'He's a very sweet boy,' said Polly, 'not half as bad as your friend makes out.'

'I'm really going to miss this room!' cried Jess sulkily, sitting down on the bed, 'it feels like a second home to me already.'
'Well you've got a much nicer one waiting for you in Leeds now haven't you?'

‘That’s true but this is special because we chose it together. It’s our very own space; our secret little den!’
‘It’s certainly little,’ agreed Sam.
He seemed nervous and distracted, constantly checking his passport, money and travel documents.
‘What will the weather be like in Oz when you get there?’
‘Not too hot, I think, which is probably a good thing. It’s winter over there so it might even be a bit dull and misty.’
‘Just like our summers, then. Wish I was coming with you.’
Sam had bought a quiche, some salad and a bottle of white wine. He calmed down a little as they sat at the table to eat.
‘Did you hear any more from your agent?’ asked Jess.
‘Yes. He agrees it might be best to have a complete break from the book for a while but he’s urged me not to give up on it.’
‘Good. That sounds sensible. How do you feel about it now?’
‘I honestly haven’t given it a second’s thought this week. It’s a good job they gave me compassionate leave at work; I can’t keep my mind on anything at the moment.’
Jess placed her hand on his. ‘Poor thing, it’s been such a shock for you. Are you looking forward to it at all?’
‘Not to sitting on a plane for twenty-four hours, but yes, it will be nice to see the folks again, and the baby of course.’
‘Yes, a visit from Uncle Sam!’
‘I should get him a present shouldn’t I? What would be suitable?’
‘Oh I don’t know, a little book or something. Perhaps we could get a London picture book from the airport.’
‘That’s a great idea. You’re so clever,’ he said, gently stroking her cheek.
‘Will you miss me?’ she asked softly.
‘Of course, that goes without saying doesn’t it?’
‘Preferably not,’ smiled Jess, ‘I’m going to miss you most dreadfully.’
‘Oh dear, I’m sorry,’ he sighed, ‘I have been a bit preoccupied this week haven’t I?’
‘It’s understandable I suppose,’ shrugged Jess. ‘Tell me you love me.’
‘I love you,’ said Sam, shaking his head in amazement.

'I know it's silly; I just really need to hear you say it.'
'I love you, I love you, I love you,' he said reaching across the table and wrapping her tightly in his arms.
'That's better,' sighed Jess, 'I love you more than the whole world.'

Sam had set the alarm for five am but was awake well before. He slipped out of bed leaving Jess to sleep, put the pan on the stove and went to have a shower. The rattling of the lid as the water came to the boil woke Jess up. Guessing where Sam was, she turned it off and got back into bed disappointed. She had so wanted to wake up in his arms and have a lingering last embrace in the sumptuous warmth of their bed before having to break the spell and begin this final day.

Sam tiptoed back into the room and, noticing the water had been turned off, whispered 'do you want a cup of tea?'
'Why are you whispering?' she asked dully.
Dimly aware that he may have done something wrong, Sam assumed that making Jess get up so early was cause of the problem.
'Sorry about the hour,' he said, starting in a whisper then quickly shifting into his normal voice.
'Cometh the hour,' she said.
'Cometh the man,' he completed.
'Hmm,' said Jess, then she suddenly leapt out of bed, rummaged around in her holdall, donned her slinky wrap and headed for the door with her wash bag and towel. 'Just having a quick shower,' she said in a stage whisper.
Sam shrugged, concluding Jess was clearly not a morning person, and made himself a coffee.

They got away a little earlier than planned and the sun was just rising over Sharphill Wood as they hit the ring road. Jess looked across the Trent Valley at the cooling towers in the distance and they did look strangely beautiful illuminated by the slanting amber light of dawn. She softened, thinking that she would never have even begun to consider this aspect aesthetically if she had not met Sam.

'Look at your coffee cups,' she said, the warmth returning to her voice.
'Sorry,' he said, placing his hand on her leg and giving it a squeeze.
'Why?' she asked.
'I shouldn't have got up before you were awake this morning should I?'
'Eureka!' cried Jess.
'Why didn't you say something?'
'Never mind,' sighed Jess.
When they pulled up at a red light in Clifton Sam put his arm around her and kissed her passionately. A gang of builders in a Transit van that had pulled up behind them hooted their horn and made gestures of encouragement. Jess sped away from them as the lights changed, hoping they would not be bumper to bumper all the way to the motorway.

They made good progress down the M1 although it was quite busy, especially with lorries. Sam was telling Jess that he had Facebooked Dan and Henry in Leeds. Jess was a friend on their pages but she rarely paid them any attention.
'They call me Poetman Sam and they've made up a little song about me to the tune of Postman Pat,' he laughed.
'That sounds about right for them,' said Jess mirthlessly.
'They've got a competition to guess the name of Poetman Sam's pussy,' he grinned.
'You think that's funny?' snapped Jess, reddening.
'Well it's quite clever because Postman Pat's cat -'
'I know,' interrupted Jess, thinking how much nicer the world would be if men were extinct. This was a perfect example of what she disliked about Dan and Henry and it made her wonder how things would work out in Leeds.
They drove in silence for a while, making good time all the way to Luton, where the traffic abruptly ground to a halt.
'If it's like this all the way round the M25, we're going to be pushing it,' said Jess grimly. When they left the M1 they made steady progress for a couple of miles then stopped again.
'What are we going to do?' wailed Jess, 'I had no idea it was going to be this bad.' It was so frustrating to be this close to

their destination with absolutely no way of getting there. Jess was consumed with helpless rage.
'Don't get mad,' said Sam calmly, 'it won't help.'
'What will you do if you miss the flight?'
'I'll worry about that if it happens,' said Sam confidently, 'just try to relax.'

It had gone ten by the time they entered Heathrow. Jess followed the signs to Terminal Four. When they arrived there was a slow moving queue for the short stay car park.
'I'm going to have to leg it,' said Sam, 'you get parked up and I'll meet you at the Qantas check in.' He quickly kissed her and jumped out, grabbing his case from the back seat. Jess watched helplessly as he sprinted for the main entrance. Whilst she was reluctant to see him go, she didn't want him to miss his plane. She felt naïve and provincial assuming that they could hit London at eight am and somehow miss the traffic. She was so mad with herself that she cried for a moment as she inched towards the barrier.

Cars were actually moving quite freely into short stay, it was just the sheer number of them that slowed the process down. She jabbed the button, took her ticket and drove in. A sign clearly indicated to park upstairs for departures so she drove round the ramps, emerging onto the open top deck, where she quickly found a space. She put the ticket in her purse, quickly fixed her face in the rear view mirror and ran through the doorway straight into the departure hall. Scanning the illuminated logos above the desks, she located the red roo of Qantas, saw there was still a queue and spotted Sam at the end of it. Her heart leapt when she realised they had not closed the flight; he was still going to make it! She raced over to him and flew into his arms.
'We did it, we did it!' she laughed.
Sam too seemed to have relaxed now that he had arrived in the right place at more or less the right time. The queue moved steadily as they hurried to get everyone checked in.
'Good job it isn't Terminal 5,' joked Sam as his turn came round and they walked forward to the counter. After rushing

through all the formalities, the clerk urged Sam to hurry straight through security and passport control because they would soon be calling the flight for boarding. They looked at each other in dismay. They had expected to have a couple of hours to kill in departures between check in and boarding, taking in a late breakfast, some shopping and generally enjoying a long, lazy goodbye. Now they found themselves being swept along in a torrent of harassed travellers all desperate to get through to their gate.

'Boarding cards please,' called a uniformed attendant as they approached a barrier. Sam pulled her to one side out of the turbulent stream.

'This is it!' he cried, 'we can't go any further.' They embraced desperately. 'I have to go now. I'll call you when I land; it'll be around noon UK time.'

'I'll wave from the top of the car park!' shouted Jess.

'I'll look out for you,' he said and with that he showed his documents to the guard and was waved through. Jess clung despairingly to the bright steel rail as Sam turned in the flood and waved frantically as he was swept from sight.

'Goodbye, take care, I love you,' she called futilely.

Jess felt empty as she headed slowly back, pressed close to the wall in an attempt to stay clear of the current. When she arrived in the departure hall it was a relief to be able to move freely again. She could not believe that their parting had been such a disaster; she had not even been able to say goodbye. Looking up at the monitors, she noted that Sam's flight was now boarding and would be leaving on time. She would wait and at least see his plane take off; it would be small comfort but better than just heading straight home. Wandering into a coffee bar she paid an exorbitant sum for a small Americano and a blueberry muffin. She sat at a table that had not been wiped and stared out across the turmoil of the departure lounge feeling utterly wretched. She jumped as her phone emitted the tone indicating the arrival of a text. It was Sam.

'Sorry about the hasty departure,' she read, 'have to turn my phone off now. Just time to say I love you and I'll see you very soon.' This was followed by a string of x's. She did not bother to reply but finished her coffee and walked dejectedly towards the doorway to the car park. Drifting through the newsagents she bought a paper and a magazine then decided to go and sit in the relative sanctuary of the car while she waited the hour or so for his plane to take off.

Walking along the open upper floor of the car park, Jess looked across the vast expanse of airport with its rows of Jumbo jets hooked up by umbilical concertinas to the walkways. She could see a Qantas plane in the distance and stopped for a moment, leaning on the concrete surface of the wall, thinking Sam might be heading down the gangway as she watched, but felt nothing. The stress of the journey and the fiasco of their parting had left her exhausted and empty. She wandered listlessly over to the Fiesta and slumped into the driver's seat. Sam's ipod was on the floor of the passenger side. Any minute now he would be settling down into his seat and searching despairingly through his hand baggage for this mission critical piece of equipment. Never mind, he would have to make do with in-flight movies, or sit gazing out of the window thinking of her as continents scrolled by beneath his wings.

Jess sat with her eyes closed, wishing she had bought some paracetamol at the newsagent. Taking a mouthful of water she flicked listlessly through the trashy celeb magazine then tossed it aside. Deciding it would be better to set off rather than hang around in the short stay feeling so grim, she got out of the car and walked over to the pay station. The dubious pleasure of the morning looked likely to cost her over sixteen pounds.

Jess was just about to insert her ticket when she noticed the Qantas plane taxi slowly by, heading up the runway for its final pre-flight checks. She may as well wait for it now. The view would be better from the far end of the car park so she walked unhurriedly down to where a middle-aged woman was waiting with two small children.

'Mammy and Daddy are off to Australia!' she said in a singsong voice.

'My boyfriend's on the same flight,' smiled Jess.

The plane reached the end of the runway, then slowly turned. It stood still for a moment, extending and retracting its flaps like an insect cleaning its wings, then suddenly began to move, accelerating rapidly as it hurtled away from her. Its nose pointed up and gradually it lifted into the air, painstakingly winning a tug of war with the surface of the earth. Climbing steeply, it banked lazily away to the south, sunlight glinting momentarily on the window of the flight deck. Jess suddenly realised that she had forgotten to wave. She put her hand to her mouth in horror. There was virtually no chance that Sam had been able to see her but all the same this ultimate failure pushed her over an emotional brink and she began to weep.

'Why is that lady crying?' piped one of the children.

'Because her boyfriend's gone away pet,' said his Gran soothingly.

'Is he never coming back again?' the child asked innocently.

'Of course he is flower,' she reassured him, 'of course he is.'